Mr Gupta goes to the Sea

Paul Comerford

GRACULUS PUBLISHING

37/50

MR GUPTA GOES TO THE SEA

Copyright © Paul Comerford 2020

Published by Graculus Publishing

The right of Paul Comerford to be identified as the author of this work has been asserted by him in accordance with the Copyright, Designs and Patents Act 1988. All rights reserved. No part of this publication may be reproduced, stored in a retrieval system or transmitted in any form, or by any means (electronic, mechanical, photocopying, recording, or otherwise) without prior written permission from the author and copyright owner.

This is a work of fiction. Names, characters, businesses, places, events and incidents are either the product of the author's imagination or used in a fictitious manner. Any resemblance to actual persons, living or dead, or actual events is purely coincidental.

A CIP catalogue record for this book is available from the British Library.

A copy of this book 00/50 may be found in the British Library Legal Deposit.

First Edition, First Impression, Hardback: 51 copies

ISBN: 978-1-8380858-0-3

Author's website paulcomerford.com

Cover art and design © Angela Jane Swinn was created using a composite of three Hubble Space Telescope images and the artist's own photography and drawing. Permission to use the three HubbleSite images: Hubble Ultra Deep Field (HUDF), eXtreme Deep Field (XDF), and the Star-Forming Region LH 95 in the Large Magellanic Cloud (LMC), is gratefully acknowledged with thanks to the Hubble Heritage Project, National Aeronautics and Space Administration (NASA) and the Space Telescope Science Institute (STScI).

Artist's website angelajaneswinn.com

Printed and bound in Great Britain
using responsibly and sustainably sourced paper.

Dedication

For Harvey, from Ecuador to Gupta, thank you.

Contents

Author's Note		1
Prologue		5
Chapter 1	Mr Gupta	7
Chapter 2	Tiger	29
Chapter 3	Cobra Investments	35
Chapter 4	Mr Gupta Falls	49
Chapter 5	Angaar and Seva	61
Chapter 6	Vasupati Chopra	73
Chapter 7	Mr Gupta Comes Back	85
Chapter 8	Angaar's Fire Dims	99
Chapter 9	Kāla-Vaz	111
Chapter 10	Mr Gupta's Trials Begin	125
Chapter 11	Freedom	141
Chapter 12	The Disc	161
Chapter 13	William MacKeeg	181
Chapter 14	A New World	195
Chapter 15	Gathering Storm	199
Chapter 16	The Mechanic	221
Chapter 17	The Final Eve	239
Chapter 18	All has Ended, All has Gone	255
Chapter 19	The Journey Begins	269

Chapter 20	Olaf and Seva	283
Chapter 21	The Drawing of the Dragon	297
Chapter 22	The Pursuit Begins	315
Chapter 23	Sahyadri	331
Chapter 24	Hunted	349
Chapter 25	Arnesh Ji and the Kuru Ki Kvark	367
Chapter 26	Convergence	385
Chapter 27	All Life's Weaving is Undone	405
Chapter 28	Endings	423
Chapter 29	All Roads Lead	443
Chapter 30	Redemption	455
Chapter 31	Mr Gupta goes to the Sea	473
Chapter 32	The Sea	491
Chapter 33	Only Angels Defeat Death	503
Epilogue		511

Author's Note

The Works of Zahan Bulsara

Zahan Bulsara, as mentioned in this book, is a Zoroastrian mystic, prophet and poet, born in 1911. He is justly famed for intoning his written philosophical poems to sitar music. From the 1980s he collaborated with composer Galen Fossa, embracing electronic music, distorted sitar sounds and the progressive rock genre.

Zahan's greatest work, Chaos Birthing, had long been held up as his magnum opus. It consists of twenty-five extended verses. Its full recital is said to take exactly one day and one hour, if performed correctly. Zahan achieved this in his first performance to the faithful, set to Fossa's enchanting music in 1986.

Chaos Birthing was eventually released as a collection of twenty-five, hour-long recordings on vinyl, then later, digitally. The twenty-fifth verse is entitled Time's End, World Beginnings.

Final stanzas from *Chaos Birthing: Time's End, World Beginnings.*

Tarnished silver,
Patinated gold,
My Lord watches,
My Lord sees,
The World is stained,
All creation laid low,
Humanity has touched everything.
Tarnished silver,
Patinated gold,

My Lord watches,
My Lord is sending,
A pure river of darkness,
The waters of Ohrmazd and Angra Mainyu,
Flow into the great water of Hammistagan,
Good and evil combine,
The waters of jet purify,
A storm of change in the swirling depths,
Arrives to cleanse all creation.

From beneath He comes,
From the abyss He climbs,
From the purity of blackness, He rises,
And gains far sight from blue sky,
He knows He will start the World again.

He will fall from heaven,
He will be seen as a man,
He will absorb the light,
He will end the World.
He will stop the World turning.
He can make Himself Demon or Angel.
In gigantic form He reaches all mankind's realm.
He is all pasts and all futures.
He can kill and resurrect.
He hears the thoughts from other worlds.
He is Kāla and He is all of us, our Hive Mind.

Kāla comes to cleanse the temples,
Kāla carries a great sword,
He will come silently to the defilers,
Kāla reaps the harvest,
Kāla collects lives,
He will sow them,
In the new World.

Purity in darkness stalks,
He is coming,
He is righteous,
Time is severed from mankind,
Darkness cleanses,

Darkness is pain,
Darkness is death,
Pain leaves with death,
Both shine with blackness.

Step onto the heavenly plane,
Bathe in the dark waters of Hammistagan,
Embracing pure black river,
As all life ends,
The seeds remain,
As all life ends,
The seeds remain,
As all life ends,
The seeds remain.

Asha and Druj become one,
Light absorbed by dark,
Day becomes night,
Hammistagan flows under the Chinvat,
In full dark,
In full dark,
In full dark,
Pain is the right for all, as impurity leaves,
Embrace your pain,
Flow on to Chinvat,
Flow on to Chinvat,
Obeisance at Chinvat,
Pour into the ocean of fire,
New life on a moonlit shore,
Stars and worlds align,
New life crawls from the Birthing Black Sea.

The sacrifice is made,
Mankind's sacrificial man,
Gophapa will be slain by Him,
Gophapa takes ruin with Him,
Tarnished silver,
Patinated gold,
My Lord watches,
My Lord sees.
Fire rages,

Fire rages,
All ruin burns away,
All ruin tempered to purity,
Rise in the new world of blue,
Rise in the new world of light,
Dragons rise in praise of Him,
Mighty serpents cold as ice,
Praise Kāla,
Praise Kāla whose will moves all,
Praise Kāla who cannot die,
The Destroyer has built the new World,
The end has become the Great Arch,
All has ended, all has gone,
All life's weaving is undone,
Chaos gone and blue light shines,
Chaos gone and blue light shines,
Chaos gone and blue light shines,
Chaos gone and blue light shines,
Chaos gone and blue light shines,
Only Angels defeat Death,
Only Angels defeat Death,
Gophapa is the World's Angel,
May the blue light shine,
May the blue light shine,
May the blue light shine,
Chaos gone and blue light shines,
Chaos gone and blue light shines,
Only Angels defeat Death,
Only Angels defeat Death,
Gophapa is the World's Angel,
May the blue light shine,
May the blue light shine,
May the blue light shine.

Zahan Bulsara 1967

Prologue

Death. Everything he had done had attracted death. Yet, as Mr Gupta's eyes focussed, colours became vibrant again. He could not move, but his mind was much clearer and he smiled. An emerald flash reminded him that life would come from everything dead, and that is how he saw things. The warmth under his hand gave him comfort as he watched all horrors washed away. Oh, how he loved the sea. From this all life came and it cleansed the world of corruption. As perception changed he saw the approaching figure, and his finger sketched his final request to an angel. Fear and terror gone, he met time face to face.

Chapter 1

Mr Gupta

At 05:30 in the morning New Delhi Station is very busy. It is not *very busy* in the sense of a London or New York rush-hour; these are western cities whose transport systems evolved from historically well-managed commuting cultures. In India things are different. *Very busy* at New Delhi Station at 05:30 in the morning precedes something to which the western mind would boggle. Most would boggle at 05:30.

There is no rush hour in Delhi, just a lull in proceedings through the darker hours and manic crescendos at various moments throughout the day. Outside, the car park, pavements and roads are gridlocked with tuktuks, taxis and battered coaches, all belching blue fumes. Man-powered rickshaws and mobile market stalls jostle for position amongst them. A few drivers curl in their vehicles sleeping through the chaos, tired from a long night gambling with the hope that late revellers would pay a little extra for their services. As soon as the noise became too much to bear, these sleepers would join the rest of the vast array of hopeful drivers touting for service.

For many, sleeping in Delhi is undertaken away from the comfort of a bed. These dreamers drowse close to their work, ready to start as early as possible in order to squeeze the last rupee from the last minute of the working day. The sleepers vary from ragged beggars huddled on bare walkways, to suited bankers lying on desks in full view through the windows. All of Delhi's bedless workers wait for the lull to end and the dawn to bring light to the proceedings.

Today was no different. The 06:00 Bhopal Shatabdi Express stood at platform 11 oblivious to the torrent of colourful humanity flowing through the surrounding buildings. Inside the E2 First Class coach Mr Gupta looked around and sighed lightly. Every seat had been pre-booked. Even the listed, computer-mapped, number-allocated, no-named promissory seats had bodies occupying them. Mr Gupta disliked computers a lot. There was a time he only sold or checked and clipped tickets. Now he was a human extension of a computer system that only did half a job and left the rest to him. "Bloody annoying," he was apt to say under his breath.

Mr Gupta eyed his computer sheet with the scepticism of experience. Whatever the computer sheet said, it would be lying. He looked up and around the First Class carriage trying personally to compute how the full seats corresponded to his printed readout. They did not. There were the right number of people and the right number of seats, but he knew that most, give or take a few foreigners, were not where they should be. The computer sheet he was checking suggested that IT was not necessarily being used correctly by Indian Railways. He had been a conductor for twenty-four years, graduating from apprentice clerk, junior booking clerk and senior administrator. A conductor was a prestigious job and he was envied by many of his contemporaries, especially as he held the dual role of conductor-superintendent. He was now based in First Class only and held sway over all except the train driver. He had seen most things and every change too, but these computers baffled him. They were a waste of time and effort. They were "bloody well annoying."

Take seat 35 for instance. It was booked to a Mr J. Chandra. In reality seat 35 was occupied by a short, portly woman in a predominantly yellow sari, bedecked in gold jewellery, and talking at twenty-to-the-dozen to her equally expansive and garrulous sister diagonally opposite. This could not be Mr J. Chandra. He was the tall man sitting beside her next to the window. Mr J. Chandra looked tense.

"Madam," he said turning to the woman of the yellow sari. "I would ask you, please could we swap seats as I am very tall and need to stretch my legs?"

She stopped the staccato fusillade of relentless chatter and gazed at Mr J. Chandra with a wide-eyed look of shock. Mr Gupta braced himself for another of the early morning spats he had so often witnessed.

"And why would I do that sir?" she asked. "I may wish to use the conveniences later and this is the ideal seat."

"Madam," Mr J. Chandra replied. "I am a very tall man and am rather crushed here. I am happy to stand should you wish to move at any time, but the journey to Agra will be hellish if I stay scrunched up like this."

"You quite happily shifted over when I came along," she bristled. "It's not my fault you are tall!"

"But madam," he said. "I was reading my paper and didn't realise it would be such a dreadful crush at first. If I sat next to the aisle it would be easier and I could stretch my legs. It's not my fault I'm tall either."

"He called you fat!" yelped her sister directly across the table to Mr J. Chandra.

"He did!" squawked the woman, turning on the hapless man. "You should not be so personal just because you look like a bamboo cane! Are you mad?"

"Please, please madam," he said desperately. "All I mean is that my ticket has 35 on it. I was willing to shift over, but it is now very uncomfortable for me. I'm tall and that is my seat really. You can sit here and talk to your friend and be comfortable. I'll let you out if needs be and I'll make sure you have all the room you need..."

"He called you fat again!" yelped her sister.

"Oh God," groaned Mr J. Chandra raising a hand to his brow and shaking his head.

The resulting double-barrelled tirade from the two women caused

Mr Gupta to sigh again and step in to the fray.

"May I help you ladies?" he asked calmly.

The barrage stopped and all three passengers looked up at his gentle face.

"This – gentleman – called me fat!" said the lady in the yellow sari.

"He did! He did!" yelped her sister. "Says he's squashed up because she's too big."

"I certainly did not," groaned the man. "I just need more room for my legs. I should never have given her my seat, but was trying to be polite."

"Suggesting a lady is fat is not polite at all!" said the woman.

"We're both big boned," said her sister. "It is awful to think there are so few gentlemen left. Such personal comments are hurtful and caddish!"

"Oh God," groaned Mr J. Chandra again. "Please try to sort this out conductor."

Mr Gupta took a breath and gazed once more at the computer sheet on his well-worn clipboard. Two of these seats were number allocated, no-named promissory seats – these were the ones the portly sisters would have on their tickets – window seats 36 and 37. Mr J. Chandra should be by the aisle. The remaining seat would be filled by a member of a group of climbers, block-booked by their tour operator months ago. This would take a little tact, he thought, looking over his glasses at the protagonists in this little farce.

"Can I see your tickets please ladies?" he asked smiling gently.

He looked at the proffered items and ticked off two more seats on his list.

"Hmm, I see you have the *Preferential Pairing*," he said, making it up as he went along. "These are usually allocated to ladies so they are not jostled by the refreshment trolleys. They are highly sought after. I feel, in this instance, your allocated seats would be best kept as you are going to Bhopal and these outside seats will change several times. I will make sure you're well looked after and, after all, it is a lovely day to look out the window."

Mr J. Chandra gave Mr Gupta a look of thanks, then looked at the two sisters with hope.

"Well, I suppose that makes sense, especially the Preferential Pairing," said the lady in the yellow sari. "And you never quite know who will sit next to you on a train – there are so few gentlemen about today."

"Yes, do sit here Anulata, it will be easier to talk," said her sister.

"OK, I shall Gungita," said the woman in the yellow sari.

"Thank you, ladies," said Mr Gupta smiling. "I have you crossed off as being in the Preferential Pairing seats."

Anulata, she of the yellow sari, shuffled on her ample bottom and stood in the aisle as Mr J. Chandra unwound himself from the confines of the window seat and towered above her. She glowered at him and shuffled back into the seat opposite her sister.

"Thank you, conductor," said Mr J. Chandra sitting down. "I'm so sorry for any inconvenience."

"These little errors happen," replied Mr Gupta, "even in this modern, computer-driven India."

The sisters were soon nattering again as if nothing had happened, and Mr J. Chandra stretched his legs whilst unfolding his copy of the Times of India. He went straight to the sports page and groaned again as he read of India's latest trouncing by England at Lords. A shadow fell on him as a large Australian man in a dusty Tilley hat thudded into seat 38. The seat made a slight sigh as the fellow's weight forced the air from its fabric. He was as tall as Mr J. Chandra but built like a wrestler – one of the climbers no doubt.

"Strewth," he said smiling broadly. "This bloody station has more people in it than the whole of Oz. Thank Christ we're in First Class. Must be bloody hell in Second!"

"It can be busy," said Mr J. Chandra lifting his paper.

"Busy! It's fucking mind blowing!" said the climber, adding, "Er, pardon me ladies."

The sisters were speechless for the first time since they sat down. Mr J. Chandra winced. The big Australian settled in his seat then turned to the sister, Gungita, who was dwarfed by his bulk.

"Excuse me lady," he said smiling. "Could you budge up a tad? Only I'm big boned and ache like a bastard from climbing too many hills. Need the room. Don't worry, I get off at Agra, we can snuggle up a bit."

Behind his paper Mr J. Chandra smiled. The two sisters gawped. Mr Gupta finished ticking boxes and escaped to the next coach.

The Shatabdi started its journey to Bhopal on time. The First Class passengers had settled into a semblance of order, with no spare bodies wandering around the coaches and no irate people left to appease. Mr Gupta considered this the end of the *first phase* of his working day. The *second phase* could now begin. He would take a further wander through the coaches to ensure named passengers were identified on his paperwork, even if they had settled in the wrong seat, and then change the numbers on the sheet rather than trying to move settled bodies. Eventually the sheet would be handed in and the computer would be changed to match.

"A bloody waste of time," mumbled Mr Gupta again.

He was thankful that he had graduated beyond the chaos of the lesser coaches further back, where one of his junior colleagues would be drifting towards what he thought of as *conductor rage*. This is the point where sharp, loud rebuffs took the place of kindly answers. He shuddered at the memory. Once back at coach E2 Mr Gupta was in a better frame of mind, even though he had developed a slight headache. Very few passengers had been in the wrong seats and those that were seemed happy enough. Whether this remained the case as the express made each stop towards its destination was in the realm of *phase three*, complete with untouched computer sheets.

E2 was filled with quiet chatter and everyone looked content. Mr J. Chandra was deeply engrossed with the Times of India business pages and the sisters were engaged in a rapid-fire speaking match. Mr Gupta was amazed at how both could talk simultaneously yet still hold a valid conversation. He thought about his darling late wife, Kiran, who had chattered the same way to her equally late sister, yet they could work at anything simultaneously with no let up at all – cooking, cleaning, and even writing.

"Anil," she would say. "Women can successfully multi-task. Men are single minded and lose the track so easily. A man can be distracted. They have focus but no sense of the whole world around them."

"I think you are right, dear," he would say. "But why on Earth does talking always have to be one of the tasks?"

Mr Gupta smiled at this memory. Kiran would scold him playfully for his cheeky answer, but both were comfortable with this ritual. It was part of their natural pair bonding. She would tweak his ear lobe, then kiss his cheek and they would both chuckle like younger lovers. They had loved each other so very much. He missed her to the point of agony at times. His little Kiran.

"Hey, Harvey!"

Mr Gupta snapped out of his reverie. The big Australian had swivelled around in his seat and called to one of his party behind. His voice had physical texture and filled the whole coach with the impact of a detonating shell. The sisters by the window started and Mr J. Chandra jumped just enough to make a small tear in the top of the Times of India.

"Christ, Jason!" said the middle-aged fellow Mr Gupta assumed to be Harvey. "You nearly made my heart stop!"

"Sorry mate," boomed Jason with only slightly less volume. "Just wondering if we get any breakfast on this train, that's all. The breakfast-in-a-bag from the hotel was like a feather in a furnace and I'm bloody famished."

"Mark reckons you ate all the complimentary chocolates too," replied Harvey smiling and pointing to the tall, slim man next to him, "so you can't be that hungry."

"Bloody hell, mate," said the Australian. "He'll never let me forget that. There was only four anyways."

"Yes," interjected Mark, "but two of them were mine. You even left the wrappers on my bed!"

Mr Gupta relaxed slightly as he could see this was a gentle persiflage. All the men and women in the group were smiling, as was the big Australian. Even the other passengers seemed more amused than annoyed. Most of the party were British, he knew, as they were block-booked with a company called Jagged Peaks UK. They had finished their expedition to a mountain up in Ladakh and were now taking a day to see the sights of Agra. The banter continued as a bearded man leaned out of his seat and added a piece of wisdom that even drew a laugh from Mr J. Chandra.

"Hey, Jason!" he laughed. "Tell Mark it's a perfect balance. If he put on any weight you'd never fit in that tent you share – you'd need some grease and a shoe-horn!"

"Jesus, mate," said Jason in hurt tones. "I'm just a bit hefty – it's a natural thing. Markie there is like a bloody stick and needs less calories. And he takes up more room than me. He's all arms, knees and elbows. It's like sleeping next to a bag of rats!"

Mr Gupta decided to answer the recently proffered question regarding breakfast in the hope that the noise level would then drop to something less strident.

"Sir," he said to the Australian. "The boys will be along with breakfast very soon now. A second snack will be served before Agra too."

The big man grinned, giving him the look like an outsized child.

"Thanks mate," he replied to Mr Gupta. Then turning again said to the man called Mark, "If you leave any of yours I'll have it. Those chocolates hardly filled a gap!"

The *second phase* was now complete and breakfast was being served. This would be a nice little distraction consisting of a Meals on Wheels Tea Kit, Marie Biscuits and a couple of sweets, closely followed by bread and jam with a small packet of cornflakes. Mr Gupta could now go and sit awhile before the first scheduled stop at Mathura Junction. He had enjoyed the light-hearted banter amongst the climbers and felt that it had made the atmosphere in the carriage less careworn. It had been just offensive enough to cause a stir, yet just funny enough to raise a smile. And the noise level had dropped as the food reached that end of the train. All in all, it was a pretty normal day in First Class.

"Normal," said Mr Gupta quietly to himself as he reached a little seating area near the catering boys. He thought *normal* was something he knew less about now than at any time in his 55 years to date.

Mr Gupta found it impossible to describe what a normal human life should be. Sitting on the train it was enough to make his mind creak. He thought there was too much to consider. He mulled it over:

With seven billion people on the planet there are far too many variables, so it is a case of cutting things down to its simplest form: we are born; we procreate; we die. If a person exists at all, the first and last part of this triptych happens. One begets the other. In this simplest of formulas, the only variable is the middle part. Some do not, or cannot, have children. For the majority that do, it becomes a major part of their lives. These two constants and one variable form the basic framework of the human condition. This is normality.

Beyond this, normality ceases to be tangible for anyone. Life becomes a complex story with increasing variables which encompass joy, tears, laughter and sorrow. That is how a human would see it; other creatures would tend towards the simple formula of normality. Each of us has a story, which is our life between birth and death, but until that final act we can only ever say 'my life up to now.' The future is a foreign land. We can have plans, dreams and tangible goals, but they can only become certain once they have passed, yet we have hope.

For Mr Gupta this *up to now* was all he had. He was bereft of plans and far from hopeful. His life had stalled. If anything, entropy had taken an early hold. This gentlest of men gazed at the flat, lush farmland of the Yamuna plain passing the window. His head thumped above his left eye and his vision pulsed on that side. He removed his glasses and rubbed his temple. The colours beyond the window blurred as he drifted into contemplation once more.

He was in his fifty-sixth year and, by modern Indian standards, would be considered comfortable. His income was greater than his spending needs and he also had some safe investments. He lived in a small house in Yamuna Nagar, with a walled garden which gave him a little seclusion. There were climbing, flowering plants flowing over the walls, potted shrubs and a little garden of herbs. He fed the local birds, the babblers, drongos and sparrows, and even welcomed the small, stripy squirrels which he loved to watch. They reminded him of clockwork toys with their stop, go, staccato movements. He kept the garden tidy and was neat around the house, which had all the necessary mod-cons. Yet it lacked that special touch a woman gave. That missing element was taken from him by a taxi driver two years earlier. Kiran had died instantly under the wheels of a rusty old Ambassador which had mounted the pavement, then sped on. The witnesses had seen very little, just a man in a white shirt, dark glasses and, possibly, a tie. The car and man combination matched thousands in Delhi. Hit-and-run was the verdict and the effect had been shattering. Kiran had been a part of Mr Gupta; her death had severely damaged that part, and it had never revived. He knew it never could. All he had left now was his daughter, Rupa, who had made his life bearable.

Yet his life had started with a series of joys in which hard work, study and good health had held the key. His father had been a successful cloth merchant and the elder son, Amit, had followed him into the family business. Mr Gupta's brother was seven years the senior, so had taken the lead and was well versed in the business as he made his way through school. Anil Gupta had assumed he was going to slip seamlessly into the business too, but his father had greater plans for him. At eight-years-old he was bright, competent in English and showing signs of high intellect; it was not to be wasted. He was to have a proper education.

He was sent to England under the care of his Uncle Nikhil 'Nik' Gupta who ran a restaurant in Brighton. His mother had cried, but was sure this was the best way to ensure he was to have the greatest chance in life. He joined an independent school, St. Aubyns, where he flourished. He missed his family at first, but his uncle and aunt were caring people and kept him happy, so he began to enjoy his time there. He wrote home weekly, letters kept neatly by his mother up to her death. By the age of thirteen he had become fluent in English, remained near the top of the class in most subjects, and became quite Anglicised. He was most fond of trains and history, especially the history of India. In his diligence he even learned a lot about running a restaurant, helping in the kitchen for some pocket money with no complaint.

Five years had passed before Mr Gupta returned to Delhi. His aunt had cried as he left and he wept quietly upon leaving, even though he was excited to be seeing his family again. The plan was for him to continue his education in India then go back to England to attend a university. Cambridge was talked of. His aged father remained kind and loving, and was very proud of young Anil. His mother had a few grey hairs but always looked the same to him. The business continued to be successful and Amit had taken on the primary role of its day-to-day management. The first few weeks of his return saw Mr Gupta re-establish ties with his old friends with whom he explored Delhi. They often ended up at the station, where they watched the trains, porters and the passengers. The latest drive towards modernisation, with new buildings and faster trains, looked wonderful to his young eyes. He found himself wishing he could work for a railway company one day, perhaps as a driver. Education had opened his mind to more of life than his friends could see, and they thought him altered and bookish.

Life changed suddenly as he neared his fourteenth birthday. His father suffered a heart attack whilst in the shop and nothing could be done to save him. He was fifty-six years old. Grief shook the family and aged his mother. His brother felt terrified at the prospect of taking over the business so soon. Yet, they had rallied, pulled through and continued to live a comfortable life, Amit's fears being displaced by the confidence of becoming head of the family. Mr Gupta was not destined to return to England. He finished his education locally, but by seventeen had lost his enthusiasm for continuous learning and wanted to work for money. Amit wanted his brother to join him as a merchant. He was doing very well and was looking to expand the business with a new shop in Agra – Anil could run that once he had made the grade. Mr Gupta's ideas were different. He had been successful with an application for a post with Indian Railways as a junior clerk. With some regret Amit finally accepted his little brother's decision and was supportive. His mother remained proud. Thus started the steady rise to his present position. Not spectacular, but comfortable. Even so, the moments of normality throughout his life were infrequent and fleeting.

A throb above Mr Gupta's left eye brought him out of his reverie and back to the present. The sudden, short stab of pain caused his left nostril to dribble into his moustache, which he instinctively wiped with a sleeve. That last, intense spasm ended the headache which had tormented him all morning. However, there was now another annoyance for him to deal with.

"Bloody hell!" he muttered.

To the far side of his small refuge a fuzzy, white, opaque cloud hovered, like a floater in his eye, just out of direct focus, but there all the same. A bead of sweat ran from the crown of his balding head adding to the dampness of his moustache. With a blink, the phenomenon disappeared. His mind became crystal clear and he felt full of relief and energy. He dug a handkerchief from his pocket and dried his face and sleeve, lifting his glasses and wiping his eyes in the same movement.

"Are you alright, Mr Gupta?"

The question had been asked by one of the boys he knew as Raj. This young man was always smiling. He wore his company baseball cap at a jaunty angle which made him look the jovial rascal he was. He was proffering a cup of tea.

"Yes, Raj," he replied. "I've had a bit of a thick head, but now... Well, it feels fine. Is that tea for me?"

"Yes, Mr Gupta," smiled Raj. "My tea will pick you up no end, sir. You will have lead in your pencil and feel jolly well wonderful!"

"Hmmm," murmured Mr Gupta smiling. "I use a pen nowadays. And thanks for the tea."

"I still use a pencil," replied Raj. "My girlfriend says I should leave it in my pencil case, and I do, but I am keeping it sharp! I drink lots of chai!"

"Get off with you," said Mr Gupta. "Show some bloody respect!"

"Yes sir!" grinned Raj. He stepped from view then briefly popped his head back around the corner, grinning even wider. "I also have a rubber on my pencil, but she still makes me leave it in the case!"

Mr Gupta laughed quietly and sipped the tea. Everyone's a comedian he thought. He blinked hard and stared – nothing. Head still clear, no headache. He finished his tea just as the train started to slow down for its stop at Mathura.

Very few changes were made at Mathura Junction. A few minutes after the train left, Mr Gupta had settled back into his little hideaway near the catering boys. Raj was singing off key somewhere out of view, clanking pots and being his usual energetic self. Outside, green farmland flashed by, revealing signs of both the past and present India. One minute a large factory, the next crude grass and palm shelters in the middle of endless lush, green cultivation. Pylons marched across both old and new landscapes. Mr Gupta sighed.

"You still miss her," he said quietly.

He had talked to himself a lot since Kiran had been taken. Although loneliness weighed heavily he bore no illusions about finding love again, for he still loved her so much. Even after two years he felt inextricably tied to her. What they had had was so strong it remained solid and unbreakable. He was also aware he was well past his prime. In his younger days he was slim with a full head of hair and had *cut a dash,* as Kiran would say. He had always sported a moustache, which he thought made him look more rugged than the gentle creature he was. Kiran told him that his gentleness was his strength, but he still wished he looked more like a warrior. Now he was stocky, balding with a few white hairs showing in his moustache. He felt he was starting to resemble his job - plain and functional.

The train decelerated quickly before he could settle. This was an unscheduled easing of progress, for he knew this was a fast section of line. He squeezed his face up against the window to see ahead. A cluster of people on the up-line pinpointed the location of the problem. He felt a twinge of anxiety. The Shatabdi did not stop, it just slowed enough for all on board to look down upon an awful scene. The last up-train had been travelling at maximum speed as an old man had chosen to cross the track with a large sack of animal fodder on his head. The express passed through him as if he had not existed, which, of course, he no longer did. How far along the line he had been when he was killed was hard to tell, but his remains had come to rest by a group of little huts, the inhabitants of which were standing next to the bloody wreckage between the rails. The torso, head and arms were intact, but the legs were crimson tatters and yellow splintered bones. A dirty white dhoti had soaked up a lot of vital fluids giving the allusion that the body was just a skin bag full of kindling. There was no normal man-shape. The villagers looked on in resigned shock. Next to them a dog barked in short, rhythmic yaps, unsure what to do next.

By the time the Shatabdi started to accelerate again, Mr Gupta had settled back into his seat staring impassively through the far window. He had seen things like this regularly over the years. Memories flowed through his head in a torrent. Kiran had died in such a way. Less bloody, but as suddenly. A wicked finality ending all life's plans in an instant. When Jhatish, his best friend, told him Kiran had been killed, it started an emotional collapse which had continued inside ever since, even after the physical expressions had gone.

Mr Gupta's life of joys had continued as he settled into his new career with Indian Railways. Amit became wealthy as his Agra gamble bore fruit. He purchased a new house there, moving his wife, new baby, and mother closer to the hub of the business. With unstinting generosity Amit gave Mr Gupta the family home in Delhi. This took care of his independence and he threw himself into his job with the energy of a happy young man. He even resumed his education and went to evening classes to study history. He became fascinated with Edwin Lutyens and the buildings he had designed, and was most impressed that he had had the main railway station relocated so it would not impinge on his plans for a New Delhi. The Moguls had also made great buildings and he often explored the local sites for the sheer joy of it. He looked fondly at the history of the British rule, especially as he felt a strong connection to England where his early years were spent. India could not have been ruled forever from London and it came to an end after the Second World War with independence. Yet India tended to assimilate, adjust and utilise the more attractive parts of foreign cultures without betraying itself, making it the most varied and colourful nation on Earth. Mr Gupta envisioned the British Empire as marble slabs laid over a rice field – eventually the marble sank to become an inseparable part of the whole. India had a lot of Raj at its core, but it was Indian still.

Mr Gupta settled into his new normality and, through the gift of a complimentary season ticket, had regular visits from his mother. Once well into his twenties, his mother started to nag him about marriage, something Indian mothers took a great interest in.

"Amit has two children, Anil," she would scold. "It is time you settled down!"

He felt a little uneasy and was aware of an undercurrent of certainty in his mother's voice. Amit had smiled a lot if he was with his mother on these visits, and suggested that his brother was due to get a surprise. Eventually it happened. She informed him they had found a nice girl who would make a good wife. He had baulked at this, but agreed to meet her, determined to go through the motions for appearance's sake and use his intellect to find a way out. Then he met Kiran, and was lost.

Nalin Shastri was one of a wealthy family of bankers. He had two daughters. Tamina, the eldest, had already married a local up and coming business man, Ravi Uppal. His quest was to find a husband for his younger girl. Nalin was impressed that young Mr Gupta owned his own home outright, that he was educated and was rising steadily through the ranks of Indian Railways. Mr Gupta was then a conductor on express trains and had good prospects of becoming a superintendent or station manager in the long term. Both families were delighted that the two young people agreed to the match and the betrothal was announced within a week. There was no doubting the main mover was the traditional bonding of two good families, yet Mr Gupta had gained everything he could have wished for.

Kiran Shastri had been small and slim and oh so shy, with a beauty beyond her looks. She was educated, intelligent and kind. She moved like a sleek oriental cat, sylphlike and fluid. She could even cook better than his mother. Best of all they had fallen in love very, very quickly, and for life.

At Agra Mr Gupta returned to coach E2. Most of the First Class passengers were alighting here, they being tourists on the way to see the fort and the Taj Mahal. The Jagged Peaks party filed past him with Jason, Mark and the bearded man bringing up the rear.

"Hey, Mark," said the latter. "Ten quid on there being a food trolley on the platform."

"How do you reckon that?" replied Mark.

"Well old Jason there is moving faster now than when he slipped down the snow slope on Stok Kangri!"

"You bastards are so bloody funny," said the big Australian. "I think I need to find a hospital to get my sides stitched up!"

"Ask them to count the chocolates in there first," said Mark.

With that they had gone.

The rest of the journey to Bhopal was routine: stops at Gwalior and Jhansi Junctions; Mr Gupta adjusting new and errant lists; the usual questions from his First Class passengers; and long spells of inactivity whilst being fed tea by Raj. The Shatabdi arrived at its destination over an hour late. Once the passengers had gone and he had checked for left property, Mr Gupta stepped off the train and went straight to the offices. Today he was doing an extra shift and was returning to Delhi on the late train. It would make a very long day. At least all he needed to do was supervise a trainee who would undertake all the onerous tasks. As he entered the office a young, smartly dressed man leapt to his feet and shook his hand.

"Good afternoon, sir," he said. "I am full of beans and ready to do the whole show!"

This was Sanjay Uddhav. Mr Gupta had been mentoring him for several weeks and this was his final day before going solo. Sanjay had been a good student and had even mastered the computer sheets with a speed and efficiency Mr Gupta envied.

"That's good to hear," said Mr Gupta. "How much help do you need today?"

"None!" exclaimed Sanjay. "I am tip-top and ready to get cracking! You can relax and just check my sheets after each stop. There is a delay on the up-train though. Did you see the accident?"

"Yes," said Mr Gupta. "Quite horrible."

"You saw the bodies?" asked Sanjay.

"I saw bits of one body. Were there more?" said Mr Gupta raising his eyebrows.

"Oh yes," said Sanjay. "The man was hit at a crossing and carried a long way. The driver did not realise until he stopped at Mathura. There was a leg stuck under the bogie and lots of people screamed. He was very upset."

"Oh my," said Mr Gupta. "You said 'bodies.'"

"Yes, yes," said Sanjay. "At the crossing they found the man's wife. She was in half and it was all terrible!"

Mr Gupta felt himself shudder. The accident had not been unusual by Indian standards, but lately every tragedy sent a shock wave to his core. His own loss had sensitised him to each new fatality he heard about, and there were many on the huge railway system. Sanjay was still talking.

"So now we have a wait until they have everything cleaned up," he said. "Let's go and grab some tea."

Mr Gupta needed tea. His head was aching once more.

Sanjay was quick and efficient and, true to his word, let Mr Gupta rest for most of the trip back to Delhi. When they left Mathura, it was dark, and the lights of passing towns and villages sparkled like stars in the gloom. Mr Gupta ran a final check of Sanjay's sheets and settled for the final stretch home. They would be late, but as the morrow was a scheduled day off, he could sleep in. He also had an appointment with his GP, Dr Chowdary. The headaches were becoming increasingly regular migraines, which had become another *bloody annoyance*.

His life had changed rapidly after his marriage to Kiran. They were so very happy in their little house and she had altered it just enough to make it theirs alone. His mother approved and loved her new daughter-in-law. The young couple had made love regularly, laughed, and grew together. Within a year, things changed again. Kiran had welcomed him home one special evening. They had eaten a beautiful meal and even drank some beer, a rarity and more of a pleasure for it. Then they had made love. Their love-making had been gentle, soft and warm. He could never be brutal. Before their wedding they had both been virgins. Both shy. Both scared. It was Kiran who took the lead. She taught him by instinct, was patient and had made him feel wanted, strong and complete. They were one. His love for her was a beautiful, constant distraction. No couple could be closer.

"Anil," whispered Kiran in breathless tones in the semi-darkness of their bedroom. "We are going to have a baby."

Mr Gupta left Delhi station just after midnight, dodging all the touting taxi drivers. He had a prearranged lift home. Slightly apart from the thronging mass of other vehicles was a battered, faded green-and-yellow tuktuk. This was Old Mr Singh's pride and joy. He was dozing inside, dressed in a dhoti, light-blue shirt and turban, waiting for his expected customer. He knew Mr Gupta's working times well, and would eschew any other fares from the time he was due to arrive, to his actual arrival. Old Mr Singh lived very close to Mr Gupta, so the arrangement suited them both: Mr Gupta got a guaranteed lift and Old Mr Singh had a paying fare home. Besides that, they had been friends for many years. Old Mr Singh had an uncanny knack of waking up as Mr Gupta got within a few paces.

"Ah, there you are Mr Gupta," croaked the old man. "I thought you were not going to be here tonight."

"Delays, Mr Singh," he replied. "Someone hit by a train down beyond Mathura."

"I heard," said Mr Singh. "Bloody farmers can spot a caterpillar a mile away, but can't see a bloody great train! I tell you India has got to bloody well wake up!"

Mr Gupta settled into the ancient tuktuk before replying.

"Right now, this Indian needs to go to sleep. How is Mrs Singh?"

"Tip-top and still talking." Mr Singh's standard reply.

The tuktuk clanked into life and they set off at a modest speed, the exhaust fumes adding a large contribution to Delhi's polluted air in their wake. The vehicle's feeble lights glowed gently as they accelerated.

"There is a tiffin-box next to you," shouted the old man over the alarmingly noisy engine. "Mrs Singh put together some food for you. She cooked far too much again!"

"You are both silly, and both very kind!" shouted back Mr Gupta.

"Well, it's either you or the bloody monkeys," shouted the old man. "And I prefer you as you don't crap on my tuktuk!"

The vehicle reached their neighbourhood without mishap and Old Mr Singh dropped his friend off in a cloud of dust and fumes. As usual Mr Gupta paid the standard fare of a few rupees, arguments of any extra having finished long ago, and took the tiffin-tin with him.

"I will drop the tin off tomorrow," he said as Mr Singh found an errant gear.

"Come for tea if I am around!" shouted the old man as his steed lurched into the night. "And it's already tomorrow..."

Mr Gupta ate the delicious food from a piled-up plate. In company he was a polite eater, but the long day had blunted any self-enforced etiquette. Outside the sounds of the city continued at a more subdued level. He sat in his easy chair surrounded by reminders of his married life: a big wooden carving of Ganesha, the elephant god; various dark-wood carvings hanging on the white walls; a scattering of ornate furniture; and, incongruously, a large, flat-screened television on an antique chest. His home was as Kiran had left it. Mr Gupta was in no hurry to change things, because he fitted it and familiarity gave him comfort. He threw his clothes onto a chair and got into bed making small grunts of effort.

"I'm a bloody old man," mumbled Mr Gupta. "Goodnight, Kiran."

He still bade her goodnight. Silly, he thought, but healthy. She would tell him off for the way he threw his clothes onto the chair, but it had never cured him. He liked the gentle scolding, the ritual, the reaffirming of their togetherness. After she had died he folded his clothes for a while, but it had been wrong. Why should her death make him a better husband, a different man? Such a self-imposed reaction of guilt was a betrayal. So he had reverted to his old habit and immediately felt close to Kiran again. He dozed in the humid night.

Their son had been still-born. It was as simple as that. *Complications* had been the verdict. In the 1970s infant mortality was very high and families accepted they had no power to change fate. The little boy had been cremated without a name as they both referred to him as Little One. Adding a name would have felt too scripted. Kiran had been a rock. He had been inconsolable. He had hurt for both of them and in his odd way had given his wife the diversion she needed to get through the following months. By the time Mr Gupta had reached acceptance, she had arrived at the same point too. She had lavished care on her lovely man as she would have on the Little One. They had emerged stronger.

Life went on. Material possessions increased, but the important, missing element, children, failed to materialise. Kiran would not conceive again for twenty years. Then Rupa was born. His beautiful girl. He would visit her tomorrow.

"It's already tomorrow..."

Old Mr Singh's words drifted through his mind as he drifted into sleep.

Chapter 2

Tiger

Great amber eyes opened. A deep breath drew air through nostrils and across the back of a toothy maw. The tiger registered his surroundings immediately. Nothing new excited him, nothing new crossed his vision. The same foetid stinks filled his olfactory organs. He chuffed out his breath clearing his senses. The stink was all him, his territory, his world. Somewhere, buried in his subconscious, there glowed an ember of wildness. His DNA held eons' worth of code for being a tiger. He needed very little of this vast library of survival tools in his present, small kingdom. The zoo kept him alive but acted as a chronic tranquilizer. The tiger had been stifled for over a decade, from cub to fully adult male Bengal tiger. Yet, that ember of his true inheritance remained.

The tiger stood, then stretched and yawned, great muscles popping along his back, huge claws pulling against the rough floor. He paced his dirty confines, the floor damp with his own excrement, his fastidious nature blunted by the inability to keep clean. Stopping at a green pool he lapped at the liquid disconsolately. The sun was rising in the watery monsoon sky. The yapping and growling of hyenas from a nearby enclosure made him stand tall, ears turning to the sounds. He took a second sighing, scenting breath; a second chuffed exhalation. He knew hyena sounds and their acrid smell. The ember of wildness glowed brighter. He instinctively hated them. He had never set eyes upon a hyena, but would kill one without hesitation. More yapping. This time the tiger took a lungful of air and tapped into that ancient part of him that could not be resisted. He rent the morning with a thunderous, bellowing roar which echoed across the park silencing every living creature. A tiger's roar is intended to freeze its prey. A hesitation which increases the likelihood of a kill. A quicker meal. But this roar faded into the distance as a sound without action. It was all this tiger could do. In his cage. In his small, foetid world.

This great beast had been taken from the side of his dead mother as a cub. Her skin was now a rug, her vital parts used up long ago in useless oriental powders and potions. A reduction of her component parts by what the tiger would consider to be clever monkeys. The tiger had never killed. As a cub, he had eaten fresh meat supplied by his mother, but since that distant time he had eaten only dead flesh. It tasted dead. A fresh kill tasted of life and excited a predator. The bland food he was given was another part of his zoological stultification. Yet still that ember glowed.

Sevak had looked after the Bengal tiger for the last eight years and was known to have a way with him. He kept the cage as clean as he could and the outside enclosure was raked and cleared of daily rubbish. He even polished the sign on the fence which stated: *Bengal Tiger – Panthera tigris tigris – Khan. Rescued from the wild as a cub in 1999.* Beneath was a map of the various sub-species' range in the world, sporadic with isolated pockets. India still held the greatest population.

Sevak, or Seva as he was most commonly known, was a small, bird-like man in his mid-thirties. He wore a white shirt, threadbare but clean, a tattered cream dhoti, and sandals he had made himself from tyre rubber and rope. He was very poor and looked down upon by most, though he was a Shudra and not an untouchable. Technically he was an under-keeper, but had made the job of looking after the tiger his own. They called him *Khan's servant*, but he did not mind. Khan was one of the main attractions at the zoo, so Seva found he was given few other tasks outside of filling in for absentees on occasion. On this morning Seva had cleaned the outer enclosure of the usual rubbish thrown in by the visitors. Plastic bottles, plastic bags and paper. A dirty nappy - that was a new one he had thought.

In his time with the tiger he had become disgusted by the crowds. They were generally scared of the tiger and could not see what he could, that beauty, that wildness inside. *Majesty* he thought was a fitting word. In their fear and false bravado, bolstered by the low wall and high fence, these visitors threw things at the tiger. He had even found a bag of rusty nails on one occasion. People were strange.

Khan was also part of the synthetic persona attached to the tiger. A creature such as this had no concept of names, his senses being the equivalent of what the humans called language. To the tiger humans smelled similar to all other primates, *clever monkey* really did fit how he sensed them. Seva had his own name for his charge, one only he used and which the tiger knew. Angaar – fire: it fitted. Over time Seva had become more tiger-sensitive, knowing how to interpret the movements and signs Angaar made. In turn Angaar responded positively and looked upon Seva as the only clever monkey he trusted. They had become as close as such different creatures could be. The tiger was a closed book to the visiting crowds. They gazed down and admired the fearsome carnivore, squealed in feigned fear if a more accurate missile found its mark and gazed in atavistic wonder when he was fed every few days. A feeding tiger could agitate a watching human, an instinctive fear of being prey, as ancient a feeling as the reality of the beast they observed. Angaar had never had a mate or seen another tiger since his mother, and remained subdued throughout his captive years. He became aloof. He responded affectionately to no one except Seva. And he had grown very large. At twelve years old he was just past his prime, but still attracted the most visitors. People enjoyed being scared, if that fear was safely in a cage.

Seva, his chores outside finished, went to the inside of the tiger house. He did not like the concentrated smells there, but tried his very best to keep things clean. He knew a tiger had a very sensitive sense of smell and felt for Angaar; if the smell made Seva's nose twitch, the tiger must find it intolerable. The early monsoon made things worse – nothing dried and the humidity encouraged fecundity. A short corridor led to the tiger's inner sanctum. Bars were all that kept the man and tiger apart, but Seva felt no fear as he stepped up close.

"Eeesh. Eeesh," he whispered gently. "Come. Come. Come."

Angaar had heard his carer's approach and turned his head before Seva came into view. A low, bass rumble sounded in the tiger's throat. He was purring.

"Eeesh. Eeesh!" hissed Seva once more, and this time used the name. "Angaar. Come Angaar. Eeesh!"

The man could never use the name Khan for his charge, it seemed clichéd, was certainly uninspired and far from original. When Seva looked into the tiger's eyes and saw the glow, the spark, he knew *Angaar* was right. Sometimes, when the tiger roared his defiance at the yapping hyenas he saw the glowing embers flare, briefly, into a real fire.

"Angaar, come," repeated Seva.

The tiger responded. He had no concept of names, but recognised it as his own special sound which reaffirmed their bond. If such a beast could feel anything like affection, he held it for Seva. Angaar reached the bars and rubbed up against them with his neck and face, his purr continuous now. Seva ruffled the orange and white fur with his thin hands and whispered in soothing tones.

"Eeesh. Eeesh, my beautiful Angaar."

A huge paw was raised and, claws safely sheathed, Angaar batted at Seva's hands with cushioned blows. He was like a kitten with this diminutive man. After so many years of routine he also knew the man had something for him.

Seva had discovered by accident that Angaar loved spicy titbits. Some years ago, he was tickling the tiger's ears in this already established routine, when the writhing stopped and he sniffed hard at Seva's pocket. Wrapped in paper was his lunch, a single keema pattie given to him by the kindly vendor of one of the stalls at the main gate. He pulled it out, unwrapped it, and proffered it through the bars. The broad, rough, rasping tongue had pulled the triangular pattie into the toothy maw in one rough, unnerving lap. The odd thing was Angaar never immediately consumed such a titbit. He mumbled it, chewed, sucked and slobbered reducing it to damp fragments; he pawed at his own face, rolled around and dribbled; he chuffed and retched and coughed. Then he took a drink and sneezed a few times. Seva thought it might be caused by an addiction to spices, chilli perhaps, which gave Angaar a mighty spike to his numbed senses. He was not sure if it was healthy for a tiger to eat spicy patties, but Angaar had never shown any ill effects from his daily treat. Apart from that the vendor now gave him the patties free as he knew the tiger liked them.

This morning the ritual was re-enacted: the dance, the slobbering and sneezing followed by a drink, a few more sneezes and the addition of a massive yawn. That mouth, big enough to fit a man's head in with room to spare. This daily bonding was important as Angaar was lonely and stifled, and Seva had no family. Angaar was his only friend. A friend who could destroy him with one blow from a paw, should he so wish. Seva made his way into a side corridor and grabbed a handle that turned some well-greased cogs. He grunted with the effort of turning the gears, which moved a toothed arm, which dragged the inner cage door open. Angaar strode out into the daylight, sniffed the air, chuffed loudly and urinated on the dead tree in the middle of the enclosure. His day had begun.

Chapter 3

Cobra Investments

Cobra Investments was located on the first floor of a modern, low-rise office block in Delhi's expanding business district close to Connaught Place. The windows were dark and reflective. Inside the furnishings and fittings were a monochrome mix of black, white and bare metal, with plain walls sporting a few well-positioned traditional carvings and pictures. The cool, sanitised reception housed a large fish tank which bubbled quietly, ostensibly to give visitors something calming to look at. Outside in the tarmacked car park sat one white BMW and one black Audi. From here the building had a slightly reptilian air: the slick and modern look encapsulated India's desired perception of itself. The company was not large in global terms, but had a wide customer base with many loyal, long-term investors which made it significant in New Delhi and nearby towns and cities. It was doing very well. Advertising was surprisingly low-key as its success was built on discretion and understatement. A large percentage of its clients were of the older generation who wanted secure returns on their investments, or privacy on legal advice, financial or otherwise. They would not appreciate obvious signs of ostentation and luxurious corporate accommodation which could hint at large profits being squandered. This modest, solid look gave Cobra Investments the profile of a modern, caring company, both trustworthy and empathetic. Insurance claims were paid out promptly, investments realised reasonable returns, legal advice was thorough, cheap and sound, and customers were treated with an almost regal politeness.

Cobra, as it was generally referred to, was a joint enterprise created after a meeting of like-minded souls several years before. Ravi Uppal was the oldest partner and thought to look a little like Omar Sharif. He was sixty-three and had a kindly bearing, soft eyes and a radiant smile which engendered trust. A veteran of the investment game, he knew his look reassured his older customers and put them at their ease. With younger clients, he was avuncular and friendly, always able to appeal to their own egos and never bombastic with advice. He had learned a lot, made a lot of money and embraced modern India. Though not overtly greedy, he loved wealth, owned the white BMW and had a far younger, attractive wife. They lived in a modest haveli on the outskirts of the city and, though Ravi was easing into old age, maintained his enthusiasm for business. He had a knack of making money and had a genius for clever investment. Ravi could make a hundred rupees of a client's money into three hundred, but would quietly keep a hundred of this for himself – he was far from benevolent. Understated trappings of modest success hid a very ruthless streak.

Just after the new millennium he met his young business partner, the owner of the black Audi. Vasupati 'Vaz' Chopra had frequented the same gymnasium in a local hotel. He was younger than Ravi, slim and athletic, dressed in expensive suits, white shirts and wore aviator sunglasses. He was clean shaven, but favoured wearing his glossy black hair at shoulder length. This, with his long philtrum and wide mouth, gave him the look of a Native American. He smiled rarely, flashing a single gold tooth when he did. They had begun to talk in the lounge after their exercise sessions. Very soon their similarities gave rise to a friendship which had never faltered, each having qualities missing in the other. Vaz had a similar love of money and the trappings of wealth, but had come to it in a different way. Vasupati Chopra had been a loan shark of fearsome reputation in the darker parts of the city and well beyond. He leant money to desperate and vulnerable people at extortionate rates of interest and had many ways of ensuring payment. Ravi realised early on that Vaz was psychopathic with some deep psychotic tendencies, yet saw he had them under a firm control, using a sharp intellect to focus such traits to his advantage. Even so, Vaz was insecure and longed for approval beyond his trappings of success: a nice house, a pretty and devoted wife and two sons. Ravi had entered this small circle as a friend. A father figure. That adult approver. This finally give Vaz confidence. Everyone outside his limited world became unimportant. A psychopath with confidence is very dangerous indeed.

Ravi had long realised that some of his clients died intestate. Eventually a distant relative might be contacted and they would inherit the estate, with a large slice going to the government and a small fee coming his way. Due to the extended nature of Indian families, which tended to be large and rambling, this was an unusual occurrence, but there were enough with enough to play on Ravi's mind. If he could put such people in a single package – investment plus will, with Ravi as executor – there had to be a way of taking everything. The amount of money he had seen slip through his fingers had been staggering. These people were consistently of the same types: older couples, vulnerable younger people or, perhaps a single, bitter miser. This source of haemorrhaging wealth had irked him for years, so he devised a way to access it. Vaz had been the final component required to activate Ravi's unfulfilled plan.

Once joined they created Cobra as the mechanism to deliver the riches they desired. It had been built upon the combination of their distinct talents: Ravi's ability to charm people; Vaz's to efficiently remove obstacles. Ravi had no moral limits when it came to making money, but his avarice had been kept in check by minor scruples and a major fear of punishment, even though he stretched the rules occasionally. He considered his clients as cash cows and, if he maintained his reputation and remained friendly, they gave more milk. Vaz had no such compulsion to remain within the law and this was a quality Ravi admired.

Ravi had also become unhappy at home. His wife, Tamina, had never produced a child and was becoming an expensive burden. Their life together had stalled, so Ravi had found a new mistress who was younger and, more to the point, was already pregnant with his child. There was the possibility that his life could unravel unless he took charge of things soon. This was difficult as Tamina's family were wealthy and would fight hard to make him pay for any separation or divorce. His reputation amongst his older, wealthier clients could then suffer. It would mean ruination. The plan, which Vaz enabled, was the answer to all his troubles.

Their meeting in the hotel had laid the ground for an alliance. Once trust was established, Ravi had invited Vaz to meet him at the India Gate to discuss their future.

The Indian Gate glowed pink in the sunshine as the men met. Hawkers were trying to sell drinks, snacks and little mementos to the tourists. Ravi extricated himself from the throng and shook the younger man's hand, guiding him to the grass alongside the Rajpath. They strolled towards the distant government buildings. Vaz lit a cigarette and smoked as they walked, negotiating the Mansingh Road, weaving through the taxis and tuktuks swarming along it. White-uniformed police yelled ineffectually at those who dared to stop to let off passengers. A wave of a sub-machine gun at waist level usually got them moving again. The two men continued onward, small-talk now finished.

"Have you ever heard of Edwin Lutyens?" asked Ravi.

"Vaguely," Vaz replied. "He liked building grand structures, didn't he? Some of this stuff", he said gesturing up the wide avenue.

"Yes. Yes, he did," answered Ravi. "My brother-in-law is always talking about Lutyens's magnificent buildings. Oddly he got me quite interested. Look around. What do you see?"

"The wide road. The park and trees. Black shite hawks. The India Gate," replied Vaz looking over his sunglasses. "And bloody street sellers."

A flock of more than two hundred black kites circled over the Rashtrapati Bhavan in the hazy distance. The hawkers formed a similar flock circling a recently arrived gaggle of Japanese tourists.

"Mmm," said Ravi. "Look around again. Do you notice the space?"

"Yes, loads of it," said Vaz. "All grand vistas and very New Delhi. Are you going to lecture me about the *cradle of power* or something?"

Ravi smiled, his bleached teeth bright in the sunshine, contrasting with his greying moustache. They strode over the grass, avoiding the footpath which was too close to the fume-shrouded traffic.

"Everything you see here is like the world we inhabit," Ravi continued. "This is important to men such as us. I often walk here at the end of the day to clear my mind. The big spaces help. I find I can make decisions. Plans. All of this shows me what I could be. What you see here Vaz, *is* power. But the other thing here is wealth. Space requires power and wealth to exist in a city; to keep it constant. Power and wealth need to be constant."

"Ok," said Vaz quizzically. "Ok, I understand that. Like I said, a cradle of power, and wealth is a given. But what are you getting at?"

"Let's get a drink and I'll explain."

They hurried across the Janpath Road ignoring yells and hooting horns, and continued to the next intersection where they bought a Coke from a boy. They found a low, shaded wall to sit upon. Vaz lit another cigarette and smoked as he sipped from his bottle.

"This stuff is warm," he said, his gold crown glinting behind a cloud of exhaled smoke. "Come on Ravi. Say what you need to – I've got work to do."

Ravi laughed. "We've known each other a while now and we are pretty similar, you and I, but you have no bloody patience!"

"Call it a weakness" he replied.

"Would you be patient for ten crore rupees?" asked Ravi.

"I'm a fast learner," replied Vaz. "Now you've got my interest."

"Well, this is what I have been thinking," said Ravi cautiously. "Everything here is a model of what my life should be, but I am falling short. We are like-minded people and have the same aims yet we are, neither of us, whole. I love this space. This space is not so much the issue, as the creatures in it. They all live in shitty little holes, come out to suck up a living, then dribble back into their middens again. They leave behind crap which is fed upon by these bloody shite hawks. Or rats. Or flies. Or other scrawny Delhi wallahs who are barely alive."

A large dragonfly rattled over their heads and alighted on a stretch of chain-link hanging between two short posts. Its head swivelled. They both watched it zoom up and catch a big fly. Above, the black kites circled in the sultry air.

"That dragonfly owns the space," continued Ravi pointing. It had settled on the wall close by and was eating the kicking fly. "It takes what it wants without scruples – zoom, grab, eat. It leaves nothing but a hole in the air. That's what I want to be. I have fed off the excess of others, skimmed just enough off to be comfortable, but there is so much more to being a hunter. A hunter takes everything. I don't want to feed off other people's waste. Not like these shitty wallahs. We're hunters Vaz, but we underachieve. We feed on scraps like flies. I think... I think we can be hunters. Like that dragonfly, or maybe a cobra!"

Vaz laughed. "I've been a hunter for years! You've lost me, Ravi. We've talked about business often enough, but what's all this about dragonflies and cobras? Get down to the money." He looked at Ravi, then at the capital buildings. "We can never own India, but I'm sure we can be richer than we are. I'm limited now and am fed up with small time stuff. Let's have your business plan. The whole thing!"

Ravi sighed. "I am over sixty now yet feel very well, very healthy. I have made money and my business is solid as a rock. It's a funny game, insurance, investment and what have you. It sharpens your mind. You see, I have found a reserve of money I cannot get my hands on, just waiting to be tapped. I don't have all the...er...skills necessary to make it mine. You, Vaz, you do! We are talking crores of rupees."

Ravi sounding frustrated, confident and angry in equal measure.

"What skills have I got that you need, Ravi?" Vaz asked.

Ravi explained about the steady flow of unclaimed money disappearing into the Indian Government's coffers and the undeserving, distantly related benefactors of post-tax cash. He explained how he could corral wills with insurances and investments, about receiving enduring powers of attorney and the ease with which he could make the money mountain available to plunder. Vaz was enthralled. Ravi got to the crux of the matter.

"You see," said Ravi staring at the Rashtrapati Bhavan's dome against the sky. "It really is easy to put everything into place...*ready*. Yes, ready. Ready for the taking. The missing part of the equation is timing – the punctual demise of the client."

There was a moment's silence. Vaz raised his eyebrows, removed his aviator shades and wiped his eyes with a finger and thumb. He looked at Ravi, then smiled. At that very moment, Ravi knew he had him. Knew a link had been forged. Knew he had been right about Vasupati Chopra. Ravi could almost feel the weight of crores of rupees in his hands. Vaz replaced his aviators.

"A punctual demise of a person is my area of expertise," he said. "I assume this is a full partnership, so let's talk some more. Crores you say?"

"Regular, annual, crores. Millions." replied Ravi.

"And the partnership?" pushed Vaz.

"We'll form a new company," said Ravi, now on well-prepared ground. "I have even got my eyes on a new suite of offices here in Delhi. The only problem is initial funding. I don't want to sell my haveli or cash in any investments, and I'm assuming you don't want to risk any of your money. But there is a way to end up as a full and equal partner with no financial outlay. Come, we must walk some more."

Vasupati Chopra had never considered a partnership with anyone. It would halve profits and require the uncertainty of trust. Why should he trust anyone when he could always rely on himself? But this was different. Vaz had felt a primal attraction to Ravi Uppal, a man who treated him as an equal. Their methods of making money were different, yet their deep, dark, psychological nuclei were identical. With little effort they fitted as perfectly as two strands of DNA, becoming a fully functional organism. Friendship had grown with respect.

Skirting traffic they approached the Rashtrapati Bhavan. Here, by the railings of Lutyens's magnificent building, Ravi took a leap of faith and revealed his innermost thoughts.

"You know of my situation at home?" said Ravi leaning against the wheel of one of the ornamental field guns. "Tamina will find out about my other woman soon and things will get a little tricky, and very expensive. But she is the key."

Vaz caught on very quickly, "That's where the money comes from?"

"My wife must die," said Ravi, the words floating in the hot air giving voice to his darkest dreams. "We have no children. She has a lot of money inherited from her parents in trust and I have a lucrative life insurance on her. I control the wills and know I'm the main beneficiary. I get all the insurance and half the inheritance. Some nine crore rupees all together. Her sister will get the other part of the inheritance, but there's not a lot I can do about that. The main thing is it unlocks far more. Far, far more. There you are, that's it. What do you think?"

"You think I can arrange that?" asked Vaz, serious now.

"I know you can," said Ravi. "It will bind us."

"Yes, I know," said Vaz. "You want it clean, quick and untraceable?"

"No suffering," said Ravi. "No cruelty."

A troop of macaque monkeys strode across the huge square inside the fence skirting the Jaipur Column. The flag high on the palace dome flapped slightly in the heavy air. The kites circled.

"When?" asked Vaz.

"In about a month," answered Ravi. They started to stroll back down the Rajpath, steering clear of the armed soldiers dotted about for security. "She is going on a trip to Mumbai with a close friend. A girlie weekend for shopping and gossip. My PA sorted the itinerary, so I know what her movements will be. Mumbai is a dangerous city. She should not return."

"How?" asked Vaz.

"All the paperwork is set up and ready," said Ravi. "The insurance; the will. Everything cast iron. Nothing is amiss and all our friends think things are fine; shit, even Tamina thinks things are fine. I've made sure we attend dinners, functions and events together and that we are happy and in love. But, Vaz, the *how* is your speciality."

"And the friend?" asked Vaz balancing along the kerb, arms aloft like a child.

"She can be the witness of a crime, the witness of a tragedy or accident," replied Ravi coldly. "Or a victim of the same. I do not care."

And that was it. Since this time of union, they had never faltered.

Vaz arranged for two murders, the simplest solution. A gangster in Mumbai, who owed him a lot of money, was contracted to carry out the executions. The deal was accepted as Vaz would write off the debt and, as a bonus, would allow any proceeds of the venture to be kept. It would also remove the shadow of violent reprisal, for which Vaz was renowned. Strict instructions were given.

Tamina Uppal and her young friend, Miss Alka Rawat, had left a

43

restaurant in the business district close to midnight. They had spent a day shopping for clothes for the younger woman's pending wedding, and had drunk a lot of wine with their evening meal in celebration of their success. A taxi had been arranged and they were called out to their lift by a turbaned doorman, who escorted them to the shiny Ambassador. The doorman bowed as the car drove off into the night. The women were never seen alive again.

A second taxi had arrived ten minutes later. The driver took issue with the doorman about the missing, lucrative fares he had been contracted to pick up by a Mr Uppal's PA. He was told Mrs Uppal and Miss Rawat had already gone. The records show that the driver had formally complained over the phone to Ravi Uppal, who assured him that there had been no other arrangement. Ravi phoned the women's hotel immediately, reporting events to the Mumbai police, once he established they had not returned to the hotel. They promised to call him as soon as they had made some inquiries. At 07:30 that morning a farmer discovered two bodies in a drainage ditch, some thirty miles from the city. The police records were very precise, as the trail was easy enough to follow. The crime had mirrored many others from that year and was part of an established pattern. It bore the hallmark of a gang the police had dubbed the *Taxi Men*. Their *modus operandi* followed the same pattern and was proving impossible to detect until a crime was completed. Victims, usually wealthy tourists or businessmen, were selected using information easily obtained from waiters, security personnel, hotel staff and taxi drivers for a few rupees. Once a taxi was ordered, the Taxi Men could get their own vehicle to a customer ahead of time. It was a simple strategy that worked. Once aboard, the victims were doomed.

The two women had been naive and openly ostentatious – classic prey to the Taxi Men. They had assumed that using a top-class hotel and taking taxis direct to their destinations mitigated any risks and would ensure their safety. Ordinarily they would have been right, but Vaz had arranged events before they had even arrived in Mumbai. He knew the city and used his network well. Vaz had no qualms about killing as the means to an end, but was always logical in the way he went about it. He never took chances. He was also not opposed to killing a person with his own hands, he enjoyed it, yet his life was now on a different course and his future with Ravi required an arrest-free record. Both deaths had to be untraceable.

Vaz had a lot of experience in obfuscating his involvement in killings. He told Ravi he knew his targets as *annoyances* and the innocent phrase became part of their darker patois. His stroke of genius was inventing phantom criminals for the police to attribute these executions. One, named by the press as *The Mechanic,* would beat victims to death with a tyre iron, each seeming to be randomly selected from the poor of Delhi. In reality, they owed money and could not pay. The killers were assassins, the victims the dregs of society, each death a warning for other debtors. In Agra a mysterious killer, dubbed *Kāla,* worked his particularly cruel art. This wraith baffled local police. Kāla had killed three victims over a four-year period. The police were led into thinking this was the work of the same monster because of his calling card: a silver medal of Shiva's death-dealing incarnation, Kāla, was left on each body. This murderer was totally elusive and increasingly violent. In the first killing a knife was used in a frenzied attack inside a disused warehouse. However, not one knife wound had been fatal. It was established the victim had bled to death as each cut was deliberately shallow, yet incapacitating. The second victim had been tied to a chair in a hotel room, beaten systematically for several hours, then strangled with a thin wire. The most recent body had been nailed to the wall of an old house and had had its legs broken. Kāla had watched his prey die whilst relaxing on a carefully positioned chair, so it seemed from the evidence. In reality these poor souls were family members of debtors who could pay, but would not. Kāla's crimes were all the work of Vasupati Chopra. He soon collected the debts after these horrific warnings.

The Taxi Men were one of Vasupati Chopra's most successful inventions: a non-existent gang brought into existence for the authorities to fruitlessly chase. Instead of clues leading to a gang, the contrived evidence had created one. Mumbai was considered the base, but their fictitious actions had recently been linked to crimes in Delhi, Jaipur and even Pune. Unsubstantiated leaks from reporters and informers led police to believe it could be a local gang slowly extending their influence across the country. This amused Vaz as he had never used the Taxi Men in these cities. Police forces tended to seek the simplest of explanation and if the clues were obvious so much the better. Self-deception made this tool of execution a self-replicating, invisible decoy of immeasurable value.

Vaz used the Taxi Men sparingly before Ravi's proposition. Now it was time his phantom gang made headlines for the abduction and murder of Tamina Uppal. He ignored Ravi's requirement for lack of cruelty for effect, he had later explained. The papers reported the women's deaths as being their most brutal yet, under headlines such as *Taxi Men Kill First Women* and *Insane Killers Slaughter Friends*. Every paper carried the story with no need for embellishing the horrific truth. Both women had been bound and gagged, and taken to a remote spot. They had been beaten, stripped, raped and abused for some hours. At the end of their ordeal they were callously thrown into the ditch where they drowned slowly in shallow water, unable to escape their bonds. Their stolen valuables added up to a substantial amount, so deemed to be the main motive for the crime. The police had concluded the simple, brutal case very quickly. No one was ever arrested and the investigation was left open in the Taxi Men file. Several follow up stories traced the husband's devastation as he visited the spot where his wife's body had been found; a front-page picture of Ravi Uppal hanging on to an equally shattered Raj Singh, the fiancé of Alka Rawat, being reproduced in papers across the whole of India. Further columns reported on the funerals, with pictures of relatives in their moment of grief, amongst them Tamina Uppal's sister, Kiran Gupta, and her husband Anil.

Ravi Uppal netted more than he had supposed – close to one hundred and eight million rupees. Cobra Investments appeared on the financial scene little more than six months later. At the same time Ravi's mistress, Suneeti Virani, gave birth to a son, Rajiv. Ravi shared his time between the haveli and Suneeti's down-town luxury apartment. Before the child was a year old Suneeti Virani became Suneeti Uppal. It was she who felt the benefit of Ravi's increasingly large holdings. The money machine had started.

Chapter 4

Mr Gupta Falls

For once Mr Gupta slept well. Delhi was never completely silent and even in the darkest hours it would be very difficult to find a truly quiet corner. At night sounds became more distant, even muted, yet were comforting to a man who had lived for so long in the city. A man who lived by the ocean drew comfort from the susurrations of the waves against the shore; Mr Gupta was eased by the susurrations of the semi-sleeping metropolis. It had a rhythm. His inability to sleep of late was more to do with his constantly busy mind – he had been unable to switch off since Kiran died. Now he had the headaches to contend with. In the early hours rain drowned out the rhythm of the dozing city. The sound meshed with Mr Gupta's dreams, easing him through the night. When he awoke, he felt both refreshed and pleasantly surprised. It was still early and the room was shadowy. He groaned as the throbbing beat started in his left temple once more, but relaxed a little as he felt no pain. Yes, seeing Dr Chowdary was long overdue. As Mr Gupta sank into his pillow the white opaque cloud appeared again, gradually materialising over the chair in the corner. He tried to blink it away, but it remained stubbornly in place. It pulsed with the same beat as the throb over his eye.

"Bloody hell," he mumbled.

He tried to relax and let it run its course. He was sure it would disappear. To his surprise an echoing, distant voice talked to him.

"You know," it said. The voice emanated from the inside of his skull and echoed from the cloud. He realised his thoughts were far from logical.

"You are not real," stammered Mr Gupta wondering if it was a dream.

"...you...know..." came the voice.

He squeezed his eyes shut and despaired as his left nostril dribbled snot again, soaking his moustache and wetting his nightshirt. This time the left side of his face went numb too. Frightened, he sat and sobbed, tiny childlike sounds escaped his dribbling lips. He finally took some deep breaths and regained control. He opened his eyes. In the chair was a wavering shape. A man. A slightly transparent, grey man. He forgot everything else, even to be worried. Mr Gupta blinked hard and the figure became a throbbing cloud once more. Just as he thought it was over there was a sudden rushing in his ears, so loud, growing to the crescendo of a storm through trees, accelerating, louder, roaring. There was a sudden *Crack!* in his head and everything was normal again. Clarity was back. There was no loud pulse in his head. No numbness. He felt perfectly fine.

"Bloody hell!" said Mr Gupta again, wiping his nose on a sleeve.

He switched on his bedside lamp, swivelled to a sitting position and got up. He walked over to the chair and was relieved to see no signs of it having been sat in, no ghostly residue and no trace of a man.

"It's all in my head," he said quietly in the gloom. "My bloody head has made this happen. It was never real. And I've started to talk to myself again!"

Cold fear gripped him. His throat felt tight, as if it was closing, so he swallowed hard. Was he on the brink of madness? He started rationalising. The fear ebbed. It was just a dream in semi-wakefulness, perhaps. Or maybe the result of the migraine? His first bout on the train was like this, starting with his headache. He felt uneasy. Could a migraine do this?

"Gupta," he said out loud. "Tea and biscuits! That will do the trick."

He shuffled into the kitchen and put the kettle on. By the time he sat at the table with a pile of digestives, for which his beautiful Kiran would have scolded him, he had rationalised his vision away. It had to be the result of his migraine, that along with being stressed and tired from the long hours he had worked the day before. That was all.

"That is all," he said out loud, adding "Damn!" as a biscuit he was dunking broke off and disappeared into his cup.

The only thing that kept niggling was the fact that, for a moment, he was sure the man in the chair had been Scottish.

The stripy palm squirrels and bulbuls scattered as Mr Gupta strode through his garden and out onto the street. Though the rain had stopped, he still had to splash along the footpath as he made his way to the Singhs' home. Mrs Singh's clean tiffin-box clanked by his side and a furled umbrella swung rhythmically in his other hand. Up above the constant black kites circled in the dank air.

The city had shaken off its night-time lethargy and raced towards a full blown, bustling day. Walking along the damp, crowded street, Mr Gupta smiled as he remembered how, upon his return from England, the madness of a busy Delhi day had stunned him. Brighton, being a seaside town, occasionally had very hot, busy summer days when the papers would have headlines like *Phew! What a Scorcher!* emblazoned on their front pages. The standard picture was of the local pebble beach packed with pale bodies. His Uncle Nik had once taken him to London, Christmas shopping along Oxford Street, and that was busy, but wonderful! Everyone seemed friendly and *minded their Ps and Qs,* as his uncle was fond of saying. His return to Delhi had rocked him back on his heels as he tried to get used to the mass of people, the litter, the chaos, the dirt.

A tuktuk rattled past belching blue fumes, splashing Mr Gupta's shoes with brown water.

"Bloody hell!" he said, helplessly.

Yet to complain would be futile. He had soon become used to the madness again, but had never fully redeveloped the Indian art of blanking out the background noises. Most city dwellers could carry on normal conversations, or go about their business and social lives, without noticing the rest of humanity. They could drift in and out of their personal, invisible, sensory isolation bubbles at will. It was simply beyond him, though he did find the gentler night-time orchestrations comforting.

He crossed the street, ducked down a back alley and stepped into a compact, pink-walled yard which served as the ground floor apartment's garden. Parked tightly against the alley wall was Old Mr Singh's battered tuktuk. The tiny enclosure had an array of pots overflowing with flowers, shrubs and herbs, was well swept, and welcoming. On the street side of the building the main entrance was a formidable, solid wooden door designed to keep out unwelcome visitors, but this back entrance had a friendly face. The door was open and sounds of music drifted from the interior on a waft of cooking smells. A short, plump, elderly woman stepped lightly into the doorway as Mr Gupta wove his way through the maze of pots.

"Anil!" she shrieked, hugging him in an embrace the power of which denied her years. "Oh, it's so good to see you again!" She continued kissing his cheek with genuine affection. "Did you eat the food? Oh, you've cleaned the pans – silly man. I could have done that in a jiffy. You look a little peaky too! Are you sleeping alright? Come in. Come in. Param is at home."

Slightly stunned by the endless stream of words, Mr Gupta allowed himself to be guided through the kitchen of his friends' home.

"Look! Look Param!" she called through. "Anil has come for some tea and cakes!"

He was steered into a large lounge-come-dining room where Old Mr Singh was sitting listening to the radio and reading a paper. He looked neat and tidy, with a freshly pressed light-blue shirt and matching turban, pale trousers, and sandals. Mr Singh was fond of light blue. He looked up and grinned through his white beard.

"Mr Gupta!" he said standing, turning down the music and putting his paper on the coffee table. "Come in and sit down."

"Mr Singh, I've just brought the tiffin box back," he said shaking the proffered hand. "But I will certainly stay for tea. This house has a way of making a fellow hungry!"

"I shall make fresh tea and I have some almond cakes cooling out here, Param loves them," said Mrs Singh scuttling out into the kitchen.

"Make a big pot!" said her husband, then he turned to Mr Gupta. "Taraa is the best cook in Delhi, but I'm still skinny as a rake!"

"I wish I was, Mr Singh," smiled Mr Gupta sitting down.

"Too many convenience meals! Taraa worries about you my friend. She misses Kiran too, you know – she worries about you and misses Kiran. Then she tells me all about it! And now I'm telling you! And she'll come in and say the same in a minute!"

"I don't mind at all," said Mr Gupta. "It is good to have friends. So many people avoid me now. At first, they didn't seem to know what to say, after Kiran, then the gap grew and, well, they become strangers. It really is a bit odd."

"You are so right, Mr Gupta," said the old man. "But perhaps it is because a strong couple is like one bigger person. Once one goes there is a stranger left! People don't know what to do. I have heard divorced people have the same problems. I hear all sorts in my tuktuk."

"But you and Taraa have never missed a beat," Mr Gupta replied. "You knew what to do, what to say and helped to keep me sane. Even Rupa knew how to cope."

Mrs Singh came in with a tray of warm cakes, the smell of almonds filling the air. She put them on the table in front of the men. She picked up the conversation.

"It is because we loved you both, as a couple, and also as individuals," she said, hands on hips. "That is the big difference. Kiran was my friend and I miss her. You are still part of that, but we love you as you are, as a single man. Men do find it hard to understand, Anil. Friendships between men are closed compared with us women. I mean, look at you both! You say 'Mr Singh' and you say 'Mr Gupta', never 'Param' and 'Anil'. Men are odd things, but luckily for women, simple!"

She left to finish making the tea, clattering in the kitchen. The men took a cake each and munched quietly. They savoured the sweet, warm, nutty mouthfuls then Mr Singh spoke.

"Have we not always been *mister* to each other?" he asked.

"Always," replied Mr Gupta.

"Women!" said the old man brushing crumbs from his lap.

Another pause.

"Mr Singh, I am a bit worried," said Mr Gupta. "I have been getting headaches lately and feel a bit below the weather. I am fretting over Rupa and worried that something is wrong with me. It feels like I'm on a never ending, bumpy road."

"Those bloody migraines, is it?" asked the old man.

"Yes, but I'm starting to think it may be more than that," he replied. "I'm just not the same any more. At my age I should be sure of so much, but I am lost. Hopeless! I miss Kiran so much still. I talk to her, you know? But I am not convinced she is there, or if it is just that I cannot let go. I've let my life drift a bit too long and I don't know how to get some structure back. It saps my will to try anything. I'm fed up with just ticking over. I think I'm having a crisis!"

Old Mr Singh laughed. "Mr Gupta. You just need to understand that you are still going through a rough time. You lost your wife! It is awful and takes time to adjust and everyone is different. Grief is very personal and there is not a set of rules for it. Never will be. It'll take the time it needs."

"Oh, but it hurts so much still," said Mr Gupta. "I can't seem to start my life again. If I did it would almost feel like a betrayal."

"Hmmph!" puffed the old man. "That is silly. Kiran has gone. Where she has gone is up to your own belief, but she would want you to carry on. She could never have seen it as a betrayal. You hold her memory close and that will never leave. But to carry on with a purpose you need to have a plan."

"Well, I have kept busy, kept working," said Mr Gupta. "That has filled the time and is almost a pleasure occasionally. It gets me out. The house is lovely and I like being home. Kiran left enough to keep Rupa safe and I have a lot invested with Ravi's people, though I need to iron out the legal bits if something is happening to me. I just cannot fill this emptiness inside."

At this point Mrs Singh came in with a tray of tea. "English style!" she announced with a flourish. Setting down the tray she served the tea in three large mugs, a gift from her sister in Manchester, each bearing a Union Jack design with the words *Keep Calm and Drink Tea*. They might be a little out of place in Delhi, but Mrs Singh said it made her feel spiritually closer to her sister. *English style* meant mugs.

"Now," she continued handing out the tea, "Anil, do have more cake. You look so glum! How can we cheer you right up?"

"Oh, I'm just having a bit of a moan," replied Mr Gupta. "Nothing to worry about really."

"He's still getting those headaches," interjected Mr Singh. "And he's not sure what to do with his life. A *crisis* he thinks."

This openness was the norm for the three friends and Old Mr Singh never felt once that he had betrayed a confidence.

"Oh my, oh my," said Mrs Singh. "It's just time you need, that's all. And some new goals in life."

"I said that," said her husband.

"Well it's true," she continued. "Look, these headaches are the first thing to deal with. Men always put things off and never listen to reason. Get to the doctors and start fixing it! Then you can deal with your future. You have friends and little Rupa to help you on, so just deal with the moment for now. See the doctor!"

"I am. I am," said Mr Gupta defensively. "Today in fact; this afternoon at three."

"About time too," she said. "Now, what's all this about a crisis? Drink your tea!"

"It's all to do with my health really," said Mr Gupta sipping his tea, which he had sweetened with four sugar lumps. "I think I could make headway if only I felt well. I miss my Kiran, but I'm dealing with it the best I can. I talk to her sometimes, you know, even though I'm not at all sure she can hear me. But if something befalls me, Rupa will have no one left to look after her psychological needs. I realise I have no real faith in anything floaty – that spiritual bunkum. If there is a divine providence of any sort it has bypassed me. Losing our baby son was a trial, but we stayed happy. Rupa's condition never dulled our love, though it was hard to take. But we dealt with that too. It was the death of Tamina which was the blow which started these last few awful years. Then Kiran's death was cruel beyond thought." Mr Gupta sipped his sweet tea and sighed. "I mean, Ravi moved on. And he supported me through my own loss, even though he's hardly my proper brother-in-law any more. He's invested Kiran's inheritance which pays for Rupa's care and bore his own grief with a strength I just don't have. He went on, got married again and had a son! He's focused on a new future. I can see I'm not badly off and I enjoy my job, but, for the life of me, I cannot see a way forward. Now these damned headaches keep coming and they drain my energy, and with it my motivation."

There was a silence. The usual lightness of their meetings had become heavy. It had been like this after Kiran's death, and now it was back. Yet, this is where the Singhs had been Mr Gupta's saviours as they took such moments in their stride, sloughed them off, and acted as a team in bringing sense to everything. They were one, just as Old Mr Singh had said earlier.

"Getting things into perspective, Anil," said Old Mr Singh using his friend's first name for once. "That is the hardest thing to do. You are so close to everything you cannot see where you are."

"Yes," said Mrs Singh. "Talking about all these things to us is healthy. You are releasing pressure. And it is important to deal with one thing at a time. Tonight, you must come to dinner! First things first, Anil, you are seeing the doctor, that is the most important task. We can talk about the rest later."

"I know. I know," said Mr Gupta. "Talking does help and I know it is the pressure that has got me down. Too much thinking. Too much time on my own. I'll come to dinner and let you know what Dr Chowdary says. I just know it is more than migraines."

"How can you be so sure, Anil?" asked Mrs Singh.

Here Mr Gupta hesitated and sipped his tea.

"Well," he began. "Er…it is hard to put into words now I think of it. You'll probably think I've gone doolally, or something."

"Don't be silly," scolded Old Mr Singh. "We know you are sane. We are your friends."

"Hmmm," said Mr Gupta. "Ok. I'm starting to see things. Every time my headaches starts I see a, well, a sort of cloud. It just appears."

"Cloud?" said Mrs Singh.

"Yes, a cloud," he replied. "But that's not all. This morning the cloud took the form of a man. I'm sure it was a Scotsman!"

The old couple stared at him for a while.

"Did he have bagpipes?" asked Old Mr Singh.

"No," replied Mr Gupta. "But I'm sure he was wearing a kilt."

Heavy showers continued through the morning; the summer monsoons were early but the vibrant city never missed a beat. Outside, the Singhs' garden looked radiant under the leaden sky, as inside the three friends talked the morning away. The old couple told him that *stress can do amazing things to the mind,* and, he *should not forget that a god could be trying to contact him and show him the way,* all of which flowed over Mr Gupta without ridding him of the knot of anxiety in the pit of his stomach.

Old Mr Singh had dropped him off at the surgery free of charge waving away some proffered cash, stating "Taraa would skin me alive!" as he clattered off. Mr Gupta hurried in, splashing through the puddles. The waiting room was compact and square with white walls, chairs around three sides and the reception desk on the fourth. The doctor's surgery was in a room behind the desk which was guarded by a formidable woman. This receptionist was a veteran of many years' service and was not easily intimidated by irate patients. She was tall for an Indian woman and had a figure projecting weight and solidity. She wore her hair in a bun and had a white coat over a skirt and blouse. It was rumoured that she had been known to physically throw miscreants out into the street if her rules were breached, and that a local policeman was her lover. With this worthy in place Dr Chowdary had never been disturbed outside of his strict appointment system. Mr Gupta was nervous as he entered. He had reached the point of panic about what may be going on in his head. There were three patients sitting in the chairs: two women and a man, the former reading colourful magazines; the man looked a little odd. He was very tall and thin with rough, black stubble on his chin and a white bandage upon his head; he was simply dressed in dhoti, white shirt and shoeless. He just stared straight forward at the bare wall, as if he could see through it thought Mr Gupta. And he did not blink. Mr Gupta stepped up to the reception desk.

"Hello, I am here to see Dr Chowdary," he stated, smiling.

The receptionist remained impassive and solid behind the tall barrier.

"You are Mr Anil Gupta?" she asked firmly.

"Yes, that is right," he answered, smile fading.

"Take a seat, the doctor is running a little late," she informed him.

Mr Gupta took a seat opposite the strange man and settled into the chair.

"You have an aura!" said the man without adjusting his gaze.

"Pardon me?" said Mr Gupta surprised.

"You see his form in the cloud. You know who it is." Mr Gupta noticed, with growing alarm, the man's face seemed to segue in features, not quite settling on a single look. The changing face flickered faster.

Mr Gupta squeezed his eyes shut and shook his head. When he opened them the apparition had vanished. The two women were staring. One was addressing him.

"Yes?" she was saying.

"Sorry, madam?" said Mr Gupta, unsure of his own senses.

"You seemed about to ask a question," she said. "You said 'Pardon me?'"

"Oh, did I?" he replied.

"Yes," she said.

"You did," said the second woman smiling.

"I was answering the man," he said defensively.

"Man?" said the first woman.

"What man?" said the second.

"The chap that just left," he said, now feeling light-headed.

"There was no one else here," said the receptionist, looking concerned.

Mr Gupta's head started to throb, his vision jumping with each beat. His left nostril ran and he convulsed back violently. Sounds distorted and everything slowed down. The rushing was back in his ears. Where the man had been there floated a white cloud. It wavered and slowly changed shape. The indistinct human figure turned its head and looked at him. The face was clear and sharp now, a white-bearded European. As the rest of reality span around him, the figure remained fixed. It spoke.

"I am William MacKeeg, 78th Highlanders," it said in a broad, Scottish accent.

Mr Gupta said, "What are you?"

The figure blurred with the rest of reality and the room faded into a storm of spinning colours. Mr Gupta saw the ceiling turning above him and knew he was on the floor. His vision went, his ears could only hear the howling maelstrom, and then blackness overcame him.

Chapter 5

Angaar and Seva

Angaar stood in the downpour. Above him the people had sought cover, so all he could see was the top of the high wall and railings. He shook his great head, drops of water fanning out like a halo around his broad shoulders. The heavy rain soaked his coat, ran from his nose and dripped off the curve of his tail. He stood enjoying the freshness of the rain. It had fallen from a pure place and briefly masked the unpleasant smells. Seva had closed the door to the inner den for cleaning. As the rain thundered down Seva hurried to complete his task, so Angaar could come in and shelter. Behind the plinth where the tiger slept he found a pile of Angaar's faeces, missed by his initial hosing. It did not look right. It was bloody. Aware of the heavy rain he thought it best to allow his charge the chance to come in. He quickly shovelled the pat into a clean bucket, scrubbed the last bit of floor, put down a good layer of bedding, and then retreated. Finally, he turned the wheel which opened the door to the outside enclosure.

"Eeesh! Eeesh!" he called. "Come. Come my beauty."

Outside, the tiger shook his wet coat once, turned to the opening, walked through the puddles and into the shelter of his den. He paused to shake again, sniffed the air and then walked over to the bars. Seva ruffled the wide head and spoke soothingly to his friend.

"Eeesh, Eeesh," he cooed again. "What's the matter my Angaar? Are you ill?"

The tiger began his rumbling purr and sniffed at the little man's pocket. He could smell the spicy residue of pattie and his mouth dribbled.

"No more today, Angaar," he said in a kindly voice. "I think too much is not good for a big cat, let me have a look at you."

He stepped back and Angaar paced up and down, realised there were to be no more treats, gave a toothy yawn and walked over to drink some fresh water. Yes, Seva could see a small smear of blood by Angaar's anus. His heart sank and he felt a wave of panic. In the bucket he could not see anything but the mass of faeces and a tiny spot of blood on the side. He would have to see Mr Chakrabarti, the zoo's vet, as soon as he could. Seva was not an educated man, but he knew that the blood could mean any number of things – none good. It need not indicate anything serious, but he had a sense of foreboding. The sun came out and Angaar strode back into the enclosure. The people above were drifting back and he scanned the figures above with little interest. He walked up to his tree, stood on his rear legs and dug his claws into the rough wood well above the height of a man. He pulled and clawed and stretched and dug, then dropped down and yawned towards the crowd. The sight of his huge yellow fangs drew gasps from them, the following murmurs of appreciative conversation showing why the tiger remained a big attraction. Angaar lay down by the tree and stretched out in the sunshine.

Vikram Chakrabarti was a good vet. Tall, slim and handsome, he was the product of a wealthy Anglo-Indian family, was educated in his land of birth and English to the core. His older brother had trained as a doctor, and had done well, and Vikram was meant to follow his lead. His passion, however, was always animals and wild ones at that, so he ended up studying at the University of Cambridge at the Department of Veterinary Medicine, became a member of the Royal College of Veterinary Surgeons, and joined a practice in London. Many of his wealthy clients' pets were exotic, and he became known for successfully treating many bizarre species from chameleons to lemurs. He later became a consultant for London Zoo, eventually specialising in cats.

Having successfully directed the new Sumatran tiger breeding project, his knowledge was widely respected and sought-after across the globe. Vikram Chakrabarti was *the* premier figure in reintroduction projects, this being the catalyst in returning him to his family's land of origin. He had agreed to spend a year based in the Mumbai Ashoka Zoo to oversee the reintroduction of tigers to the wild in selected locations. The idea was to open corridors between isolated populations, working with local villagers and conservation bodies. He felt he may be based in India for longer than that initial year. However, from Mumbai he could catch a plane to anywhere in the world should he need to, so he never felt trapped. He missed his wife and three children, but visited them regularly in London and could use Skype through the intervening months.

Part of his remit was coordinating a breeding programme amongst India's zoos. His easy-going nature had won him many friends which opened the door for the necessary cooperation. The magnificent Khan had prompted him to find a suitable mate to ensure such fine genes were passed on. Vikram had become used to the limited local facilities and was happy to forego luxury if he could get the breeding programme up and running.

There was a compact laboratory and Veterinary Centre near the administration block, which had been refurbished once Vikram answered the call from Mumbai. He had organised the funding, gleaning it from the local government and various wildlife charities, especially in the United States and Britain. There were facilities for several students from the city's veterinary college, which attracted extra income. Vikram had settled in well and agreed to manage the big cat section's staff as they were crucial to success. He required a dedicated team of enthusiastic people and had identified those he wanted. Seva was one of the least educated men he had worked with, but he had a natural genius with Khan, and Vikram had grown to like the little man.

On this rainy morning Vikram was treating a very lively young manul, a Pallas's cat, which spat and hissed from its swaddling blanket as he tried to give it an injection. He succeeded, but was too slow to avoid the needle-like teeth as the little beast squirmed in response to the sting. "Ouch you little bastard!" he yelled as the manul bit his finger, drawing blood. He dropped the writhing creature into a basket and quickly secured the door. As he sucked the painful wound reflectively he noticed Seva hurrying across the lawn outside the window carrying a bucket. Seva clanked to the door. Vikram opened it, still sucking his finger, and smiled at the diminutive keeper.

"Hello, Seva," he said. "What have you got there, a bucket of gold?"

"Sahib Vikram," answered Seva, flustered in high company. "It is the tiger. I think I may have found the sign of trouble for him. But it may be nothing."

"Come in, come in," said Vikram smiling. "Let's have a look at it."

Seva walked gingerly into the white laboratory, jumping slightly as the still fiery manul spat from the basket as he passed. He placed the bucket on the floor, the smell was very strong and not for the faint-hearted.

"Sorry Sahib Vikram," intoned Seva quietly. "It is very smelly, but I have noticed blood in his shit, and a smear on Angaar's arse. He is acting very normally, but I felt you should look at this."

"Angaar's a better name, I think, than Khan," said the vet.

"Yes," said Seva, unsure how Vikram may react to his secret, "He knows his proper name and responds to it. You have seen how he purrs!"

The little man became very animated.

"Hmm, it means *flame*?" asked Vikram.

"Yes Sahib," answered Seva, "*Fire* really. It fits him. Please, what do you think?"

Vikram gazed at the foul lump, then picked up the bucket and placed it on the counter.

"Pass me that wooden spoon," asked the vet, pointing at the counter opposite. Seva complied. Vikram carefully moved the stinking mass and saw the blood immediately. It was very red, which was good, but then noticed a darker mass smeared through the faeces. This could mean deep internal issues, rather than a superficial bleed. This was not a good sign.

"I think I'll need to take a good look at this and have a few tests done," said Vikram. "You say he's acting normally?"

"Yes. Yes, Sahib," replied Seva. Then looking downcast he asked, "Er, do you think the wrong food could do this?"

Vikram watched the cloud of despair move over Seva's face and felt for him. He knew about the patties and never had any concerns. Indeed, Seva had let him watch the tiger's reaction to eating one, and he had found it amusing and interesting at the same time. He thought the spice acted like catnip did on domestic cats. He quickly reassured the little man.

"My good chap," he said. "It's not the patties so don't go getting down. Tigers have a pretty robust constitution and he would avoid the treats if he felt they were bad for him. This is something else completely."

"Thank you, Sahib Vikram," said Seva with obvious relief. "What do I do now?"

"Carry on as normal. Watch our friend and let me know if his behaviour changes at all. You know him better than anyone else." Vikram paused and eyed the bucket again. "I will start on this now and pop over later. If anyone asks you to do anything else today give them this note from me."

He took some paper from his desk and scribbled down *Seva is to keep Khan under constant observation today. He must not be disturbed or given other duties.* He signed it, read it out loud to Seva, whom he knew to be illiterate, and gave it to him.

"Thank you, Sahib," said Seva. "I am very worried."

"Chin up, Seva," said Vikram. "I'm sure things will be fine."

Seva was gazing down into the tiger's outer enclosure as Vikram visited some time later. The sky was blue, but painted with dark thunderheads which threatened rain again. The enclosure had dried out in the warm sun and a noisy, colourful crowd watched the tiger.

"Seva," said the vet gently. "Let's have a look at Angaar."

The little keeper started slightly. He had been so engrossed looking at his charge he had not noticed Vikram approach.

Seva pointed down at the tiger. "You see, he looks perfectly fine."

Angaar was lying sphinx-like in the sunshine, rear legs tucked up under him, forelegs straight out in front, head held high. His eyes were half closed in a feline reverie and he seemed quite content. The tiger was enjoying the heat.

"Is there any way I can get to see his rear end?" asked Vikram.

"Oh yes, easily!" said Seva. "But we need to go inside, Sahib Vikram."

Seva led Vikram down the gently sloping path which would take them into the tiger's inner sanctum. He asked the vet to keep back. As he approached the bars of the gloomy interior, a bright shaft of sunlight shone through the outer door illuminating dust motes floating in the air. Vikram watched with undiminished interest.

"Eeesh! Eeesh! Eeesh! Come. Come. Come beautiful Angaar," Seva called.

Vikram had seen this a few times now, but it always surprised him how this tiny man could exert so much control over such an animal. He realised that Seva was a rarity: illiterate and uneducated, but incredibly switched on to the biorhythms of the tiger, almost if they were soul mates, which he felt was a fanciful notion. The doorway darkened and Angaar strode into the den, heading for Seva with purpose. Vikram caught his breath. The tiger dwarfed the little man, yet there was no hint of fear from him as Angaar rubbed up against the bars and patted Seva's hands with his huge paws. Vikram heard the deep, rumbling purring. With Seva the tiger was like a kitten. Angaar's wide nose pushed through the bars as he sniffed at the little man's pockets.

"No more today my Angaar," scolded Seva gently. "No more patties. I'm just saying hello."

The tiger shuffled back and yawned, the great maw level with Seva's head. Vikram swallowed anxiously as he noticed how Seva's skull would comfortably fit inside. Angaar shook himself, stared directly at the vet in the shadows, sneezed and turned away, walking towards the door.

"Look now. Look!" said Seva.

Stepping up to the bars, Vikram crouched and eyed the tiger's anus and large testicles. Nothing.

"Hmm. No blood now," he said.

"He has cleaned himself," said Seva.

"And he looks well enough," continued Vikram. "I'm wet-sieving the faeces to see if there is anything obvious we may have missed. I've already sent some samples to the lab boys. Not a lot more I can do for the moment, Seva."

"Thank you, Sahib Vikram," said Seva, "for coming so soon."

"There's no need to thank me, Seva," replied the vet. "Tigers hold a special place in my heart and this lovely fellow is invaluable. He has precious DNA. Do you understand?"

"Oh yes, Sahib Vikram," said Seva. "He is like a god. You talk of his seed, of future tigers. Magnificent tigers! They are all in him. He has fire within him. He is not tame. He has old tigers inside. He holds people in disdain. He could kill a man easily!"

"Not you," said Vikram turning to leave.

"Sahib," said Seva pointedly, making Vikram pause. "He is like this with me because it is his choice. He chooses not to hurt me, that's all. I have no power over him, none. Perhaps friendship... Perhaps." He tailed off as he watched Angaar walk out into the sunshine.

Vikram strode across the park towards the Administration Block, a frown taking the place of the smile he had worn for Seva. He had found something. He had found a piece of black, corroded metal in the faecal matter – an old nail perhaps. The dark mass had contained some putrid tissue showing there was something wrong inside somewhere. Ulceration? He was not sure. He knew the metal had been in the tiger for some time and had a strong hunch that damage had occurred, but he could not tell

Seva until he knew exactly what the extent of the problem might be. He had some calls to make.

Evening fell and Seva remained with the tiger, even after the park had closed. He had started to notice subtle changes in Angaar's behaviour, little nuances which most would miss, which made him realise all was not well. He leaned against the wall of the outer enclosure, keen eyes hooded by a frown. Over the last hour the tiger had settled into an undisturbed semi-sleep next to the tree. Every so often he would yawn, but each time he retched as if trying to dislodge something from his throat. Seva did not know if tigers got fur-balls like domestic cats, yet that is how it seemed to him. Angaar had also started to pant a lot which formed part of an odd, new ritual: he stood suddenly, panted for a few seconds, yawned and then retched before settling down again. He was drinking more often too. The head keeper, Sandeep Pathak, found Seva as he made his final round of the zoo and walked over to join him.

"I hear the vet has asked you to watch old Khan," he said in his usual friendly manner. Sandeep was an easy-going man and liked Seva, a man he could trust regardless of his lowly status.

"Yes," said Seva. "I think he may be a little ill. Blood in his shit. He's not quite right. I thought it may be nothing, but he's not himself."

Sandeep looked down at the tiger and the two men enjoyed a silent moment, listening to the various animals calling. The traffic of the city could be heard in the distance but the background hum was of no significance in this green oasis.

"Sir?" asked Seva, without looking up. "Could I stay here tonight? Just to watch over him. To make sure I can report anything more to Sahib Chakrabarti."

Sandeep considered this for a moment, scratching his ear. "There would be no extra pay for it," he said.

Seva looked up. "Money is not in my mind at all. I can sleep in the back of the den. There is a wooden pallet there. I could not rest if I left here tonight."

"Well, I'm leaving shortly," said Sandeep, "but I'll square it with security. Get them to call me from the gate if anything comes up. Vikram's number is there too."

"Thank you, sir," said Seva with obvious relief.

"Goodnight, Seva," said Sandeep as he left.

"Goodnight," said Seva returning his gaze to the tiger.

Seva made up the pallet bed in the access passageway at the rear of the inner den. In amongst the pipes and switchgear, he would be quite comfortable. Angaar had long since wandered in and settled on the fresh bedding Seva had put down; his drinking trough contained fresh, clear water. Darkness had come early due to the rain clouds above and a single, dim bulb bathed the inner sanctum with a yellow light.

Seva made his way to the security office at the zoo's main gate. It was pay-day and the little keeper would need some money to buy breakfast in the morning and get Angaar his daily treat. Money was not something Seva had in abundance and he often went hungry, even though he had never starved. Every Friday employees would queue for their wages at the cashier's office, but as he was an hour later than usual the night security guards would have his pay packet. They had already come on shift and were smoking and drinking tea in an anteroom. Seva knocked, and hearing a cheerful voice shout, "Come in!" entered. This was the ever smiling Bandi Sinha, head of security. He was a man who liked his job, liked the park and liked the animals. He hated criminals and was not averse to using violence if any interloper was caught doing harm, damage or tried to resist being detained. As an ex-army sergeant, he was perfect for this role and was respected by all staff, though not universally liked, mainly because he did not have a blind-eye to any irregular behaviour.

Most of the staff were already out on their rounds, but Bandi had a new, younger man with him, someone Seva did not recognise. This newcomer turned out to be temporary cover for a holiday absentee, sent by a local agency. He did not look as polished as the other guards and wore a stained khaki uniform, had uncombed, greasy hair and sported several days' growth of stubble on his thin face.

"Hey, Seva," said Bandi. "Come in and have some tea!"

"Tonight, I cannot, Bandi," replied Seva. "I am observing Khan for the vet."

"Yes, he told me. Have you come for your wages?"

"I have," said Seva. "It will be easier to have them now as you will be busy in the morning."

Bandi fished in his top pocket and pulled out a brown envelope with printed details of the contents on the outside. He then opened a red bound ledger to the required page and placed it on the table facing Seva, asking him to sign it. Seva took the proffered pen and very slowly wrote his name, the only writing he had ever mastered, accepted the envelope and thanked Bandi.

"Oh, this fellow is Suman's replacement," said Bandi pointing at his scruffy companion. "Whilst Suman is swanning around down in Pune, Mukul here will fill in. Mukul, this is our tiger keeper, Seva."

The two men shook hands. Seva immediately felt like washing his, Mukul being grubby with an almost sticky touch and weak grip. His smile was equally as unpleasant, his brown-toothed grin reminding Seva of the drain cover in Angaar's den. His breath was sour.

"I'll be doing the rounds later, so don't you worry about a thing," said Mukul.

"Thank you," said Seva edging away from the smell of old cigarettes and stale sweat.

"If you need to get in touch with the vet or Sandeep, just come running and I'll make sure they are called. They are both pretty fond of our old tiger," said Bandi.

"Thank you," said Seva backing through the door.

He quickly walked back to the tiger's den and looked at Angaar's recumbent form in the dim light. The rhythmic rise and fall of the animal's ribs told Seva that he was sleeping. He retired to his makeshift bed and wrapped himself up in an old tarpaulin. Beside him was a threadbare cloth bag in which he kept all that he owned in transportable goods. He withdrew a couple of cold chapattis rolled around a filling of rice, ate them and drank a little water from a plastic bottle. Then he placed his wages in the bag where it would have the company of an ancient wrist watch with a broken strap; a tattered NYC baseball cap; and a moth-eaten spare blanket. He rolled the bag up and used it as a pillow.

Seva dozed and, in his semi-wakefulness, watched Angaar through the darkest hours. Sometimes the tiger slept, sometimes he was awake watching over his keeper like a feline sentinel. Night in the den felt surreal. The dank, sealed womb seemed isolated from the rest of existence. Eventually Seva slept and dreamed of his beautiful Angaar standing in a forest, free and fully alive.

Chapter 6

Vasupati Chopra

Ravi Uppal was anxious. He had been unable to contact Vaz all day and he paced his large office looking out over the streets. It was almost dark and Suneeti would be expecting him home soon. They had a dinner party arranged for several local politicians and business people, all of whom had dealings with Cobra Investments. Although he found most of them tedious, and he was paying for the annoyance, the advantages to be gained in local political circles were not to be sneezed at. Suneeti loved arranging these sumptuous affairs and was very strict when it came to timing. Despite her young age, she was an asset and had learned quickly how to positively influence her husband's business contacts. They made a good team. She never asked too many questions and was the perfect woman to be seen on his arm – beautiful and intelligent. Yes, the money he could make using these people made any annoyance pale into insignificance.

Cobra was flying high and the partnership with Vaz had proven to be an inspired move. The money machine had quickly found a rhythm and the regular, annual millions Ravi talked about had materialised so easily he was shocked at his own foresight. Vaz was very, very good at his specialist role in the business and Ravi had quickly grown confident in his ability. Vaz became fixated on Ravi as a mentor and always understood what was necessary, never took chances and always delivered. There were usually three or four clients a year whose files were moved from the conventional side of the business to the hidden side. Ravi would, after a great deal of manipulation of figures and legal aspects, tell Vaz that there was a job to do, whereupon they would discuss the next target for an early demise. They discussed details on their traditional walk along the Rajpath. Nothing was ever written down or filed in an IT system. No one else but they would know. This walk was effectively the signature on a death warrant. Usually a victim's money had already disappeared into Cobra's various investment schemes before the final, brutal act, and would never figure in a subsequent reading of wills or police investigations. There was simply no audit trail and no way of linking the two. There was only the legitimate link of insurance and executorship which Ravi always oversaw with professional courtesy. Greedy he might be, but never careless. Once the details had been debated, Vaz would embrace the task and clinically finish the job. It was never a rushed process, but methodically worked through, using intelligence gained from his many sources. None of these avenues could be traced back to Cobra. It might take weeks, but the net result was a death far from the shiny offices in Delhi.

The latest annoyance to be removed was the one which had caused Ravi's anxiety. Vaz had been quieter than usual and had left in a strangely pensive frame of mind. Ravi had no reason to be concerned about the completion of the task, but it was not a normal, strategically planned case. It had to be an uncomfortably quick job. The long-standing client was a single, retired pilot who had a large house in Agra. He worshiped money and had invested heavily in some of Ravi's riskier, but high profit ventures. Lalit Mahto did not spend his money unnecessarily and his pleasure came from watching the figures on the balance sheet get bigger. It was not his only pleasure. He was also a pederast and had a reckless addiction to young, attractive boys. Lalit Mahto was a very special client to Cobra. Their history went back some years and Ravi had treated his client's deviant form of homosexuality as a bargaining point, showing empathy and faux sympathy. It helped that Vaz could supply his addiction, sourced from the streets of Delhi and Agra, each one increasing the grasp Cobra had, even if the tightening grip was clothed in the velvet glove of presumed understanding. Ravi had been so clever in his handling of Lalit Mahto that the latter's complete financial portfolio belonged to Cobra Investments. His tendencies required multifaceted, skilled management. At seventy-one years old, Mahto had relaxed into wealthy retirement and gave no thought to the possibility that the trust he had in Ravi Uppal could be used against him. He often socialised with the Uppals and felt something akin to friendship for the family. Vasupati Chopra, however, made Mahto uneasy, so was kept at arm's length.

There had been a sudden change in the old man's circumstances and, as a confidante, Ravi was contacted by his excited, wealthy client. Lalit Mahto had fallen in love. Independently of Ravi, Mahto had picked up a perfect, effeminate teenager, whilst frequenting the Blue Clouds wine bar in downtown Agra. This new beau, Sethi, was proving to be a very expensive distraction. Lalit Mahto had recently taken to making regular calls in order to retrieve large sums of money from previously untouched investments. In the last two months he had added to his lover's wardrobe, taken him on a trip to Singapore and had even purchased a new car. Mahto had lost his resolve not to spend and Cobra was going to lose a golden client. That was unacceptable.

Cobra was a complex beast, but far from fragile. It was designed to cope with people like Lalit Mahto. It thrived on them. Ravi had wrapped Mahto's affairs in tight, invisible bonds and was even the executor of his will. He had Mahto's estate tied to a charity, Fallen Angels, which had been set up to help young street urchins gain an education and climb out of the gutter. Fallen Angels had become a national organisation and was often in the press where good works were reported. It also soaked in ten times more money than it used. It was part of the Cobra machine. It made money for clients and was tax exempt.

On Mahto's last visit to the Cobra Investments offices he had brought his pretty lover and talked expansively about changing his will and a possible permanent move to Britain, or even America. Ravi Uppal had smiled at the old man as the fool had discussed his plans, the effete Sethi sitting in the manner of a theatrical queen, smiling through whitened teeth.

"I can have most of the paperwork completed in five weeks," Ravi had said, Mahto accepting that these profitable investments would need a trouble free, if prolonged, extraction. The detailed arrangements were skilfully mapped out by Ravi and he suggested wiring the proceeds to various overseas accounts to gain maximum benefit. Mahto agreed with everything and they set a date for the severance of their ties.

"How much am I worth now, Ravi?" Mahto asked. "I mean cash wise, not other assets."

"A ball-park figure?" asked Ravi.

"In American dollars," said Mahto.

Ravi noticed Sethi's eyes light up at the sound of money – he already hated the fop with a burning intensity belying his calm exterior.

"After Cobra's small commission we are looking at one million, two hundred thousand dollars. Close to nine crore rupees," he said coolly.

"Ravi! You have nearly doubled my money!" gasped Mahto. Then turning to Sethi said, "I think we will have some fun."

"Oh yes, Lali," said Sethi, squirming and clasping his knees. "You are so lovely."

Ravi had cringed at the boy's slight lisp and wished he could strangle him right there and then. Instead he rose, shook both their hands and guided them out of his office.

"What is the best number to reach you on?" asked Ravi as they reached the reception.

"Use my landline," said Mahto. "I will be in Agra for the next few weeks. I'm getting the house valued – I already have a keen estate agent chap interested."

With that they had left. Ravi's smile had disappeared immediately and as he strode back towards his office he had said to his personal assistant, "Jyoti, I want you to get Vaz to call me as soon as you can. Even if you have to stop all other work."

"Yes Mr Uppal," she said.

Without breaking stride, Ravi closed his office door and sat down hard.

He had been so angry.

"Fucking queer bastard!" he had muttered.

Now, three weeks after their walk up the Rajpath, Vaz was overdue sending news of the closing of their dealings with Lalit Mahto. Ravi had given up waiting and was getting into his BMW when his phone beeped. To his relief it was a text from Vaz. It quite simply stated, *I am become death*. Ravi grinned. His evening had become much brighter.

I am become death.

The worms inside his head were writhing. It was an itching, rhythmic, almost pleasant feeling. The Destroyer surfaced from the deep, black, secret pool of his mind into the outer world. Kāla had been set free. It was the time of Kali Yuga; the world was in ever greater chaos and Shiva had become death. In this muddled mind all the stories were reality. Whilst hidden in the lightless depths, this incarnation of Shiva remained masked from all. Ravi had been the giver of power, yet even he only saw the glint of the reality in the eyes of Kāla's human vessel. Kāla's recent deeds echoed briefly in the outer world, but journalistic prose could never do him justice. Their words were just a blip on the radar of reality. A ghost and nothing more.

Shiva begat Kāla. He became one of Vasupati Chopra's executioners, a wraith to carry the blame for the deeds of others. A scapegoat from the same stable as the Taxi Men and The Mechanic. The perfect weapon. A silent, invisible deliverer of death. But Kāla was special. Vaz was one with Kāla. To him Shiva was incarnate. This alter-ego had journeyed with Vaz for years, slowly growing from a subliminal idea into part of his consciousness. A specialist would call him schizophrenic, but Vaz was aware he was two beings and fought neither. Dominance of one relied on the cunning of the other, just like Cobra; Ravi had given Vaz the freedom to be what he yearned to be.

It had never been easy for Vaz to control the creature inside and he was frightened what Kāla might do unchecked. However, with the invention of his phantom killers Vaz had a functional pressure-relief valve. Kāla could hide in plain sight amongst them, so caution became less of a prerogative. Kāla-Vaz was a deep and deadly secret.

It had been Ravi who became the unwitting catalyst for this monster's release into the world. Musical verse had been the key. Ravi had given Vaz a rare compact disc by Zahan Bulsara for reasons forgotten. When Vaz had listened to the haunting intonations of the great Zoroastrian mystic, his world changed. *Chaos Birthing* made the worms in his head writhe. He was driven to find out more about this hypnotic Parsi music. Zahan was famed for intoning his written philosophical poems to sitar music. In more recent times he embraced electronic sounds, collaborating with the composer Galen Fossa. *Chaos Birthing* was Zahan's greatest work, long regarded as his magnum opus. It consisted of twenty-five extended verses. Its full recital is said to take exactly one day and one hour, if done correctly. Zahan managed this feat in his first performance to the faithful, set to Fossa's enchanting music. *Chaos Birthing* had been released on a series of hour-long discs, the final one entitled *Time's End, World Beginnings*. This was the recorded verse that opened Vasupati Chopra's mind. He eventually purchased the other twenty-four discs, but kept the original, auspicious twenty-fifth. Zahan's words had freed the dual being: a man who is a god, a god who is a man. He was not scared of release anymore. It was easy: Kāla only wanted to appear to kill, to feed; then he would retreat and stay hidden. Vaz was a god, Zahan the key, infinity his right to inherit. He no longer needed an excuse not to kill.

He had tested it on that third reported victim. Kāla-Vaz had nailed the man to a wooden wall, watched from a chair as he regained painful consciousness, then used a lump of wood to break the horrified man's legs. Sitting, watching he could feel Kāla rise from the depths inside, become him and at once the balance was right; a resonance that calmed the writhing in his brain and charged him with power. Watching death was all. The cognitive dissonance he had suffered was gone.

The worms inside his head writhed. He was watching a large house in Agra, the rambling shrubby garden walled in for security, with lengths of iron railings giving glimpses of the rich man's world beyond. In India status is writ large. He could smell the Yamuna River and feel a warm breeze on his face. He stood inside the grounds cloaked in evening darkness staring at the brightly lit building. In this form, as a man, he could finalise plans before opening the doors for the god within. For many days he had watched and followed the pair, buying information from reliable informants from the underworld with which he was so familiar. He had built up a picture of daily routines. Mahto was a man of habit. This was to be the final night of watching. As the time for Kāla approached, the vessel, Kāla-Vaz, trembled with excitement. The worms writhed. He could feel the power inside building; pressure of an almost orgasmic force. Once the lights went out, the watcher disappeared into the dark. Avoiding the ragged rough-sleepers and pariah dogs, he stepped lightly through the night to a grand hotel.

"Ah, good evening Mr Vaida," said the receptionist, "I trust you had a good business meeting."

"Yes," said Vaz. "Very profitable. My keys please."

"Certainly, sir," said the receptionist.

With a mutual "goodnight" the receptionist watched the man step into the lift, the doors sliding shut behind him. Mr Vaida was no stranger here, but remained mysterious and aloof; never rude, yet not one to pass time with idle chatter or gossip. There was something cold about him.

Vaz pressed the button for the top floor and made his way to room 555. He stripped, lay on the bed and relaxed as the worms settled in his mind, Kāla slipped back into the depths and he drifted into a deep, undisturbed sleep.

Dawn heralded the morning. No cleaners would bother him as there were strict instructions that their valued customer was resting, preparing for a night flight to London, and should not be woken. Mr Vaida paid top prices and tipped generously. The sun moved towards the west and he still lay on the bed as evening fell upon Agra. Only street lights and car headlamps illuminated the room. He was the vessel. It was time for the doors of perception to open. The transformation of man to god. The buds of an iPhone sat snugly in his ears and he wore a pair of round, blue-lensed sunglasses. Kāla's world had a blue cast. The vessel listened to the mesmeric voice of Zahan.

"Tarnished silver, patinated gold, my Lord watches..."

The sound of Zahan's voice reverberated in his mind; the rhythm of Fossa's music had found his cognitive worm. The self-proclaimed Mystic Prophet had opened the doors to the inner god.

"My Lord is sending, a pure river of darkness, a storm of change..."

The man, the vessel, had been still for most of the day. The worms inside his head had woken, started writhing and were now irresistible. It felt good. It was the precursor of the arrival of Kāla.

"He will fall from heaven..." he was now the god *"He will be seen as a man..."*

"I am become death," he muttered, the transformation was complete. He listened and muttered his mantra.

"Kāla carries a great sword..."

80

"Destroyer of worlds…" Kāla was out. He was in the room. The naked body on the bed was no longer Vasupati Chopra. The body spasmed and relaxed.

"Kāla reaps the harvest…"

A slow release of breath.

"He will absorb the light…"

As the cadence of the music rose and accelerated the body's energy was increased, it arched upwards as an erection grew and exploded into an orgasmic climax. Kāla was Vaz; Vaz was Kāla.

"Darkness is death…"

He sat up and rested his feet on the floor.

Lalit Mahto sat in a plush armchair watching a large, flat-screen television. He was clad in a maroon silk dressing gown, cream homespun pyjama trousers and a pair of green and gold velvet slippers. He held a tall glass from which he was sipping an ice-cold white wine spritzer. He was engrossed in a show featuring a colourful pageant of dancers moving to Indian music: all were male; all were youthful. His foot tapped out the rhythm and the ice in his glass followed the same cadence, tinkling musically. He was happier at this moment than he could ever remember in his adult life. His early years had been spent at an all-male boarding school in England where his tendencies to prefer same-sex liaisons were occasionally reciprocated by those of like mind and body. Being a homosexual by nature, but a pederast by inclination, his existence had been

81

a roller-coaster of tension and relief. He had lived through the full history of anti-gay prejudice.

Becoming a pilot had helped him keep his tendencies hidden, the 1960s and 1970s being far from enlightened, especially in India. He managed to have fun in western cultures with New York, San Francisco, Sydney and London allowing him a lot more freedom to express himself. Unfortunately, as he got older his affections remained with the young and this had caused him more tension than relief over the years. Money, however, fixed most things and being a high earner and sole beneficiary of his wealthy mother's estate had pushed his life to a very comfortable level. She had been the widow of an Anglo-Indian businessman, many years his junior, and Lalit had been his only issue. She had been his rock and spoiled him as a child, but bowed to the pressure of travel and reluctantly gave him up to an expensive boarding school system. He hardly saw his father, who died when Lalit was sixteen, but his relationship with his mother was always very strong. She ended her days in a New York apartment overlooking Central Park, her son being a regular visitor during transatlantic flights. Mahto had inherited everything. The more money Mahto acquired the less tension he found he had to deal with, so his pederastic balancing act became inextricably linked to the increase of his assets. Money became his second vice. He became greedy for both – fast money and safe boys. Then he stumbled across Cobra Investments.

After retirement he settled in Agra in his late father's Indian residence, quickly selling his mother's remaining estate. The West was exciting, but boys there were too dangerous to coerce. India was different for the likes of him. His penchant for rent-boys or the more innocent, vulnerable victims of poverty, had cost him a lot of money, but he could not subdue his desires. Eventually a local pimp started to extort hush-money from him. Mahto had become trapped, yet fate had intervened on a night some years before. In a seedy downtown hotel room, he had completed the violation of a new boy after paying an exorbitant sum to his blackmailer. The pimp had arrived after a pre-arranged call and had escorted the distressed victim back to the streets. Mahto had showered, dressed and left the room quickly, only to come across an alarming scene in the car park. The pimp was lying on the ground being kicked repeatedly by a younger man in a suit. As he watched, the man stamped on the pimp's head. This figure was strange and out of place. He showed no sign of excited emotion and calmly carried out his vicious assault as if it were a mundane chore. Eventually the young man stopped and spat on the still figure at his feet. The pimp was dead. So shocked was Mahto that he dropped his car keys and trembled in disbelief as the assassin turned towards him. This cold, violent man had just smiled, taken out a cigarette and lit it.

"Mr Mahto," he said. "You really should be more careful with whom you do business."

Mahto could only stare in shock, surprise and shame – he always felt shame after the climax of his uncontrollable actions. The man had walked up to him and offered an outstretched hand, which he took even though he continued to tremble.

"Call me Vaz," said the killer.

Cobra had been a revelation. Cobra had freed him of tension. Cobra had made him money and found him boys; cheap boys. Scrubbed, compliant boys. Mahto knew Ravi Uppal and Vasupati Chopra were making money out of him, but his capital was growing and they had protected him from his own proclivities. Ravi Uppal had become his friend. Vaz remained a shadowy figure, a provider and fixer. A reliable constant. Mahto never took to this killer yet felt safe in the protection of such a man. The scene at the car park was never mentioned. Cobra had become his sole business and legal service provider.

Now, after five years, his life was perfect. Sethi had made it so. The Blue Clouds wine bar was a private club that Mahto often frequented when he was not flying. Once he retired he still dropped in to enjoy the company of likeminded men, but as these were mature in years his interest was limited. Sethi appeared several months ago, and despite some gentle warning from some of whom Mahto had considered old queens, he fell under the spell of the young man's charms. Sethi was very young, yet was a clever manipulator of those who wanted him. Lalit Mahto was a dream come true. Mahto's desires finally overcame his miserly tendencies and common sense, making his fall complete. He had unconsciously allowed lust and then love to cloud his judgement – but, at his age, why not? He could deal with any heartache later.

Lalit Mahto looked at his watch, 21:35. Sethi would be home from his dancing lessons at midnight. Until then he could enjoy the luxuries life had bestowed upon him.

Chapter 7

Mr Gupta Comes Back

He floated in a sibilant ocean of jet, a being of consciousness without physical form. Was he in the sea? How did he get to the sea? Were the susurrations waves lapping a sandy shore? His eyes were open yet he could see nothing but darkness and hear only a beat…a rushing…and a beat.

Thump. Thump. Thump.

He became aware that he was leaving a place where consciousness did not exist. An ocean of nothingness. He was moving fast, rushing upwards through a black void, rising from the inky depths.

Thump. Thump. Thump.

The rushing accelerated in his ears, rising in pitch to a deafening whistle, then a full-bodied scream. He felt lighter, buoyant, alive. He was reaching the surface, the pressure beneath forcing his fully conscious body up to the light. He needed to breathe. It became unbearable. The noise, the relentless scream, the howling in his head…

On the bed Mr Gupta's body twitched. A huge breath was taken. A sudden juddering tension. Then it was still again. No one saw. There was an almighty *crack!* in his head. His lost mind came into sharp focus in an instant. Clarity. Clarity held. The background beat remained as a receding echo from the emptiness he had left behind. Slowly his senses returned, his body being painted back into the physical world by a growing ripple of feeling. His ears began to pick up faint electronic sounds – beeps and clicks. A growing sensation of pins and needles prickled his skin, first across his face, then down his body. Then smells registered – disinfectant, something that reminded him of sticking plasters and a waft of carbolic soap. He was nearly back.

"I am blind," he said. His eyes were open and he could blink, but nothing in his brain registered vision. His tongue felt dry, leathery and fat in his mouth, his teeth wooden against its surface. Such a thirst he had never known. His penis felt hot. A tube? He could feel the tube against his thigh. He managed to move slightly and he felt the tug of tubes or wires against his skin. As understanding returned he ran an inventory of his body: fingers; toes; arms and legs. There was no obvious pain. He felt relief. His chest felt fine – good, it had not been a heart attack! Full cognition and a coruscating wave of colours flashed in his eyes as sight returned. Slowly it cleared and shapes appeared around him, wavered, wobbled then formed crisp, clear lines. He was back. His return from oblivion complete.

Mr Gupta was on a bed in a softly-lit hospital room attached to a wheeled box of electronics – the box was beeping and clicking. His last conscious moments in Dr Chowdary's waiting room drifted through his mind and he winced at the scene he must have caused. Relief flooded through him, a primal feeling beyond clinical explanation, something hard-wired in his chromosomes. There followed a wave of doubt and a series of questions. Had he had a fit? What condition would render him insensible? Was he now recovered? All he knew for sure was that he lived and was desperate for a drink of water. So, how to get it? A cord hung down from the ceiling ending in a small globe with a red button. He instinctively grabbed it and pressed the button – a button was meant to be pressed, he thought, especially in hospitals. In the distance he heard the faint sound of a bell followed quickly by the rapid footfalls of someone approaching the open door to his room. A pretty, young nurse dressed in white danced in and, upon seeing Mr Gupta looking at her, replaced the look of concern she had been wearing for a beaming smile.

"Hello, Mr Gupta," she sang. "It is so good to have you back!"

Mr Gupta tried to speak, but could only manage a dry croak, a residual bubble of thick mucus popping in the back of his throat. He tried again.

"Wuh!" he managed.

The nurse instinctively poured some water into a plastic cup and fixed a spouted top onto it. The sound of the water was as much as Mr Gupta could bear.

"Here you are dear man," she said. She helped raise his head with one arm and lifted the spout to his lips with the other. The cool liquid poured into his parched mouth. Never in all his life had he felt such relief.

"Careful now," cautioned the nurse. "Too much and you'll throw it all up again!"

He stopped drinking and smiled.

"Thank you," he said. "What the hell happened?"

"The doctor will answer all your questions in the morning, Mr Gupta," she said, still smiling. "Tonight, I am here to make sure you stay with the living and remain as comfortable as possible."

"Where am I?" he croaked.

"In the New Delhi Gandhi Hospital Intensive Care Unit," she said. "It means you are in good hands as we are the most modern hospital in India. You are being looked after by Mr Radhika, one of our top consultants who seems to have taken a special interest in you. He's a close friend your own Dr Chowdary. They play golf together."

She helped prop him up on pillows. He noticed the smell of sweet soap from her clear skin and saw her badge gave her name as Wamil. He felt unworthy of the attentions of such a beautiful young woman, yet it gave him a strong feeling of his maleness. It felt good.

"I need to make a phone call," said Mr Gupta. "I was due to be at a friend's for dinner tonight. They will worry. I need…"

"Enough for now," she interrupted. "At least your recall is good, my father would never have remembered a dinner appointment so far in advance."

"What time is it?" asked Mr Gupta a little confused.

"Nine o'clock," replied the nurse.

"Yes, a call will put their minds at rest," he said.

The nurse paused in her fussing, a quizzical expression on her face. Then realisation made her smile again.

"Do you mean Mr Singh?" she said. "He knows already, as does his sweet wife."

"What?" said Mr Gupta.

"You've been here two days, Mr Gupta," she chuckled. "I think your dinner must be cold by now!"

The night had played the sorcerer and shrank the world to room size, which had given Mr Gupta comfort. When he woke for the second time it was morning and the harsh light made his surroundings stark and far less cosy. Outside he could see it was raining. He felt quite well. His door was open and the busy sounds of a hospital reached his ears. A different nurse bustled in and saw to his needs. She was slightly older than Wamil and had a blue piping to her uniform, was quick and efficient and lacked the broad smile. She was, however, almost as pretty and her badge gave her name as Pia.

"How are we today Mr Gupta?" she asked.

"I feel well enough," he said, offering a smile.

"That's nice to hear," she said, smiling in return. "First things first I have to remove your catheter, after that you will feel more comfortable and less like a packet in a shop."

Pia was quick and not at all rough, but he was painfully aware that his body was not a joy to behold and felt ashamed of his lack of fitness, his tummy and his lifeless penis. He realised he was no longer a sexual being and had lost a part of his masculinity; he briefly felt like crying. Her last touch cheered him up as, when she replaced the sheets, he felt his old knob grow slightly across his thigh and he even watched her bottom as she washed her hands in the nearby sink.

"The consultant will be along later to see you and have a chat," she said, drying her hands. "First of all, a little breakfast."

"That sounds lovely," he said. "I'm not very hungry though."

"Some tea, a little toast and some fruit, perhaps," she said and left.

Mr Gupta surprised himself by eating everything put before him. The tea tasted so good too, the best he could ever remember. A rotund girl in a green uniform whisked his dirty crockery away and he was left, propped on pillows, to wait for the doctor. To his right the large window gave him a good view of the shrubby gardens. He was pleased he was on the ground floor and was delighted to see a pair of the stripy squirrels chasing one another around the branches of a small tree. It made him think of home. A pang of loss rippled through him and a vision of Kiran's sweet face entered his mind. The house was a refuge where he could hang on to the life he once had, yet, deep down, he knew this was an illusion. As he waited and watched the playful squirrels chasing around in the rain he tried to take stock of the events of the last few days and what it meant for him. He was trapped in a time capsule which would one day seamlessly evolve from what *was* to what *is*. Since Kiran died he had ticked over and managed to slip into a tedious routine which had, at best, given him comfort. He had done nothing to drag himself into the present and, despite his friends gentle cajoling, he had remained in a very deep rut. The one thing he had relied upon to keep him in this self-imposed stasis was his health: as long as he had kept this, he had plenty of time to pull himself together and start again, or so he had reasoned. That reliance on good health had now gone, leaving him in a state of growing anxiety over how late he may have left things.

Mrs Singh had been right – get the medical stuff done, then start a new life – but right at this moment Mr Gupta could see no further than the walls around him. Were the headaches migraines? Was his collapse stress induced? Had it been a culmination of many things or something far more serious? Not knowing had been a comfort, now it scared him. A sense of foreboding threatened to overwhelm him. Then there were his *financial affairs*, a term he used as a catch-all for insurances, investments, wills and last requests. To say he had ignored them would be an understatement. He was so lucky to have had Ravi Uppal as a brother-in-law, a strong man who had taken the financial burden from him and put his affairs in order after Kiran's death. Indeed, he had helped Kiran to invest her inheritance too, a tidy sum of forty million rupees, which had given them a steady income to cover Rupa's needs. Ravi had also managed Kiran's life insurance money into various funds and had told Mr Gupta to rest easy until he was ready to sort out his affairs properly. This help was given at no cost and showed great empathy from a man who had lost his first wife in such violent circumstances. Ravi had also shown righteous strength when he had successfully sued the hotel, from where Tamina and her friend were taken, as a matter of principle, and was rumoured to have given the proceeds to charity. Mr Gupta was pleased that Ravi had managed to rebuild his own life. Yes, it was time to talk to Ravi and get some advice, especially the best way to use the money he had at his disposal to consolidate Rupa's future. How much had there been all together? He could not remember. Ravi would. His mind whirled as he realised he was planning for the worst-case scenario – his own demise.

"Bloody hell," he muttered.

He cleared his mind of glum thoughts and focussed on the squirrels. Then he noticed his mobile phone on the cabinet next to him.

Across the city Rupa sat in her wheelchair looking at another shrubby garden in the rain. Outside her window three striped squirrels were quartering the lawns oblivious to the weather, flanked by some common mynahs. Wherever there were gardens and trees in Delhi one could see these creatures, but seldom were they scrutinised with the intensity of the girl in the window. Her darling father had taught her to watch everything around her, to see what others could not see, and to use everything she learned to make her world more complex and beautiful. He told her that life was a journey, travelling along receding parallel lines on a plain white canvas. Everything learned would add another layer of colour to the picture, thus brightening her journey. One should never be ignorant of the surrounding world. She had embraced this philosophy. It kept her mind sharp and exercised the high intellect her father had recognised.

When she was little her father would spend long hours pushing her around the city, through parks and gardens, explaining everything they saw. Most of all she had enjoyed the birds and other creatures, especially those that visited their little garden. Since her mother had died he had changed. His vitality had been drained. He had become gentler, but less anxious to know why mynahs were mimics, how so many kites found enough food in the city, or where their squirrels spent their resting hours. He had stopped painting his journey.

Rupa Gupta suffered from cerebral palsy. She had been unlucky as her condition had progressed rapidly from birth and all semblance of a normal life had gone by the time she was four years old. In spite of her disabilities her parents had managed very well whilst she was young and were pleased that Rupa was a very bright girl. By the age of six Rupa had started to show an astounding level of intellectual understanding, spoke both Hindi and English, and was pushing boundaries her loving parents were unable to cater for. This is where Lord Ernest Beaufort, 1878 – 1961, came in.

Lord Beaufort had been born at an Assam hill station into a wealthy Anglo-Indian family who had become rich by growing and exporting tea. After private schooling in India he was sent to England for an education at Oxford, where he took a degree in engineering. After graduating he worked on civil engineering contracts across the British Empire. He eventually returned to his beloved India to work on a variety of projects, including railway construction and hydro schemes. He returned to the family business at Dibrugarh in his late fifties. His sons took up the day-to-day running of the plantations and he controlled the administration, including import and export management.

Although from aristocratic stock he remained a humble man and felt his riches should be used to help those less fortunate than himself. During his travels it was seeing the suffering of children that had stirred him, especially the broken and disabled who were so often coerced into being beggars. That was where he decided to focus his attention. He established the Beaufort Homes Educational Trust of which he became the director and sole benefactor, allowing him to make it independent of all political or religious interference. It was unique in selecting disabled children of high ability, giving them the care they needed to fulfil their intellectual potential. He was convinced great minds could operate in broken bodies and that this would contribute to society in future generations. His wealth was the mainstay of the charity and during his lifetime built more than sixty homes. They could be found in places as unlikely as Quito and Reykjavik, but the bulk remained in Great Britain and India. He also managed to extract funding from governments and rich altruists, with contributions from student's families always based on their ability to pay. His charity had fought criticism, takeovers and direct political attack. An education for severely disabled children was no simple affair, but such an established, well-managed system had created success after success. It was Beaufort's hard work and dignified responses that gave the Trust international respectability and him a life peerage. He was made a Companion of Honour in 1956.

Delhi's Beaufort Home was located in a large, red-brick ex-military barracks, which catered for and educated up to thirty-five youngsters. This had been Rupa's home since she was seven, and here where she had blossomed into a talented and fearless teenager. The key had been Kiran being the heiress of a large inheritance. Kiran Gupta and Tamina Uppal's father, Nalin Shastri, had left his two daughters a substantial sum of money in trust, which they were given access to upon their mother's death, several years before Rupa was born. Ravi Uppal had convinced them to invest the money in a high-yield account which he would administer and from which they could glean a regular income, should they wish. He had become the sisters' executor and the Gupta family's financial and legal advisor. Tamina had left her money as a growing investment, but Kiran was able to use some of her income to help fund Rupa's entry into the Beaufort system.

Ravi had been so kind to the Guptas and used his relationship with the Beaufort Homes Educational Trust board chairman to bring Rupa to their attention. Her assessment showed an IQ of above 120 and she was offered a place on ability alone, with a 60% grant for her projected time there to the age of eighteen. Ravi Uppal's management of Kiran's lump sum ensured there would be ample annual income to cover the fees remaining after the Beaufort grant was paid. Since her mother's death, Rupa's father had allowed her Uncle Ravi to place the money in trust for her and also to invest a large amount of life insurance money which had, in effect, secured their future. Cobra Investments had served them well.

Rupa remembered how upset her mother had been when she moved to this permanent boarding school, but unlimited access, first-class pastoral and medical care, and the mental stimulation of good teachers made it an inspired decision. She had become a bright and popular student and enjoyed the relative quiet solitude of her own room, with its view onto the gardens. The tumbling squirrels made her smile. She loved the way the rain sprayed off of their tails in a watery fan. Her bright, pretty face bore the clouds of concern as she thought of her dear father. Her Uncle Jhatish had told her of his collapse and hospitalisation, and had just left a message stating that he had regained consciousness, so it was hard not to worry. Just then a squirrel slipped and rolled onto the wet grass and briefly lay on its back, unhurt but with a comical air of surprise, and Rupa beamed again. She dribbled as she chuckled, but was used to it. Happy as she was, she still missed her mother and needed a hug from her father soon.

Jhatish Das frowned at the clock on the wall at the back of the classroom. In front of him sat a mixed class of diligent students stooped over their desks writing a short English essay.

"I want two hundred words explaining what your favourite pastime is," he had stated earlier. "Take your time – you have an hour before the lesson ends. Make it interesting and do not worry too much about spelling – I want to see structure! It's like building a house – structure first, decorating last."

Now his smartly dressed pupils were beavering away whilst he watched the clock. Jhatish Das was a short, dishevelled man in his mid-forties, his slightly spreading frame kept in check by regular games of tennis and a tendency to rush around *getting things done* as he was apt to say. His wire-rimmed reading glasses were slightly buckled and swung gently from a long, black boot-lace tied around his neck. He was what the old school would call a *bit of a duffer*, but he was ever popular as a teacher due to his patience and ebullient encouragement of creative work. In his language classes he had found that correcting sentence construction and punctuation was learnt quicker if students could apply it to their own creations, thus his now accepted cliché about frames and decoration. He was clock-watching as he was anxious to see his best friend, Anil Gupta, who had been in the hospital for a couple of days. He had been the one to inform Rupa of her father's collapse and was desperate to give her better news. Since Param Singh had phoned him with the shocking news, he had not been as attentive in class as he usually was. His students had noticed their favourite teacher's appearance was rather more crumpled than normal. To his shame the mobile phone in his pocket chirruped into life – he had broken his own strict rule about not using them in the classroom. With a brief, "Continue working!" he stepped quickly into the corridor and took the call. To his surprise and delight he had seen it was Anil's number on the screen.

"Hello, Anil?" he said in his quick voice.

"Yes," replied Mr Gupta. "I'm back from the dead!"

"What is going on, Anil?" asked Jhatish.

"Well I feel fine and have just found my phone on the cabinet by my bed, so I thought I'd better call you," said Mr Gupta. "I'm probably breaking lots of rules, but I'm bored and worried about Rupa."

"Rupa is alright, but needs to know when there is any improvement," said Jhatish as calmly as he could. "Now, what is the prognosis? What happened?"

Mr Gupta told his friend the full story of his collapse at Dr Chowdary's surgery and of regaining consciousness at the hospital. Much of this was already known to Jhatish but it was good to hear Anil's voice again, especially as he sounded pretty normal. Mr Gupta explained that he was waiting to see the consultant, then he would find out more. He asked Jhatish to let Rupa know he was feeling fine and to reassure her that he would visit as soon as he could. Jhatish told his friend that he had seen Rupa each day since the incident, and that the Singhs had also been regular visitors.

"Can I come and see you in a couple of hours?" asked Jhatish. "You were always asleep when I visited!"

"I can't see why not," said Mr Gupta. "It would be nice to see a familiar face."

The sound of moving chairs from the classroom alerted Jhatish that things may need his attention, so he reluctantly ended the call. Stepping back through the door he saw the scrabbling figure of a boy under a desk and the rest of the class could not suppress a giggle.

"What are you doing, Raj?" he asked.

"Sorry Mr Das," replied the grinning boy. "I dropped my phone!"

Jhatish Das raised his eyebrows, took a deep breath, and then laughed along with the rest.

"Raj," he said. "Today is your lucky day! For once we'll call it quits. But do remember to look up the word *once* and absorb the meaning."

"Yes, sir," said Raj quickly returning to his seat.

Order, silence and stooping over essays resumed, the occasional little chuckle punctuating the air. He believed a happy class was a productive class. Fear taught fear. Kindness taught everything. Apart from that Raj was a very bright and equally funny boy: why snuff out comedy? Life would find its own seriousness without adding to it.

Jhatish Das was an old friend of Mr Gupta's even though he was several years younger. They had met whilst attending a series of lectures on the history of Delhi at a local college, and finally began to meet socially after a lecture entitled *The Consequences of the Indian Mutiny for Modern India*. They shared a love of history and it was this that had sealed their friendship. Jhatish had been a poor student-teacher at the time and Anil Gupta had just moved onto trains to be a conductor as part of his training to be a supervisor. There was an imbalance in their means, but Mr Gupta was happy to let Jhatish join him on trips across the city and he became a frequent guest at the house. Occasionally, Jhatish would take Mr Gupta out for a meal which was accepted as a gesture of friendship and respect for the younger man's generosity with limited resources. The bond strengthened over the years and Jhatish had become a surrogate member of the Gupta clan. Amit's children called him *Uncle* without hesitation and they all attended his graduation as a teacher. It was unthinkable to leave Jhatish out of the reckoning at weddings, funerals or births, and even Kiran's appearance on the scene changed little. She learned to love the dishevelled, gentle teacher and was overjoyed that her lovely Anil chose him over Amit as his best man at their wedding. Amit's approval was sealed when he paid for a suit for Jhatish, made from cloth he chose and using a tailor on the payroll; for once he had looked very smart. Later Mr Gupta was present at Jhatish's wedding, and comforted the young man a year later when his wife ran off with a fellow teacher. It had been Jhatish who told Mr Gupta that his wife had been killed, and he who had caught and held him as grief took its course.

Unlike the Singhs, the teacher had been allowed into Mr Gupta's inner sanctum of hopes and fears and personal problems, and Jhatish had shared his worries and dreams with his older friend. The eight-year age gap faded into insignificance and they found no hardship in their close communion. Rupa had grown up knowing him as Uncle Jhatish and even when she could grasp the formal structure of a family's blood ties he remained so. It was he, along with the Singhs, who had kept Mr Gupta sane as grief over Kiran threatened to overwhelm him; and it was he, whose prompting it was, who had made Mr Gupta take stock of his life and carry on living. He had taken him by the hand and brought him to his grieving daughter and embraced them both, cried along in the triple embrace and cemented the diminished family into a unit that would survive. In recent months they had talked about the future a lot and Jhatish had told Mr Gupta to take his time, but to at least have a plan, especially as Rupa would need security and also because there was *life in the old dog yet* which drew a laugh. The headaches had been discussed, yet both had dismissed the seriousness of them, drawing false comfort in a denial which reflected their gentle nature rather than blind hope. They had last met the day before Mr Gupta's long day to Bhopal and back, when they had talked about positive things; Jhatish's dearest friend seemed to be coming out of a two-year trek in the dark.

Today, however, Jhatish had felt a great dread as there was obviously an underlying problem with his friend, something he knew they had not taken seriously. Now that Mr Gupta had finally regained consciousness he was determined to do all he could to get him through it and was relieved he had the chance to do so. His two days of reassuring Rupa had seemed disingenuous, so now he felt a profound relief and a little heroic.

Jhatish and Rupa were very close. It was her response to his effective mentoring that was the main factor in her being accepted into the Beaufort education system. His greatest pleasure was reading to her, something he had done since she was tiny and his visits always included a session. Over the two days of her father's incapacity he had been reading from

Seal Morning by Rowena Farre, an English classic about life on a distant Scottish croft. Although Rupa found it hard to imagine the strange animals and landscapes described in the area called Sutherland, she loved the song-like prose and the visions conjured of a girl free to enjoy life without fetters. She loved the pencil drawings in the book, the easy way her uncle read and the distant look he got in his eyes as they were transported to faraway places.

The school bell shook Jhatish from his reverie and he took each student's work as they filed out of the classroom. He quickly tidied his desk, popped the essays into his well-worn briefcase and hurried out into the corridor. His phone beeped as he reached the main gate and he checked the message. It read: *Goodnight Mr Das. I have looked up 'once' and will absorb it – Raj.* He chuckled to himself as he hurried out into the warm evening air.

Chapter 8

Angaar's Fire Dims

The rain washed the air without cleansing. Thunderclouds over Mumbai could sometimes stir an artist's heart to capture the ever-changing scene in oils or watercolours; or perhaps even to store it in the electronic memory of a camera. Sometimes however, on days of sultry, windless heat, the clouds looked old and oppressive, condensed from the putrid, humid airs that hung over the city more often now civilisation had advanced on a sea of oil. The filter of the water cycle seemed broken. The rain, when it came, smelt of the drains to which it raced in greasy rivulets, down fouled gutters, into black holes which were the gateways to the Stygian depths of the sewers, a horror of viscous liquid, roaring to a stagnant sea. Beneath the corrupted clouds Mumbai lived on, people damp with effort, the extra burden of weather borne with resigned shrugs. The fug of moist air served only to increase the symptoms of over-population: a few more passengers fell under the merciless wheels of crowded trains; a few more babies perished in the arms of hopeless, wailing mothers; tempers flared a little quicker; and reactionist plots bloomed into action, only to be swept away by hails of righteous, democratic bullets. Mumbai suffered a few more things a few more times. This was such a day.

Seva watched the tiger. He could see that wild glow had dimmed a little more. His vigil had continued unabated and his presence became an accepted part of the normality of the zoo. He had not left for several days now and his sleeping niche at the rear of the den resembled a permanent shanty – tidy, but incongruous. Yet, it was as good as his usual lodgings in the windowless garage behind a workshop in which a grimy blacksmith toiled. The little bird-man kept Angaar's routine the same. The great cat still performed every morning then went about his limited life with little diversion. He had even managed to roar at the hysterical hyenas, but the edge had gone. Fresh blood no longer appeared in his waste, but little flecks of the darker mass were always present. Angaar was ill.

Mukul had taken to visiting Seva in the hours of darkness for a few minutes after midnight when his shift allowed it. This made Seva uncomfortable as Mukul smelt bad and his faux friendliness seemed to hide other intentions. Seva kept a close eye on his belongings and had hidden his small stash of rupees in a hole inside Angaar's enclosure where a brick had come loose. Yet Mukul had remained polite and his actions never indicated any intent other than the need for company. It was his eyes that gave him away: they darted hither and thither, missed nothing and never staying fixed, even in conversation.

Seva was in his customary early evening stance at the wall looking down at Angaar in his outside enclosure. The heat had been oppressive all day. A mighty rainstorm had driven the clouds away early, but the stifling heat remained, humidity redolent with vegetation, dark earth and city drains. It was as if the metropolis had a fever. To Seva it seemed the tiger's illness had infected everything around him, heating the atmosphere as quickly as it cooled his wildness. The thunderhead above was charged. Everything became still and Seva instinctively looked up as the hairs on his arms raised with static. Angaar stood up and gave vent to a colossal roar at the very moment the cloud discharged into the ground nearby. A banyan tree exploded and an eerie silence followed as the world was struck deaf. Seva's heart beat in his ears – one, two, three, four – then a breeze took the smell of ozone away and the heavens opened. Huge, warm drops crashed down, the early darkness lit by lightning painting the world monochrome in a series of white strobing flashes. He felt a presence beside him and turned as a final flash lit the face of Vikram Chakrabarti.

"Let's get into the den, Seva!" he shouted. "We need to talk."

The den echoed with rain. Angaar had retreated from the deluge to settle onto a fresh pile of bedding into his sphinx-like pose, eyes half closed facing the two men, ears swivelling to the sound of their familiar voices. Seva was soaked to the skin, but showed no sign of discomfort even as water dripped down his neck. He looked up at the vet, small in his ignorance and respectful of the taller man's knowledge, education and ability to cure. Seva knew that the vet had news about his Angaar. He already knew there was something bad lurking in that great body. The storm became the harbinger of ill omens. He felt sure Angaar's strength would rise to any challenge. He believed there was a greater destiny for all of them. What he needed was confirmation of longevity from this learned and great veterinary surgeon; for him to lay down a hopeful trail to recovery and not a short road to doom.

"How has Angaar been?" asked Vikram. "I have heard you have been here since our last chat."

"Yes, Sahib," said Seva. "This is as good a place as any to live for now. Angaar needs me."

"I would never try to stop you," said Vikram.

"Angaar is unwell," continued Seva, "but it is a strange affliction. He eats, though without enjoyment. He keeps himself clean. When he shits there is no pain. He drinks a little more and retches occasionally, but he does not seem to be suffering. He ate his last food yesterday and took his time. But finished the meal. But… but I know he's ill. He has faded a little bit, though he still plays in the morning. Are the things I have seen of value to you, Sahib? I cannot write things down like a doctor."

"That is perfect," said Vikram with a smile, looking at Angaar. "These are all good signs. It says to me the trouble may not be too far advanced."

"You must tell me what's to do," stated Seva. "I know he is in trouble. Only you can tell me the possible futures."

"Ok, Seva," replied Vikram. "I'll keep it simple. There are bad cells in the samples I took from his shit. Right now, Angaar's symptoms tell me if we act quickly all may be well. I've contacted a friend down in the Wai

Farm College and I can use the facilities there. Rupak Kunwar has worked with me on Project Tiger and he knows his stuff. And, most of all, owes me a few favours. I have managed to get some funding for his education trust so there are a lot of young student vets who will be happy to see us."

"What does this mean?" asked Seva, anxiousness obvious in his voice.

"Nothing to worry about," reassured Vikram. "In a couple of days Angaar will be sedated – that means I'll give him an injection to make him sleepy – and driven out to Wai in a secure truck. I need to X-ray him, then cut out whatever it is that should not be there."

"An operation?" asked Seva.

"An operation," echoed Vikram. "That is the simple version. I will carry out any procedure and the Tiger Rescue Fund will cover the cost. As you said, this lovely fellow has valuable seed. DNA we call it. We have to give him the chance to make some cubs."

"Oh," said Seva looking at the floor.

Vikram could see the little bird-man's mind was conflicted by the expressions on his face. He smiled slightly, unseen by Seva, and turned to the tiger again before saying, "Of course there is another problem."

"Another?" said Seva, defeated.

"Yes," replied Vikram frowning slightly for effect. "Our old friend Angaar will be away for some weeks. The cost is high, but tigers are mainstream conservation targets and funds are generous once secured. His quarters will be clean and modern and the environment peaceful – the college is set in acres of parkland on the edge of a wildlife reserve – but he will not have companionship. For recovery to be assured Angaar will need to feel as much at home as possible…" The vet's voice faded away as he feigned deep thought.

Seva shuffled his feet and scrutinised the hairs on his arm. His mind grasped the possibilities, but could not see a mechanism to accompany his fearsome friend. He had no transport, little money and he felt he could never become a part of such an important group of people. Men in white coats. Men who would all be Brahmins, foreigners and wealthy, both in mind and possessions. Seva had never missed a day with Angaar. Even on his days off he would use his free pass to be with his friend. Money, though such a useful tool, was secondary to the bond between the man and the tiger. Weeks without Angaar would be more than he could bear.

"Seva," said Vikram after a short time of reflection had passed. He turned to the little man and looked as earnest as he could. "I need to ask you a big favour. I think you are necessary to the whole thing. You are crucial in this tiger's life. I'm sure he'll respond better if you are there. Look, if I arrange things... if I make sure you have paid accommodation and enough expenses for food, things like that; would you be happy to be part of the team? I need you there."

Seva's mind flipped in his head – half thoughts, half plans, ways of travelling to this college place and watching from a distance – all disappeared in an instant. Vikram's words became a banquet to replace famine. A starving man could but boggle. Seva reacted instinctively from his ingrained position in caste. He grasped the vet's hand and placed it upon his own bowed head.

"Thank you, Sahib," he said quietly.

The power of the emotion behind the words was not lost on Vikram. For several long seconds he left the hand in Seva's gentle embrace before the feeling of unwarranted superiority made him withdraw it. He had felt Seva tremble under the involuntary touch. It was the nervous energy one feels when a bird perches on a finger. During those few seconds Vikram knew he had been accepted into something very special; something far more important than the structured bureaucracy of his professional existence. He had worked with wild creatures for many years, strove to improve their lot and, for convenience sake anthropomorphised his charges so as to feel a greater attachment to them. This way he felt he could understand each animal at a deeper level. This in turn would help him cure or conserve as necessary. But here was a small, uneducated man who had crossed the boundary that isolated species; the boundary that was even greater between predator and prey. Vikram felt both ashamed at his thinly veiled condescending request, well intentioned as it was, and warmed at being part of a new triumvirate of friendship and trust. His mind had been able to extrapolate much in that brief time in the den. All this made manifest under a darkling monsoon sky.

"Believe me, Seva," said Vikram placing his hand on the man's shoulder, "you are a key part of this. And you will be expected to be on constant duty. It won't be easy."

"Is not life a constant duty anyway?" said Seva. "A duty to make the most of what one has and not to waste time wishing and hoping? Angaar is a king. He is different from all the others of his kind. He holds greatness in him from times long ago. He has echoes of tigers going back to creation. I do not know why I know this, but I do. He is my friend and to look after him is part of my life's constant duty. If I was not to come with Angaar what would I do? The other creatures are beautiful, but they would not see me as he does. I will stay with him without question. You have lifted my heart. If you do all you say it will be miles beyond anything I could imagine. You are an honourable man and I know you will help Angaar and because of this I am your servant. I know together we can help him travel his true path."

"You are a good man," said Vikram. He took Seva's small hand and shook it as men should do. "It's a deal Seva. I'll sort out the details. Together we might fill India with tigers."

Vikram Chakrabarti was in his element. The facilities at Wai Farm College were perfect and he was able to use his influence to call in two more big-cat specialists who devoted a lot of time to Project Tiger. The philosophy of the group was to preserve, conserve, protect and study; they knew the future of the tiger as an existing species relied on people such as them. The treatment of Angaar's condition (he always thought of the tiger as Angaar now) may help to plug more gaps in their knowledge about *Panthera tigris tigris* and the more complete their database, the greater the chance of success. True to his word, he included Seva in all decisions regarding Angaar's coming journey, confinement and recovery. He also managed to supply him with an olive-green baseball cap and fatigue jacket, both emblazoned with an embroidered Project Tiger badge: green and gold with the central feature being the head of a tiger. Seva insisted on keeping his dhoti and home-made sandals but was delighted with the kit-bag that Vikram had also managed to purloin from Project Tiger stock – his worldly belongings found their way inside quickly. Even though the jacket was the smallest size available, Seva still had to roll back the sleeves as he was so slight, but the hat fit well enough. The vet mused at the fact that Seva looked remarkably like a freedom fighter in his new clothes and felt sure he would sacrifice more than most for a tiger. He determined to take the little bird-man wherever Angaar ended up. In turn Seva walked slightly more upright than usual; for the first time in his life he felt part of something bigger. Yet he remained the same gentle soul; his newfound status, minor though it was, required no compromise. Seva smiled at the reflection of himself in the windows he passed, thinking he looked like a green duck, especially with his tyre-rubber sandals flapping on the ground. He had no pretensions. Angaar regarded him the same, and that was all that mattered. Whilst Vikram planned the tiger's journey, Seva remained for the most part at the zoo. The blacksmith agreed to keep his lowly lodgings for him as long as the rent was paid. This large, dirty man had come to like Seva and trusted him around the foundry and was not a greedy landlord, but rent was money and children had to be fed.

On the day Seva had had to see the blacksmith in order to pay a month's rent in his absence, Mukul had been covering the day shift. Bandi, the head of security, had called him in and offered him a special job. He was to be part of the team to transport the tiger to Wai, *riding shotgun* Bandi had joked, but then added, "You are used to night shifts, so why not?" which made it a matter of convenience. Mukul agreed, especially as there was a modest bonus to be paid, and then asked why the tiger was being moved at night.

"It's simple," said Bandi. "There's a lot less traffic on the bloody roads at night and it will mean a simple A to B journey. Less stressful for the tiger and an easy shift for you. Straight down the main road to Pune, along the nice fast by-pass, then Wai. Bob is your uncle!"

"Who will be driving?" asked Mukul.

"Not the tiger!" laughed Bandi. "We've got a converted horsebox coming down from Hyderabad. It's all fixed up to move tigers around and Khan will be secure in there. One of Mr Chakrabarti's pals from Wai has arranged a driver. Anyhow, we will all be told the plans in a briefing tomorrow morning. Khan will be moved the night after that."

This had not been news to Mukul. He had a habit of keeping his ears open and knew the tiger would be moved. Such information could earn him money. He had left the office, smiling, and made his way to the wall overlooking the tiger's enclosure. He looked down on the great cat with dark, narrow eyes, rasping the stubble of his chin with a black fingernail. After a little while he made his way to the restricted area in the den, took out a phone and punched in a number.

"Cho," said a voice on the other end.

"It will be the night after tomorrow," said Mukul.

"Then we will meet soon," said Cho.

"I'll be in touch," said Mukul ending the brief conversation.

Angaar had wandered in to his inner sanctum, curious as to the unfamiliar voices he had heard. He stood near the bars and growled at the clever monkey standing in the gloom. Its smell was offensive to the tiger – bitter and unclean. He growled a second time, eyes boring through the space between them. Mukul stepped back involuntarily. Very quickly the hot pang of primal fear dispersed and Mukul grinned at the beast. He stooped and picked up a shard of concrete from the floor and threw it through the bars catching Angaar above the left eye, a more accurate shot than Mukul had really intended. In an instant everything changed – perspective, scale and speed. Angaar made a coughing growl and sprang the short distance to the bars. A paw the size of a dinner plate armed with razor sharp claws raked the air but an inch from Mukul's face, continuing its arc and slicing the man's shirt at the shoulder making a small but painful wound. Just enough to bleed a little. Mukul was so taken by surprise that he screamed, fell back and hit the rear wall, sinking to a sitting position. All this happened in seconds. The sudden charge of fear was such that a squirt of urine had voided into his trousers, but he just managed not to fully soil himself. It had been the speed and relative silence that had been so terrifying. The tiger was staring at Mukul. Mukul had been very close to death.

"You fucking bastard!" he yelled panting and getting to his feet, making sure his back was tight to the wall. "I'll kill you!"

Then he calmed down quickly and noticed the tiger staring at him. Just staring. Mukul spat on his thumb and rubbed the wound with saliva, wiped his sweaty forehead with a grubby sleeve then left the den muttering darkly. Mukul never reported the incident.

The meeting room in the Admin Complex was abuzz with conversation. It was a relatively small gathering as moving a tiger was a specialist task and hangers on had been discouraged. There was Rupak Kunwar, Vikram's veterinary friend from Wai, and a student called Vinay; the security contingent wearing their Kohli Security uniforms, Kohli being the zoo's security sub-contractor; and Seva. Vikram Chakrabarti moved to the front of the room and called for quiet. He sat on the edge of a table and addressed his Tiger Team, as he had named them.

"I won't keep you here long as we are pretty clear as to what's happening. Just bear with me. Our mighty Khan has a nasty little infection inside. It is ulceration brought about by having ingested a nail sometime in the past – nice people the public – but it is not fatal. That's why I need to get him down to the nice facilities they have at Wai Farm College. There I can zero in on the problem and excise it. Team Tiger's task is to get Khan there quickly and safely.

"To do this I will knock him out with a tranquilizer. We'll shift him into the converted horsebox, which will be here in the morning, and drive to Wai down the main highway by night. We can do it in four hours, five if there are any delays. I've driven the route both ways twice in daylight, so know it's doable. Rupak managed it in three hours this morning so it's simple enough. We have the funds, so it is just a logistics problem now."

Vikram pointed to the map attached to a flip chart holder.

"Here we are. I've marked the route in yellow. Straight down the Expressway. Once we're clear of the city all we have to do is avoid any new potholes and stay in convoy. We'll make a stop at the service area near Pune, stretch our legs, then on to Wai.

"Bandi has had a chat to his cousin in the police and we will have an escort over the bridge and out of the city. Rupak will be in our lead car with young Vinay – it's a nice Wai Farm College Land Rover with a yellow beacon. There's a driver coming down in the Tiger Taxi, our converted horsebox, and I'll be in there with Seva and the tiger. Behind, Ranjeet Kohli has a couple of his lads driving an Ambassador as a rear guard. Ram and Mukul will be in there and will fight any dacoits who try and rob us – they are brave and will give their lives so we may live!"

The two men chuckled, Ram beaming under his khaki turban.

"We will leave tomorrow night at about 01:00 and should arrive in Wai by 06:00. Simple stuff. Any questions?"

The plan really was simple, so simple that all in the room nodded sagely.

"What state will the tiger be in on the journey?" It was Mukul.

"Good question," replied Vikram. "I'll feed him a light sedative in the afternoon then just before the transfer to the Tiger Taxi we'll pop a tranquilizer into him with a crossbow. He'll be totally zonked when we load him up and he should sleep all the way. It's more of a semi-conscious daze, really, but for all intents and purposes he'll be asleep. That's why I have to stay with him. This stuff can be unpredictable and dangerous for an animal, but Rupak and I have shifted a lot of tigers so it should be alright. As I said simple."

There were no more questions so the meeting broke up. The converted horsebox arrived in the afternoon driven by a round, hairy man called Pak.

"My name is Rupak really," he had growled extending a hairy hand to Vikram, "but we can't have two – so everyone calls me Pak."

Everything was set.

Mukul was given the evening off. He left the zoo and disappeared into the backstreets of Mumbai, just one man amongst many millions. He did not head home as he had an appointment in the Chinese quarter. There, in a small café, he was to meet with a couple of people he had often done business with. Cho and Dong helped run a meat export business.

Chapter 9

Kāla-Vaz

Outside it was very dark and relatively quiet, this residential area of Agra having been chosen by Mahto's father for its seclusion; the high cost of properties kept this exclusivity intact. The house was well lit, though drawn curtains had shut out the night. The silent watcher could see nothing inside; conversely there had been no witness to his movement through the shrubbery of the garden. Kāla-Vaz had arrived. Dressed in black he was all but invisible in the shadows and stood looking at the backlit windows of Mahto's lounge.

Kāla-Vaz was a lethal, heartless creature, devoid of all emotion except for the overwhelming desire to exert ultimate power over others. He was a god-man who held the gift of death. Kāla-Vaz – god and vessel. The lust to dominate and kill had become insatiable. His long hair was loose and dark glasses tinted the world blue. He carried a heavy black cloth shoulder bag which contained all he would need. He loathed the old man inside. He had been tolerated due to his wealth and Ravi's expert use of it. Now a young gold-digger had signed a death warrant and it would be served this very night. The god-man could hear music from the television and knew Mahto was alone. It was time to move. He crossed the lawn to wide French windows. Keeping close to the wall he studied the closed drapes and found a small chink which allowed him a limited view of the lounge. The back of the man was framed perfectly. Mahto was engrossed with a large screen showing dancing boys and had a fairly full glass in his hand. Kāla-Vaz had the few minutes he needed to make things safe.

He moved quietly to the back of the house and drew a bunch of keys from his bag, then found they were not needed as Mahto had left the kitchen door unlocked. The silent killer felt even more disgust for the aged, effeminate human inside. The kitchen was dark and redolent of spicy cooking, the only illumination coming from the hallway beyond. Death entered quietly. The sound of the television was loud and would mask any sounds Kāla-Vaz might make. The worms inside his brain started to writhe more urgently. The vessel was controlled by Kāla. He paused and listened. At the far end of the hall the wooden door leading to the lounge was ajar; the music seemed even louder, Mahto was singing. A sudden brushing against his left calf made Kāla-Vaz jump. He soon relaxed as he saw the fluffy, flat face of a cat looking up at him expectantly. It was purring. Stepping quickly back into the kitchen he fished inside his bag and withdrew a bush hammer. This stone mason's tool had taken his fancy as he watched restoration work at the great fort; it had a toothed face a little like a meat tenderiser, but far heftier, and was ideal for making new stonework look weathered and ancient. It felt good in his hand, the balance perfect. The cat wove around his legs some more. He hated cats. As the fluffy feline paced to and from its empty food bowl the hammer rose. The single blow caught the cat between the shoulders and neck smashing every bone in its path. Blood spurted from the animal's nose and it twitched but once. The only noise had been a wet splat, unheard in the lounge.

Kāla-Vaz turned and stepped into the hall. All was safe, the music and singing had not missed a beat. The death of the cat had animated the god-man. The light in the hallway shone blue through his glasses and echoes of the key calmed his mind.

He will come silently to the defilers...

He stopped beside the lounge door and glanced in. Mahto's back was to him and he was humming, waving his now empty glass in time with the beat. The colourful boys on the screen gyrated and circled a man in a blue face-mask; ironically it was Shiva as the Destroyer. The real Death in the doorway put the bush hammer back into the bag and withdrew a short length of thin rope, wrapped it around his right hand and closed it into a fist. He took a deep breath then walked boldly across the room and stood in front of Mahto.

"No!" yelped Mahto dropping his glass and freezing in disbelief.

Kāla-Vaz punched him once to the side of his head, a fist made solid by the rope bindings. The pain was instant, but brief as Mahto lost consciousness. Kāla-Vaz punched him once more just below the ear. Simple. Death prepared to receive his next guest.

Sethi sat cross-legged in the taxi singing along to popular songs on his smartphone playlist. He enjoyed his new leisurely lifestyle and was now being indulged in his first love of classic dance. He enjoyed rubbing shoulders with the middle-class and upper-class students and tutors at the Kathak Academy. He felt alive at last! Not bad for a slumdog.

It was his beauty and natural feminism that had given him the edge over the other street boys he had grown up with. All had learned the tricks of the streets quickly. Rent boys who did not sharpen their wits soon starved. Sethi was the smartest. He looked like a class act, belying his squalid origins, and had rationed his favours to richer men who desired him. He was never pimped and was always his own boy. He knew instinctively which clients posed a threat, honing his senses after one brutal beating early on. He had followed the money and now he had hit the mother lode, with a chance to set himself up for life with little effort. Lalit Mahto was a lovely old queen and had chatted Sethi up in Blue Clouds for several weeks before finally asking if he was *so*. This was a sweet way of referring to being gay, thought Sethi. He confirmed that he was indeed *so*, but was not obviously *out* and was rather shy about it. His Lali had almost dribbled with lust as Sethi played him expertly, flirted and became more tactile. Mahto wined and dined him, indeed wooed him with gifts and money and promises, finally begging for sex. Once at this point the old man was snared. A gift of 10,000 rupees and a trip to the Maldives became the perfect way to consummate the relationship. From then on it was easy. Mahto was not grotesque, just old, but the wealth he had carefully managed had made him infinitely more attractive.

By the time he moved in to Mahto's home, Sethi was able to promise total loyalty, to be his and to share his life forever with some confidence. Now, after very few months he was on the verge of becoming Lalit Mahto's sole beneficiary. Sethi would have total control over a fortune and it had been easy. Even the sex was easy. Sethi was an expert and the old man easily pleased, yet the young man never acted with petulance and never sulked; his power over Mahto did not require such tactics. All that was required was for him to be a beautiful and faithful companion, and then he would have it made. After all, Mahto would probably die before Sethi was out of his twenties and, odder still, he had started to feel real affection for the first man to give him stability in his life.

The taxi came to a halt outside his Lali's big house. *My house*, Sethi thought. He paid the driver and danced nimbly across the pavement, whisked through the wrought-iron gate, being careful to click it shut behind him ready for the alarm to be set, and sashayed daintily up to the front door. There was only a single lamp burning behind the closed drapes – asleep, thought Sethi. He fished in his pocket and took out his keys. He would surprise the old man, then make him a drink. He stepped into the hallway and closed the door quietly. Sethi eased open the lounge door, took a pace inside then made an involuntary squeak as the dead body of the cat dropped from the top of the door, draping itself over his wrist before sliding to the floor. In front of him Lalit Mahto was bound to one of the heavy wooden chairs from the dining room, dressed only in silk shorts. His arms, legs and body were duct-taped securely in place, his mouth taped shut. His eyes bulged as he started to struggle with his bonds; his frantic gaze seemed to look past Sethi. Sethi turned. A blow rendered him senseless; the second sent him into unconsciousness.

Kāla-Vaz saw the dimly lit lounge tinted blue through his glasses. Mahto had long since given up struggling against his bonds. The tape yielded not an inch, his skin was sore and his nose had blocked with snot. He felt as if he were drowning. Panic almost overwhelmed him before the mucus dribbled out, freeing him to breathe normally. He knew it was best to keep calm. He had watched the dark man strip his unconscious lover down to tight silk briefs, cutting off the clothing with a kitchen knife, occasionally nicking that fine skin with a sharp point. The beautiful boy had stirred slightly at this, but the man had punched him again, hard, and Sethi remained in oblivion as a second, matching chair was brought in. Sethi was hefted in and taped firmly in place, the final piece sealing those beautiful butterfly lips. Kāla-Vaz had placed the two lovers three paces apart facing each other. Then he had drawn up a third chair, positioned it to one side, between them, so they had a view of his profile and could see each other's faces too. The dark man sat silently.

Mahto had calmed a little as time passed and tried to figure out what was happening. He was an intelligent man and felt logic must prevail. The old man had no enemies of importance and could think of no one he may have upset, so felt that this could be more to do with his young lover. That had to be it. Mahto sat uncomfortably staring at the side of the dark man's face. A twist of unease cramped his stomach. He knew this man – he knew him! He doubted his own mind at first but there was a change in this person before him that almost disguised his identity; he looked very different with his hair down and those glasses on, the change in demeanour was the obfuscating point. This was Ravi's partner! The pimp beater. A man whom he had rarely seen since that first encounter, so long ago. A man who quietly arranged for him to be supplied with safe boys, before Sethi had reformed Mahto, of course. Dread made his stomach cramp again. What *was* this about?

The man stared into nothingness. This was even more disconcerting to Mahto. What had he done to upset him? Vasupati Chopra was his name – *Vaz,* he remembered. This was Ravi Uppal's fixer, but the transformation was almost physical – did he have a twin? Mahto settled again and breathed slowly through crusted nostrils, remembering how cool he could be when flying in bad weather, how in control he had always been as a pilot. He would wait and see. If it was a blackmail attempt he could handle that. That was it; it always came down to money. Ravi and his business were mutually profitable, so was Vaz trying to make a quick rupee on the side? Mahto began to have doubts again, more snot dribbling from his nose as he breathed too deeply.

A muffled moan broke into his string of thoughts as Sethi stirred. The left side of that fine face was red and puffy. A red bubble grew and burst from a nostril as he exhaled in wakefulness. The young man's eyes flickered and the light of realisation snapped them open. Sethi panicked and tensed against his tight bonds. He swivelled and rocked his head in wide-eyed fright, cries muted beneath the silver-grey tape. The need to breathe finally stopped his thrashing. All the lovers could do was stare at each other, and at the impassive, motionless man who sat silently between them.

Time passed. Kāla-Vaz remained still. Mahto had become extremely uncomfortable. The spritzers he had enjoyed earlier had filled his bladder. How long had it been? Two hours? Three? He could not see a clock, but had been conscious through everything since Vaz had strapped him into this infernal chair. It seemed an eternity. Mahto was very, very scared. The sight of his Sethi being so cruelly beaten had made him weep. Now his young lover was awake Mahto felt better, no longer alone, yet all they could do was stare at each other. His head thumped as, for the hundredth time, he tried to extrapolate their possible futures from this insanity. Not knowing why he was in this position was the most frustrating and frightening thing. Ravi was a gentleman and had always been so very kind. Surely, he could not know of his partner's latest venture? Mahto was not naive. He knew that Ravi had helped supply his addiction in return for all his financial business, but all men had their quirks and none of this made sense. It was not rational. Money. It had to be money. It was what made men tick. This man had to be here to frighten them. To extort money. If it involved Ravi too, then Mahto had enough to settle any dispute with Cobra. Then he would run with his Sethi and sort them out through legal channels from the security of London or Milan. That disquieted him. If Ravi was party to this, all his business was so woven into Cobra that it could prove very difficult to extract himself. Not if Ravi and Vaz were locked up, however. Yes, if he fled with Sethi he could buy off a police chief and make Cobra a memory. He wriggled his bony buttocks against the hard teak seat as they became numb and sweaty. He gazed into Sethi's beautiful eyes and tried to convey reassurance, but the young man was frozen in terror. If only Vaz would talk, or even look at them. If only his mouth was not taped he could reason with the man. If only. *If only* were becoming the saddest two words in Mahto's lexicon; three syllables which could convey the sadness of generations.

Kāla-Vaz's mind was in heaven. It was full of images of the Bhagavad Gita and the words, *I am become death, destroyer of worlds,* echoed in his brain. He had killed before Kāla's release and each had been clean and quick – business with but a spike of pleasure. However, the most recent three killings had been different: Kāla had partaken in the deaths. The god had been kept safe for so long behind the strong door of the vessel's mind. It was Ravi who had shown the way and had allowed a complete being to operate. *Your Lord gives you leave to be yourself,* Zahan had once said, and so it had been. Ravi needed results and he had empowered his partner to bring them about, regardless of the means. Dividing Cobra into two separate entities had been a stroke of genius. The light side catered for souls who would draw sustenance from Ravi's skills, never to be touched by death. The dark side received souls for dispatch. For change. For destruction. Ravi gave life and Kāla-Vaz was the taker of souls – all was balanced. Vasupati Chopra's duty was to ensure any trace of Cobra was eradicated from the deceased's physical world. Ravi took care of the paper trails; Kāla facilitated Vaz's plans. It was an unholy trinity. Vaz saw Ravi as Lord Rama, and himself as a duel incarnation. They were all one. Somewhere Ravi was wiping accounts from computers, expunging Lalit Mahto from the light side; Kāla-Vaz was to complete the balance sheet: final total, nil. The state would happily take the house without enquiry.

Time passed.

Sethi's mind raced. He had known violence before, young as he was, and knew something bad would happen here tonight. He would use all he had learned to survive. He had been so close to reaching security. So close. He stared at his Lali in the chair opposite, had seen the reassuring look and had relaxed slightly. But a smear of blood from the cat – the wet, cold slimy, dead cat – was still on his hand. Horrible. Yet he would survive, if he could.

Time passed.

The worms inside his head writhed.
Purity in darkness stalks, He is coming, He is righteous...

It was time. Kāla filled the vessel; Kāla-Vaz was complete. Mahto and

Sethi heard a loud inhalation of breath and the dark man stood, walked forwards a few paces, turned then spoke.

"My Lord is sending, a pure river of darkness, a storm of change, to cleanse all creation." His voice was deep and resonant, commanding and clear.

The men in the chairs stared and trembled. Time had become a fickle comforter and now it had gone.

Kāla-Vaz spoke again. *"To waken in the real world takes purity of mind. It is not light that cleanses darkness, but the blackness that absorbs mankind's deeds. With the coming of the black river, we can begin."*

Flat round lenses suggested deep holes where eyes should be. Light sparkled like stars in the blue discs. He smiled, his single gold tooth flashing.

"I want you to listen," he said. "The key-master says, *'Purity in darkness stalks, He is coming, He is righteous, time is severed from mankind, darkness cleanses, darkness is pain, darkness is death, pain leaves with death, both shine with blackness. Love gives you pain, it is right to be cleansed, to embrace your own pain.'*"

Mahto and Sethi could only stare, neither understanding the complex outpouring from this creature.

"I will let you talk soon, but first you will listen. I will collect two souls tonight, and this will be, but life is arcane and mystical. Your creature is a soul. It will suffice for one. Remember that. Do you understand?"

Mahto and Sethi both nodded quickly after eyeing the remains of their cat by the door. Both men were aware of what was meant yet could not grasp the reality of what was happening. Lalit Mahto's stomach knotted again and he nearly wet himself. Sethi's thoughts were more basic: he saw a chance and knew he was more street wise than his old lover.

"Each of you will have the chance to explain why it should be the other who will die. Each of you may ask one question which I shall answer honestly. I reserve the right to tell one lie in all that follows as a token for the life I spare. Do you understand?"

Again, the nods. Kāla-Vaz paused, emotionless and still. He felt immensely powerful and knew he could exert it as he chose. He would tell the truths and single lie. This would intensify the feeling of power he wielded over life and death. He could do anything.

He spoke again. *"Kāla reaps the harvest, Kāla collects lives, He will sow them in the ground of the new World.* There will be clarity here." He then turned and left the room.

The two lovers stared at each other close to panic. Their planned future had become a fiction, reality was this dark horror in which they lived. Neither could divine meaning from the other's wide-eyed stare; each gathered small comfort for the seconds the man was missing. He came back all too soon carrying the bush hammer. Mahto knew what it was. Sethi could only boggle at the odd tool. It looked heavy. The man placed it on the floor between them. It sounded heavy – *clunk!*

"Do you understand what I have said?" asked Kāla-Vaz.

Both men nodded, minds grasping for impossible remedies.

"You first," pointing at Sethi. Kāla-Vaz stepped over and stripped the tape from his mouth in a single movement. Sethi squealed and dribbled blood-stained spittle.

"Why should I kill him and not you?" asked Kāla-Vaz.

Sethi breathed deeply and started to cry. "Why are you doing this?" he managed to ask between sobs.

"Because you interfered with business," Kāla-Vaz replied, "and because I do not like you. I have answered your question. Now, why should I kill him and not you?"

Sethi's gaze drifted to Mahto. The old man's blank look belied the fact that he was starting to understand and could see a way money could get him out of this. His feelings for the beautiful boy were strong, but capricious, the animal urge for survival winning the internal battle. He would salve his conscience once he was out of this. Sethi could not read the old man's mind, but intuition gave him the kick he needed.

"I am young and have nothing to lose," he gabbled in his high voice, "I am sorry to have interfered with business, but I did not know. How could

I? Let me live and I will just go. I cannot hurt you." Sethi turned his gaze upon the old man. "He got me into this. That old dog there. He hurts helpless people…kids…street kids, boys. He's foul and greedy…"

"Enough!" said Kāla-Vaz stopping Sethi's diatribe. The tape was replaced. Sethi blew bubbles from his nose as he wept again, little groans muffled by the tape.

The same swift movement and the tape was ripped from Mahto's mouth.

"Ghaaah!" gasped the old man. The top set of his false teeth followed the exhalation, skittering across the hard floor. Mahto's face collapsed around the resulting, fleshy sink-hole, drawn in cheeks emphasising his skull. His lower teeth were real, irregular and yellowed. He looked comical and tragic.

"Ghaaah!" he gasped a second time dribbling heavily.

"Talk to me!" barked Kāla-Vaz, crushing the dentures under his heel.

"Ghaaah!" from the diminished figure once more struggling for breath and finally speaking. "Why can't we sort things out without this insanity? It is not necessary!"

"Because Ravi has moved you into darkness. Things can never be the same," said Kāla-Vaz. "So, why should I spare you?"

Mahto's mind picked up the change in Vaz's words. He had used the word *spare* for the first time. Was this a sign? Mahto was having a real problem controlling his old body, slobbering from his collapsed mouth, the upper gums a pink, crinkled wall through which his usual eloquent speech had fallen into moist babble. With a final sniff he pulled himself together his urgent need to urinate sharpening his resolve.

"I…I have money," he said, slobbering. "Lots of money! Please, Vaz. We can just go on like before. I'll leave my investments in place. I don't need to waste it on this…this rent boy. He's used me. And you…Cobra, I mean. There's no need to kill anyone – just kick him out on the streets where he belongs!" At this point Mahto ran out of breath and gasped again, "Ghaaah!"

Kāla-Vaz spoke. "The answer has to be death. Do I kill him? Or you?"

"Ghaaah," uttered Mahto, quieter now. Then, in despair and shame, "Him."

Kāla-Vaz spoke again. *"Pain is a part of your reality. Pain cleanses. You should stand up for your right to feel your pain."* He was making quotes neither man could identify. Zahan was not widely known in India. The worms inside his head writhed faster. He bent and picked up the bush hammer.

"Only the living feel pain. Kāla demands the maximum from the living and my judgement is based on your own words. One of you will feel more pain by watching, the other by dying. That is all I have to say."

With one swift movement the bush hammer proscribed an arch, up and down, connecting with a left elbow, smashing it between wood and metal. The pain flared as a purple nova in Sethi's head and the muffled scream emitted with such force that the top corner of the gagging tape came loose above his mouth.

"Pheeeh!" wheezed Sethi, head rocking, eyes popping wide in their sockets.

The hammer continued its work coming down without pause on the left wrist.

Crunch!

"Pheeeh-eee-eee!"

Mahto blew more snot from his blocked nose, gagged and involuntarily released his bladder; a stream of hot urine soaked his lap and poured onto the floor. When the hammer struck an ankle, the pressure blew the tape completely from Sethi's top lip allowing a high-pitched whinny to escape. The once pretty boy was now insane with agony, fear and despair. Kāla-Vaz reached a steady, slow, but relentless rhythm: ankle, elbow, wrist; knee, shin, knee. Sethi's bowels released and the stench filled the room. All existence was in this room. There was nothing outside the will of Kāla. The hammer rose and fell. Mahto was making keening noises beneath the tape as he watched the destruction before him. The beautiful boy he had condemned to death was still conscious. How could he be? How? *At least kill him quickly*, thought Mahto, then understood how pain was being mined from watcher and victim. Kāla-Vaz maintained the rhythm, grunting with effort, slow and precise, electrified by the power over two souls, feeding on pain. The part that was Vaz, the vessel, could barely control the overwhelming urge to frenzy. Frenzy had taken over with the first real victim. Since then he had evolved the process to become tantric for Kāla. This time it would be perfect. Pain was being systematically harvested and none of the crop would be wasted.

The limbs were now smashed. Kāla-Vaz stopped and stared. Sethi's voice had broken under the strain, his head lolled but he was still conscious. His bloodshot eyes wandered to the dark man before him.

"Please…" was the only soft word he could manage.

The hammer rose and took up the rhythm once more. The two bound men inferred the pause as the end. The continuation harvested more despair.

Shoulder, collar bone, ribs; shoulder, collar bone ribs. On and on.

Kāla-Vaz paused again and turned to the skeletal figure of Mahto. "This is the fruit of your choice," he said. This time the pause would be different. The worms in his head writhed slower now. A comfortable itching replaced the thrashing need to impart pain and harvest fear. The pursuit of the art of death took over.

He spoke again. "The pain you inflicted on so many boys is no different to this, Lalit Mahto. Pain takes many guises. Look at your lover, Lalit Mahto. He looks at you."

Kāla-Vaz ripped the tape from Mahto's mouth.

"Ghaaah!" Another tortured breath. Mahto did indeed look at the broken boy and wept for him. He was still conscious. The beautiful irises now floated in red pools. The beautiful face was intact, but no longer vibrant.

"Seshi…" mumbled Mahto. "Oh Seshi…"

In one fluid movement the hammer was driven into the centre of

Sethi's skull killing him in an instant. Blood exploded from his ears, nose and mouth. The hammer was lodged so deep that Kāla-Vaz left it in place like a grotesque headdress. Sethi's smashed body remained strapped in place. Mahto continued weeping.

"That is two souls," said Kāla-Vaz. "Now you must stay silent. Cobra owns you. Do you understand?"

"Yesh," said Mahto.

Kāla-Vaz left the room.

Lalit Mahto could not look at his young lover's corpse or the mess that had been his kitty-cat. He wanted his teeth back. He felt old and broken. Yet through all this he was alive and that glow of hope flickering from the word *spare* was now growing in him. He would go on. His mind raced as he thought of a story to concoct for the police. Robbery would do it. He could easily make up a story which would fit the scene in the house. The threat of violence to Sethi would have made him give up cash, yet the robbers still killed him as a warning. He could say it was a lot of money! He could even claim it on his insurance. Yes, he could. Mahto baulked at this thought, but it was there and had merit. He would go along with Vaz and Cobra. Then get out of Agra. Out of India. For good. Yes, he would be their puppet, but get away as soon as he could. Then, safe in New York, or London, or Singapore he would show Ravi Uppal what ruination was. A seed of anger grew with the glow of relief. A pilot had to be sharp. He could get boys anywhere. Rio, maybe. Mahto relaxed. He took a breath and savoured his survival.

The room turned translucent as a plastic bag was pulled over his head. Strong hands taped it in place around his neck.

A voice said, "This is the lie I reserved for myself."

Kāla-Vaz sat and watched Mahto die.

Chapter 10

Mr Gupta's Trials Begin

Mr Gupta had just turned his phone off when Pia rushed in, taking him unawares.

"Mr Gupta," she said, panting, "Mr Radhika is on his way and will be here soon. I must get your chart up-to-date and make sure you are ready!"

She busied herself with his pulse – normal; blood pressure – slightly raised; and then propped him up on his pillows, adding an extra one for luck.

"Goodness me, you are in a tizzy," said Mr Gupta. "This chap must be a stickler for the rules."

"Mr Radhika is very particular, you know," said Pia. "He has held high posts in London and Chicago, and is determined to make this place look modern and Western and professional."

"Well, if cutting a patient in half with tight bed sheets is part of the plan," he said smiling, "it is certainly being applied with gusto!"

The sound of voices drifted in through the open door as the legendary consultant's party approached, at which point nurse Pia squeaked, "Oh dear!" and adjusted her hat. The door darkened and the imposing figure of Mr Radhika stepped in, closely followed by a trio of white-coated students. He was a big man in all regards – tall, heavily built, but not flabby, with a round face bordered by bushy black sideburns. His hair was black, though thinning on his pate, and he sported a tremendous pair of unruly eyebrows. A pair of thick, gold rimmed glasses gave him an owlish look. His face was enhanced by a round nose under which he cultivated a luxurious moustache, which almost joined forces with his sideburns. He was unseasonably dressed in tweed trousers and waistcoat, with fob watch, a white shirt with a red and white-spotted bowtie and brown brogues. This man had presence. He made the room look small. He beamed as he looked over his spectacles at Pia and Mr Gupta.

"Good afternoon nurse!" he boomed. "How are you today?"

"Fine, thank you," she replied standing slightly more to attention.

"Ah! You are my Mr Gupta," he said possessively, turning to the figure in the bed. "You look jolly well compared to the last time I saw you."

Mr Radhika proffered a large hand which Mr Gupta shook with some trepidation. The grip was firm but comfortable, perfectly gauged to send a message of confidence into the recipient.

"Hello, Mr Radhika," said Mr Gupta. "I'm feeling surprisingly well at the moment."

In the doorway two young men and a woman, bright-eyed and attentive, all white coats and new stethoscopes, watched their mentor.

"Come in my children!" bellowed Mr Radhika increasing his volume to uncomfortable levels. "Mr Gupta won't bite!" Then, turning to the same, added jokingly, "Will you?"

"No," replied Mr Gupta instinctively.

They gathered at the foot of the bed whilst the consultant dragged up a chair which protested by squealing against the polished floor. He sat down so he was level with Mr Gupta. He beamed once more.

"I was talking with Nihal about you yesterday, Mr Gupta," he said a little quieter. "He's a great GP but a bloody awful golfer! He spends more time in the rough than a bare-arsed dog sat on sandpaper!"

Mr Gupta chuckled – he liked this man. "I take it you mean Doctor Chowdary," he said. "I must admit I never did get to see him this time. I was rather indisposed."

"Quite! Quite so!" bellowed Mr Radhika, volume rising again. "As indisposed as a corpse! Now, whilst you were busy sleeping we conducted some TESTS. TESTS. That very word is supposed to strike awe into the layman and allow me not to drone on with over-technical nonsense, which could drive you into unconsciousness again!"

"That's fair enough with me," said Mr Gupta. "So, what have you discovered?"

"You show all the symptoms of having something wrong with your noggin," said Mr Radhika a little more seriously. "We've taken a couple of X-rays and there is a very clear, sharp shadow just above your left temporal lobe – that is not good. Thus, I shall get you scanned by our magnetic resonance imaging machine – that's bollocks for MRI scanner – so I can be absolutely sure of my hunches. I think it's pretty likely to be an oligodendroglioma. A very special tumour!"

Mr Gupta's stomach tightened. This was confirmation his subconscious was right. There was far more to his headaches and collapse than mere stress or a migraine. The consultant saw his patient's face drop. Mr Radhika quickly carried on – he was not fond of pauses for emphasis.

"Now, don't you get all het up, Mr Gupta," he said. "You are a long way from a fiery end on the ghats and reincarnation yet, but I think, from what Nihal has told me, you are a pragmatic man of some intellect. Sometimes I beat around the bushes, but in your case, being succinct is better. Much better. I can prevaricate if you so wish, but I think we should get the hard bit out the way now, then we can plan for a realistic way forward. How do you feel about that?"

Uday Radhika was a good judge of character. Mr Gupta smiled as he noticed he had become the sole focus of the big man's attention. In spite of the others in the room it was as if they were having a private conversation between equals. Mr Gupta was grateful for this and in spite of his worry, and the obvious techniques Mr Radhika was using, he already felt confident in any potential course of treatment. So, he answered honestly.

"It has been a very hard few years, Mr Radhika. You know I lost my wife not that long ago and since then I have drifted a bit. Right now, I am afraid of knowing what is wrong with me, but terrified of not knowing. All things considered I think it is time to make some decisions. So,

127

Mr Radhika, I want to know the most likely prognosis. Your best guess. A realistic take on my chances of survival."

Mr Radhika beamed again, his eyebrows lifting high above his glasses, his dark eyes gleaming.

"Just the ticket, Gupta!" he said genuinely pleased. "Just the ticket! You have to know you're in one of the best hospitals in India. No. It is THE best! I am regarded as a first-class oncologist…"

"So, it is cancer," interrupted Mr Gupta, almost to himself.

"Hmmm," resumed Mr Radhika. "That, sir, is a very general description of so many things that are specific. A bit like saying 'so it's a virus' which means nothing. A virus can cause anything from a common cold to HIV! But, for simplicity, cancer is loosely what you have."

Mr Gupta was filled with dread. Knowing the truth was no easier. His mind flashed with a thousand unrelated thoughts and memories. Foremost was Rupa. His beautiful girl. He had left so much undone. He always thought he had plenty of time. Dragging his heels had given him the perceived sense of normality he always sought. What now if his one major currency, time, had run out?

"Ah," said Mr Gupta after his contemplative pause. "I have a cancerous tumour *'in the old noggin.'*"

"Yes, quite," said Mr Radhika. "As I said, a shadow."

"A tumour on this side," said Mr Gupta indicating his left temple.

"Yes, that's the place," said Mr Radhika. He beamed again. "Now, chin up and let me fill you in on my thoughts! Ah, but first a few questions. I have chatted to Nihal and your friends, but it is now time for me to confirm your symptoms, from the horse's mouth, if you will."

At this point Mr Radhika noticed the students once more.

"Mr Gupta," he said. "Do you mind if my students take a few notes? It is good experience for them."

"No," said Mr Gupta. "Let's get this over with."

"Quite! Quite! Just the ticket!" continued the consultant. "What symptoms have you been getting? I know about the headaches. But any little thing you can tell me will be a step to starting a counter offensive!"

"The headaches have been coming along for several months now," said Mr Gupta. "I did see Dr Chowdary at the start and he gave me some painkillers. He also told me to go back in a week if things did not improve, but I just left it really. They were never regular things and I put it down to stress...and grief, maybe. But recently things began to change."

Mr Gupta went on to explain the sudden onset of the attacks and the escalation he had experienced on the train. Then he described the running nose and the cloud-like floater in his vision. He told of the sudden clarity and ensuing sense of relief. Then he described the events in Dr Chowdary's waiting room. He went through all these things slowly, step by step as best as he could remember. Even so, he missed out the part about the man his mind had produced before his collapse, and he certainly could not discuss the later apparition, one William MacKeeg. He felt it bore no relevance. As the minutes passed Mr Radhika asked a few more probing questions and the three students scribbled away, each looking slightly uncomfortable, but focused intently on the two men. Finally, Mr Radhika sat back. His smile had drifted away as they had spoken, but now it returned.

"Right! Excellent!" he said. "Everything you have told me has not changed my prognosis, but the MRI needs to do its work so I have a good picture of the extent of the invasive mass."

"The tumour," stated Mr Gupta.

"Yes, quite," said Mr Radhika. At this point he stood and chivvied the students from the room and closed the door, leaving only nurse Pia as witness to the coming discussion. The room immediately became cosier and more private. A green light filled the room as the sunshine filtered through the lush vegetation of the garden. It served to calm. A single striped palm squirrel sat on a leafy branch eating a berry from its front paws, looking in at the scene. Mr Gupta saw it and smiled. The consultant turned to see what had grabbed his patient's attention and smiled too, as did Pia.

"They are lovely fellows," said Mr Radhika. "I seldom notice them, but they seem to thrive in Delhi."

"Yes," said Mr Gupta. "Do you know they live in holes in buildings? My daughter used to ask me where they slept, when she was very young, so I found out. The first clue I got was on a visit to the fort at Agra. As I walked over the bridge across the moat I saw one peering out of a hole in the brickwork of the retaining wall."

"Well I never," said Mr Radhika.

"And eventually, with a little patience I found the home of the squirrels that visited our garden. They lived in my house walls!"

"Don't they do any damage?" asked Mr Radhika with genuine interest.

"No. None whatsoever," said Mr Gupta. "We built a city on their ancestral homes. The very least we can do is allow them to share our accommodation."

Mr Gupta took a deep breath.

"Now, Mr Radhika," he said. "Tell me what it is and what my options are."

"Right! Yes. Of course," said Mr Radhika. "Within the brain there are nerve cells, and cells that support and protect the nerve cells, these are called glial cells. A tumour of these is known as a glioma. An oligodendroglioma is a type of glioma that develops from cells called oligodendrocytes; these cells produce the fatty covering of nerve cells. This type of tumour is normally found in the cerebrum particularly in the frontal or temporal lobes. The tail end of the shadow, however, intrudes into the occipital lobe – that's the visual area. You know the symptoms and signs as you have just described them. The odd vision abnormalities are produced by the pressure on the left ocular nerve. Your runny nose and blackout all tally, and it is just a case of finding just how deep this bugger is! One thing to remember is that you may have symptoms never recorded – nothing is certain with these things. The brain is a very complex organ."

Mr Radhika took a deep breath and looked at Mr Gupta sitting passively in his bed. The evening was coming on; the light from the window grew darker, the green tinge being replaced by yellow. Mr Gupta felt empty and forlorn, haunted by his inertia of the last two years. He could feel the energy drain as he had so often before; when he got like this even getting dressed seemed an exhausting chore. He felt weighed down by the baggage he still carried from the past. A Sisyphean curse, he often thought. His eyes had lost focus as he stared into his lap, then snapped out of his brief reverie.

"Right!" he said. "The question is, can it be treated? Am I a goner, or is there hope?"

Mr Radhika smiled again. Mr Gupta thought it was strange how this great owl of a man could make him feel confident and less anxious with a look. Was it a skill inherent in the consultant, or just an ill man grasping at a straw? Had he become a sponge ready to soak up any reassurance on offer?

"Tomorrow I will look at the scans," said Mr Radhika. "The tumour is not overly large, but I need to see how deep it goes. Once I've established that, there are several courses of action, all of which involves the excision of the mass at some point. A gut feeling is you have an 85% chance of getting through this. It will take time, and patience. You have good insurance and, may I say, a bloody good surgeon. So you must rest, eat normally and go about your life positively."

"85%," repeated Mr Gupta. "That's good."

"Of course it is!" replied Mr Radhika. "It's bloody good odds. In some parts of the country it is 90% sure that the age of fifty will not be reached, so you are already six years ahead!"

"85%," repeated Mr Gupta again. "Will I be able to go home soon?"

"After I've seen you tomorrow," said Mr Radhika. "There will be a few dos and don'ts to tell you about, and some sorting out with pills and the like, but things will move quickly. I will see you tomorrow."

Mr Radhika stood and swept to the door.

"It's already tomorrow," mumbled Mr Gupta quietly.

"It is somewhere in the world!" laughed the consultant as he left in a waft of displaced air.

Jhatish Das had crossed Delhi as quickly as the jammed roads allowed him. He had decided to take one of the ubiquitous Ambassador taxis as the frequent rain made tuktuks uncomfortably damp. It was not so much the rain itself, but the low-level waves of muddy water displaced by passing traffic that made a tuktuk trip unwise. He had often seen these small vehicles completely inundated during the monsoon. Evening's gloom had descended as he made his way into the corridors of the New Delhi Gandhi Hospital, the city's lights having switched on whilst he was in the taxi. Above him the kites were joined by huge fruit bats, both species wheeling briefly together in the sky at dusk. The girl behind the reception desk eyed the dishevelled teacher as he walked up.

"Can I help you?" she asked.

"Yes," he said. "I have come to visit a patient. One Anil Gupta. I have been here before."

He gave his name and the girl busied herself on a computer, slowly tapping the space bar a few times before speaking once more.

"I can see you have been before. If you show me some identification you can take a pass and pop along to his room. The consultant has finished with him."

A few minutes later Jhatish burst into Mr Gupta's room, a wave of relief passing over him as he saw his old friend sitting in a comfortable chair by the window, drinking tea.

"Anil!" he cried out rushing across and dropping his brief case. He shook Mr Gupta's hand and crouched next to him. "Thank goodness you are back with us. And you look so well!"

"Jhatish!" said Mr Gupta smiling. "I'm so glad you came. I am bored and ready for some proper company. Grab a chair. Sit down, sit down."

For several minutes they talked nonstop about the events of the last few days, Jhatish reassuring his friend about the wellbeing of Rupa, the Singhs and the general state of the world since his spectacular collapse at Dr Chowdary's. Jhatish had even phoned Indian Railways and notified Mr Gupta's manager about his temporary incapacity.

"I thought it best you gave him the details," said Jhatish. "After all I don't know what the position is with you yet."

Mr Gupta thanked his friend and felt a little less anxious about Rupa, but the knot in his stomach remained. Jhatish's last sentence had brought his condition back into focus. He knew he had to attempt to explain what had been found lurking in his brain. It was absurd, thought Mr Gupta, but he found himself talking reassuringly to his friend, so as not to shock him. Giving voice to a possible death sentence also seemed to ease his own burden. *Very odd*, he thought.

"I suppose it best I talk you through the things the consultant has just told me," he said. "It seems my collapse was the result of something growing in my head. A funny name, but ultimately a tumour. Cancer. Cancer is what it is, but of a very specific type. It means they have to get the bloody thing out. Apparently, it is a routine procedure with a high success rate. That's it in a nutshell. The main thing is it changes my life completely; I have some weeks of treatment ahead, then, with luck, recovery. I have no clue as to what condition I shall be in then. I may be a dribbling lump! But, yes, with luck and a following wind I can be back to normality by the end of the year."

Normality, that bloody word again, he thought. He was now less sure what normality was than ever before. He could think of no one who would fit *normal*. Jhatish was stunned, staring at his dear friend, unable to articulate anything worthwhile for a moment.

"Oh, goodness me Anil," he finally said. "Oh my. Oh my. What on Earth is to do? I …I don't know what to say."

"Calm down, Jhatish," said Mr Gupta. "It seems I have an 85% chance of survival, by all accounts, according to Mr Radhika. This has just shocked me into taking stock of things. Once this is over – because I will get through it – I must get my life in order. It is time I did. I am going home tomorrow, after some fangled scan, and then I will need your help to get sorted. Sorry if I'm not sounding rational, but I am a little rattled."

"I will help you in any way I can," said Jhatish, squeezing Mr Gupta's hand, "anything at all. My word... those headaches. I should have nagged you a lot more... yes I should. Goodness me – a tumour! Does it hurt?"

"Oddly enough, no," said Mr Gupta. "The headaches are frustrating, but not unbearable. The biggest problem is the effect on my vision especially on the left side..."

"You mean the Singhs were not joking about you seeing things?" interrupted Jhatish.

"Well...no," said Mr Gupta. "I sometimes see a translucent, cloudy disc. It is the tumour's effect on what Mr Radhika calls the *optical path*."

"But Old Mr Singh says you saw a Scottish man!" said Jhatish.

"Ah," replied Mr Gupta, "I see. Well, yes, I did. But now I know it was just my brain short-circuiting and making me imagine a shape which was not there. Mr Radhika did talk about our DNA being hardwired to infer patterns into shapes; we naturally assume a pattern relates to something known to us. It was all rather above me I'm afraid. It does explain it all.

"Look, Jhatish, I am serious here. It is time I got my act together. Ravi has been looking after my affairs since Kiran's death. I owe him a lot. But it is time I took control and secured Rupa's future, especially as my own is far from assured. I want to go through my finances and legal stuff so I can figure out what to do for the best. I may be able to retire and spend more time with my daughter. Go and visit Amit – I've put that off for months. Maybe take Rupa to England. So much I can do if I pull myself together."

"That's more like it, Anil," said Jhatish. "Get through this and start living again! Rupa is fine right now, but I have promised to give her the latest news on my way home. Shall I pick you up tomorrow?"

"I was hoping you would," said Mr Gupta.

At this point Wamil walked in, she having relieved Pia in the morning.

"Hello Mr Gupta," she sang. "I hear you are leaving tomorrow."

"Hello, Wamil," he replied. "Yes, after some scan or other. What time do you think they will release me?"

"The evening, after tea," she said. "No earlier than four p.m. That way I will see you off before I go home."

"Right," said Jhatish. "I shall drive over and be here to pick you up then."

Wamil took Mr Gupta's temperature and blood pressure then left the room.

"I have a favour to ask," said Mr Gupta once she had gone. "I need you to go to Ravi and let him know I will want to see him sometime next week. Give him the low-down on my condition and epiphany, and let him know I will want his help to finally get my estate in order. He's been nagging me for years. Kiran dealt with everything through him, but I only ever signed a will and agreement on the transfer of Kiran's accounts. I don't even know how much money there is! He'll be shocked and pleased that I take the burden off his shoulders."

"I'll do that," said Jhatish. "I have taken tomorrow off, just in case, and can pop in to Ravi's offices on the way here, so it's no trouble."

The two men talked for the next hour or so, then Jhatish, realising the time, got up to leave just as an orderly walked in.

"Mr Gupta," she said. "There is a gap in our schedule and you are going to be taken to the MRI scanner in ten minutes. I'm afraid your friend will have to leave." She left.

"I have to catch Rupa before she goes to bed," said Jhatish, shaking his friend's hand. "She'll need to know you are OK."

"Don't tell her too much," said Mr Gupta. "Let me be the one to talk her through this."

"Of course, of course," reassured Jhatish. "I'll tell her you look fine and will see her tomorrow. We can pop in when we're on the way to your house."

"Thank you," said Mr Gupta. And he meant it.

As it turned out Jhatish arrived at the Beaufort Home a little on the late side, or so the receptionist informed him with a frown. She expected Rupa to be going to bed within the hour and told her visitor to bear this in mind. Rupa was sitting, as was her wont, by a large window, her flawless face beautiful, the dribble on her chin a signature of her cruel affliction. Yet she smiled at her beloved Uncle Jhatish and cared not for the bubbles she blew as she spoke in uneven, but measured tones, the content giving the lie to any preconceptions to mental frailty.

"Uncle Jhatish!" she exclaimed, eyes wide with expectation. "How is my Daddy? Do tell me he is getting better. Is he bright and sharp? Is he the same sweet Daddy? Is he scared? Oh, do tell me. Do tell!"

Jhatish Das kissed the girl's forehead and allowed her to give him a clumsy, but heartfelt embrace, then tapped her nose with affection.

"Goodness me, Rupa," he smiled. "One question at a time! He is fine and bright as a button right now. We chatted for a long time. He wants me to tell you not to worry. He's being released tomorrow! In fact, I shall be picking him up and bringing him here. So calm right down."

Rupa gave a little laugh of delight, blew more bubbles and said, "Wipe!" to her uncle. Upon command Jhatish pulled some tissues from a colourful box on the windowsill and dried her face.

"Bubbles! Bubbles! Bubbles!" Rupa chuckled. "I love you Uncle Jhatish! You always save me from drowning!"

They both laughed. The bond between them was simple and strong. He saw beyond her incapacity and knew Rupa had inherited her mother's love of life, joy in everything and intellectual strength. Sometimes he felt reincarnation was involved, the likeness was so perfect.

"*Seal Morning!*" she giggled, changing the subject. "If Daddy is alright, read me more about the seal creature who plays a trumpet!"

And so, he did. He read about lakes called *lochs* and mountains called *bens*; of cold and ice and snow. He read from Rupa's favourite book: Rowena Farre's *Seal Morning* was set in Scotland after the war and told of a girl's life in a distant land. He read about the trumpet playing seal called Lora and of creatures they may never see, pausing only for a "Wipe!" ending only when Rupa's assistant, as Lord Beaufort had insisted they should be referred to, came to take her to bed.

"I love you Uncle Jhatish!" she called as her chair was wheeled away. Then, "Bubbles! Bubbles! Bubbles!" her voice fading into the distance.

"I love you too!" he called after her.

"I love you three!" echoed Rupa.

For his final visit of the day, Jhatish's energy propelled him into the dark and fragrant garden of the Singhs. They had come to know the dishevelled teacher through their friendship with Mr Gupta and always welcomed him with open arms. Old Mr Singh had told him to *drop in no matter what the time, if the lights are on, we are up*, so he felt duty-bound to see them. They fretted so about Mr Gupta. Sweet scents surrounded him as he approached the back door, the zooming shapes of feeding moths hovering on blurred wings in front of sweet-smelling blooms. The door opened before he managed to knock and Taraa Singh swept out gathering him into a firm embrace.

"Jhatish!" she cried smiling, but anxious. "Come in! Come in, do. I have just made Param some tea. He's having some biscuits too. Join us, and tell us the news."

He was ushered through to the sitting room where Param Singh was losing an unequal struggle with a small-handled china cup, a dainty saucer and cinnamon biscuit.

"Look, Param!" his wife declared. "Jhatish has come with news. Sit! Sit my boy. I'll get tea. Have some biscuits, I made them today."

Jhatish had barely managed to mumble a word of greeting as he was propelled through the house, redolent with baking smells, into the self-same chair Mr Gupta had occupied a few days before. Old Mr Singh gave up his struggles and plonked cup and saucer noisily on the table.

"Bloody fiddly cups!" he said, scowling at the offending objects. "Why can't we have tea English style this time of night? Hello son, how is Mr Gupta?"

Jhatish Das sighed, grabbed a cinnamon biscuit and answered as he nibbled.

"Well, Param, he seems fine," he said, crumbs falling. "He is coming home tomorrow afternoon, so that is good news."

"Hmmm," said Old Mr Singh, decrumbing his beard. "Good. He gave us a real scare. Now, if that's the good news, specifically, I am thinking there may be other news to add. Am I correct?"

Mrs Singh bustled in and poured their visitor a mug of steaming tea, English style.

"Bloody hell!" said Old Mr Singh. "He gets a mug whilst I, with these numb old fingers, have to struggle with a bloody thimble."

"Shush!" scolded his wife. "Let Jhatish speak. You do go on."

"Hmmph!" grumped the old man.

Jhatish told them of his visit and gave them all the missing details of Mr Gupta's travails of the last few days. He could not bring himself to give voice to the main issue and glossed over the consultant's findings, trying to compress everything remaining into the phrase *further tests*.

"Yes, that's it," he repeated. "Anil has to await the results of further tests. He is having some kind of brain scan this evening…"

His words petered out. He stared at the cups on the table. Jhatish finally saw the gravity of his friend's predicament. He thought of Kiran. He thought of sweet Rupa. The sad pondering opened a well of despair inside him, dragging thoughts of his own emotional baggage from the depths – the sorrows of life had a strange attraction. Joys beget joys; sadness begets sadness. His eyes welled with tears unbidden and he looked up at the old, sweet faces now silent before him.

"Cancer," he managed to spit out. "After everything else, Anil has gone and got a bloody brain tumour."

Jhatish Das hunched over and wept, his pent-up energy having no release, except in tears. He had dashed about so much in the past days without thought for himself, but now, with these dear people being journey's end, he had let his guard down. The releasing of pressure gave vent to a wave of sorrow and now he was inconsolable. Taraa Singh ran to him and put a motherly arm around his shoulders. She clucked and hushed and soothed, and then she wept too. Old Mr Singh sat quietly staring at his wife and young friend. For once he remained quiet and just floated passively in his own pool of tacit grief.

Chapter 11

Freedom

Shortly after 01:00, some thirty hours after Vikram Chakrabarti's briefing, the four-vehicle convoy left Mumbai Ashoka Zoo. The lights reflected on rain-damp streets as the tail end of another heavy storm eased into a gentle persistent drizzle. Leading was a white City Police jeep, blue and red emergency lights flashing, serving to clear any night traffic from their course. They were followed by a green Land Rover with a yellow beacon driven by the Wai Farm College veterinary surgeon, Rupak Kunwar, accompanied by one of his young students, Vinay Sharma. Behind this the tiger lay semi-conscious in an aluminium barred cage fixed to the floor of a converted horsebox, the Tiger Taxi. Vikram and Seva sat on the bench-seat in the cab alongside the driver, a heavy set, hairy man who had been introduced as Pak – "I am also Rupak, but we can't have two." He was on familiar terms with Rupak Kunwar, so it was assumed they had worked together before. Bringing up the rear was a dark Ambassador carrying Mukul and driven by Ram Singh. They headed for the Vashi Bridge over the Thane Creek.

Earlier, the Tiger Taxi had reversed up to the rear service doors of Angaar's den. Rupak, under the gimlet eye of Seva, had fired a tranquilizer dart into the tiger's rump with a crossbow. Once it had taken effect, the team coaxed and carried the beast into the back of the waiting vehicle. Vikram had kept a close watch on the tiger's vital signs, ensuring he was settled comfortably and reassuring Seva that all was well. The plan was to keep Khan, as Vikram and Seva referred to their charge in public, sedated until the Wai Farm College was reached, any additional medication being delivered en route if necessary. Vikram had in his possession a small black plastic case with five syringes inside set in a dense foam lining – three with red bands, two with blue.

"The blue is a fast-acting antidote," he had explained to Seva. "If there are any signs of distress this stuff will bring him round fairly quickly. At that point we will need to be at least a good paw-swipe away!"

"No, Sahib Vikram," Seva had replied firmly. "If he becomes distressed and he is injected with the blue, I must be here when he wakes up. I do not think he will harm me."

Vikram had cautioned the little bird-man as to the strange effects a tranquilizer can have on an animal, but Seva was adamant. The vet saw no issues anyway, Angaar's vital signs being strong and steady, so dismissed such concerns from his mind.

The Tiger Taxi had indeed once been a horsebox, donated to Project Tiger by the Indian Army. It had been modified by the simple installation of an aluminium travel cage which had been bolted to the floor. The cage entrance was a drop-down door hinged at the bottom, held in place by pins at the top, facing the rear doors. Plywood covers could be slipped onto locating pins around the otherwise exposed cage in order to give an animal a little privacy. The cage was set to one side allowing passage for people via a narrow entrance door from the cab. A wooden bench-seat had been constructed over the wheel arch for two people. Vikram had left the rear-facing door and bench-seat sides open for access. The conversion of the Tiger Taxi had been carried out by enthusiastic army engineers, so was a solid piece of work. The vehicle had also been given a new coat of dark green paint and a Project Tiger logo added to each cab door.

Rupak had helped Vikram several times before and was relaxed. The drive to Wai seemed a formality. It was not an inordinately long trip and the bulk of the route along the expressway would be fairly traffic-free at night. Even so, Vikram would not really settle until Angaar was awake and feeding at his new quarters in the Farm College. He had moved seventeen tigers like this since his involvement with Project Tiger and each time he had felt the same unease. It was all about getting the right balance between sedation and deep coma. Even the sudden introduction of the antidote could prove fatal in less robust creatures; the measured doses in the blue-banded syringes should be right, but one could never be completely sure. It could be pretty unpleasant for the administering vet too if the tiger came around quicker than planned. He had three parallel scars on his right calf as proof that waking tigers were unpredictable. To Vikram every tiger was precious and Seva's Angaar was a beauty. He could not remember seeing such a large male of any of the sub-species, including the very rare Siberian, and he wanted to weigh this one as soon as they got him to Wai. Angaar had to be 260 kilos at least – that was huge. If Vikram's gut feeling was correct, and it usually was, he should be able to cure this lovely animal and have him ready to meet the young, productive female he had coming from Basle Zoo.

The police jeep led the convoy over the Vashi Bridge and into the darkness beyond the city limits. The police driver was glad of a simple night duty in which he did not need to be out in the rain. He had agreed with Vikram Chakrabarti that he would continue as far as the Turade service road, an hour's driving at their slow pace.

"The roads are not in the best of repair, sir," he had told Vikram, "so we should not go fast," he had warned.

Pak, the Tiger Taxi driver, was a heavy-set man who was running to fat. His shirt buttons were straining under the pressure within and a wide neck filled his open collar. He was hirsute apart from his balding head, with many days' growth of stubble on his double chin. Tufts of black hair protruded from his shirt collar, sleeves and between buttons. He settled into the driving seat like a bag of loosely tied grain, filling all nooks and crannies. He was a man used to sitting down. As they set off, Vikram, who was sitting in the middle between Pak and Seva, tried to start a conversation.

"It is a damp night," he mused.

"The monsoon's a long one," growled Pak.

"At least we have a clear road, and a police escort leading the way," continued Vikram.

"Scorpions!" growled Pak with venom, keeping his eyes on the road.

"Eh?"

"The police are scorpions!" stated Pak once more as if to a simpleton. "They sting you for bribes. Scorpions!"

"Oh. I see," said Vikram, holding back a smile. Then asked, "Have you worked for Kohli for long?"

"Ranjit Kohli is a snake!" growled Pak with even more feeling.

"A snake?" asked Vikram.

"He makes money any way he can," said Pak, glancing briefly at the vet. "He kisses bottoms. I say he could crawl under a door wearing a top hat. A snake!"

"I see," said Vikram, amused by the big man's faux fury.

"I don't work for Kohli," said Pak in a sudden show of verbosity. "I am a friend of Rupak. He knows I am a careful driver. Knows I drove for the army. Kohli still charges him for a driver, *'A part of the overall package'*," he growled mimicking a prissy voice. "*'It's in our contract.'* A snake!"

"I see," said Vikram smiling openly at Pak's imitation.

The cab settled into silence for a while, the flashing beacons of the two lead vehicles having a mesmerising effect. The Tiger Taxi rocked gently as they made their way onto the expressway, the smooth surface only occasionally blighted by the ubiquitous Indian pothole.

"Sahib?" said Seva, after a few minutes.

"Yes."

"Should we not look at the tiger?"

"A good idea," said Vikram. "Pak, we will just pop back for a short while. Try not to hit too many potholes."

"Ha, at this speed you are safe," he growled. "Any slower and it would be quicker to walk."

They squeezed through the narrow door and settled themselves onto the bench-seat. Seva leaned forward and stroked Angaar's stripy haunch.

"Eeesh. Eeesh," he intoned quietly.

Angaar's ear twitched, but he was deeply sedated, only hearing the sound on a subliminal level.

"He looks fine," said Vikram reassuringly. "He will hardly know anything. He'll wake up in a beautiful enclosure with his best friend next to him."

"Yes, Sahib," said Seva. He then asked an unexpected direct question. "The plastic case down here by our feet. These are the needles?"

"They are. Why?"

"I worry about the blue ones – you said they can be dangerous," said Seva.

"Angaar will be fine," said Vikram opening the case. "This blue banded one is for manual use. See the plunger? It is a very carefully measured dose, specifically for his size and weight. Take this white cap off, jab the needle firmly into the haunch and gently press the plunger. Then stand well back. You don't want to be close to a wakeful tiger!"

"I see," said Seva. "I worry about Angaar that is all. I find it hard to understand this medicine and science. I regret I will never be clever."

Vikram felt unsettled at Seva's self-deprecation. His worry was genuine and Vikram hoped he had put Seva's mind at ease.

Behind them Mukul sat nervously in the Ambassador's passenger seat. Beside him was the young Kohli driver, Ram, who seemed very enthusiastic over the task ahead. Ram Singh was a proud Sikh, crowned with a khaki turban, sporting a neatly tied beard and wearing a standard khaki Kohli uniform. He told Mukul he was *jolly well delighted* with the change in his usual mundane tasks and *wide awake with overwhelming senses of duty.*

"Don't get too close," Mukul kept nagging.

"I count five seconds gap every now and then," Ram had replied eventually. "That is very safe."

Mukul fidgeted and chewed on a dirty thumbnail.

"Look, Ram," he eventually confessed, "I'm not feeling very well so I may need you to pull over in a bit."

Ram frowned with concern and agitation at the possible unplanned stop, especially as Mukul kept whining about the state of his rebellious bowels.

The convoy reached Turade and the police jeep dropped back alongside Rupak's Land Rover, the driver yelled 'Goodbye!' through an open window and sped off into the night. Rupak took over leading the convoy heading along the expressway towards Pune, having no qualms about driving as he knew the route very well. Vinay Sharma dozed next to him. He had brought the student along to show him the sharp edge of veterinary conservation work, but staying awake all night was proving beyond the young man's ability. Rupak let him sleep.

About halfway into the journey Mukul's mobile phone peeped twice. He had received a message; a single question mark. He read it with a shaking hand and sent a one-word reply: *ready*.

"Who's texting you at this time?" asked Ram.

"My girlfriend," replied Mukul scratching his stubble. "She gets lonely."

Ram was too polite to voice any surprise, but thought Mukul must have a girlfriend with very low aspirations and a strong stomach. He stank. His teeth looked green at the gums and his fingernails were filthy. Ram's eyes watered at the thought.

A few kilometres away Cho lowered his phone. He and Dong were sitting in a dark Mercedes van, lights off, parked well back on a rough service road.

"About twenty minutes," said Cho.

"Hm," grunted Dong.

Cho speed-dialled a number on the phone.

"When?" asked the voice at the other end.

"Twenty minutes," said Cho for the second time. He finished the call.

"Is it all set?" asked Dong.

"Yes," replied Cho. "Let's get moving."

Cho nodded to the driver who started the van and set off up the service road into the hills which formed the southern end of the Western Ghats overlooking Pune.

On the expressway the bulk of the night-time traffic comprised of great, multi-coloured trucks which supplied the towns and cities with the raw materials of existence. These great machines varied in age and state of repair, from new and sparkling, to gun-metal grey and heavily soiled. It was the latter type which caused Pak the most ire.

"Bloody fools!" he growled, as a particularly raddled truck of vast dimensions began to overtake, forcing him to drop back for safety's sake. Vikram and Seva leaned away involuntarily as the huge vehicle loomed over Pak's window. It eventually made a lumbering turn into their lane separating them from Rupak's Land Rover, slowly pulling away, but dowsing the Tiger Taxi in a steady spray of muddy water.

"Bastard dog!" rumbled Pak darkly and allowed the truck to get to a safe distance away.

Vikram's phone rang.

"There's a bloody great truck behind us, you OK?" asked Rupak.

"Fine," replied Vikram. "We know the way. Pull over at the service station as planned and we'll all regroup."

"OK. It's less than an hour now. I'll see you there. How's the tiger?"

"He's sound asleep and healthy enough," said Vikram.

"Great, see you at the se..." Rupak's voice faded to nothing.

The reception had gone. However, the pre-arranged plan was sound enough. More trucks went by followed by a couple of vans, Rupak was well

147

ahead. After a while the vehicles in front started to slow down, brake lights shining through the drizzle. The queue of traffic ground to a halt. Pak pulled out a little to look ahead.

"Scorpions!" he spat.

"What's going on up there, Pak?" asked Vikram.

"Police. Scorpions!" he replied matter-of-factly. "They have stopped the traffic."

As he spoke a uniformed figure appeared and gestured Pak to unwind the window.

"There has been a crash up towards Pune," said the policeman. "It will take hours to clear so I have to hold the lorries here."

"We have a tranquilized tiger back here," said Vikram gesturing to the rear. "We need to get to Wai Farm College as soon as possible."

"It is OK, sir," said the policeman smiling. "We know about you from the Mumbai fellows. I've sent your colleagues up the service road over there." He pointed across the opposite carriageway where some temporary barriers had been pulled aside. "I'll guide you over and if you go up there for a few minutes you'll join another good road and that will take you past the obstruction and drop you back to the expressway near the Pune services. So, it's up, left, along and first left. A detour of about twenty minutes or so. Your chap will wait up where the service road joins the old Pune road – you'll see his lights. There are a few corners, so be careful."

"Thank you," said Vikram. "There should be a black Ambassador back in the queue. There are a couple of Kohli Security men in it. They are with us. Can you send them after us and ask them to meet at the rendezvous at Pune?"

"There's no car there, sir," said the policeman looking further back. "Just two more trucks. When they come along I'll make sure they follow."

Pak left the queue and drove the Tiger Taxi across the central reservation to the service road behind the jogging officer. The road looked reasonable so they set off glad to be on the move. Behind them the policeman pulled the barriers back across the road entrance and flicked on a flashing beacon. He dashed across the expressway and after consulting with his partner waved the traffic on.

Mukul convulsed in his seat.

"You are fidgeting a lot," said Ram, eyeing his scruffy companion. "You do not look top drawer."

"You have to stop," groaned Mukul. "I need to find a bush or I'll shit my pants!"

"OK, hold on," said Ram, horrified at the very idea. "I'll pull in here."

Mukul smelt bad enough without an additional stench being added to the miasma. Ram had spotted a muddy lay-by and pulled in skidding to a halt.

"Be as quick as you can please."

Without comment Mukul dove out into the darkness to some nearby trees pulling at his belt. Ram pulled out his phone and scowled at the *No signal* legend.

"Damn," he muttered.

However, Ram was a steady man and was generally unflappable. He reasoned he could catch the others up at the Pune stop, earmarked by Vikram in the briefing just for this sort of development. After all, disruption to India's traffic was commonplace even on these ultra-modern expressways. Ram sat and waited. Large trucks rumbled past.

Pak scowled through the windscreen at the winding road in the headlights. The Tiger Taxi was an old vehicle of solid military pedigree and coped with the gradual climb easily enough. However, it was dark and wet and it took a concerted effort to remain vigilant.

"We must reach the Pune road soon, surely," said Vikram.

"Nothing yet," growled Pak. "The scorpion is laughing as he knows this road is much longer than he said. They are like that. He could not ask for a bribe, so he has his fun. Son of a camel!"

"Should we look at Angaar?" asked Seva. Vikram had almost forgotten the little bird-man sitting next to him. He could tell Seva was anxious again as it was the first time he had used Angaar's name in front of a stranger. Pak did not notice.

"You slip back and sit with him, Seva," said Vikram smiling. "Let me know if he does anything but snore and twitch."

Seva disappeared into the back hanging on tightly as the Tiger Taxi lurched ever higher up the bumpy road. Eventually it levelled out and Pak became less tense. Vikram was suddenly struck by a thought.

"There are no other cars on the road anywhere. Nothing behind; no red lights ahead. You would think we'd see another car."

"It is probably because we did not offer him a bribe," stated Pak. "Then he would have let us go on. His scorpion friends would have led us past the crash for yet another bribe."

"You may be right," said Vikram, concerned now.

"There are lights ahead," said Pak suddenly.

"Good, that must be Rupak waiting for us," said Vikram with relief.

As they turned a final corner to a straight part of the road, the lights turned out to belong to a dark idling van blocking their route, lights ablaze. A man was waving a torch.

"Looks like they're in trouble," said Vikram.

Pak stopped the Tiger Taxi and wound the window down.

Ram was annoyed. Mukul had disappeared for a long time. When he finally returned he had muddy boots and damp clothes, which enhanced his stink no end. They were now travelling as quickly as they dared in the rain, windows steaming and vast sprays of water coming from the trucks they sped past.

"Mukul, you stink!" said Ram after a short while.

"That is a personal remark," said Mukul looking hurt. "I am ill and that mud was full of cow shit."

"Well I am damned well annoyed," said Ram. "I am trying to make a jolly good impression on Mr Kohli and I have already been delayed in my first important task. Please call Rupak on my phone."

Mukul picked up the device and navigated his way to the relevant number. They finally had a signal. Mukul was nervous, but felt certain his subterfuge was undetectable. Even so, his stomach lurched when he saw the faux police vehicle parked across the front of the barricaded service road just before the long sweep to Pune. As he looked the jeep set off towards Mumbai leaving a flashing beacon over the *Road Closed* sign. It was done. That road led up into the hills. Mukul had no interest as to what was happening up there – he could comfortably plead ignorance and happily live the lie he had been party to. He could still stick with his regular job with its small wage, but now he was due a big bonus. The call reached Rupak.

"Hello, Ram?" came the voice.

"It is Mukul," said Mukul. "We had a delay, but are not far from the service station."

"Good," said Rupak. "How is the Tiger Taxi doing?"

"We are still trying to catch up," said Mukul swallowing back his nerves. "I had to take a…er…rest break. They should be with you any time."

"Righto," said Rupak. "See you in a few minutes."

Ram passed several more lumbering trucks and turned into the surprisingly busy service area. He spotted the Land Rover to one side in a clear space. There was no sign of the Tiger Taxi. He parked the Ambassador next to Rupak. The rain had stopped.

Rupak was frowning. "Where the hell is Vikram?"

"We've not seen him. No sign at all," replied Ram.

"That's impossible," said Rupak. "Just impossible! I hope to god he's not gone off the road. There is no answer from his phone – it must be in an area with no damned signal."

"We only stopped so I could take a shit," mumbled Mukul. "I have a bad stomach."

The others barely noticed him.

"The last time he called he was stuck behind a truck," said Vinay. "He said he would meet us here."

"He could have gone past in error," suggested Mukul.

"No," answered Rupak. "We would have seen him. There is not that much on the road. But you must have passed him. You had to have! Mukul, did you say you stopped?"

"Yes," said Mukul. "I have had a bad stomach and had to take a shit in some trees."

"Where?" And for how long?" asked Rupak.

"In a muddy lay-by," cut in Ram, "he was blooming ages, maybe twenty minutes or so, but I was sure we would catch up. Or at least rendezvous here, like we planned."

"Twenty minutes," repeated Rupak. Then louder, "They would have reached here just before you did at the speed they were doing. They can't have been more than ten minutes behind us."

As they debated a tall, skinny Sikh in overalls strode by, and then paused.

"Are you talking about that van with the picture of a tiger on the door?" he asked casually.

"That's right," said Rupak. "Did you see it?"

"Yeah," he said. "I overtook him a way back. That's my truck over there." He pointed at the raddled vehicle in the far corner. "He was stopped at the road block."

"What road block?" asked Ram.

"The one with the two policemen and a jeep," said the Sikh. "This cop stopped me and said to wait as there was a crash ahead. There was a queue behind; your chaps were there. The swine kept us there for ten minutes, took five hundred rupees off us all then waved us through. There was no fucking crash. The odd thing was they sent that tiger thing up a side road. The cop said it was a detour for smaller vehicles. I saw them drive up into the hills."

"I don't like this," said Rupak. "Something's wrong. But I just can't figure out what."

"Well it ain't far back," said the driver. "Fifteen K or so. You'll see the road on the left as you head towards Mumbai. It's not big but obvious if you're looking."

"Thanks," said Ram.

"We'd better look for them," said Rupak. "They can't be far away. Ram, you and Mukul stay here and watch just in case we missed them. We'll take the Rover back and check it out."

The Land Rover left in a spray of gritty water.

"Your shit has dropped us in the shit," said Ram to a silent Mukul as they watched the others go.

Pak wound the window down as the figure of a man approached, silhouetted by the headlamps of the vehicle ahead of him. Pak got ready to ask if he could be of help, then froze. Vikram looked across and saw the reason why. The barrel of a gun was pointing at the big man. The figure outside wore dark clothes, a black baseball cap and a scarf obscuring the lower half of his face.

"Get out!" barked the gunman. "Engine off!"

"What's this about," grumbled Pak as he opened the door and stepped out. The gunman hit him in the midriff with the rifle butt, doubling the big man over.

"On the floor and stay there!" said the gunman unnecessarily as Pak was in no fit state to move.

There was a metallic tap on Vikram's window. A second man used a gun barrel to draw his attention. He beckoned Vikram out.

"No one will get hurt as long as there are no heroics!" the second man said.

Vikram had the impression of an Oriental accent, Chinese perhaps. Japanese? It was too dark to make out features as the two men kept in front of the headlamps.

"Sit down by him!" shouted the second man gesturing to Pak, who still lay on the floor making mooing sounds.

"We have no money," said Vikram in confusion.

"You have valuable cargo!" said the first man standing over Pak. "Don't they Dong."

"Shut up!" said the one referred to as Dong. Then to Vikram, "Where is third man?"

All at once Vikram put it together. Dong was a Chinese name. If they knew Seva was in the truck, the *third man*, they had inside information. His stomach turned over as he figured out what these men wanted. Angaar. A dead tiger was worth more than fifty thousand U.S. dollars on the Chinese traditional medicine market. Double that once it was rendered down to its component parts. This simple heist could net these thieves a fortune. He also knew he could not argue with guns.

"I'll call him," said Vikram. "He's in the back. Seva! Get out here and keep your hands where they can be seen. And no heroics, these men have guns! We are being robbed!"

Seva's small form appeared in the cab and he stepped out rather dramatically with his hands raised above his head.

"Over here!" barked the first gunman.

Seva complied and stood shaking next to Vikram and the gently moaning Pak.

"They have come to take Angaar," stated Seva. It was not a question. He knew.

"Shut up!" said the one called Dong. He seemed to be in charge. He leaned into the Tiger Taxi, turned the lights onto parking mode and removed the keys.

"You!" he yelled at Seva. "Show me tiger!"

Seva went to step into the cab but Dong shouted, "Back door!" He led the man to the rear of the Tiger Taxi. He opened the door and pointed at the still, helpless form of the tiger.

"He is asleep," said Seva quietly. "Please do not harm him."

"Shut up!" snapped Dong. "Shut door!"

Seva did so.

"Over there!"

Seva re-joined the others. Pak had been helped to a sitting position by Vikram and seemed to have recovered.

"Listen," said Dong, "and you will not be harmed. Get up!"

The three men stood.

"Start walking back down road. Do not look back. Walk until you get to expressway. You get lift there if lucky! Look back or come back and I will kill you. AK47 good for this job! Search them, get phones."

The first man roughly patted them down and retrieved two phones. These were stamped on and thrown into the undergrowth.

"Now walk!"

"Do not hurt the tiger," said Seva stopping by the masked figure of Dong. "He has a destiny which is not here."

"Shut up!" barked Dong and hit Seva in the back of the ribs with the gun butt. The small man crumpled and fell making an involuntary "Eeeh!" sound. Vikram and Pak helped Seva up.

"OK, OK," Vikram directed at the two men. "We're going. There was no need for that!"

Vikram pulled Seva gently by the arm and led him down the road, with Pak falling in on the other side to add support.

"Bastards," grumbled Pak having regained his composure.

The three men walked not daring to look back, the fear of a barking gun adding death to their plight. Fear, anger and disbelief filled Vikram.

He knew now the fate of yet another of the world's diminishing population of tigers — to be used in quack medicine which did not, indeed could not, work. Human beings could be the foulest of creatures.

"He will not die here," said Seva quietly as they walked slowly around the first turn in the road, losing sight of the two vans.

"I cannot tell you how sorry I am," replied Vikram putting a hand on Seva's shoulder. "They are bad men and they do not care about tigers. Only money."

"They are swine," rumbled Pak darkly. "They will kill the beast and make a lot of money. I hope they make it a clean shot."

"No!" said Seva with conviction. "He has a chance."

Vikram stopped and looked down at his small companion. He saw the certainty in his face.

"What do you mean?" asked Vikram.

"I stabbed him with a blue one," said Seva.

Dong and Cho watched the men disappear around the bend in the road. Dong turned to Cho.

"Never use my name in situations like this!" he snapped. "It was stupid."

"Sorry," replied Cho abashed. "Fuck them! Let's get this tiger shifted."

He gestured at the Mercedes van, the engine was started and the driver moved it to the rear of the Tiger Taxi so the vehicles were tail to tail, the rear lights bathing everything red. The plan was simple: the tiger would be shot through the anus to preserve its skin — that alone was worth more than twenty thousand dollars — and they would drag it into their van. They would be back in Mumbai before dawn, the tiger hung in a deep freeze container with racks of sheep carcasses, bound for Hong Kong. Dong had run his illegal trade in exotic animal products alongside Cho's family export business for years. The ever-wealthier Chinese economy was hungry for many modern luxury items, but the trade in traditional medicines had soared. The rarer the beast, the higher the price. Rhino horn, ivory, leopard parts and even pangolins were valuable, but the king of all remained the tiger. Mukul had given Dong the nod about movements of animals on several occasions, had even obtained the bodies of exotics who died naturally, or had been put down humanely, but this was something special. He would have earned his 5000 rupees.

With an air of consolation Cho offered Dong a cigarette which he accepted with a grunt, both men shouldering their AK47s as they lit up. The driver joined them.

"Open door!" barked Dong blowing out a plume of smoke.

The driver turned the handle.

Angaar's mind floated, his senses dulled as he slumbered. He was aware of the van's movement and also aware that his clever monkey companion was nearby, but nothing registered on a higher plane.

It was Seva's final visit that had changed the tiger's world. The little bird-man had felt the Tiger Taxi stop and had clearly heard the shouted words, but to his credit had not panicked. He knew what the men with the guns were going to do; Vikram's explanation of why Project Tiger was so important had been accompanied by some graphic pictures of slaughtered victims of poachers. He had been horrified. He knew that these men intended to kill Angaar as he lay in a stupor. Before his presence was discovered he opened Vikram's black, plastic case and grabbed a blue banded syringe, quickly pulling off the cap. He plunged it into the tiger's rump, pressed the plunger and withdrew the needle throwing it into a corner. He just had time to pull the pins from the cage door when Vikram had yelled for him to come out. He made sure the front access door was secured after he stepped into the cab making a great show of squeezing through, hoping they would prefer to open the rear of the truck, and stepped out with his hands held high. He hoped he had not killed his great friend.

Angaar had not felt the sting of the needle, but the effect of the antidote was swift. His senses began to register and his brain started to evaluate information. Time began to accelerate with his metabolism, yet he was still only semi-conscious when the doors were opened the first time. He heard Seva's voice and his ear twitched. The door slammed shut just as the great amber eyes opened. He chuffed out his breath, panted to drag in oxygen then, with a final deep breath sat up and yawned, his nose pushing the unsecured cage door against the main truck doors. After another minute he was fully awake, synapses firing, his senses working flat out. It is seldom fully understood how long-term captive animals may react to extraordinary events. Reptiles and frogs retain their wildness and are able to survive release with ease. Mammal minds are more complex. Some captive animals could never cope with freedom, so dulled are their instincts, so reliant are they on humans. Not so Angaar. He was atypical and, Seva had been right, he had fire within. In spite of his nascent illness, Angaar's senses raced. Smells told him what was outside, sounds gave him direction, danger informed his flight mechanism and his haunches gathered as he made ready to spring and run. A sound from outside changed the information and altered his focus.

"Eeeh!"

Angaar's ears swivelled towards the sound, his eyes fixed at a point beyond the door where he would have seen the events outside had the solid barrier been transparent. The tiger changed to attack mode. He felt Seva's pain. This diminutive clever monkey had been his only companion. He smelled like a tiger combined with calming scents and exciting tastes. There were also foul-smelling monkeys outside – acrid, bitter and dangerous. Inside Angaar the fire grew. As the door opened a second time it was white hot.

Cho and Dong puffed on their cigarettes, AK47s slung across their shoulders, as the driver turned the door handle into the fully open position. They knew nothing would be along this stretch of road as they had placed barriers at each end; it could be days before the highways department discovered the nefarious evidence of their crime. It would be hours before the three men they had sent off reached the expressway and by the time they summoned help, the tiger would be stored, safely frozen in the confines of the city docks.

The door clicked open.

The driver would relate the events of the following minutes to no one. He would also have nightmares for years to come, unbidden. The handle released the catches on the double doors and the world exploded. The driver was brushed aside, rolled into the roadside ditch and hit his head on a tree root. He became an invisible witness in the darkness, watching the horror unfold in the red glow of tail lights.

A petrifying roar rent the air causing Cho and Dong to freeze as prey are programmed to do. The tiger was huge and unbelievably fast, emerging as if from the very air into the red world. It hit Dong in the chest with a muscular shoulder as it passed by on its way to engulfing Cho's face in open jaws. The teeth clamped down as Cho toppled and a crunch stifled his screams aborning, his lower jaw snapping under the pressure. Angaar's upper canines broke through bone, the left locating into an eye socket, the right through the thin temporal covering. Cho died instantly. The tiger turned, leaving his body where it fell.

Dong had fallen on his back. There was a black mark on his lip where the freshly lit cigarette had seared the skin. The AK47 had slipped over his head and was now behind his back, the lanyard like a belt, almost comical, but absolutely fatal. Instinct drove the tiger. Its cold, highly evolved killing system was fully engaged. Angaar covered the ground between the body of Cho and the now screaming, struggling Dong, who was crawling away frantically along the road. Ironically, the AK47, his talisman of power, slipped further down impeding his legs. Angaar loomed over him, a huge black hole in the night sky, and clamped those fearsome jaws around the man's cranium. The upper canines broke into the soft organ beneath and for a moment all was a grotesque, floodlit tableau.

The driver knew his only chance of life was to remain still. A hand was trapped under his body against a rock, but fear overcame pain and, even as a finger fractured, he remained motionless. He watched. The tiger had pulled Dong to the ground in the beams of the Tiger Taxi's headlights, all colours starkly defined. The terrible beast stood astride the man, jaws clamped to his skull. Dong whimpered and started to reach behind him, clawing at the warm white-furred underbelly, trying to push away his doom. The driver's pulse thumped as his blood pressure rose, his body shaking with the release of adrenalin, flight or fight responses nullified by fear. He prayed quietly for redemption.

Angaar's initial instinctive burst of energy was slowly flowing away. The thing in his jaws tasted foul – not food, an enemy. Something to kill. Dong was pulling his legs up underneath him, trying to gain purchase with his feet. This broke the impasse. Dong felt a slight tension quiver through the tiger's mighty frame. He barely had time to gasp "Ma!" as the jaws closed. Angaar dropped the body, turned and walked slowly back down the road.

The tiger was briefly lost to sight, then emerged into the red glow of the vehicles' tail lights. The man remained still. He had almost stopped breathing. So silent. But he had to watch. Angaar sniffed the ground and made a mournful sound.

"Geerumph! Geerumph!"

The driver continued to watch as the tiger walked into the darkness towards the higher hills. Just once more the melancholy "Geerumph!" echoed back from the black night.

An hour later the driver crawled from the ditch. He ignored the two vehicles and made his way down the hill through the scrubby undergrowth towards the distant expressway. In the morning light he caught a lift with a truck to Mumbai and went home to his new world of recurring nightmares. He never broke the law again.

Chapter 12

The Disc

Ravi Uppal frowned as he looked through his window at the black Audi pulling into its reserved parking space. Vasupati Chopra stepped out, straightened his dark suit, stretched and walked into the building. Vaz was different. Ravi could not see exactly what had changed, but his gait was smoother and he seemed taller. He almost danced as he walked and looked very well. And so he should, thought Ravi, as his young partner had been away for nearly three weeks. A strategically planned absence.

Vaz had quietly disappeared from Agra. Mr Vaida, businessman, remained as just a name in the hotel's guest book. He paid in cash and left a false address. Cobra's records showed receipts from Mumbai for Vaz, a contact had a credit card which he used as prompted, no questions asked. Then Vasupati Chopra had flown for a luxury break in the Maldives via Delhi – a genuine trip and solid alibi. As Vaz had lain in the sun the headlines in Agra papers screamed *Serial Killer ups His Game*, *Torture of the Innocents,* and *Horror in Agra as Kāla Calls Again!* The police had already placed their resident killer in the frame, for they had found *irrefutable similarities* with previous slayings. A medal bearing the image of Shiva had been found in both victims' mouths. Ravi had read the graphic stories and wondered who on Earth Vaz had working for him.

Ravi expunged every trail that may lead to any investigation of Cobra. As soon as he was sure of his work, he checked everything again. He was always thorough. Always. There had been enough in Mahto's estate for the local government to grab and not ask too many questions. All legal dealings with Cobra had been very informal, for good reason on Mahto's side. Every trace disappeared at the press of a key. Pederasts had a lot to hide and Ravi's blackmail had been clothed in friendship. Their mutual, profitable business ventures, spiced with the supply of anonymous boys, had fatally dulled Mahto's sense of caution. Lalit Mahto had fooled himself.

The door burst open and Vaz strode in almost glowing with energy, well-groomed with neatly tied hair. The two men embraced with genuine affection.

"Good to have you back, Vaz," smiled Ravi. "Did you enjoy the break?"

"Yes indeed," said Vaz. "My wife said I had earned a break. She says you work me too hard! She loved the gold bracelet I bought her though. I told her Ravi is a slave driver, but the business pays us well."

Ravi stepped to the door, asked Jyoti to bring in some coffee, and then closed it. Both men settled into the soft chairs.

"All has gone well since your holiday," said Ravi. "Our recent ... erm ...*investment* has paid out and has been...well... *reinvested*."

"How much?" asked Vaz smiling. "In US dollars."

"Nine lakhs. Nine – hundred – thousand," said Ravi slowly and quietly.

"Dollars?" asked Vaz, incredulous.

"Dollars," confirmed Ravi.

"Fucking hell," gasped Vaz in genuine surprise. "You are a genius Ravi."

"Shhh," reproached Ravi gently. "We'll talk later."

Jyoti came in with the coffee, smiled at Vaz and Ravi, then left. Both men sipped their drinks and chatted over neutral business matters. The intercom buzzer sounded.

"Yes Yot-Yot," said Ravi in his usual suave voice.

"There's a Jhatish Das here to see you," she answered.

"Is it urgent?" asked Ravi, frowning.

"He says it concerns Anil Gupta," was her soft reply.

"Hmm, OK," he said. "I've not seen Jhatish for a while. Give me five minutes and I'll be out."

Ravi broke the link and turned to Vaz.

"I suggest you take a long lunch," he said. "Your work has been first-class. Relax a bit. Show Hemlata I am not so bad! Tell her to phone Suneeti and arrange a night for us to have dinner, my treat."

"Anil Gupta," said Vaz getting to his feet. "I'd forgotten about him."

"I'd better see what's going on," said Ravi opening the door, "after all we owe Gupta's wife's family a great deal."

Jhatish Das staggered into his apartment after midnight. He had left the Singhs in sombre mood, but the comfortable air of affection gave warmth to their parting. They gained strength from each other and had committed themselves to be as strong for Mr Gupta in the coming months. None of them had given voice to this pact. For them it was what good friends naturally do. Jhatish was part of a close, extended family.

He woke from a deep, dream-filled slumber, sweating and groggy, so took a cool shower to sharpen his mind. He dressed in his usual careless way, tattered jacket and all, before hurrying down to the block's secure parking area where he kept his raddled car. This ancient vehicle had served him well and continued to survive its travails on Indian roads with honour. It was an old Ambassador Classic ISZ of dubious descent which he had hand painted years before, in a shade formally known as duck-egg green. It was now more *duck-pond-grim*, as he was wont to say if trying to describe the colour. When asked about its mechanical qualities, Jhatish would defend its prowess with some vigour. He was proud of it. It started first time, every time, though he tended to wince as the engine made alarming noises until it had warmed up. Then, it was smooth, if sulphurous, and, though not rapid in nature, could match the speed of Delhi traffic. In addition to the colour there was a rust patch on the rear wing shaped somewhat like a mallard, so he had named the noble machine *The Duck*. It roared into life and left the car park wallowing on uneven suspension, a waddling progress to justify its appellation.

Once into the slow-moving crush of traffic The Duck blended in with the other eclectic mix of vehicles, a large number of which were far less roadworthy and more ancient. Jhatish was as patient as any Indian driver in that he was resigned to delays and madness, but loud in his protestations. He viewed the yelling, posturing and honking as parts of a daily musical – unavoidable and everyone playing their part with gusto. The horn on The Duck sounded at regular intervals making a robust *phooeeoop!* which held its own amongst newer, less fatigued types. It was a sound that suited the Ambassador's personality. After an hour of vehicular madness Jhatish waddled The Duck into the car park of Cobra Investments, bringing it to rest alongside a black Audi. As he walked around the beautiful car he heard the ticking of the cooling engine and wondered if Ravi may be busy with a newly arrived, well-heeled client, and if he should have made an appointment. A pretty girl in the reception put him at his ease with a smile and it was quickly established that Ravi would see him if he could just wait a few minutes. Jhatish sat down and studied the fish tank. After a while a smart man came out of the door marked *Ravi Uppal Managing Director*, and walked across to a door opposite marked *Research & Security Manager*. He paused and smiled at Jhatish.

"Hello," he said. "It's Das, isn't it? Jhatish Das?"

"Yes," replied Jhatish, standing.

Vaz walked over and shook the teacher's hand.

"We've met before," said Vaz. "I'm Vaz Chopra, Ravi's partner."

After a brief exchange of niceties, Vaz went into his office. Jhatish blinked through his glasses at the closing door. He remembered Vasupati Chopra, but was not quite sure of his role at Cobra. Both research and security covered a vast spectrum of possibilities, so the sign on the door gave little away. All Jhatish knew was this man's eyes seemed to look right into him. His smile hid something so primal an atavistic alarm circuit triggered in Jhatish's subconscious. He shook the feeling off as Ravi stepped into the reception. They shook hands.

"So good to see you again, Jhatish," he said, in his avuncular fashion. "Yot-Yot. Could you bring us in a tray of tea and some of those nice little cakes? Thank you. Now Jhatish, come in. Come in. Tell me what is all this about Anil? How is the dear man?"

Jhatish was steered into the surrounds of a plush office where he joined Ravi on the chairs by the coffee table. Outside the green avenues of Delhi looked clean after the recent rain, but the city smog tinted the upper air yellow.

"Now," said Ravi settling opposite, "tell all. I'm guessing something has happened."

"I'm afraid it has," said Jhatish. "Anil has been hospitalised for the last few days and has a serious medical condition. He is being allowed home, in fact I'm fetching him later on. He asked me a favour – said you'd understand. He wants you to sort his files out as he feels it's time he made sure his affairs are in order. I think he may want to move some investments to secure Rupa's future, that sort of thing."

"Hmm, I see," said Ravi smiling. "Well, that should not be too hard. In fact, it is about time – I have nagged him. What is his condition, by the way?"

"Cancer," blurted Jhatish, still uncomfortable using the word in relation to a friend. He felt as if he should spit the word out. "A tumour. Operable, but he sort of…well…he wants to finally sort things out. Since Kiran died he has let things go…you know, all the stuff he's left you to deal with. And now…well, he wants you to guide him, I think. Anil is a little lost."

"I see," said Ravi, with the air of concern. "That is truly awful news. Awful. Our destinies seem to be linked by tragedy and sorrow. The poor fellow. What to do? What to do? We are similar men, Anil and me. I miss my darling Tamina so much and know Anil is still grieving for Kiran. So very sad."

"Yes," said Jhatish, "but you have moved on and used your strength to watch over Anil's family. He is a gentler, less robust creature. He wants for little, but you are right, he has been plagued by ill luck. I fear for him, really I do. But ... but I think he can get through this and finally start anew."

The door opened and Jyoti delivered a tray of tea, small cakes and biscuits. The two men spent the next hour talking about families and fates, drank tea and cleared the tray of food. Eventually, Ravi said he had an afternoon appointment and must reluctantly bid Jhatish goodbye.

"Tell Anil not to worry," said Ravi. "Any time he needs this sorting out I am here. After all I still see him as my brother-in-law."

Jhatish Das shook Ravi's hand and left to make his way to the hospital. As The Duck bounced out of the Cobra Investments car park, Ravi looked down and frowned. Anil Gupta was worth a great deal of money; most of it was held by Cobra. Ravi decided to wait and see what Mr Gupta had to say. He buzzed Jyoti.

"Yes Mr Uppal?"

"I need a job doing quickly, Yot-Yot," he said. "I want all the files for a Mr Anil Gupta. The latest figures on investments, shares, the whole thing."

There is a saying that it rains on the just as well as the unjust. It did upon Delhi: on all its early morning commuters, vendors, beggars and Sufis; criminals, husbands, schoolchildren and squirrels. Everyone shrugged and mumbled and continued with their lives. Even though the monsoon rains were finally abating, there were still aftershocks of heavy showers to contend with. Delhi steamed in the rising sun.

The previous evening Ravi Uppal had sifted through all of Anil Gupta's files, paper and electronic, revisiting the portfolios set up via Cobra. Jyoti had set out everything in order, Ravi had chosen her for brains as well as looks, a perfect PA. Vaz had left early to spend some time with his family and Ravi had yet another dinner to attend in his home. Suneeti had really gone to town on this one, but Ravi did not mind the expense as it was part of his drive to get into politics. It was a meeting of backers for the powerful Indian Patriotic Union Party and they had earmarked Ravi Uppal as an electable candidate. He wanted to become a Member of Parliament. It had gone well. He had money, support and influence; now he had endorsement for his march into government, and the possible gift of a safe seat. There lay power and wealth, each fuelling the other. He could already see the space opening before him in which he could exercise power amongst Lutyens's grand buildings. Yet, he had not slept well. Anil Gupta kept drifting through his subconscious.

He stood in his office looking at raindrops running down the tinted window. Even though the dinner had continued well into the night, he had risen early, driven to the office and arrived before Jyoti. He had been through the pile of papers on his desk once more, searched the computer files and started to weigh up hazards and risk. All the figures were up to date, all of the facts were in; these data were complete. But, he could not stop thinking of an error of judgement. A tiny seed of improbable calamity. Everything had been perfect, but he had let his guard down.

Next to the Gupta documents lay a morning copy of the Agra Record, a broadsheet which dealt with that city's local news. Inside was a certain Lalit Mahto's obituary. It had published details of the recently deceased's will and a potted history of the life of a well-connected, but private man, who had left his property to the people of Agra as thanks to the place he loved. He had, it seemed, apportioned his non-physical assets to various local charities and one large donation to the Delhi based international charity, Fallen Angels. Ravi smiled at this; even as Lalit Mahto burned on a ghat somewhere, the $900,000 contributed to Cobra without leaving a trail had disappeared into the complex laundering system that was the child of Ravi Uppal's genius. The irony was that Ravi had drafted the will, had it signed by the pederast, and had been the executor as well. Cobra was seen to be acting altruistically, all reports were positive noting the local government coffers had been gifted a large sum of cash from the estate. Many from the previous night's dinner party approved of this overt publicity stunt as it would boost Ravi Uppal's coming election campaign. Ravi was surprised by his own subterfuge at times. Lalit Mahto had taken a high-risk strategy, had trusted those with knowledge of his depravities, relied on his wealth to shield him, enjoyed the nefarious profit of his investments, and thus had become profitably expendable. Lalit Mahto had refused to acknowledge his own self-deception until the bag was pulled over his head.

Ravi turned and picked up half a cup of tepid coffee and sipped at it pensively. His political ambitions meant he had to be squeaky-clean, at least when it came to an audit trail. In this he had succeeded very well, so far. Since he and Vaz had joined, every action they took had been re-examined and sterilised where required. No evidence of wrongdoing could be traced to them. The dead had no living relatives to call out foul play. They had been expunged from history and no one cared. Vasupati Chopra's side of Cobra was the perfect black hole. *Perfect* mused Ravi as he put his empty cup on the window sill. As the stage was set for him to become a national figure, Ravi Uppal had been ever more forensic in his dealings in business. He had spent months cross-referencing the legitimate side of Cobra. All was correct. All taxes had been paid; he had even allowed a few errors into the system which tax auditors had picked up. Sometimes he had a little more to pay, occasionally he had a rebate. All clean. All contrived. Fallen Angels had become iconic in doing good works across Asia, and was freely endorsed by the rich and the famous. It was so intricately interwoven into the fabric of high society that it was bomb proof; the best money laundering system in India. The trick was never to get careless.

The dark side of Cobra was all profit. Every victim selected had their files erased or modified to fit Ravi's purpose. Fictional reasons for cessation of business were inserted, and any legitimate discharging of wills and distribution of estates were on public record. Ravi's carefully crafted new reality hid brutal truths. The mantra had always been, one job at a time, each seen to its conclusion before a further, carefully selected victim was eaten by the machine. What Ravi was capable of in corporate subterfuge, Vasupati Chopra matched in the removal of those with erased portfolios. Vaz never left a trace. His genius was weaving the *modus operandi* of a fictitious perpetrator into each killing. He even watched for news reports on real killers, then choreographed a murder to match reality. The police expertly identified these hallmarks, and attributed them to unknown, but obvious killers, or lumped them with similar killings already on file. As the police pursued wraiths, Vaz could hide in plain sight.

Ravi was aware that he held a certain paternal power over his younger partner, but never abused it and, even though they both dealt in gross dishonesty, they both trusted each other implicitly. Each held the family unit close and inviolable, including each other's. Anyone else was fair game. They were the yin and yang of a whole entity. It was perfection.

Ravi's pondering was interrupted by a knock on the door.

"Come in, come in!" he said, a smile replacing his pensive frown.

Jyoti swept in wearing a white, two-piece suit and a pale lemon-yellow blouse which set off the golden jewellery she favoured. Her brown legs were well toned from regular visits to the gym and her feet were shod in medium heeled, designer shoes which matched her ensemble. She was beautiful. Her smile had the effect of making Ravi feel clumsy and inarticulate from which it always took a few seconds to recover. It was not an unpleasant feeling for a man who was strict with his outer persona.

"Hello Mr Uppal," she said, her voice as lovely as the rest of her. "You are in early. Coffee?"

"Yot-Yot," he replied using his pet name for her, "that would be marvellous! The one I made myself looked and tasted like the water from a paddy-field. I'm going over Anil Gupta's files. I'm helping him finally get his mind back on living."

"Dear Mr Gupta," she said. "He has had some rotten luck over the years. Truly horrid. You both lost so much. Is there a financial problem?"

"Oh no," said Ravi, "but Anil has some new health issues and I shall be taking care of his files from now on – personally. I still feel responsible for my brother-in-law, after all our losses were so similar, so dreadful. I must make sure he finally takes control of his affairs and that my niece has a secure future."

Unbidden, Jyoti stepped forward and kissed Ravi's cheek. "You are the kindest man I know," she said. "Now, let me get you that coffee."

She swept out leaving the faint hint of perfume. Something expensive Ravi did not doubt. His groin ached as he watched her leave, the spot on his cheek where those soft, warm lips had barely brushed, burned. He sighed and cleared his mind of erotic fantasy. A politician could not to take any risks; anyway, his Suneeti was as much as he could cope with and there had never been a time when he felt frustrated. It was another added strength, another boost of confidence that he was still desired by a beautiful woman – wife or not. If anything, he needed vitamins just to remain an active husband, he thought with a wry smile. Jyoti came back into the office carrying a coffee maker, turned it on and then brought in a small silver tray with a cup and some cinnamon biscuits and dates arranged on a white plate. The smell of coffee filled the air.

"There you are," she said. "A couple of minutes and you'll be in heaven. If you need anything else just buzz."

She left Ravi gazing after her once more. He paid her a very high salary, a white Volkswagen Golf in the car park bore witness to this, but she was worth every rupee. She seemed to read his mind and pre-empt his wishes, looked after him well and never dallied; Jyoti switched into work mode very quickly even after light persiflage, a trick most women never learnt, he mused. He sat by the low table with a cup of coffee looking out over the leafy trees which grew profusely in this suburb.

What was he to do with Anil Gupta? He should have known Gupta would raise his stupid head eventually, and with his reappearance came the reminder of Ravi Uppal's only errors in creating the wealth-making, power-enhancing device that was Cobra Investments. These errors were forced upon him, but he still wondered if he had not acted too rashly and was now due to be punished by his own unusual laxity. Something would have to be done to finally close this possible route to ruin. Mr Gupta's future was at a crossroads. Ravi Uppal had to weigh everything up and look for the most beneficial solution to a problem he had ignored for too long. He stared at the pile of papers on his desk then out the window once more. If those files went back to Jyoti in the next few days Mr Gupta would remain in the light. If Ravi kept them to begin his well-practised purging process, then his brother-in-law would be a dead man walking. He would become a temporary citizen of the dark side ruled by Vasupati Chopra. But, Anil Gupta was not an individual. He had family, friends and a will. Amit Gupta, the brother, was a virtual stranger, but the Shastri family still kept an eye on Rupa Gupta's welfare via her father. Mr Gupta had tendrils weaving through many lives any of which could become annoyances. Then there was that basic error. Two events, years apart involving the sisters Tamina and Kiran. And a computer disc. A seed of disaster.

Ravi drank the coffee and came to a decision: he needed some space. He stood and buzzed the intercom.

"Yes Mr Uppal?" asked Jyoti's sweet voice.

"Order me a taxi, Yot-Yot," he said politely. "Tell them Indian Gate. I need a walk and to get some air."

"Of course, right away," she said.

Ravi stood, gathered the Gupta files and placed them in his secure filing cabinet, locking it after him.

"Ten minutes," came Jyoti's voice again.

A walk up the Rajpath was required and for once he chose not to call Vaz. Not yet anyway.

Ravi Uppal paid the taxi driver twice the required fare and stepped out onto the hard standing surrounding the India Gate. Sir Edwin Lutyens's mighty designs set in wide-open spaces freed Ravi's mind. Today the hawkers were selling rubber-band-propelled darts which, when fired into the sky, sprouted a trio of rotors at the zenith of their arc and helicoptered to the ground. Clever, but with a limited fun factor. Yet children, parents and hawkers were firing the multi-coloured missiles into the air all around: blue, yellow, pink and green projectiles zooming into the clear sky where they became gentle flowers as they fell. Ravi purchased an ice lolly and began his walk towards the distant Rashtrapati Bhavan as he had done so many times before. He knew by the time he flagged down a taxi or tuktuk at the Motilal Nehru Marg he would have made a decision. He negotiated the Hexagon road and started to stroll along the long lawn, taking nibbles at the hard, fruity ice, enjoying the cool of it melting down his throat.

Tamina had been suspicious of his long absences and the tension had grown over many months. He was always sure things would be alright, even if it came to a divorce, which he did not really want. Then they had a single row. This was no ordinary argument, but a full-blown vituperation which distorted reality, ire outweighing sense. Just one row. That is all it had taken. It had started over an outfit she chose to wear for a business dinner. In a moment of thoughtlessness, he suggested its look was *perhaps a little mature*. Mature was never a good word to use about a woman reaching middle age. She had exploded and he had tried to defend himself. There followed an intricate verbal battle, fuelled by intimate knowledge and remembered mistakes. Everything grew out of proportion with Ravi taking a conciliatory stance, calming, soothing and cajoling, but just before tears claimed the field of conflict she had made her mistake.

"Ravi Uppal!" she had yelled. "You be careful with me! Don't you forget I am one of the trustees of the Fallen Angels – your nice, new, innocent charity." She had spat those last words at him. "I adjust the books before the accountants get hold of them. Cover up those little holes – your skimmed profits. This is tax avoidance, not evasion. And I help!"

Ravi had quietened – he had never thought of this fact in such a context. He felt trapped and vulnerable.

"Now, now Tamina," he said. "The charity will do a lot of good…"

"For you!" she barked. "Always for you! Well, I have taken a few precautions, Ravi, just to make sure we are equal partners no matter what. I have a copy of the first year's work on a disc in a safe deposit box. Don't look so worried, Ravi. There is nothing on the company hard-drive, but it may come in handy if you have eyes for another bitch! Like that Virani girl. She is not *mature*, is she?"

The tears were bitter, borne of a woman scared of rejection, scared of ageing, scared of a younger woman's influence on the man she still loved. Ravi knew she needed reassurance and gave it.

"Why all this?" he had soothed. "We are a good team. I don't want anyone else – this is just a row – nothing. I love you and just want us to be comfortable. We built the business. We should have the benefits. All you have helped me do is to make sure the crooked tax men do not rob money from those who earn it. Please. Let's forget this and go to dinner."

And so they did and nothing was mentioned again, Tamina eventually apologising for her stupidity, Ravi sealing forgiveness by taking her on a luxury break to Sydney and adding to her wardrobe. Tamina had felt secure again, but Ravi remembered the disc. And Suneeti had missed a period.

Tamina was clever, but Ravi was a man of deep cunning. His wife's bank was known to him and the manger was not averse to bribes, especially clothed in untraceable investments cloaked in a charity. Within a month of the argument Ravi was in the secure booth in a branch in Mumbai, a city favoured by Tamina for shopping, hotels and taking her friends, opening her single safe deposit box. There was jewellery, amongst which was a diamond-set brooch inherited from her mother and a single computer disc in a plain plastic case. *Fallen Angels* had been written across the cardboard frontispiece, behind the plastic. Ravi took the case, replaced the locked box and left. He flew back to Delhi that same day and went to his small office in Chokhandi. It was only when he opened the case that an alarm bell sounded in his mind and the shock of realisation passed through him. It was not a computer disc he was holding. It was a music CD entitled *Chaos Birthing, Verse 25 - Time's End, World Beginnings*, by Zahan Bulsara.

No mention was ever made about the incident. Tamina had to know her decoy was gone, but it remained a closed subject. If he said nothing there would always be doubt that he had been involved, though it did not detract from the fact that his wife had him at a disadvantage. Until he teamed up with Vasupati Chopra. Until he rationalised the risk to himself. Until he realised the law of probability was with him. The great leap to Cobra would solve everything. Tamina's miscalculation centred on her belief that her husband could not harm a fly; she never considered he could facilitate murder. When she and Alka set off to spend, spend, spend in Mumbai, her miscalculation had cost them their lives. Yet, even as she died so cruelly, she did not once think of her husband as anything but her love.

The Rajpath was not so busy. The long lawns had groups of office workers and tourists strolling around or sitting in the shade under trees, sharing the grass with the ubiquitous mynahs, but Ravi had plenty of room to saunter in peace. The ice lolly finished, he casually flicked the stick into the grass ahead of him; a mynah sidled up, grasped the stick in its bill, shook it, dropped it and marched off. Ravi smiled at the bird as he passed.

"Always check," he said to the mynah. "Always check and never leave anything to chance, little bird."

Anil Gupta's request via Jhatish Das had re-emphasised Ravi's mistake, his single error in all things Cobra. The disc his murdered wife crowed about must exist – he just knew it. He had kept *Time's End, World Beginnings* in a drawer at the office as a reminder for him to always check, always make sure and always watch his back. After Tamina was gone, and once Vasupati Chopra ignited the all-consuming Cobra Investments, Ravi had meticulously excised any trace of nefarious dealings. He had done a good job too; years of success passed and then came the aftershock – Kiran Gupta.

Kiran was very bright and had no issues investing her inheritance with Ravi's company, even letting him draft her and her husband's wills, building in a total wipe-out clause with Ravi being named as Rupa's guardian. Ravi Uppal had remained close to his late wife's family, helped with Rupa's education and never left them out of social gatherings. He needed them close to ensure nothing about his dealings was compromised by Tamina's link to Cobra. Keeping them close kept them in his sight. Here he had made his second mistake and overplayed his hand: he had invited her to become a board member of Fallen Angels when linking Lord Beaufort Homes to his charity. In the media Rupa Gupta became the face of his altruistic creation and the beneficent union. This gave him greater legitimacy. Kiran Gupta only had to attend meetings and fundraisers, and sign the annual accounts. Therein lay the problem. She took her job too seriously. Some thirty months ago she had set up a private meeting with him, and it was not at all pleasant.

Kiran Gupta had not wanted to meet at the Cobra Investments office, instead arranged their appointment to take place at The Callanish, a cool marble-lined hotel near the Delhi Race Club. Lunch was convivial and light and Ravi enjoyed their conversation about his charity, family and life in general. Kiran was a more attractive version of his dead wife and he was genuinely fond of her, admiring her resilience in the face of such an unlucky life. Business was not discussed until they settled in the large lounge in one of the quiet areas set aside for such meetings. They sipped tea and nibbled on cakes. It was at this point that Kiran fished in her bag and placed a computer disc in the table.

"Ravi," she said, "this seemed to belong to Tamina. It was in a box of bits from our parents' house she retrieved when mother died – you sent it on to me when Tamina was killed. I had only given it a cursory glance and left it where it was, but since being involved with Fallen Angels something niggled my memory. This was it. I remember reading the scribbled name around the centre. See – it reads *F. Angels*. Do you know what it contains?"

To Kiran's surprise Ravi answered without pause, "Yes. It is her pre-filtered first year accounts for the charity. She kept it to ensure she did not miss out on the profits. Tamina was fond of the good life and we made a good team – but she did not fully trust that I would share any, shall we say, bonuses."

This had silenced Kiran for a moment. She was sure Ravi was a legitimate businessman and trusted him with her affairs, but this disc had the hallmark of deception. She also knew her sister had indeed enjoyed the luxury lifestyle her husband had provided, and did not doubt she was complicit in something untoward. Yet Kiran was not her sister, and if she was involved in what was perceived as a great charity, she had to know there were no nasty secrets under the surface, even from years before.

"I trust you Ravi," she said, "but right now I am a little concerned about what is on this disc. It shows a large influx of money with no link to its origins. This would stand out in an audit, but it seems an adjusted set of figures became the accepted version. What I want to know is if Fallen Angels is just a scam? I need you to tell me what went on."

"Kiran," said Ravi smiling. "Fallen Angels is a clean charity and I am proud of the good that it does. I can back this up at any time you want. But…" He had paused for effect. "But at the start I was in trouble. I was forced to pay bribes and this money was not easy to get. I ended up borrowing money from some bad men – Tamina knew this – and I was paying them off, but it was crippling me. I worked out that I could rid myself of the debt and the extortionate interest in a single year if I could reduce my tax bill, so that is what I did. The charity absorbed a lot of potentially taxable income and by the end of 1999 I was free of them. I had this one blot on my copybook and I have been unable to erase it.

"I vowed to make the charity huge, viable and worthwhile, which of course it is. It was to be my redemption. This disc is the only thing that could have ruined everything – and for no good reason – it was purely Tamina's insurance for a life of luxury."

Kiran had wrestled with this for a while as she sipped her tea. It was more than plausible. Probable even. And Ravi had selflessly helped her and her family. Was this proof of an altruistic homage to a life of goodness set against a mistake? Kiran's good nature took over.

"Oh, Ravi," she said. "I knew there was a reason for this. I know Tamina loved fine things and I also know her death hit you hard. I think we can forget this."

"Well," said Ravi relieved, "that is a weight off my mind…"

"But…" Kiran had interrupted. "There is one condition. I want a full independent audit of Fallen Angels' finances for the last five years. That will miss the first few years and will miss this silly issue. I have to be sure things are in order."

This bombshell had almost caused Ravi's composed mask to crack into rage. He felt sick with the effort of staying outwardly calm, yet stay calm he did. He even smiled and kissed Kiran's cheek.

"Of course, Kiran," he had said. "Let's meet next week and we can agree on a firm of auditors. I'll get my new girl, Jyoti, to set up a meeting – she'll contact you."

They had parted on good terms, but she had taken the disc.

Ravi paused in his walk at the Janpath intersection. He remembered overcoming the panic and talking to Vaz the same day – right here, oddly enough, close to where Tamina's fate had been sealed. He sighed and jogged across the Janpath to the next stretch of lawn.

For the first time Ravi had ordered an execution without meticulous planning. Kiran's innocent interfering was as dangerous as her sister's crafted blackmail. It came down to weighing up the odds and this time it had to be done quickly. A decision was not that difficult to make he had often told Vaz, it was just a point in time where direction was chosen; it was the aftermath one had to deal with. He had stood here with Vaz and explained the problem. Both were in immediate concord. If Fallen Angels became the focus of a full and proper audit, a loose thread to Cobra could be found and pulled. Things would start to unravel and with every tug more would be exposed. The disc was useless without intelligent direction, but Kiran gave it that. If Ravi reneged on the audit promise he felt sure the disc would be used as a bargaining chip, just as Tamina had done. To nullify the disc and avoid an audit only one thing needed to happen.

"Killing Kiran Gupta is a tough one," Vaz had said. "There's not enough time to do much planning."

"All we have is the weekend," Ravi said. "Friday's tomorrow, maybe Monday I can give you, but Jyoti will be setting up a meeting on Wednesday. Kiran may choose Tuesday. Who knows? Can it be done?"

Vaz had lit a cigarette and smiled. Ravi knew that smile and his nerves settled. He hated the feeling of not being in total control, but that was now melting away.

"Yes, it can be done," said Vaz. "The big problem is the short time frame. It means arrangements will be basic. It is a tough one. No time. Hmmm."

"But?" asked Ravi.

"But," said Vaz, "I can do it."

"How?"

"Leave it to me," said Vaz. "If it goes wrong, you know nothing. If it goes well only we know the truth."

And so, it had come to pass. On the following Sunday morning Kiran Gupta was killed in a hit-and-run accident. The car had been an old taxi, number plates obscured by dirt, the driver nondescript. Ravi Uppal had been surprised how easy it had been. A road accident. One of thousands recorded every day in India; a single statistic diluted out of existence by the weight of similar fatalities. It was not unusual and drew no attention. The great irony was Anil Gupta's reliance on Ravi to sort out Kiran's affairs. Beyond irony was the reappearance of the disc in a box of Fallen Angel papers the grieving man had plonked on Ravi's desk, apologising for not knowing what to do with it. Ravi had disposed of the item as soon as his brother-in-law had gone. He even burned the original case. He gave no mind to Zahan's CD, which he had given to Vaz one day during a rather alcoholic business meeting. Yet both discs had been keys. One had closed and locked the past. The other unlocked a door which would influence all their futures. Kiran Gupta had been as dangerous as her sister. Anil Gupta was no major threat, just a sad and pathetic figure, but he knew the Shastris. The Shastris, if prompted could become Ravi's nemesis. Ravi feared the honest financiers. Mr Gupta's inherited money was originally Shastri money and they were casually linked to everything. And some of that money had already been tapped and filtered through Fallen Angels via the Beaufort Homes Trust. This, if revealed, could expose Cobra. This, in turn, would ruin Ravi Uppal's political future.

By the time he reached the Motilal Nehru Marg and hailed a tuktuk, he had weighed up the odds and the decision was easy. Anil Gupta had to go, just like Kiran and Tamina. Rupa Gupta would then become an annoyance but, as he would become her legal guardian, he could arrange her demise too. After all it was the Age of Kali – chaos was to be expected.

Chapter 13

William MacKeeg

Mr Gupta sweated through pyrotechnic dreams. Delhi sat hot and airless under the heavy monsoon sky. City lights painted the dark clouds a dirty orange, a poor substitute for the obscured full moon. The rains had been long in coming, but now they lingered. The life-giving water, once yearned for, was now a wearisome daily companion. Though they longed for drier days, Delhi's people knew rain would eventually end, so went about their lives stoically, patient with events considered ordained by greater minds. It was visitors from foreign lands who suffered in the humidity. Cloistered in thick-walled, air-conditioned hotels the brutal shock of stepping out into the warm liquid air, fogged glasses, misted cameras and dampened skin. A walk through the wide-open spaces of Delhi induced perspiration, even though blue skies gave the impression of dry heat. Tourists rushed: Indians sauntered. Once sweating it was impossible to stop.

The modern New Delhi Gandhi Hospital was climate-controlled and the atmosphere cool and dry, but hot dreams affected the sleeping man's subconscious. Mr Gupta had entered a world he could hardly have imagined in daylight wakefulness. Such dreams he had never known before, even after the mental torment of Kiran's death. These were visions. Vast pictures in colour, not monochrome hints of what may be, unfixed after waking. The pictures burned into his consciousness and would remain as long as he remained. Deep in slumber's febrile embrace Mr Gupta's mind was still sharp. Time became obsolete. Who knows if short dreams take hours or extensive visions take seconds? Relativity defines a dreamer.

Cognisance increased Mr Gupta's anguish, made manifest in the sweats he was suffering. Coruscating colours, snapshots of pure clarity and panic filled his head. The cyclonic winds of fantastic thoughts gathered in a scream. Then *Crack!* His mind broke through a barrier and he reached a calm equilibrium. Clarity held.

Where Mr Gupta was he could not say. He knew he was asleep, but knew equally that this felt very real. Where his mind had taken him, what world he was now in, proved beyond his reasoning. Even so, he felt able to relax and take in his surroundings. He was standing on a white beach fringed by palm trees, bathed in bright moonlight. The sea was calm, the water very dark, edged in sparkling wavelets along the shore. But the sky was all wrong. The huge, shining moon did not block out the spangled darkness of black space: it was full of stars in their millions, clear and bright, sparkling with rainbows of elemental refraction. Beyond the great globe moon was Saturn, tilted to reveal its rings. There was a tightness in Mr Gupta's throat as he perceived the revelation before him. If he just concentrated he could know everything. Joy filled him, tears dripped down his cheeks. He reached out with his mind. Projected thought raced towards infinity and nearly, so nearly, touched this well of knowledge, the sink of everything. Nearly. Then clarity let go and in a rush of dizzying, unbidden thought he fell, and fell, and fell, lost in endless space and time. He felt the jolt and, opening dream-eyes, found himself on the same beach. This time all was as it should be. Perspective conformed to perceived human logic. He was sitting on an ancient rock, not anxious, but feeling the loss of the vision that was pulled away. He looked to his left and there he was, the silver-grey, luminous man he had been trying to fix in his mind.

"Och, it's about time laddie," said the figure in a Glaswegian accent. "You've been awhile."

As dreams went Mr Gupta had to admit his was a blinder, as his Uncle Nik would have put it. Somehow, he had reached a place of calm. For the first time since Kiran died felt he could rid himself of some inner anxiety by the simple process of talking. The relief he felt was palpable.

"Who are you?" he asked.

"Ach, I've told ye afore," replied the Scot. "William MacKeeg."

"But…" said Mr Gupta struggling with the concept of this new reality. "But, how on Earth do you exist in an Indian's head? If you were a fakir I could grasp it. But you are Scottish, in a period costume and we're speaking English."

William MacKeeg laughed. "I've been called a fucker, but never a fakir!"

"Now I'm in a comedy show," groaned Mr Gupta. "Am I dead?"

"Och, no," said MacKeeg. "It's your mind playing fast and loose with the help of a tumour, I'm guessing. And ye know who I am, really you do."

The silver moon shone brighter. The silence seemed scripted to fit with Mr Gupta's need for a pause. An idea flickered in his mind. MacKeeg had dug out a short clay pipe from a pouch in his battered webbing, filled it with dark tobacco and lit it with a match. The match and pipe burned with a blue flame. The Scot drew in a lungful of smoke then blew it out into the still night air.

"It's the first time I've had a smoke since I got killed!" he said laughing again. "Old Fergus used to say it would kill me – he was like an old crone mithering on. Now I can smoke and it fucking well can't. Ha ha ha. Fuck you Fergus!"

Mr Gupta was adjusting to this altered world. He thought the odd events of recent days had conspired to give him the weirdest of breakdowns.

"So, you are just a figment of my imagination?"

"Aye," said MacKeeg. "Close your eyes and wish me away."

Mr Gupta closed his eyes. He quickly opened them and MacKeeg was gone. All at once he felt grief for a lost companion.

"See!" said MacKeeg.

Yet he was not there. What there was, on the sand by his feet, was a fat toad.

"That's your mind," said the toad. "Now for fuck's sake blink again!"

Mr Gupta did and the soldier was back smoking his pipe.

"I just do not get this," said Mr Gupta.

"In that case laddie," said MacKeeg, "I had better introduce myself without explaining the *why*. Just concentrating on the *what*, eh? What do you see?"

Mr Gupta relaxed. He recognised the uniform from his studies of Anglo-Indian history. Then remembered the few sketchy words from MacKeeg's previous, brief appearances. Mr Gupta had it.

"You are a member of a Highland Regiment of Foot!" said Mr Gupta feeling pleased with himself.

"Private William MacKeeg, 78th Highland Regiment of Foot, at your service," said the Scot saluting with his pipe. "My clan is a sept of the MacLeod so I am duty-bound to utter the motto *Hold Fast* in any situation of conflict...including ale houses. I was killed in Lucknow on 30th September 1857. Now, that's a bit of a bastard for a fellow to bear. I shall tell ye all. The odd thing is ye are telling yourself and ye don't even know it!"

MacKeeg laughed and coughed and, as he was thus engaged, Mr Gupta finally took the whole person in. William MacKeeg was a tall man with white hair and full white beard. As the Scot had materialised in monochrome his hair could have been blond, but he looked old, so the implication was white. He was heavily built, compared to Indian men, and his body looked hard and muscular. He wore no hat, had a plain tunic with crossed webbing, and a thick belt holding up a knee-length kilt. He was shod in boots with sagging, calf-length stockings. MacKeeg looked a little out of place in a coloured dream, but black and white suited him. After all he had died 155 years before.

"Och, ye see me now," said MacKeeg, fully recovered from his coughing. "Good. As we are we, and I is ye, there is little to say, laddie. I know what ye see, and know there is confusion, so I'll tell ye more."

MacKeeg drew on his pipe, settled on his rock and told his tale.

"I was born on the island of Skye in the year of our Lord 1824.

Scotland had been through quite a time by then, mainly 'cos we tend to fight everything and learn fuck all from getting a hiding! Ye see, laddie, defeat was like a fight up the pub. A tale to tell and drink over. It is our way. I once saw a Highlander cut off by rebelling Sepoys on the far side of a battle field. He just smiled at them and, as they charged in, he shouted, 'Fuck you!' That's a Scot for ye.

"Anyhow, my life looked pretty bleak. I had no education and found the dreary, grey world of the Presbyterian life a burden. My father was a compulsive drunk, and my mother a brood mare producing excess labour for the fields. We had nothing at all. Och, it was ten years before I wore shoes! A kindly lady, Isobel MacDonald, did teach me to read at Sunday school, but there was nothing on the island for me. Just sheep and shovelling shite."

MacKeeg looked across to Mr Gupta and smiled.

"You know all this, man," he laughed. "It's your mind this comes from! But, we're both getting used to this, so I'll plough on.

"In the end I ran away and joined the Ross-shire Buffs as a drummer boy. They looked after me and I grew up a soldier. See, a lad needs guidance, discipline and somewhere to belong that's based on honesty and prospect. I had that. By the time I got to twenty-one I was an old lag, knew nothing but soldiering, yet I had food in my guts, clothes on my back and boots on my feet. And I'd travelled to India just in time for the Indian Mutiny. I got stuck in Lucknow as the second siege got underway. That's where I saw the lad I told ye about getting killed all alone. I got killed on my birthday at 33 years old. Now I'm here."

MacKeeg drew on his pipe, looked at Mr Gupta and smiled again.

"What thinks ye laddie?

Mr Gupta recognised the brief history MacKeeg had talked about and knew that the facts about 78th Highlanders had come from somewhere in his subconscious. He felt perplexed at the possible meaning of MacKeeg's appearance in his life.

"You are here to help me?"

MacKeeg laughed again. "Aye," he said.

"Through what?" asked Mr Gupta.

"Everything that's coming," said MacKeeg. "I'm here to illuminate what you already know. Here to build the bricks of knowledge into a house of understanding. Here to thrash out the best way to get through this part of your life…"

Mr Gupta could hear the rushing in his head again. The night sky began to waver and the moon receded slowly. MacKeeg's luminescence started to fade.

"MacKeeg!" shouted Mr Gupta.

"Aye laddie?" came the reply above the increasing noise.

"If you died in 1857, and you were 33, why do you look so old?"

"Cos ye'd never listen to anyone younger!" came the voice just audible over the storm.

Rushing, screaming wind. The beach had gone and the universe span wildly. Mr Gupta called out in his bodiless world "Kiran!" For an instant she was there, ephemeral and fleeting and beautiful and…gone.

Mr Gupta's eyes snapped open. The morning light had intensified colours in the room. He could remember every detail of his dream. He also felt refreshed. By rights, he thought, he should feel distraught, especially as he was beginning to consider the possibility that he was mad. Something in these visions, William MacKeeg perhaps, made him feel very different. Gone were the apprehensive emotions and strangling knot of grief. His anxieties were still there, but they had changed. Diminished, he thought. Could a tumour produce such reality? Was there a pre-ordained meaning to any of this? Or was everything in his life the product of a diseased mind, god-ridden, a product of gambling deities with the fate of mortals being their wagers? He had no answers, but he did have his feelings, and right now he felt surprisingly good. He felt sure new and beneficent truths were to be revealed. He thought his dreams were like his vivid imaginations as a child, though not absolutely. MacKeeg was too real. Mr Gupta smiled to himself.

"Only children have imaginary friends," he quipped aloud.

"Talking to yourself?" asked the sweet voice of Wamil. She had arrived in a waft of perfume.

"Oh … yes," said Mr Gupta, "I've had some quite vivid dreams. Realistic too."

"That's quite normal, Mr Gupta," she said, smiling.

Normal again, thought Mr Gupta.

"Now, I shall bring you some tea and toast soon. Mr Radhika is seeing you earlier than usual and asked me to make sure you are clean, dressed and ready to go. He's told me to make sure you maintain your dignity!"

"It's about time," said Mr Gupta, "I am ready to leave. I have never felt better!"

"That is good," said Wamil. "You are a strong man."

"It must be the moustache," he replied.

"I do not think so," said Wamil with a sudden intensity. "It is your cloak of gentleness that makes you strong. Strength and kindness in a man is rare. It is very sexy!"

With that she swept out leaving Mr Gupta red-faced and surprised at the forward way of modern women - and with a little glow of pride.

A while later Mr Gupta was fed, washed and dressed in his freshly laundered clothes. Dr Chowdary's waiting room seemed like ancient history to him now, though the vision of the tall, ragged man was still clear in his head, as was the much more solid form of William MacKeeg. He wondered about this. The thin man had looked normal for Delhi, but his transformation, if that was what it was, to a Victorian Scottish soldier was weird and beyond his reasoning. He rid his mind of incipient pondering and carefully checked his possessions, what there was of them: his clothes;

phone, keys and wallet; spectacles, though he seemed to be seeing better of late; and a ballpoint pen. Not much, he thought, but he had left his house with no intentions of a prolonged absence and was glad of a light burden. Wamil had even charged his phone; an ungentlemanly thought drifted through his mind as he remembered her teasing. He smiled, *must be the moustache,* he thought remembering Kiran's gentle ribbing. This was a good hospital, though he felt sure the level of service reflected the quality of his insurance. Eventually, he settled in a chair by the window and looked for the palm squirrels. Today they were not around, just a lone mynah pacing the lawn and a babbler looking brown and dowdy in the bushes. The monsoon was persistent this year.

"Bloody rain," he mumbled.

Barely a week had passed since the Shatabdi trip down to Bhopal and back. That was the day his perception of normality had been altered irretrievably. His job had kept him stable and he had clung to it tightly, the effort counterbalancing the emptiness of missing Kiran. He knew this was just procrastination, sooner or later he would have to get on with his life and that journey was the tipping point. He was mortal and getting older; he was ill; his equilibrium had gone. An echo of that day came to him...*it's a perfect balance...* it was something the bearded climber had said. Mr Gupta remembered him as a solid man, sun darkened skin and bleached hair, strong. Kiran said *He* had strength. Did he really? He had Rupa and knew this was where his priority must lie. His train of thought ended with Old Mr Singh's words echoing in his mind like a mantra, *it's already tomorrow.* This shift in his life had placed him in a constant tomorrow, so it seemed, and he was racing away from the past with some speed. Maybe William MacKeeg was his way of finding some sense in it all.

"Bloody hell," he said to the rain. Then he smiled at the thought of his beautiful Rupa. He had *today,* of that he was sure. Outside, as if by magic, two striped squirrels appeared on the lawn paralleling each other across the grass looking for food. They held their tails out behind, transparent, bushy filaments bejewelled with water. Every few paces they paused to shake the drops to the ground in spiral arcs of perfectly symmetrical synchronicity.

Yes, thought Mr Gupta, it had been a strange week. Seeing that glimpse of Kiran before he woke fixed the change in him. Indeed, Wamil had been right, he was strong in his way. His fears were for others, not himself. His life had not been one of great achievements. This was the issue. He was just one more human being amongst the billion or so in this diverse land. It had made him sad. He wanted to make a difference.

"I haven't done anything yet," he said to the squirrels.

He missed Kiran; he missed Rupa; and, rather oddly, he missed William MacKeeg. Before he had time to become glum the door burst open and Pia rushed in, said a quick, "Good morning," and made a rapid visual check of the room. If she saw anything amiss it was too late to do anything as close on her tail loomed Mr Radhika. Today, he wore light brown trousers with a large check design and matching waistcoat, pale green shirt and an emerald green, white spotted bowtie. His brogues were almost yellow. He was a visual shock to the system.

"Good morning, Mr Gupta!" boomed Mr Radhika. Outside both squirrels jumped simultaneously, froze momentarily and then bolted for the trees. In a single, fluid movement he had crossed the room and settled into the chair opposite, leaned forward, grasped his knees and looked Mr Gupta in the eye – a perfect owl.

Mr Gupta barely managed a startled, "Good morning," any longer reply being thwarted by the consultant's quick, sonorous switch to meaningful dialogue.

"Now, Mr Gupta," he began, staring fixedly through his glasses. "I have had a good look at the scans and, well, they are not what I had expected from what I could see in the initial x-rays. In short, things are not quite as simple as I had implied."

Mr Gupta's capricious emotions instantly fled to the realms of anxiety. He had made the 85% chance of survival his anchor, his fear deflector, his comfort; now the word *cancer* looked huge again, fatal and uncompromising.

"So, what you are saying is my chances of survival just took a dive?" he asked.

"It was my fault to quote a specific percentage," boomed Mr Radhika, "I was being a bounder to do that. Unprofessional! I misled your perception of things. Unpardonable! You see, Mr Gupta, each case is different, but the layman, that's you, requires a simple explanation. Your chances of survival have not reduced, don't you see?"

"Er, not really," said Mr Gupta perplexed. "Why?"

"Well, the same as a squirrel was a squirrel yesterday!" said Mr Radhika triumphantly. "If I called that squirrel out there in the tree 'Ganesh' yesterday, but today you told me it was 'Colin', all well and good, but it is still a squirrel!"

Mr Gupta gaped for a moment, even looking out at the nervous squirrel, then realisation dawned.

"I see," he said. "You mean my chances are the same because ultimately I am no worse off. It's the same tumour today as yesterday."

"That's the ticket!" roared Mr Radhika with obvious delight. "Absolutely! All we have to do is work out the best route to take for survival. The percentage will look after itself!"

"Alright," said Mr Gupta, a cold weight of dread in the pit of his stomach. "So, what has changed your diagnosis?"

"The diagnosis is the same," replied Mr Radhika. "The same oligodendroglioma, it is just that it goes deeper than was first obvious. It is very odd. It looks as if it is rooted in several parts of the cerebrum as well as the occipital lobe. It is still curable, still operable. It is just that the process will be longer, more delicate and will call for a solid disposition!"

"From me," said Mr Gupta.

"Yes, from you Mr Gupta."

"How long would I have if it was just left?" asked Mr Gupta.

"No prevarication!" stated Mr Radhika. "An educated guess from this bounder before you – six months and it will kill you stone dead!"

"Bloody hell," said Mr Gupta.

"But," interjected the consultant, "with treatment, if successful, it is as long as a piece of string!"

"Can I still go home today?" asked Mr Gupta.

"Yes! Why, yes!" replied Mr Radhika. "You will be an outpatient. My own outpatient. There will be tests and initial treatments and all sorts of paraphernalia to set up! But I want you back in a week, or before if things get obviously worse. So, there you are!"

"Bloody hell," repeated Mr Gupta.

The squirrels returned when Mr Radhika left, though they kept looking nervously at Mr Gupta's window.

Mr Gupta spent the rest of the morning having instructional sessions with Pia. He was given his list of dos and don'ts; some pills *to keep you calm*; some pills *to help you sleep*; and some pills *to bring down your blood pressure*. Finally, with his window-side table filled with forms, contact numbers and pills, including a freshly delivered batch *for the headaches*, he was left alone to wait for Jhatish in pensive mood. He had lost control of his life. Two years of moping and living with the baggage of the past had turned him into a dithering, doddery old fool. Just as he was gathering himself to make a leap into the future, it had come to this.

"I'm lost," he said to himself.

He smiled, even as a tear formed at the corner of his eye. His habit of talking to himself was amusing and probably another sign of age. It was his way of figuring things out, he thought. Just then he saw movement at the window. A striped squirrel had jumped onto the windowsill. Its black eyes, shiny beads of jet, gazed straight at him. Lifting itself onto its hind legs it stretched up the glass staring upwards as if looking for an opening. The fine white belly fur went all the way to the little down-turned mouth which was soft and pink. A pair of orange teeth gave it a buck-toothed look. Mr Gupta thought it looked like a slightly worried climber seeking a handhold. The squirrel sat back down, washed its face with its front paws, then spoke.

"Boo!" it said in a Scottish accent.

It jumped down and disappeared beneath the window sill. Mr Gupta raised his eyebrows and smiled. His inner unfettered emotional butterflies settled and the feeling of despair faded a little.

"MacKeeg?"

"Aye, laddie," said the soldier who was now sitting opposite, over the table. This time William MacKeeg looked different. He had lost the eerie glow and was now more solid, more defined – sepia-washed, like a faded daguerreotype picture. In trying to deal with his latest setback, Mr Gupta felt the appearance of MacKeeg was not unexpected, but the solidity of the man was. Could a mind do this?

"Och, thinking too much again," stated the Scotsman drawing on his short clay pipe. "Ye just have to accept the fact that I am here. I'm your irrational attempt at rationalising things!"

"Bloody hell!" said Mr Gupta. "Well, it does make me feel better having you around. Unless, of course, I have actually gone mad!"

"Rubbish!" barked MacKeeg. "It's the tumour. As I am you rationalising – and I'm not explaining that any fucking more – I'll set it out before ye. Ye are too gentle to face the facts, yet strong enough to cope with all that you have, so listen. The pressure on your occipital lobe formed the cloud thing. Your mind has shaped the cloud into me, laddie. I'm your memories. All the knowledge yev stored in your head – like one of those hard-drive things. I'm your thought activated search engine. Does that make sense?"

Mr Gupta could only accept everything MacKeeg said. He had read somewhere that no thoughts or memories or knowledge were ever lost to one's mind, so assumed he might well have found a way to access all his hidden data banks.

"Decoupled cognition," they said together.

"Och, we got there at the same time laddie! Yev read about decoupled cognition allowing us to believe in gods, and people believe in all sorts of spirits. But it's shite, man! The brain and thought are the same thing; the brain's an organ and thinking is what it does – too much in your case. But…"

"But what?" said Mr Gupta.

"But ye can project thoughts using your mind, so you can see me here like this, or as a squirrel, or a toad, and no one else can see me cos I'm just a thought. That's all. Mind you, if people see ye talking to y'self they may think you mad. Or a sadhu. Right now, y're thinking too much so let's get down to it. What do you want answers to?"

Mr Gupta was starting to like his invisible friend and the confidence he carried. A little echo of Kiran's insistence of him being a strong man? It had taken a potentially fatal growth to sharpen his senses which, he reasoned, smacked of…

"Irony!" continued MacKeeg. Then he laughed, "Old Fergus thought irony described something made of iron! And, laddie, yer mind is wandering again. I've been dead a long while and I'm too tired to wander. The more y'think, the more I know, but I'm impatient to start using it. Now, questions?"

"This is all very peculiar," mumbled Mr Gupta, "but I think I have a grip of this…"

"Jesus! Ye're tiring, but I can't kill ye as I'm already fucking dead!" chuckled MacKeeg coughing on his smoke.

"So, what do I do?" asked Mr Gupta finally.

"A pretty general question, so I'll set it oot afore ye," said MacKeeg in a noticeably stronger accent. "The chances are ye're fucked. Even if treatment is successful, the road is the same Gupta – ye have to tie up all the loose ends. Get young Rupa secured. Get yer legal stuff in order. Spend time with yer friends. Only then can ye relax a wee bit. Simple!"

Mr Gupta rarely looked directly at his problems. He tended to circuitously edge himself gently towards what he knew to be the obvious. He lived in hope that the problem may have gone before he arrived. As quick as he was to help others, either practically or with sound advice, he procrastinated with himself. The simple task of opening an envelope containing something official was at first put off, then ignored, then hidden under more unopened mail. Eventually, after waiting for a nice day when he felt brave, he would tackle his priority mountain of mail and clear it in one exhausting lump. Now here was MacKeeg, who was ostensibly himself, laying everything out in one go, and Mr Gupta knew he was right. Short, sharp and simple.

"Yes," he said," that is what I must do."

"It isn't going to be that simple," cautioned MacKeeg. He looked wiser now, avuncular, with his long, white hair and tobacco stained beard.

"The worst that can happen," said Mr Gupta, "is that I die. If Rupa is catered for, my job is done."

"You forget Ravi Uppal," said MacKeeg. "And you forget Vasupati Chopra."

Mr Gupta stared over his glasses at MacKeeg. "Ravi has been good to me and will help. Vaz is quiet and, although a bit of a strange one, has always been supportive. So what do you mean?"

"I...I don't know that yet," was the unexpectedly vague answer. "Just leave that thought in yer head and I'll figure it out. Watch everything and I'll have plenty to work with. It reminds me of a Sepoy we called Abu. We trusted him, but I knew he weren't right. At Lucknow he left one night and joined the rebels. First, he cut Sergeant Grieg's throat. Bastard. Uppal gives me the same feeling as Abu – he ain't right."

Mr Gupta felt he should argue, but, with a blink, William MacKeeg had gone, the discordant thought seemed to have cancelled him out.

Chapter 14

A New World

The Western Ghats stretch from the border of Gujarat and Maharashtra and spread a thousand miles through the states of Goa, Karnataka, Tamil Nadu and Kerala, ending at Kanyakumari near the southern tip of India. Rather than mountains, in the true sense of the word, they are really the edge of the Deccan Plateau, a vast, ancient area of stratified lava flows known as the Deccan Traps. It is a jagged edge where India broke away from Africa to drift north where it collided with Asia fifty million years ago, pushing up the great Himalayan range. The Western Ghats are now well weathered, with rich soil and lush forests, cascading rivers and, in spite of an encroaching population, plenty of untrodden ground. It has a vast and complex biodiversity and contains many nature reserves – and is home to perhaps five hundred tigers. The northernmost of these Sahyadri, holds a small population, but north of this they had not been seen for many years. The appearance of a huge beast near the small village of Palahmin, well south of Pune, high in the Ghats, started a legend that would be recounted for years. Its coinciding with a night of thunder and lightning, followed by a surreal misty morning, added to the facts like spice to food; myth grew as fast as the original event grew distant.

It was cool in the early morning mist outside Palahmin where Pelhi's family lived. Pelhi was a small, thin boy of average height for a rural eight-year-old, with the careworn look of an adult. Hard work was required to keep full stomachs, even for one so young. Yet the changes in India were gradually taking hold, even in so isolated a spot. His parents were enlightened and they sent him to school, knowing that a vein of educated people would be beneficial for all in their community, themselves in particular. Pelhi still had his chores to complete before walking more than four miles to the school, but with the energy of the young the only burden was time and not the effort.

At first light he set off on the long trail which wound up through the trees above his village, a small bag of books and his lunch over his shoulder. Bulbuls, thrushes and flycatchers tuned-up in the leafy canopy above him and somewhere in the gloom an owl *hoop-hoop-hooed* a final call to the retreating night. He could hear the occasional dog bark down in Palahmin, but it was distant, muted by the low cloud. At the top the swirling mist made him feel unusually edgy as he followed the winding trail across a grassy plateau interspersed with clumps of ragged scrub. Looming rocks took on the form of twisted demons to his young, impressive mind, so he hurried on. Ahead he could just make out the edge of the escarpment, marked by the tops the trees through which he would soon descend to the school at Muhn. He paused. If he was lucky he would meet some friends where their paths converged and chatter excitedly about the weekend's adventures. Pelhi's father had killed a cobra near the goat pen, a tale hard to eclipse. His nerves subsided. In the distance he thought he heard a rumble of thunder and to the east the rising sun showed as a milky blur through the moisture laden air.

"*Geerumph!*"

The sound he had mistaken for distant thunder came to his ears from just over the incline, where the trail dipped down to the trees.

"*Geerumph!*"

The hairs on Pelhi's neck stood on end. He froze, staring into the whiteness. Something was coming. The mist swirled. His toes wriggled in his old sandals and his hand tightened instinctively on the strap of the shoulder bag. He had never heard such a sound before. Pelhi was aware there was nowhere he might realistically hide. He was petrified. A breeze blew a thicker layer of mist across the track and he was enveloped in whiteness. This perceived isolation made him feel safer and he found the wisdom to sidle quietly to his right. He stopped at a large clump of grass and crouched behind it, knowing if he could reduce his outline in this open area he would be hard to spot.

"*Geerumph!*"

He gazed towards track where it disappeared over the slope. It was hard to make out, but he was sure there was definitely something there. Pelhi shook in his sandals and dared not breathe.

"*Geerumph!*"

The mist cleared and Pelhi's eyes popped from his head. It was a tiger! It was enormous and strode up the track to the place he had been standing minutes before. The enshrouding whiteness no longer felt safe. Pelhi had never seen such a beast. His grandfather had told frightening stories of long ago when India had tigers everywhere, but now they were the stuff of legend. To most youngsters they held a similar status to dragons. Tigers ate people, the boy knew that much, and he was small enough to make a single mouthful for this huge creature.

"*Geerumph! Geerumph!*"

Pelhi quaked. The tiger was now close enough for him to make out the stripes through the mist. It looked bigger than he imagined a tiger could be. Yet, something was not right. The tiger's tail drooped and the great head hung low beneath the rolling feline shoulders. It looked for all the world as if it was sad. Pelhi's bag suddenly slipped and made a soft thud as it struck the ground, spilling its contents. A new terror filled him and he could bear the tension no longer. The boy jumped up and raced into the mist squealing in fright, his feet barely touching the ground.

Angaar had walked ever higher away from the scene of his wilding. Instinct had taken over, driving him from the smell of humans: oil, tarmac, petrol and rubber. It was as if the cleaner air purged him of the years of incarceration and reignited dulled senses. Scents were sharp, clear and no longer masked by foetid stagnation. The dawn lightened the eastern sky

197

and a thick mist condensed in the thin air. He lapped fresh water from a stream. He had had a raging thirst and his mouth still tasted of the bad men. The mineral rich water cleansed his palate. New and fresh as things were, he still yearned for the company of his clever monkey companion. He called as he would for a lost mate.

"*Geerumph!*"

The deep sound carried, but no answer came. He was tired and as the climb levelled out he called again.

"*Geerumph! Geerumph!*"

A noise to his left changed his whole aspect. His head rose and he chuffed the air across his tongue, through his nasal cavity, over the Jacobson's organ – tasting, analysing. He grumbled hungrily as he smelled food. He hurried across the ground towards the sound of a scurrying creature, picking up the pace and eventually bounding – once – twice – and he was on it. In the distance the sound of parting vegetation and squealing filtered into his ears as he tore open a bag and ate Pelhi's spicy lunch.

Chapter 15

Gathering Storm

By the time Jhatish Das manoeuvred The Duck into the hospital car park Mr Gupta had dressed, gathered together his few belongings and made his way to the cool, marble-lined reception area. He had with him a bag of medication with a printed list of instructions along with his admittance appointment for his coming treatment. Pia had escorted him and had kept up a reassuring dialogue which he had appreciated, even though the false comfort of that 85% had long been disavowed. He sat watching people coming and going, trying to make sense of his last few chaotic days. He could not. All he knew was that his comfortable world of inertia had gone.

"Anil!" Jhatish's shout broke Mr Gupta's reverie. "Let's go – I'm double parked!"

The friends embraced and Jhatish steered Mr Gupta from the cool hospital, through the doors into the humid madness beyond. Mr Gupta's glasses steamed up and several drops of rain pattered onto his shirt.

"Bloody hell," he muttered.

The Duck was parked at an obscure angle blocking in the shining cars that belonged to various consultants, as noted on the *Reserved for...* signs in front of each bonnet. They pulled away just as a uniformed attendant had started to make a purposeful move towards the offending machine. The Duck popped out into the Delhi traffic eliciting a fusillade of multi-toned honks, as is the tradition in any Indian conurbation, *phooeeooping* back with gusto.

"This car is astounding," said Mr Gupta.

"It is a car, Anil," said Jhatish, "and it works, that is the main thing. Where to?"

"Rupa," answered Mr Gupta without pause. "I need to see her, now more than ever. I have nine days to sort out the muddles I have left so long. Nine days! Everything I will do is for her. Rupa is all I am and all I shall leave. Oh Jhatish, what is to become of me?"

This show of emotion took Jhatish by surprise. Glancing sideways at his dearest friend he struggled to find anything of value to say. The Duck wallowed and a series of angry beeps made Jhatish return his attention to the road. He punched the horn twice, the *phooeeoops* lost in the surrounding cacophony. What to say? Once he began to answer the words came well enough.

"Anil," he said. "You have nine days before you start your cure. Think of it like that. CURE. Not execution. C-U-R-E. In nine days you can sort out a lot, but plan your own future life too. That is what you have never done and are not doing now. If you have to plan for the worst-case scenario at least call it Plan B. Rupa needs you to be positive. Goodness me she doesn't even know about the tumour! If you go planning to die it will break her heart!"

Jhatish paused to hit the horn and shout abuse through the window before continuing.

"You have been ticking over since Kiran. So you cannot give up – you've not even *given down!* DO stuff now. Get up to speed. Lean on your friends. Get everything in order and only bloody give bloody up if you feel like it when you're where you blinking should be!"

Mr Gupta raised his eyebrows at the diatribe which had peaked in this rather confusing rant. After a brief silence Mr Gupta laughed.

"I hope you do not chide your students like that!" he chuckled. "They would think you had gone bonkers! I know what you say is true, it is just so bloody unfair, so crushingly hard. I will keep things as positive as I can, but my condition isn't as straightforward as Mr Radhika first said."

"Eh?" said Jhatish.

"This tumour. It is larger than he thought. It has deep roots I think he means. Whatever happens they have to open up my skull. That is scary. That is the bit I can never have control over. I cannot be sure I will wake up. That is the long and short of it."

"Oh dear," said Jhatish deflating at this new intelligence. "Look. I have some days off booked. I will help. The Singhs will help. Ravi will help. For once share the burden and then you have the best chance."

Mr Gupta patted Jhatish on the shoulder, "I will," he said. "I am not scared, just frustrated at my own laxity. Let's see how Rupa is, and then all will be clearer."

The Duck bounced along the city streets engulfed in motorised mayhem, bearing the two men to the quieter suburb where the Lord Beaufort Home broiled in the heavy air. As they drew to a halt Mr Gupta saw the honey-coloured face of his daughter watching and smiling. She gave a clumsy wave and blew bubbles as she mouthed "Daddy!"

Ravi Uppal shuffled in his seat beneath the impressively ornate veranda of his summerhouse. His property was extensive, the old house renovated in the traditional manner with large, high-ceilinged rooms set around a paved courtyard. The outer shell was a worn, but stylish, red brick – a colour reminiscent of Lutyens's choice Delhi colonial architecture. The summerhouse was isolated, some way from the main buildings along a natural stone path which meandered over lush lawns, between verdant hedges and skirted colourful flower borders. Suneeti had prepared a large pitcher of iced mango juice to keep him cool in the humid air. Vaz had just arrived and was walking purposely down the path. Ravi raised an eyebrow as Vaz had changed his usual appearance. He was still dressed in dark trousers and shoes, with a crisp, white shirt, but his hair was down and his usual aviator glasses had been changed for a pair with round, blue lenses. Ravi dismissed it as a quirk of fashion.

"Vaz," said Ravi shaking a proffered hand. "Come and sit down. Have a drink."

Vaz filled a glass and sat down.

"I'm guessing we have a problem," suggested Vaz, smiling.

"Yes. Yes, we do," said Ravi sipping his drink. "We may need a quick fix, but this time it is very close to home. That's why I invited you here. It is an unusual situation. And it may be beyond us."

"Even me?" asked Vaz.

"I hope not," replied Ravi. "In the last few days another Shastri related headache has arisen."

"Anil Gupta," said Vaz, confidently. "I already had an idea he was about to finally wake up and thrash around."

"You are spot on," replied Ravi, encouraged by his partner's perception. "It is my own fault. The sisters should have been an end to it, but I fear that Anil Gupta is about to withdraw funds and, even worse, to ask questions. He has become ill and seems to have had some kind of epiphany. We can live with it, I suppose, but it really is a lot of money. Then there is the possibility his wife said something to him. Any whiff of a scandal and my political career would be finished before it had even started. I think it is time to wipe the slate."

"Before next year's elections?" smiled Vaz.

"Before the campaign even starts!" snapped Ravi. "But it is too close to the Mahto affair. And in Delhi. Then again, I could sort out the paperwork as soon as I know what he wants, settle up with him and keep his business. I can do all that. But, Vaz, the money is tied up and doing well. And it would take money from our pockets. It is far more cost effective to remove the annoyance. The trouble is I am stuck. I'm not quite sure what I want you to do even."

"Ravi, you worry too much," said Vaz. "All the removals I have managed have been well spread and old news. So much happens every day!

Mahto's death was replaced in the news within a day by the big train crash near Hyderabad, and that shifted even quicker when we lost the last test against England. What we have created is invisible, Ravi. We always take care – always. Let's start from the beginning with a simple question. What is best for us, Gupta's continuing presence or his removal?"

"If he is removed we consolidate enough resources to enhance our lifestyles and fund my way into parliament," said Ravi. "The only problem is he is very close to us. If this was handled clumsily even Delhi's police may figure out the Cobra connection – and *we* are Cobra."

"Hmmm," said Vaz. "So, it will be an accident? A criminal act?"

"I have no clue," said Ravi, sighing. "That is the difference this time, I have no plan and it has to be quick. Too quick. I will have to rely on your judgement completely. If you say it's too risky, we'll leave Gupta in peace. But…"

Vaz laughed.

"You can rely on me. Anything is possible. Gupta will go. The next question is, what about the girl?"

Ravi felt uneasy. This was the issue his musings along the Rajpath had failed to sort out in his mind. He just did not feel safe ordering a child's execution.

"If Anil Gupta is removed I become Rupa's guardian. It would be a legal tie and impossible to remedy. She would be useful in my campaigns, but then we could never safely remove her. You see, Vaz, it is now or never for the whole shooting match."

"Her too then," said Vaz.

Ravi nodded, unable to say the words.

"But," he managed, "it needs to be totally plausible. See what you can come up with, but be fast. Anil Gupta is coming to see me soon, so I will have a better idea what he is after."

"How ill is he?" asked Vaz.

"I'm not sure yet," said Ravi, "that's what I need to know. Anyway, enough for now. Let's go in and eat."

The two men sauntered through the garden towards the house where Suneeti and the housekeeper had laid out a light lunch.

Mr Gupta hugged his little girl. The embrace was genuine and primal. Both had tears in their eyes.

"Oh Daddy," said Rupa. "I have missed you so much. Uncle Jhatish said you had been in hospital, but never explained. How are you, Daddy? How are you?"

Mr Gupta wiped his cheeks and then his daughter's face.

"Always bubbles!" she giggled.

He sat beside her and Jhatish did likewise, all three looking out the window.

"I had a bit of a…collapse," he said holding Rupa's hand and squeezing it reassuringly, "in Dr Chowdary's surgery too. All rather embarrassing."

"Yes, and you were asleep for three days!" said Rupa. "That seems more than a bit of a collapse."

"Well, yes, I suppose you are right," said Mr Gupta. "But, look, I seem to have recovered, don't I?"

"So, what *aren't* you telling me, Daddy?" she asked.

Mr Gupta was not at all good at telling untruths. He had always been honest with Rupa and she knew him too well for subterfuge. If his life was in danger he felt he had to tell her all. At this point Rupa's assistant, Sarasa, came in with a tray of liquid refreshments, setting it down on a nearby table.

"Here you are," Sarasa said, smiling at them, "all fresh and icy cold."

She swept out. Mr Gupta was glad of this brief respite. They sipped their drinks quietly, Rupa by means of a colourful blue and white striped straw. She then turned to her father.

"You have to tell me, Daddy," she insisted. "We said 'No secrets' when Mummy died. 'No secrets!'"

Mr Gupta was stunned by Rupa's simple statement about her mother's death. His daughter had never used terms like *passed away, reincarnation, heaven* or any other such hopeful language. Her mother was dead and that was it. Her love survived, and that was enough. This always disarmed him – her strength was gentle, but irresistible.

"I think your father will be forthright with you," said Jhatish. "It is our way. Isn't that so, Anil?"

"Yes, it is," said Mr Gupta.

So, he told his daughter about his headaches and the recent rail journey down to Bhopal and back; about the terrible accident he saw and how his nose had begun running; and about the white cloud. He told of his collapse in Dr Chowdary's waiting room and his meeting with Mr Radhika, but had to pause for a drink. His throat had dried up.

"Dear, dear Daddy," said Rupa. "I wish I could help you more. I wish I could."

"I know, I know," he said patting her hand. "Your smile gives me plenty of strength to keep my chin up."

"You have more big things to tell," said Rupa sternly. "Let me know everything…bubbles, wipe!"

Jhatish smiled and wiped the drooling girl's face. She grinned back.

"All of it?" said Mr Gupta in a daze.

"All of it," she replied.

"Well…it seems I have a tumour. In my head. It is causing these headaches and…and vision problems. It is serious, but survivable."

He sighed and realised a sentence simply spoken really was the easiest way. Rupa was the master of that.

"Anyway, that is why I have to return to hospital in a week or so. Treatment has to start and I have to be operated upon. It will mean a long recovery period so I have to get all my affairs in order…just in case."

"'Just in case,'" paraphrased Rupa, her resolve collapsing. "Now I'm

205

scared of losing you, Daddy! Oh, Daddy. How does it feel?"

"Oddly enough I've not had a headache since my collapse," he said. "And I feel remarkably well which makes the need for treatment seem silly. I think MacKee…"

Mr Gupta paused and sat up straight, consternation written across his face. He had let his mind wander and nearly stepped into the Scot's world.

"All of it," repeated Rupa. "There is something big missing."

"I…I cannot," said Mr Gupta swallowing hard. "It is all too strange."

"All of it."

Suddenly it was easy. "I have started to have regular talks with a Scottish soldier called William MacKeeg. And he's dead."

Both Rupa and Jhatish gawped at him.

"Who?" asked Rupa.

"He came with the tumour," he replied. "An illusion, I suppose. I guess you could call him a symptom, a figment, but he seems real to me. If this means I am bonkers, then I am, but I feel alright."

After a little thought and with a smile Rupa asked, "Is he nice?"

"Yes, very nice," he said, smiling back.

"Then that is alright," she said. And she laughed. And Jhatish laughed. Then Mr Gupta laughed. How, he thought, could so much bad news be turned into laughter?

Mr Gupta was tired. He had spent a long time with Rupa arranging for her to come home for a long weekend – their last before his treatment. The house was familiar to her, so coping would be easy enough. Her room was on the ground floor and had been set up especially for her independent use. Kiran had been insistent upon that. And then there was Jhatish and Mrs Singh who had already offered help. Those few days with his daughter would give him the strength to persevere, whatever the outcome. Rupa managed to turn everything around her into sunshine and laughter, so Mr Gupta was happy. But, he was tired.

Jhatish had driven him home in The Duck by way of the Singhs', which became a house of tears, hugs and smiles. They were inconsolable with the news of his coming treatment and offered to do as much as necessary to make things easier, insisting on providing breakfast the next day. Then his friend had seen him into his house, carrying an array of provisions bestowed upon him by a robust Mrs Singh, *enough to feed a bloody army*, he had mumbled. Then Jhatish had left, his progress in his car tracked by increasingly distant car horns and the occasional bellicose backfire. Mr Gupta had stayed by his gate staring into the busy, leafy streets, then turned to walk through his flowery garden. He felt like a stranger, the scents of gardenias and hibiscus evoking memories of that which he once was a part. The house looked as it always did, but it had lost its family redolence. It held past memories, not future dreams.

"Thank you, Jhatish," he had said as his friend left.

"I'll see you tomorrow," Jhatish had shouted from the car window as it waddled into traffic.

It's already tomorrow. Old Mr Singh's phrase had become a permanent echo. Yet, he knew his future was concentrated into a timeline just eight days long. Beyond that, tomorrow was an unknown land. Since Kiran had died he had come to rely on the future, the promise of time without obvious end, time enough to get his life in order. For now *today* and *tomorrow* had become arbitrary words he could not define. A bit like trying to explain *normal*, he thought.

He made tea and sat in his chair in the lamplight. He decided to end his day's proactively by phoning Ravi Uppal. He was surprised when Ravi answered immediately.

"Hello, Anil," said the smooth voice.

"Are you a psychic now?" asked Mr Gupta.

Ravi laughed – a comforting sound that gave Mr Gupta ease.

"No. Not at all, Anil. This is a very modern country now. Your name pops up on my phone's screen! I have also been thinking a lot about you since Jhatish visited. Tell me, how are you, Anil? What have you been doing to yourself?"

"Dear Ravi, it is good to hear your voice," said Mr Gupta, genuinely pleased. "I have just returned home and thought I'd call you on the off-chance you'd be in. I need to talk to you very soon."

"Jhatish Das told me all about it," said Ravi. "You must not worry, your estate's in good order. I have your files all ready. I can talk you through the figures anytime. First of all, what on Earth has been wrong?"

"You would not believe my luck, Ravi," said Mr Gupta, for once feeling a little sorry for himself. "I have been diagnosed with a tumour..."

"What?" interrupted Ravi's shocked voice. "You mean cancer?"

"Yes," said Mr Gupta, words catching in his throat, "and it is in my brain. It is operable, but the problem I have is making sure my affairs are in order...in case anything happens...you know?"

"All your affairs *are* in order, Anil, and you must not worry." Ravi deliberately chose positive phrases. He had a sharp mind and he knew Anil Gupta well. His avuncular way allowed him to steer the vulnerable and nervous to his way of thinking, by application of overt positivity, or flannel, some might say.

"Thank you, Ravi," said Mr Gupta. "I really do need your help...advice, really. After all you know more about my finances than I do, much to my shame. I have left you with a duty you should not have shouldered. I have to make sure Rupa is well catered for, should I...should the treatment fail. It is time I recognised my responsibilities."

"Anil, enough of that. I can see you before the weekend. How does tomorrow sound?" Ravi had taken control.

"Why...well, yes," said Mr Gupta. "That's Thursday? Yes. Rupa's due Friday. For a weekend. So tomorrow is perfect."

"Right, I'll have a car at your house by eleven," said Ravi with finality. "We can have a light lunch."

Mr Gupta agreed and they ended the call. He had done it. That last big step. Getting his house in order was not as hard as he had imagined. He smiled at his own rather inflated view of his modest achievement. This was the jolt he had required.

"A fire under your fucking arse is what you needed," said William MacKeeg.

Mr Gupta jumped. He felt ridiculous being startled by his own mind, then realised he had missed his imaginary friend regardless.

"*Friend* is it now?" MacKeeg chuckled. "A Sergeant Fitch called me that once, then ran off with my doxy!"

MacKeeg was sitting in the chair opposite. He looked more solid than before – he had a shadow. He was still a sepia tinted grey, but there were flecks of colour in his uniform.

"And why not have a shadow?" asked MacKeeg.

"I thought you had gone," said Mr Gupta, "now here you are reading my mind..."

"I am your mind, ye dopey 'apeth!" laughed the Scot.

"I was not thinking about you, so why are you here?"

"Resonance," said MacKeeg cryptically. "Something lurking in the back of yer mind is twanging like a whore's knickers."

"And what would that be?" asked Mr Gupta. He had starting to gain comfort in this unexpected friendship. The less he resisted, the more real MacKeeg was becoming. Was it madness? Could he become dangerously unhinged?

"Mental illness is many things," offered MacKeeg, "but mad, bad men know they are insane! They just prefer doing barbarous things than seeking help. Suffering has a fascination, but most of us are unwilling voyeurs. Ye looked at that mangled farmer on the railway. Everyone did. Yet we're not all of us cruel. It is those mad bastards who take the step, to create suffering in order to watch and enjoy it, as makes the difference. Ye will never be dangerous."

"Of course, you are right," said Mr Gupta. MacKeeg had become the visible manifestation of his altered mind with which he was able to converse, however odd that seemed. He was aware that he now had a source of finding and rationalising information hidden in his memory. MacKeeg allowed him to perceive and qualify those memories.

"So, what is my new perception, one William MacKeeg, able to tell me?"

"Watch out for Ravi Uppal," said MacKeeg without hesitation. "Something is not right with him. Not right at all."

"But he has been so very good to my family," said Mr Gupta.

"You are looking at the wrapping of his words! Think! Think, laddie!" demanded MacKeeg.

Mr Gupta did so and the divided Gupta mind became whole and a moment of brilliant clarity was gained.

"I have it!" yelled MacKeeg. "Money! Shastri money. Charity! And so much death. Two dead! …But it's gone. You shut your mind, laddie."

"You scared me," said Mr Gupta, throat dry. "Did you mean…the two…did you mean Kiran and Tamina?"

"Aye, I did," said MacKeeg, looking confused and tired, "…but it was too much. I've lost the thread…"

William MacKeeg was no longer there. Mr Gupta fell into an exhausted sleep in the chair until discomfort woke him, whereupon he drifted in semi-dreams to his bed.

Vasupati Chopra was sitting quietly in his study as the phone rang.

He was surrounded by a collection of antique ornaments which gave the room a redolence of age. His house was out of the city, not far from Ravi Uppal's, a renovated colonial bungalow with wide verandas. He loved the high, cool rooms and wide spaces. Hemlata, his wife, had loved it at first sight and together they had made it a family home to reflect their wealth and status, something she cherished. Vaz was the perfect husband – she wanted for nothing and he was a devoted father. She liked Ravi Uppal and his wife, Suneeti. They had become an extended family. Vasupati Chopra was fiercely loyal to Ravi Uppal and embraced the life style that Cobra provided. He was supremely confident in their partnership, their dealings and their ability not to fail. He also understood Ravi's overwhelming desire to enter the political arena in order to own the space people existed in. Power over the masses was Ravi's aphrodisiac. Vaz was happy to help deliver this for his partner. However, Vaz was a very different being. He desired power over individuals, the power to grant life or death, and needed to witness it first-hand. He was a psychopath. He still had room for family and lived the part, but what Hemlata did not realise was if she wanted to leave, she would never be allowed to.

The phone continued to ring.

His study was out of bounds. He cleaned and tidied it himself, and rarely invited people in, Ravi being the sole exception. Vaz looked around at the patina on the dark wooden shelves and carvings; at the hand-painted figures of Shiva and Kāla he had had made by a specialist idol maker, Gangesh, in Shimla. Gangesh's family had been idol makers for generations and had moved to the higher hills to be closer to the gods. He was famed for ensuring his figures held the power of the god they represented. Vaz knew this was so as Kāla rested there when he did not need his human vessel. The study was a temple.

He picked up the phone.

"Vaz," he said.

"It's Ravi."

"I have done some homework and can set the job up very quickly," said Vaz. "It will be sub-contracted to a preferred source."

"And it will remain…separate?" asked Ravi.

"The Mechanic is good. Cobra is separate – I guarantee it," said Vaz.

"First of all, I need you to pick up Gupta at 11:00 tomorrow. Can you do that and bring him here?" Ravi did not want to rush things unnecessarily. "It could be that he is very ill indeed, and that may rid us of all our problems without any effort. Let's see what he has to say, then we'll take it from there. Does that work for you?"

"Yes."

"Good," said Ravi. "Just remember, if he wants his money immediately, we will need to remove him quickly."

"Everything is in hand," said Vaz.

"One more thing," said Ravi. "There is an outside chance the sisters had a copy of some sensitive material. It could be in the house – can we ensure nothing remains?"

"Anything I should be aware of?" asked Vaz.

"Tamina once did the F.A. accounts. The adjusting – if you understand? I destroyed a disc, but there could be a copy at her sister's house. His house. The issue is pretty dead, but I want nothing left. Nothing at all."

"It will be so," said Vaz.

The call ended. Neither man needed an extended conversation in these circumstances.

Mr Gupta was sitting on the same rock on the same beach in his otherworld. He had resigned himself to the fact that sleep had become be a series of adventures in tangible dreams.

"Ye're a ninny," said MacKeeg.

"And why is that?" asked Mr Gupta.

"Because y'are pulling the tiger's tail," said MacKeeg.

"Surely it is not beyond the realms of possibility," said Mr Gupta, "to have a conversation with myself without the need to be mysterious. What tiger and what tail?"

"Ravi fucking Uppal," said MacKeeg, loading his short pipe. "He is the tiger. Time is accelerating, or getting shorter, one of the two, whilst ye be circling a dangerous flame thinking it's warmth and safety."

"I have no idea what you are talking about. And you are mixing metaphors," said Mr Gupta.

"Whataphores?" said MacKeeg.

"Ravi has never done my family any harm and tomorrow I shall sort out my affairs. Rupa will be secure and, if I am lucky, I'll survive the next few months and make up for lost time." Mr Gupta knew he sounded weak and hopeful. Also, something niggled. MacKeeg niggled.

"Ye're a ninny."

"It is pointless repeating yourself," said Mr Gupta. "You have yet to tell me why."

"Ye're like a young soldier at his first battle," said MacKeeg. Then feigning a timid voice, "*It'll be alright MacKeeg, won't it? Won't it, won't it?* Well it fucking won't. Think, man, think hard. It's to do with Tamina. And Kiran. Think and it will help me."

Mr Gupta struggled with this rationalising. He found it difficult to conceive that he did not know what he knew. MacKeeg stared at him from beneath bushy, white eyebrows. Mr Gupta thought hard, focussing on memories. Roaring wind filled his mind and the world about him whirled. Colours flashed, a smashed rainbow lifted into the maelstrom of his altered mind. The sound grew in volume and cadence, faster and faster and faster...

Crack!

He floated in space looking down at the blue world. The cosmos stretched away in the spangled velvet of space and time – beautiful and terrifyingly enormous. And Mr Gupta thought as comets drifted past and meteors flashed bright on the atmosphere below.

"What have you got there, Kiran?" asked Mr Gupta.

"A computer disc my darling," said Kiran.

She looked lovely and he felt proud to be with such an intelligent, vibrant and beautiful woman. He felt confident in their solid bond. He knew she loved him.

"Do I know what that is?" he asked. "You know I struggle with this I.T. malarkey."

He felt happy. It was as if Kiran was here and real, at least as much as MacKeeg was.

"I explained before," said Kiran patiently. "It is to do with my new charity role with Ravi. I'm meeting him later. It made sense to carry on Tamina's work, so I agreed to take on the position."

"I remember," said Mr Gupta smiling. "'The chance to put something back,' you said."

"Yes, my darling," said Kiran. "I just have to see Ravi about an anomaly. So, I did see him…"

"…and events overtook intentions," said MacKeeg.

Kiran had gone. Her conversation had been disjointed, but he thought it may be his own mind mixing past and present events as much as badly conjugating verbs. Mr Gupta felt a pang of loss.

"Back up!" said MacKeeg. They were together on the beach once more. MacKeeg took a long draw on his pipe.

"What?" said Mr Gupta now confused about location, verbal forms, which dream he was in, and the non-existent, but persistent characters he was in conversation with.

"Back up. Kiran always used her laptop thing," said MacKeeg. "She was good at it. Not like you. Look at those bloody sheets on the train…"

"Bloody annoying…"

"…Aye, but Kiran knew her way around spread sheets and things. She said to you twice…"

"I always back important things up, Anil," said Kiran from where she stood on the sand. "I popped the disc contents onto the memory stick you bought for me in Bhopal."

"I…I," Mr Gupta was thinking in three minds which was hard to

214

qualify, even if the quantity was sound. "I…remember. Kiran, you told me that, but it seemed so unimportant that I hardly listened. That memory stick was blue with 4GB on it. I still have no clue what that means."

"And I had to see Ravi," said Kiran. "You and I made love that night darling man, and…"

"…Kiran was killed a short while later," said MacKeeg, Kiran had winked out of existence.

"…*was killed*," echoed Mr Gupta. "*Was killed* as in accident? Surely it was an accident?!"

"Watch Ravi Uppal," warned MacKeeg drawing on his pipe. "I'll do the thinking for ye now. The disc belonged to Tamina. Tamina got it to Kiran somehow. Ye gave the disc to Ravi. So what is the link?"

"Fallen Angels," said Mr Gupta.

"And Ravi fucking Uppal!" said MacKeeg triumphantly. "I knew I'd get it! We're a good team, even if we are the same. Add young Kiran, and the papists would call us a trinity!"

"Was it an accident?" asked Mr Gupta.

Mr Gupta opened his eyes. He was in his bed. His adventurous dreams were clear in his memory, but he must have slept as he felt refreshed. He stumbled out of bed and shuffled into the spare room which Kiran had used as an office. There was a small guest bed, often used by Jhatish, and a desk. Next to this was a free-standing cupboard which he had seldom opened, but now he looked inside and immediately found a bag. Once unzipped it revealed an old laptop, which he presumed to be well out of date by now; he would not know how to start it let alone use it. However, he was looking for something else, something he knew, at least by sight. He found it in one of the pockets: small and blue with 4GB etched on the side. The only changes were a lanyard advertising Indian Railways (borrowed by him) and a small sticker with 'F.A.' printed on it. He had been so pleased she had liked it and had agreed that the man in the shop was right in saying it was a handy thing to have. He replaced the laptop and went down stairs placing the memory stick on the coffee table.

"Back up," he mumbled.

Mr Gupta did not go back to bed. He showered and changed and strolled to the Singhs' house, where he was greeted like a long-lost son.

"I cannot stay for too long, Taraa," he said, "I have some rather urgent business matters to sort out before…"

"A good breakfast is what you need," said Mrs Singh, dragging him into her house and coaxing him into a chair near her husband.

"Good morning, Mr Gupta," said Old Mr Singh.

"Good morning, Mr Singh," replied Mr Gupta.

"She will feed you to death and beyond," said Old Mr Singh sipping some tea.

"I have enough food for an army at home already," replied Mr Gupta.

Before long Jhatish arrived and breakfast was set out before them: fruit and tea, fresh cakes and rolls, eggs and cheese with spicy chutney. They talked about Rupa, the weather and cricket. The obvious subject for conversation was being avoided.

"There is an elephant in the room," said Mr Gupta, "as the British would say."

"A what?" asked Old Mr Singh.

"An elephant," said Jhatish.

"There are no animals in my house," stated Mrs Singh firmly, "and certainly no elephants! I think I may have noticed one of those!"

The men laughed, even though Old Mr Singh was slightly perplexed.

"It is an expression," said Mr Gupta. "It suggests everyone can see what needs to be discussed, but no one will. Let me try to make it easier and get it out the way. I have a tumour in my head and it may prove fatal. The mad thing is, I have never felt better, but it is there and that is what I must deal with."

Mrs Singh sobbed. "It is just that we do not know what to say or do," she said wiping her eyes with a handkerchief.

"Taraa is right, you know," said Old Mr Singh. "All we can do is what we always have – be there and help where we can. Yet it seems to be insufficient."

"Oh Anil," said Mrs Singh. "You have had so much to put up with. It is not fair at all!"

Mr Gupta smiled at his friends.

"You are my closest friends," he said. "You have watched me blunder on, taking my time to get over Kiran's death, but I have never really got my act together. My life hit a wall in Dr Chowdary's surgery, and it has changed forever. I had taken time for granted, now I find out it may not be there. I do not feel frightened, but have got a lot of things to sort out – loose ends and such – and that is what I will do. The only way I can face my illness is to make sure Rupa is catered for and my friends have only my health to worry them – not my estate. That is why I'm seeing Ravi later on. He has power of attorney over everything at the moment, and that is not fair on him, and not fair on Rupa. Ravi has done more than enough. Jhatish, I want you to take over that role and the Singhs can be executors. Ravi will remain as an advisor, but he has done so much with no talk of a fee, so he should be paid an agreed sum for any further help. Are you happy to do that for me?"

They all agreed. Jhatish reassured the Singhs that it was not a complicated matter, but an honour and something they could accomplish without stress.

"I do not *intend* to die," said Mr Gupta, "but there are only two variables in this whole matter: I survive, or I don't. You are allowing me to concentrate on living."

"It is not fair," said Old Mr Singh, "but here we are and *fair* means nothing. We will do all we can."

Breakfast came to an end and tea drinking took over. Conversation was less constrained now and kind words flowed from all directions. Finally, Mr Gupta broached a subject which relied on the tacit input of his MacKeeg mind.

"There is one more thing," he said, immediately getting their attention. "I may need you to look after Rupa sooner than I planned. She may need to get away for a little while. If so I will make sure you have instructions. It sounds odd, but can I rely on you?"

"Without question!" said Old Mr Singh, before his wife could agree for them. "You can trust us to do anything."

And that was all Mr Gupta needed to hear.

"What was that last bit about?" asked Jhatish as he drove Mr Gupta home. "The bit about Rupa?"

"I am not totally sure myself," confessed Mr Gupta, "but you have to be aware that a few strange things might happen. If I ask you to do something a little out of the ordinary I need you not to ask questions and just do it. Is that clear?"

Jhatish raised his eyebrows at such a show of directness from his usually capricious friend. His voice had an edge. Had it been an accent? A swift manoeuvre through a particularly tight gap in the traffic snapped him back to the here and now.

"Phooeeoop!" went The Duck's horn.

"Bastard!" yelled Jhatish.

"Bloody hell!" said Mr Gupta.

Eventually, The Duck bounced to a stop by Mr Gupta's house and the men went in. Mr Gupta made some chai. They settled in the lounge.

"I need to give you this," said Mr Gupta handing over the blue memory stick. "I am leaving for Ravi's in half-an-hour or so, but you have to take this and check it out. I want you to copy it and send it to Sudhesh Shastri. It has some information on Ravi's charity, Fallen Angels, and it may hold the key to some unanswered questions. You must tell no one else about this. If something happens to me tell Sudhesh to follow where it leads. If not, tell him to let me know what he thinks. In fact, see what you can figure out – it's all beyond me, but I know it is important."

"Is that what you meant in the car?" asked Jhatish.

"Not entirely," said Mr Gupta, "but, for now this is enough. Come on, Jhatish, I have to go and I don't want Ravi knowing you were here this morning. It's not a major issue, but…"

"Is this memory stick anything to do with Kiran?" asked Jhatish as he got into The Duck.

"Kiran. Tamina too, perhaps," said Mr Gupta. "They both worked for Fallen Angels."

With that Jhatish said his goodbyes and steered his noble carriage into the traffic. Mr Gupta walked back into the house.

"Was that wise, laddie?" asked MacKeeg.

"Back up," said Mr Gupta. "It is all I could think of doing. Let's face it I am running out of guaranteed time."

"It's already tomorrow," said MacKeeg just before not being there.

Chapter 16

The Mechanic

Mr Gupta had a persistent knot in his stomach. Yesterday, he thought nothing of seeing his brother-in-law. Now, MacKeeg had sowed a seed of doubt in suggesting Ravi Uppal's possible link to all his woes. That it could be true felt so unlikely his nerves seemed misplaced.

"It is just paranoia," he said as he sat, knowing MacKeeg would not be far away.

"Aye," said MacKeeg from the opposite chair. "Seeds of doubt I have sown. Into what shall they grow? Och, I cannot tell. But I know one thing – something is due to happen."

"How do you know?" asked Mr Gupta.

"Soldier sense!" said MacKeeg confidently, scratching a bare knee. "I've had it many times. Y'can wait with yer company for days – polishing buttons, cleaning rifles, honing bayonets – just waiting for the enemy. Ye all carry on as normal: then everybody feels it! It isn't just silence, nothing like that, but similar to that moment before a thunderstorm. Och, I don't know, maybe it's electricity, or energy – one of those modern, invisible things – but all the boys know what's coming. That soldier sense is never wrong. That is what I have now."

"Perhaps you are wrong," said Mr Gupta. "All I know is that I am possibly going to die in the next few months and the only thing upsetting me is my belated attempt to put my house in order. I can harm no one and I have nothing anyone would want. Rupa can harm no one and she will be my only lasting legacy in this world."

"But ye have that knot in the pit of your guts," said MacKeeg. "Mark it well. Never mind, I'll be with ye all the time so I reckon we can get through it. Now, laddie, just one more thing."

"And what would that be?" said Mr Gupta.

"There may come a time soon when y'are too scared to think," replied MacKeeg, leaning forward. "Panic is setting in at such a moment. That is the time ye listen to me and let me take over. Do not resist, just leave me to it. I will flush the real Uppal out. Sometimes a soldier has to do his job. Do y'understand?"

Mr Gupta nodded, blinked and MacKeeg was not there. This time the Scot's words were darkly prescient and did nothing to assuage the trepidation he had felt since waking. A rapping on the door made him start. He looked at his watch and saw it to be eleven o'clock. It had to be his lift to Ravi's house. He opened the door.

"Hello, Anil," said Vasupati Chopra extending a hand. "I have come to take you to Ravi's place. Good to see you again."

The handshake was firm, with a granite-like solidity. Vaz looked all the world like an animated basalt statue. His hand had been cool, even in the heat. Raven black hair and dark suit added to the impression. His skin was smooth and flawless, and seemed to absorb light. Mr Gupta saw his reflection in the blue-lensed sunglasses. He shuddered. It was like being appraised by a predator.

"Good to see you, Vaz," he said. "It has been a long time."

Mr Gupta grabbed a jacket, closed and locked his door, then followed Vaz to the brooding black Audi ticking over in the street. It was cool inside. Once in the driving seat Vaz seemed to become a part of the machine.

"Malevolent," said MacKeeg inside Mr Gupta's head.

"Sorry?" said Vaz.

"Oh," said Mr Gupta, realising he has mumbled the word in tandem with his familiar, "I said 'Marvellous.' I have never been in such a car."

Vaz stared at Mr Gupta through round lenses. He was blue-tinged, small and vulnerable. Kāla stirred, but it was not yet time.

"Yes, it is a beauty," said Vaz, "but it is a waste on these bloody roads. Let's go."

Vaz manoeuvred the machine smoothly through Delhi, never getting flustered, never hitting the horn and not once showing annoyance. As cool as the car, thought Mr Gupta. The air conditioning kept the interior at a constant, dry 16 C, according to the digital indicator – he was glad he had his jacket.

"Do you mind if I play some music?" asked Vaz.

"Not at all," said Mr Gupta. He expected something Bollywoody perhaps, but what he heard was new to him.

Step onto the heavenly plane, bathe in the Dark waters of Hammistagan...

A deep, intoning voice filled the car. To Mr Gupta the singer sounded entranced. The haunting music behind the voice spiralled in his ears. He guessed it to be a mystic work, but it was so unfamiliar that he felt compelled to ask who it was. Vaz pre-empted him.

"It is Zahan," he said, eyes fixed on the road. "A mystic poet. A prophet who is now 105 years old. The music belongs to Fossa. Zahan wrote a great work called *Chaos Birthing*. This is the twenty-fifth and final verse, *Time's End, World Beginnings*. When Zahan found Galen Fossa, he found the perfect composer to lift his words to a higher plane."

Even though Mr Gupta had known Vasupati Chopra since Cobra's inception, this was the most he could remember the man saying in his presence. Further conversation was displaced by the music. By the time the car turned into the drive leading to Ravi Uppal's haveli, Mr Gupta had started to appreciate the dark, lyrical poetry. As the car stopped the final words were playing: *As all life ends, the seeds remain, as all life ends, the seeds remain, as all life ends, the seeds remain...* These words increased his anxiety. They carried a prescience that made him feel sick to the stomach. Kiran and Tamina: were their deaths contrived? If so it changed everything. He was in the dragon's den. He stepped from the car and looked at the haveli. Magnificent as it was in the bright sunshine his thoughts had given it had an air of menace. It seemed huge and brooding. Was Ravi a friend? A killer? Catching his reflection in a window Mr Gupta saw a small, old, balding man. He felt hopelessly insignificant as he stepped through the main door into the ornate hallway.

"Anil!" Ravi's voice drew an unexpected smile. "My dear chap."

Ravi was descending a wide staircase, arms wide in greeting. He shook Mr Gupta's hand. A chill ran up Mr Gupta's spine. His senses were sensitive to everything. The hallway was a trap and he the prey. Paranoia? His heart raced and the clarity with which he now perceived things prompted a rush of fear and a surprising rage. All this during a brief handshake. An irresistible urge to flee filled him. Then a soft voice whispered in his ear.

"Do not panic, laddie," said MacKeeg. "Now is the time to be the same actor ye are when dealing with those bastards on the train. Ye're safe for the now. Trust me."

If Ravi had noticed anything amiss he gave no indication of such. He led Mr Gupta into an extravagantly furnished lounge and steered him to a soft chair. Ravi sat opposite.

"I have some things to do," said Vaz. "I'll see you later."

When Vaz left, the room seemed lighter. Ravi's smile was disarming and Mr Gupta felt a little less paranoid. He had certainly changed since his collapse. His newly enhanced senses, his MacKeeg mind, took some getting used to. Even though he wanted to see the best in everybody, he now felt increasing doubt and mistrust.

"Hold fast," whispered MacKeeg, and Mr Gupta finally felt able to cope.

The lounge seemed as big as Mr Gupta's house. Carvings, gilt framed

224

mirrors and original paintings; ornate lamps; metal idols depicting the pantheistic nature of Hinduism; deep carpets and old, solid wooden furniture with a patina of use, reflecting age and permanence. Such opulence made a statement of power. It made Mr Gupta's unravelled life seem even more insignificant. If MacKeeg was even partly correct, how could he pit himself against the power that surely hid behind this façade?

"Steady," whispered MacKeeg.

"Pardon?" asked Ravi.

Again, his other-self had intruded into reality. He would have to take greater care in the future.

"I said I feel unsteady at the moment," said Mr Gupta. "I have the tendency to mumble of late."

"It is hardly surprising," said Ravi, "after all you have had a lot to endure. Now, just relax and tell me how I can help my brother-in-law."

Ravi leaned forward and poured out two glasses of juice from a jug in which floated small pieces of fruit, ice and mint. Mr Gupta settled and decided to be honest as he would not know how to weave lies into his tale – the facts were bland thus harmless.

"As you know the last couple of years have been hard for me," he said. "Since the accident I have lost my way a little and have left far too much to chance. Had it not been for your kindness I may have drifted into some kind of financial disaster without knowing it."

"I would hardly say that," said Ravi. "It was only a case of watching your investments. Kiran, bless her, had left you a lot of money in trust. All her investments have continued to work for you, and do not forget I do make a little by way of fees, so business is a factor. I am no saint, Anil."

"Yes, I accept that," said Mr Gupta, "but you continued to hold the reins for far longer than necessary. It should have been me sorting my own affairs, with your guidance obviously, but with me taking responsibility, even if the amounts are modest."

Ravi Uppal looked startled and raised his eyebrows.

"Do you have any idea what money you actually inherited?" he asked.

"Well, enough to keep Rupa at the school," said Mr Gupta sheepishly. "And enough to put by for my old age, perhaps?"

Embarrassingly, Mr Gupta had no clue as to what his estate was worth.

"'Enough to put by,'" echoed Ravi slowly, smiling. "My dear man, you have sufficient invested to retire in comfort for a hundred years! In total it comes out as roughly six crore rupees!"

Ravi had quoted a low amount compared with the real figures, which had grown and been harvested regularly. After all, if Anil Gupta was really that clueless, Ravi felt he would only volunteer enough information to retain a generous advantage. He had become so practised in this he did it automatically.

"Goodness me!" said Mr Gupta, genuinely shocked. He sipped his drink and blinked through his spectacles. He let out a long breath. "Then you must help me understand what I should do for the future. It is so much money."

"Take it as read," said Ravi. "Now tell me, what is wrong with you, Anil? It came as a shock to hear you had been in hospital. Tell me all, brother-in-law, tell me all."

Mr Gupta told the now familiar story of his headaches, collapse and hospitalisation, diagnosis and projected treatment, and the operation he was soon to have. Ravi sat forward, listening intently, with concern clear upon his face. Mr Gupta relaxed and started to feel comfortable, just as he felt in his home, in his small, undemanding world. Ravi had helped him settle. The atmosphere in the room was far from threatening so Mr Gupta embraced the calm – he gave into the weakness of wanting to feel safe. They talked openly, as would friends, words coming freely. They talked of Tamina and Kiran, relived shared pain, reaffirming a bond which had seemed frail. Ravi evoked the image of Rupa, assuring Mr Gupta that he took his role as her named guardian very seriously and that she would be looked after, no matter what. After all, he reminded Mr Gupta, she had been the face of Fallen Angels in its first year.

"Darling Kiran was so keen to help out with it too," said Ravi. "Then, well..., then the accident..."

...the accident...

Time slowed. The words echoed in Mr Gupta's head. All emotions fled, leaving him in a frozen body. Ravi was a monster. His comforting doubts were draining away. Everything greyed out and he was on the brink of rage, panic and madness. But MacKeeg was with him.

"Let me take over, laddie," he said. "Trust me, the now, trust me."

And Mr Gupta let go.

...the accident...

Ravi had paused for effect, to consolidate the bond, to open his brother-in-law's heart, to gently winkle out every scrap of information. The desired effect never materialised. Mr Gupta had entered a fugue state, seemingly unaware of his surroundings.

"Anil?" asked Ravi, uncertainly.

A force hit Mr Gupta. He was aware of a terrible pain in his head, it knifed into his brain and he convulsed in the chair. His foot flew up and kicked the heavy table knocking over a glass.

"Anil!" shouted Ravi, leaping to his feet and stepping to the stricken man. Then, after a few seconds, it was passed. Mr Gupta resumed his stiff sitting position staring blankly ahead, a dribble of mucus draining from his left nostril into his moustache.

"Anil?" asked Ravi, gently touching his shoulder. "Are you alright?"

"The accident," said Mr Gupta robotically. *"The accident. We don't know if it was, do we Kiran? We have backup. The disc was not all..."*

Ravi felt his heart skip a beat. Mr Gupta's voice was all wrong and he was obviously ill, having a fit of some kind, but whatever he was saying, Ravi could not ignore it. It was fascinating.

"...safe at home. Safe at home. Fallen Angels is our fallen angel. Not Ravi.... the accident.... What do we do? Kiran, what shall we do... I'm sorry, sir, but the ticket is for the dead on the line. Do...do...do you...MacKeeg, is it you?"

A lesser convulsion shook Mr Gupta. Ravi crouched before him and held his hand. He could see no artifice in the stricken man, just sickness, a confirmation of his illness, but the words had compounded Ravi's fears. His course of action had become self-evident.

Clarity returned to Mr Gupta's mind as MacKeeg let go. The pain had been real and for a moment he was dizzy and disorientated, not remembering too much at all. He relaxed and opened his eyes drawing in a deep breath and looking at the concerned face of Ravi.

"Hmmm," he managed, blinking rapidly. "What am I doing here? Ravi? I...I seem to be in a bit of a state."

"Thank goodness," said Ravi, smiling nervously. "Are you alright? Talk to me."

Mr Gupta felt himself return to the room and remembered where he was.

"Oh dear," he said. "I'm so sorry, Ravi, this is the first time this has happened since Dr Chowdary's surgery...I seem to have made a bit of a scene."

"You talked to me, Anil," said Ravi. "Do you remember?"

"Yes, of course," said Mr Gupta. "We were talking about Kiran and Tamina and Rupa.... I think we were anyway."

"No," said Ravi gently, "over the last few minutes. You seemed to have a fit or something. You talked then, don't you remember anything?"

"No...No I can't," said Mr Gupta looking genuinely confused. He rubbed his eyes and face with a hand, then wiped his moustache with a napkin. "Did I make any sense?"

Ravi gave a considered answer.

"Not really," he said. "Just a few words about Kiran and Rupa and a train ticket, or something. And another odd name. It made no sense to me. I think you had an epileptic fit, or something. The main thing is, are you alright? Should I phone for a doctor?"

"I will be fine now," said Mr Gupta smiling, confident he was right. "Yes. I will be fine"

"Who is MacKeeg?" asked Ravi suddenly.

Mr Gupta laughed.

"Goodness me," he said. "MacKeeg was a soldier from Scotland who died in Lucknow in 1857. He's a figure from my history studies. He's lodged in my memory for some reason – I must have sounded quite mad!"

"Well, irrational, perhaps," said Ravi returning the smile. "Look, you must not worry. I will make sure all is in order. I'll talk you through things next week and we'll take things from there. Anil, I know this tumour is awful, but I will do all in my power to make any transition as easy as possible. Let's assume the best. That's the only way to think. Shall we have lunch?"

"Perhaps I should go home," said Mr Gupta, desperate to escape from this awful place. "I'm not really hungry and I need to rest. I'm sorry to be such trouble."

"Stop apologising," Ravi scolded gently. "I'll get you home."

He shouted loudly for Vaz who appeared from an adjoining room.

"No lunch?" he said smiling at the empty table, eyeing the pool of juice.

"No," said Ravi making direct eye contact. "Anil is a little unwell and needs to return home. We will sort out business next week – I have all I need to make sure I can get things ready as Anil wants it." Then turning to Mr Gupta, "Anil, I will get Jyoti to call you on Monday to arrange a visit. I'll arrange a car, or I can come to you if needs be. Now, let Vaz take you home. Try to have a quiet and restful weekend. I will make sure your will is ready for review and will have some suggestions to make life easier for you."

Mr Gupta stood, still in a daze, and shook Ravi's hand.

"Thank you yet again, Ravi," he said. "All I want to do is take control of my life."

"It has been my pleasure, Anil," said Ravi. "The important thing is for you to get through this."

Ravi escorted Mr Gupta out to the black Audi which Vaz had already started. As he opened the door the sound of distorted sitar music floated out. It was more of the strange Zahan-Fossa recording. The interior was too cool again. Vasupati Chopra manoeuvred the car out of the haveli's extensive grounds and onto the main road.

Gophapa will be slain by Him...

Mr Gupta felt overwhelmingly tired. The music made the journey surreal.

Gophapa takes ruin with him...

He felt on edge. Was he *Gophapa*? Trapped? He glanced at Vaz.

Pain leaves with Death, Both shine with blackness...

Round, flat, blue lenses. Vaz never made an error, drove smoothly and used the engine's power sparingly. He seemed part of the machine. The car felt solid, unstoppable and relentless. Cold.

"Are you alright?" asked Vaz without taking his eyes from the road.

"Yes," replied Mr Gupta, startled. "The music is rather strange, but I'm sure I have heard this before."

"*Zahan - A day and an hour* concert, New Year's Eve 2011," said Vaz. "It was his only full recital of *Chaos Birthing* shown on television. He said, to be perfect, it must take exactly twenty-five hours. The old day goes, and new life arrives in the dark morning. Zahan managed this feat in this performance to the faithful, set to Fossa's music. Few understand it, but it is like a key. If you really listen, and let it in, it can unlock your mind."

All ruin burns away...

Mr Gupta shivered in the chilled air. He was unsure whether he was dreaming or awake – everything was cold and dark and enclosed. Outside on the footpath he saw the strange man from Dr Chowdary's waiting room staring at him. How could this be? His world was skewed, his perception off kilter. He blinked and the man was now William MacKeeg standing in all his military splendour watching. MacKeeg tapped the side of his nose and winked.

All ruin tempered to purity...

Mr Gupta descended into a reverie.

Rise in the new world of blue...

The world adjusted around him. The car became a cold monochrome cell where gravity had increased. The music pulsed. He looked at Vasupati Chopra – he was an ebony figure, the only colour the shiny blue of his lenses; neon lights in the blackness of infinity. Time slowed and the pieces fell into place. They came together in a moment, and he knew he was in the presence of a malevolent force. Kiran's death was not an accident. *Not…an…accident. Not…an…accident.* He felt very close to knowing everything, but it remained just out of reach. The car was cold. A snake is cold.

Rise in the new world of light. Dragons rise in praise of him, mighty serpents cold as ice…

The car suddenly swerved and in an instant Mr Gupta was fully aware of his surroundings.

"Bloody old fool," said Vaz calmly.

An elderly, skeletal man had pushed an ancient rusty bicycle into their path. It was laden with onions – a huge bundle held together by faded orange netting sacks. The bicycle looked far too big for the man. It was more a beast of burden. He stared without reaction as the Audi missed him by inches.

Praise Kāla, praise Kāla whose will moves all…

The song was still playing. The incantations were very long thought Mr Gupta. Had Vaz replayed it? He couldn't remember; all he wanted to do was be free of this cold steel enclosure. His MacKeeg mind had brought to him the unquestionable conclusion that he was in a car with a very dangerous man. His fear was primal. Instinctive.

Praise Kāla who cannot die,
The Destroyer has built the new world,
The end has become the Great Arch,
All has ended, all has gone,
All life's weaving is undone,
Chaos gone and blue light shines,
Chaos gone and blue light shines…

Vaz turned off the music.

"Enough of this Mr Gupta," he said. "Such lyrics are a little dark for a lovely day."

"It is very strange," said Mr Gupta.

"Zahan first released this on vinyl, it is that old", said Vaz. "I think Zahan is possessed of a god. Fossa's music fits the lyrics perfectly. He is from Madagascar, but his mind is Indian in its make-up. Their journeys brought them together and they reached perfection."

"I do not know of this," said Mr Gupta.

"It is rare to hear this music unless you are Parsi," said Vaz. "I only found this by chance."

Mr Gupta became transfixed as he stared into the blue lenses. They glowed with cold light.

"Home," said Vaz.

The car had been stationary for a while.

"Oh! Thank you Vaz."

"You are most welcome," replied Vaz, smiling. His gold tooth flashed.

Mr Gupta watched the car until it was lost from sight in the busy street.

"He is death," said MacKeeg.

"He is death," said Mr Gupta.

Kush Karnik watched. Vaz saw him, but drove past without acknowledgement. Ravi Uppal had sanctioned the removal of Mr Gupta whilst he was being driven home. The Cobra machine had started. Mr Gupta watched the black car disappear, then went into his house.

The Mechanic had been busy. He had a job to do and a short time in which to complete it. Karnik had worked for Vasupati Chopra before. He was ruthlessly efficient, meticulous in his preparation and left nothing to chance. His skill was to obfuscate the real nature of each execution, leaving false, but tangible clues for the authorities to interpret. Karnik was of medium build and height, clean shaven, dressed in dark trousers, blue checked open-collared shirt and a dark waistcoat. He was invisible in a crowd, nondescript, just a businessman out for a walk. He operated in Delhi only for Vasupati Chopra and had enjoyed creating The Mechanic for the police to chase. It had been Vaz's idea and it had worked beautifully. Now this phantom was to commit a further atrocity. Kush Karnik found The Mechanic's calling card, a tyre iron, to be a messy weapon. However, primitive as it was, it was effective and quick, if wielded correctly. It was unusual for Vaz to ask for a job to be done at such short notice, yet it seemed easy enough and he had managed to do a lot of ground work in a short space of time. The only thing he needed to establish was a daily routine, so he would watch, be patient and complete his contract the following night. He could foresee no problems. It was easy money.

The monsoon rains were giving out and Delhi dozed through its first dry night for some time. The moon rose in a clear sky. It shone with a tranquil light on those below, dragging whole oceans in its wake, affecting the lives of millions of creatures. The rough sleepers could feel the difference in the air and confidently curled up on streets and pathways knowing their travails would be reduced just a little, and sleep would be less troubled. One more night and the moon would be full, lighting the dark places in silver and, this year at least, marking the end of the heavy rains. It would be a time for festivals to multiply and pilgrimages to begin; a time for journeys across the ancient land.

Far to the south a fellowship of five settled in a clearing beside a stretch of silvery water, talking well into the night, watching the moon transcribe its arc across the sky. To the west in rich volcanic hills a tiger roared over its first kill; the goat was not much of a test, but would give sustenance for a few days. The moonlight turned the blood black. The echo of the roar drifted across a river-cut ravine to the ears of a sleeping giant. He stirred in his sleeping bag, opened his clear blue eyes and watched bats weave intricate patterns across the bright lunar surface.

Mr Gupta looked up at the same moon. He could not rest and had decided to sit in his garden to drink his tea. He could see craters and the lunar seas of dust, smiling as large moths flew by, dipping and twirling, all in sharp silhouette. With astonishment he realised he had not worn his glasses all day and had seen with no trouble at all.

"Bloody hell," he mumbled.

A large gecko scrambled up the garden wall its jaws snapping shut on a careless beetle. Beyond the house Delhi still throbbed with the rhythm of life, the moonlight encouraging sleeplessness and revelry. Mr Gupta sipped his drink and wondered why, with a tumour in his head, he felt so well. Was there purpose to this, some blessing bestowed by a merciful deity? He dismissed the idea as he was not a fatalist as was prevalent in India. His time in England had educated the superstition out of him. As he watched he realised that he was exposed out here. The hairs on his neck stood on end. Could it simply be instinct? The change Mr Gupta felt was like the tidal pull of the not-quite-full-moon. Whatever was happening under this beautiful night's sky was irreversible.

The source of Mr Gupta's growing discomfort watched from the shadows. The Mechanic could strike now, but Kush Karnik had his instructions. He knew both targets would soon be in this one place and thus easier to dispatch. As the moon drifted west he left Mr Gupta to enjoy a final undisturbed night. He stepped across a shaft of moonlight and looked back quickly to see if he had been noticed. Did the seated man's head move? No. Mr Gupta remained intent on staring at the moon. And seemed to be talking to himself.

Mr Gupta finished his tea.

"The moon is beautiful, laddie."

"Yes, it is," he replied, no longer surprised by MacKeeg's appearances.

"You felt something?" asked the Scot.

"Yes," said Mr Gupta. "I know change is coming and there's nothing I can do to stop it. I'm not wrong, am I?"

"Nay, laddie," said MacKeeg, "trouble is coming and that's no lie. Ye have to forget trying to decipher what you think is normal the now. *Normal* is just temporary moments of peace, mundanity if you will. Everyone yearns for it – grasps for it even – a bit like the lady in the blue dress."

"You have lost me again," said Mr Gupta turning to his constant companion.

William MacKeeg had gained more colour; the sepia wash had gone. He looked every inch an imposing soldier, even if white-haired. He was sitting, gazing at the moon, puffing away at his short pipe.

"When the lads and me fought our way to the Residence, ye know, in Lucknow, I couldnae believe my eyes. I thought the poor devils would be crawling around half mad. I clambered through a hole in the bricks with Fergus whilst the others finished off the Sepoys. We must have looked a sight covered in shite and blood, powder smuts and dirt, stinking and wild-eyed. We'd been pushing on for hours y'see, and I must have killed a dozen of the bastards, but now it was done. Fergus had our colours and wanted them hoisted first."

MacKeeg blew out a cloud of smoke and turned to Mr Gupta.

"So, we clambered over the bodies and rubble, through that big hole, and do y'know who met us?"

"I have no idea", said Mr Gupta, half thinking he must do on some level, but dismissed this idea aborning to preserve a semblance of rationality.

"Well, I'll tell ye. I came to a stop, snapped off a salute and gawped. The soldiers, officers and wives were all dressed up to the nines in order to greet us. A wee bit tatty, mind you, but smarter than me and shite-for-breath Fergus. This officer stepped forward, dolled up like a lord, all shiny buttons, but with the arse out of his trousers, and says, 'Good afternoon gentlemen. May I congratulate you on a fine display of soldiery?'

I says, 'Ye're welcome, sir. The lads will be along in wee while, they're just kicking the shite out of the last of the feckers.'

He says, "May I remind you, sir, there are ladies present. Kindly temper your language.'

I says, 'Fuck me, Sir. Begging your pardon, but I've just this moment been having a quick war.'"

Mr Gupta laughed, "So what about the lady?"

MacKeeg raised his eyebrows and blew out another cloud of smoke.

"Ye wait for this! Behind Colonel Snot was this pretty lady in a long, blue dress, jewellery and everything. She sort of comes to my defence.

" 'Charles,' she says. 'Leave the chap alone.'

"Then she turns to me and says, 'Did you bring any milk with you? We've not been able to take tea for a few days.'

"I just goggled, lost for words like, but Fergus laughed like a fucking drain. Then I did. Cried with laughter we did. And all the time this group of dolled up buggers just stood and watched.

"Then the lady says, 'You've no milk, have you?'

"And I says, 'My lady, for you I shall fuck off and get some cos that's the best laugh I've had since Fergus coughed and shat at the same time!' Then they all laughed and huzzahed us. And I got them their milk."

Mr Gupta chuckled again. "Were you a bit annoyed with them?"

"Why nay, laddie," said MacKeeg. "They were fucking heroes, the bravest people I met before I died. You see, out of all that mess – only one in three survived that bit – they just wanted to dress for tea. All we had to do to cheer them up was milk a cow! Make things normal again."

Mr Gupta became silent.

"I cannot protect anyone, MacKeeg," he said. "I do not know what to do."

"I told ye man," replied MacKeeg, "a time will come when ye'll be in big trouble. When it does let me handle it."

"I do not understand," said Mr Gupta.

"Did ye see him?" asked MacKeeg.

That question gave him pause. He cast his mind back a few minutes. A tingle went through him. He was looking at the moon, at the craters and moths. He felt anew the shock of realising his sight was better, and what depth of perception he now seemed to have.

"Could this tumour cure my vision and give me a quicker mind?" he asked.

"Aye, it seems so," said MacKeeg. "I'd call it a couple of advantages wrapped in a huge pile of shite myself. Think, laddie, did ya see him?"

Mr Gupta continued to stare at the moon. His subconscious memories were drawn into the light. They became clear. He glanced across to the shadows shrouding the corner opposite. The patch of moonlight had moved and his mind released the latent image of the watcher. A slim man, his upper lip protruding a little over large teeth, with bright eyes and a smooth walk. He had passed briefly through the moonbeam, was cautious, then relaxed and walked on.

"Yes, I saw him," said Mr Gupta.

"I did too, laddie," said MacKeeg. "We have a fan."

"It could be nothing," said Mr Gupta without conviction.

"Remember that face," said MacKeeg. "We have the advantage of knowing it now, and that will give us the edge."

"I am no soldier," said Mr Gupta quietly.

"Nay, laddie, ye're not," said MacKeeg smiling. "But *we* are!"

Chapter 17

The Final Eve

Mr Gupta slept, for once calmed by soft visions of brighter days when the world gave the promise of fulfilled dreams. Whilst sleeping he rose and walked through the darkness of his house, his movements smooth and natural in the familiar surroundings. Once in the kitchen he went to the narrow door of a cupboard in which he kept a jumble of household tools, opened it and stared into the darkness.

"Now laddie," said MacKeeg, "let us dig and delve."

Together they searched, guided by lost memories, and what they needed. The prize was grasped and hidden in a place of MacKeeg's choosing. It was upon such things survival rested. It was said that the flap of a butterfly's wing has an effect on all futures. MacKeeg had set Mr Gupta on a path that philosophers and scientists could never explain, the effects of which would echo through countless lives.

Above Pune, many miles south of his encounter with Pelhi, Angaar finished eating. The goat had been young and foolish, escaping from the safety of its pen to wander and browse until it reached a high trail leading through dense undergrowth. The great weight of the tiger had fallen upon it before dulled senses had the chance to set it to flight and the jaws crushed its windpipe, suffocating it in less than a minute. Angaar had instinctively eaten the liver, heart and kidneys first, before bulking out his empty stomach on the muscle tissue and flimsy ribs. The goat had been his first real kill. His nascent hunting instinct had flared into life. Angaar's wilding was complete.

Sated, he moved on, then picked up a familiar odour on the breeze. The scent was reminiscent of Seva, but it drifted away on capricious eddies, leaving only the instinctive longings of his inner cub.

"*Geerumph!*" he called.

He continued to walk south along the high trail. A while later he entered a clearing and stopped. The breeze swirled and brought to him the scent of clever monkey from close by. His senses constructed a picture. This was nothing like the smell of those he had killed, but closer to his companion of so many years, spices and sweetness, scents that made the tiger purr. Across the clearing was a shelter. It was a tarp, a half-tent similar to those used by the armed forces, or long-distance mountaineers and trekkers who shunned weight. Beneath, cocooned in a sleeping bag, was a man. Angaar could tell he was asleep and quietly paced the edge of the trees until he was just twenty metres from the hidden figure. Here he settled down and, comforted by instinctive trust, went to sleep.

The moon drifted higher. It eventually shone into the face of the man. He opened his eyes and looked at the silver disc, smiling as he remembered where he was – free of everything. From the forest an owl called and a nightjar churred as it flew across the clearing. He watched the bird hawking for insects, silhouetted against the moon, and snuggled into his down-filled bag to keep the chill at bay. As soon as the monsoon had given way to drier weather he had set out on the long trail to Goa, determined to explore this ancient volcanic range of mountains, keeping to as high a trail as possible. He was a tall man, two metres high in bare feet, with long blond hair and beard, blue eyes and tanned skin. His Scandinavian origins were obvious, though his accent would be more at home in Dublin. He stood out in India and had grown tired of the crowds of urchins that followed him as he wandered the cities, preferring the solitude of where he now was. Raising himself onto one elbow his gaze drifted across the clearing to the unmistakable outline of a sleeping tiger. He had read there were no tigers here, yet this was such a beast, and a big one at that. He was not a man given to panic, so weighed up his options: to run would be silly; to try and tip-toe away seemed as daft; to stay and wait for the tiger to go? This last option had merit, drifted in his mind, settled and made peace with the world. The man closed his eyes and went back to sleep.

To the south of Bhopal, next to the great Indira Sagar reservoir, an unlikely group of itinerants sat around a camp fire, faces lit by the orange flames. They had recently attended post-monsoon festivals in and around the city under the leadership of their sadhu, Nawal Ji. He sat in the fire's glow, the light illuminating the stylised roundel of a yellow sun on his forehead, and looked with affection at his four companions. Nawal Ji was unusual for a sadhu. He often mused that if religion was a stable atom, he would be an escaped particle. He was a *thought quark*. His philosophy was not theologically based, but set squarely in the rational world of logic, science and mathematics. This gave him the luxury of free thought rather than any stultifying set dogma. A free particle could escape from anything. He had no time for reliance on authority and blind faith, instead extolled the value of evidence-based reason in an empirically beautiful universe. He had built a network of followers, in the loosest sense, as he had travelled, but never regaled them with nonsense and metaphysical sophism. He enjoyed jarring authority with statements of the obvious. The pluralistic, pantheistic nature of India had allowed him to discuss theology across a wide spectrum, so that, after many years on the road, he was comfortable in his own skin. Under the same moonlight which lit Mr Gupta's distant house, his *Kuru*, as he called his group, had debated their future. They were

241

waiting for the return of their stricken vehicle which was being repaired in Bhopal. Before coaxing the lorry to the city, it was the driver who had asked Nawal Ji the most important question.

"Where shall we go?"

After each had spoken, they waited for their sadhu's recommendation.

"You may all go where you wish," said Nawal Ji. "As for me, I have decided to allow the laws of probability to give direction. This is one thing I know – something will inject energy into our mass and produce movement, so to speak – it is just a case of waiting."

It was decided this was a wise thing to do. Thus, they all waited and talked under the not-quite-full moon.

Kush Karnik was sitting in his hotel room holding a cheap, new phone. His plan was set. He was content that The Mechanic would be the ideal wraith to execute the Guptas. Vasupati Chopra trusted his judgement and was waiting for confirmation. Karnik speed-dialled the single stored number.

"Speak," said Vaz.

"Both – by The Mechanic," said Karnik.

"Tomorrow night," stated Vaz.

"Yes," said Karnik. "Do you have the weapon?"

"By the morning," said Vaz. "I have to give it *ownership*."

"Who delivers it?" asked Karnik.

"The Rat," said Vaz.

"Contact once it is complete?" asked Karnik.

"Text the word *End*," said Vaz.

Kush Karnik put the phone in his pocket and looked through the window at the moon.

The car was parked in a small industrial complex where Vaz leased a lockup. Now everything was settled he could finish the preparations. He put the phone in the Audi's glove box. Reviving Delhi's notorious serial killer, The Mechanic, to perpetrate the execution of both Guptas was a master stroke, but staging the killer's death after the fact was sublime. With The Mechanic dead the local police would close the cases on several murders. The police would celebrate, the politicians would crow, and Cobra would grow stronger.

He stepped from the car and paused as Kāla filled him. The merging was becoming easier. He was Kāla-Vaz: god-man, mad-man and killer. He lifted a heavy sports bag from the boot, walked in the moonlight to a side door, unlocked it and stepped into the windowless interior. He closed the door before switching on a single, low wattage light bulb which dangled from a twisted flex. Before him, hanging by shackled wrists from a hook attached to an overhead beam, feet barely touching the oily concrete floor, was a skinny man wearing nothing but a pair of filthy jeans. His mouth was taped shut. He rotated slowly, his grimy, calloused toes taking a little of the weight from his aching arms. At some point this man had taken a severe beating. He was covered in bruises; one eye was swollen shut and the other stared at the man before him with bloodshot resignation.

Malik owed money to a man known as Mr Black. Not a great amount and nothing ordinarily to worry about, but Mr Black was calling in the debt. Malik had never seen him before, but had used his loan sharks in Agra to borrow high interest money for quick-fix drug deals. Malik would borrow money, buy drugs, cut them and sell them at a profit, then pay the money back, with interest, on time. It was a precarious living which finally crumbled a few months earlier. He had set up a deal to buy cheaper heroine from a new source. It was too good a deal to miss as it would allow him to make six months' profit in a few weeks. Malik had been set-up, beaten and robbed of the borrowed cash. The deal was too good to be true and the cycle was broken. Accumulating interest had driven him to simple crime, but he could never make enough money. Then he was given a lifeline and told that if he did Mr Black a favour, his debt would be wiped. Malik knew he was owned and had no choice but to agree, especially as he had developed a taste for the product he had been dealing in – he was chasing the dragon most days. He came to Delhi knowing he would have to do something seriously illegal. Several men had been waiting for him at the lockup. They talked and he was sent out to buy a new tyre iron. Upon his return they had attacked him and beaten him to insensibility. He was hoisted into his present position a few hours before. Stranger still he had been given enough of his chosen drug to alleviate his suffering. It had long since worn off. Malik was confused and very scared.

The man who entered was dressed in black, had long hair hanging down to his shoulders and wore round, blue-lensed glasses which reflected the dull light in neon sparkles. He knew this must be Mr Black. Malik would have felt easier had it been one of the heavies who had left him there. The apparition strode forward and tore the tape from his mouth.

"Welcome to Delhi," said Kāla-Vaz.

"I'll pay you the money," gasped Malik.

Kāla-Vaz stared at Malik for a while then turned and walked across the space to a white chest freezer which hummed quietly in the corner next to a battered table and bamboo chair. He placed the sports bag on the floor then picked up the well wrapped tyre iron from the freezer lid. He placed it in the sports bag. Then he pulled out a pouch and flicked it onto the dusty table.

"I...I'll pay you double," whimpered Malik.

Kāla-Vaz walked back.

"You are paying your debt now. Listen to me and do not talk – I am not a patient being."

Malik nodded, grasping the crumb of reassurance in those words.

"I will let you down soon. When I do I want you to take this pouch and do something simple – chase the dragon. You know how. I need to know how good this sample is and you, being an expert, are my quality control. Do you understand?"

Malik nodded again. He racked his brains for an explanation, for a trick, but what Mr Black had said made some sense. "And after?" he blurted.

Kāla-Vaz stared at him again and spoke: *"We have been drawn to this ancient space to purify light with black water. Our lust for life will take us all through the Great Arch, Chinvat.* For your debt I take these words and throw them to the wind…"

Malik understood nothing, so just quietly groaned.

"…And after, I will not kill you. I will leave, you will be alive and the door will be open. I will put two thousand rupees in your pocket and you will never hear from us again."

In a swift movement Kāla-Vaz hefted Malik's arms up releasing him from the hook, then stood back to let him crumple to the floor.

"When you are ready," said Kāla-Vaz, pointing to the table.

Malik stood unsteadily and freed his wrists from the buckled leather straps, the connecting chain rattled to the floor. He wandered over to the table. Everything Malik would need was in the pouch and within a few minutes he had entered a different world and his pain was forgotten.

"Hey, Mr Black," slurred Malik, "this stuff is first-class. Very good. Good good good…"

Kāla-Vaz watched dispassionately as the man drifted into a helplessness, then took out two bank notes wrapped into a ball and stuffed them into Malik's pocket. He stepped to the freezer and opened the lid before pulling Malik to his feet. Bending forward, he lifted Malik over his shoulder, spun him round and dumped him into the icy, silver box. It happened before Malik could react, but something in his brain functioned well enough to realise what was to be his doom.

"Hey man…" he spluttered. "Hey, hey… Not this."

Then louder, "Not this! NOT THIS!"

He tried to rise but could gain no purchase on the icy sides. The drug and the cold sucked the last of his energy and he slipped, cracking the back of his skull. Dazed he looked up and could see his own horrified face in the lenses of Mr Black's glasses.

"NOT THIS! NOT THIS! NOT…"

Kāla-Vaz slammed the lid shut, turned the key and left, leaving the door open as he had promised.

The day dawned bright and the fruit bats retreated to their roosts as the kites rose to fill the air. Delhi shrugged off the night and the inhabitants set out to join the daily dance of millions. Under the India Gate the plastic toys were already being catapulted high into the air, arrows with folded rotors, becoming gyring many-coloured helicopters as they fell to the ground. They had joined hunting dragonflies in the spaces which emphasised Lutyens's grand buildings. High amongst the domes of Hyderabad House monkeys sat in the morning sun looking down on their clever cousins, unaware of the effect this grandeur had on one Ravi Uppal.

He had risen early and breakfasted with his family knowing this was a pivotal day which could put him a step away from joining the government. He had a luncheon appointment with Dr Pallab Bhanot – a Delhi Member of Parliament for the fast-rising Indian Patriotic Union Party – who was sponsoring him to be named as a candidate for a local seat. It was a marginal constituency and would suit a well-known, well-liked local man perfectly, especially one with such an altruistic profile. Later that day, Ravi would be announced as the nominated candidate at a dinner with the IPU's selection committee. Dr Bhanot had assured him they were convinced of his credentials and were certain the marginal seat would be theirs. At home in his office, Ravi saw on his desktop calendar it was the eve of a full moon which he considered auspicious.

"Destiny," he said absentmindedly rubbing the top corner of the frame with his thumb. In an instant he saw the evening as it would be: announcement, applause and dinner. Then, later, an end to any chance of scandal with the removal of the remaining Guptas and consolidation of funds. Ravi had no qualms in sacrificing his former brother-in-law, considering him and his daughter to be collateral damage for a greater good. There had been moments of doubt, but these had been replaced by waves supreme confidence. Cobra was unstoppable and Vaz would work his unfailing magic. Fallen Angels had become the perfect disguise for his schemes, laundering and obfuscating money transactions with the outer façade of an altruistic temple for good and very public deeds. This was the trump card Dr Bhanot had used to convince the IPU selection committee that Ravi Uppal would take his local seat with a landslide and make it safe. Once in parliament he could rise through the IPU ranks, then his party would be able to make deals with the larger parties and hold the balance of power. Then his walks along the Rajpath would be as a powerbroker, not a citizen.

As he rubbed his thumb against the calendar frame a little twinge of uncertainty rippled in the ocean of confidence. After this evening, that too would be gone.

The squirrels scampered from Mr Gupta's shrubby garden, stormed the house wall and dived into their hole in the brickwork. A pale blue ambulance, doors emblazoned with the Beaufort Homes logo – a truncated tree with new shoots overarched with BHT, underscored with the words: *From Hope to Reality* – was reversing into the tight alley beeping noisily.

Kush Karnik watched over the rim of a coffee cup from the corner café. He watched Mr Gupta wait patiently as Rupa was lowered in her wheelchair by way of a powered tailgate, after which he pushed her into the house. Her assistant, Sarasa, followed with Rupa's overnight bag, then left after promising to pick her up the following Monday morning. The ambulance sped out of the alley leaving father and daughter together. Karnik would watch all day from various vantage points, but for now he waited where he was. He opened a paper and read the latest cricket news.

"Do you know Mr Black?" asked a squeaky voice.

Looking up Karnik saw the strangest fellow. He was no taller than a ten-year-old child, and clad in huge khaki shorts, a ragged green vest and enormous sandals. His thin body was lost in his clothes. He stooped with rounded shoulders and his pointed face had two large teeth protruding from the upper lip which was decorated by a wispy moustache. He looked like a rat.

"Rat?" asked Karnik.

The tiny man danced with nerves and grinned, making the question redundant.

"Yesh," said Rat. "That'sh what they call me. I have thish for you from Mr Black."

He held up a brown paper parcel, long, thin and well packed, which Karnik took. He gave Rat a thousand rupee note.

"Mr Black saysh it'sh marked as requeshted," said Rat, who then turned, danced out of the shop and disappeared into the crowded streets.

Karnik placed the package into his bag and ordered some lunch.

For the first time in months Mr Gupta felt he was truly home, Rupa's return having brought a sense of family back to the house. Her disability was of little consequence here as Kiran had overseen the adjustments necessary to ensure her daughter could move around with relative freedom, on the ground floor at least. Within an hour of Rupa's arrival Mrs Singh had bustled in, clucked over father and daughter, and then took over the kitchen. She popped in and out seamlessly re-joining the conversation whilst supplying them with snacks, tea and juice at regular intervals.

"You need to keep up your strength," she would pronounce with each delivery.

Without prearrangement she produced several meals which could be easily reheated for consumption over the weekend, thus giving them more time to enjoy their time together. Mrs Singh also invited them to tea at her home the following afternoon so Rupa *could get some air*, then left, promising to return in the early evening to prepare dinner when Jhatish was due to join them. Mr Gupta and Rupa retreated to the rear garden, sitting quietly under the leafy canopy shading the back door. The bustle of the morning had not given them much chance to talk, but once Mrs Singh had been driven home by her husband, they could finally relax.

"How are you feeling, Daddy?" asked Rupa.

"Fine," he answered settling into his chair. "I am much better now you are home my girl. I feel as if I have a billion things to say…well, to tidy up, if you see what I mean?"

"I know, Daddy," Rupa replied smiling, "but you have no need to explain anything. I'm pretty well versed in our domestics."

"I just miss your mother, and feel I have let too much time pass without getting properly on my feet," he said gazing with sorrowful eyes at Rupa.

"I know, Daddy," said Rupa. "Uncle Ravi will soon help put everything right. Uncle Jhatish will help. There is very little to do, don't you see? Wipe!"

Mr Gupta gently wiped his daughter's face with a tissue, then hugged her and kissed her forehead.

"I miss Mummy too," she whispered in his ear. "But I know her strength is in me, so you must not worry."

He sat back down with damp eyes, smiling at his extraordinary girl. So bright, so very bright. He could see Kiran in her, of that there was no doubt. He felt a huge mixture of emotions, then a sharp pain in his head. Closing his eyes, he let out an involuntary groan and rubbed at his temples, head lowered.

"Is it the tumour?" asked Rupa, gently.

"Yes," said Mr Gupta. "But it has passed now."

And so it had. He sat up then started. William MacKeeg was sitting opposite.

"Is it the Scotsman?" asked Rupa.

Mr Gupta goggled and realised this was the first time MacKeeg had arrived in company, so he could not be denied. His goggling changed to a smile and he gestured to the empty seat.

"Rupa," he said, "I can see him in the chair. I know you cannot, but he is as real to me as you are. So very real."

"Is he talking?" she asked.

"He's just sitting there…"

Mr Gupta's voice trailed off as he settled back in the chair. Rupa watched with alarm, then relaxed as her father looked at her and smiled again. When he next spoke, she could only just understand the strangely accented English.

"…Och, I'm not sat there, but affront of ye," said MacKeeg's voice.

"What? How?" asked Rupa, somewhat startled, wondering if this was an elaborate joke. "Are you a spirit? A god?"

"Nay, lassie," said MacKeeg. "I am yer father. Ye are bright enough. Forget the improbability and, for the sake of experiment, accept me as ye'r inner father, so to speak. Aye, that's what I am."

Rupa chuckled and complied with MacKeeg's suggestion. She trusted her father's judgement and accepted the Scot into her life – well, his voice anyway.

"Alright," she said, curious now. "Why are you here?"

"Well, lassie," said MacKeeg, "I need to say things yer father is too gentle to. I will keep it brief as this is hard to sustain. Very hard. There is something coming which will change everything. Ravi Uppal has a lot to do with it and has set a watcher on the house. He plans to do us harm, of this I am sure, so forget Uncle Ravi as a good man – he is far from it. Y'will need to be taken to safety. Tonight, someone is to end and we have to take on the forces set against us. I am a soldier and yer father is strong, but I cannot say who will end even if I can protect us. An assassin is coming and ye, lassie, should not be here…"

Mr Gupta convulsed in the chair.

"… He has gone now and I am scared," said her father's voice.

Her father wept quietly as he regained full awareness. He sniffed, wiped his face with a tissue and smiled.

"Bubbles," said Rupa smiling too.

"Bubbles," her father agreed.

It was early evening when The Duck waddled into the back street where Mr Gupta's house stood draped with flowers and leaves. Jhatish Das parked the vehicle as close to the low garden wall as he could, scraping a cloud of rust from the nearside door.

"Bugger!" he muttered.

The Duck bounced gently on its worn suspension whilst Jhatish made his way through the garden to the open door.

"Anil!" he called, noting the residual smells of Mrs Singh's cooking frenzy.

Mr Gupta stepped from the lounge. They shook hands enthusiastically and embraced.

"Has Rupa arrived?" he asked.

"In here!" she called from the lounge.

Jhatish strode through with Mr Gupta and kissed Rupa's cheek.

"I have met MacKeeg!" she cried with delight.

Mr Gupta looked slightly embarrassed.

"Who?" asked Jhatish.

"Daddy's invisible man!" said Rupa.

"Ah," said Jhatish.

"His voice, anyway," added Rupa. "He sounds very strange, but is very nice, like Daddy!"

"Then all is well," said Jhatish.

"No secrets," said Rupa. "Wipe!"

Mr Gupta dried his daughter's face once more and looked at his friend. Jhatish stared back.

"Where are your glasses?" he asked.

"I no longer seem to need them" replied Mr Gupta. "One advantage of a brain tumour, I suppose."

Jhatish smiled, but looked pensive.

"Have you looked at the memory stick?" asked Mr Gupta.

"Yes," replied Jhatish frowning.

"And does it contain anything of interest?"

"Kiran was very tidy when it came to figures," said Jhatish. "Everything is laid out in order and she had marked selected parts with a bracketed blue question mark. I'm guessing these are the areas where things are not quite right. There seems to be two identical files, but the balance on each is different – I think these are two sets of the same financial process, each with a different outcome. I've yet to decipher everything, in fact it may be beyond me, but there is a discrepancy of many lakh rupees – millions even – between the two documents. This needs expert eyes."

"Ah," said Mr Gupta sadly. "If what you say is so, it supports the things I have discovered, but explains very little of motives. The upshot is, Ravi wants rid of these records, or us, or both."

"Is this why we are in danger?" asked Rupa.

"What danger?" asked Jhatish.

"MacKeeg has warned me," replied Rupa.

"He has warned all of us," said Mr Gupta. "There is no time to explain as tonight is all that is left and you will both have to accept what is said."

Jhatish felt the world rushing away from him, gears engaged in his mind and a new reality rattled into view. His friend had changed so much in a few days and Rupa seemed wise beyond her years. He felt lost and separate from everything, mind racing as he tried to find a less brutal explanation for recent events and possible outcomes. Yet the data on the memory stick, if accurate, proved Ravi Uppal was a crook. But a killer? Ruthless? Mr Gupta became still, then spoke in a strange voice.

"Laddie," said MacKeeg. "I do not expect you to understand and if ye run screaming from the house I would not be surprised, but ye must listen to me now."

Jhatish was beyond shock.

"To…to whom am I speaking?" he asked.

"Anil Gupta," said MacKeeg, simply. "He is me, so to speak. I am William MacKeeg, but that is all ye need to know the now. There is a man watching the house and I have a mind that he is making a move to kill us tonight. But Gupta has me, and I am a soldier. Ye must pay heed to all I will say."

"I am scared, MacKeeg," said Rupa, softly.

"I know, young lassie," he said, "but ye are in the greatest danger as you cannot move like me. Ye can be safe, but it will take action and my plan. Now listen to me…"

Kush Karnik watched from the shadows. He saw Jhatish Das rumble up in his old car. Later he watched Mrs Singh jump from her husband's tuktuk loaded with bags and disappear into the house. He watched her leave as evening descended and saw the full moon rise, huge and amber, above the city, and saw it shrink and become bright as it climbed. He watched the tuktuk return and saw Mrs Singh climb aboard and leave. Kush Karnik was calm. In another hour or so he could return to his hotel and prepare for the night ahead. He leaned against the wall to wait for his victims to go to bed when, for once, he was startled. Mr Gupta stepped into the street and walked towards him.

Chapter 18

All has Ended, All has Gone

The blond giant had spent the day climbing ever higher through the ancient hills. A pack, a Bergen as he knew it, sat snugly on his hips. His strong legs, clad in dusty trousers, covered the ground with ease. It was cool at this height, pleasant to walk in and he relished the fresh air and solitude. Several times he had spotted the orderly green rows of tea plantations on the lower foothills where they thrived, but he was not tempted to drop down into the more civilised world, preferring the company of animals to multitudes of people.

He had woken just before dawn immediately aware of a close presence. He could smell the tiger's aroma, but more to the point could hear the chuff of inhaled breath and feel the exhalation against his cheek. His right hand, hidden in his sleeping bag, found the handle of his knife. Without moving a muscle, he opened his eyes. There, not two feet away, was the tiger's face. They stared at each other and there was a long moment of stasis, yet neither registered any threat nor felt the need to panic.

"Good morning feller," said the man in a deep, soft voice. "It's good to meet you. I am Olaf."

The tiger's stare did not waver.

"We were tired and shared a cool night," continued Olaf. "Are we to remain chums?"

"Geerumph!" sighed the tiger loudly making Olaf jump.

A few more moments passed then the beast turned and walked away, heading south out of the clearing towards even higher ground.

"Phew!" said Olaf sitting up, brushing his blond hair against the tarp. He pulled out the big wooden handled survival knife and stuck it into the ground next to him. He looked at the knife, then thought about the size of the tiger and laughed quietly.

Not a chance, he thought. "We seem to be heading the same way," he muttered as he watched the tiger disappear.

Within an hour Olaf had packed his Bergen and followed the trail, watching all the time for signs of the tiger. He found pug marks, noting one had a distinct diagonal line on the impression of its pad – a scar perhaps? By the evening he had covered a lot of ground, but did not see the tiger again. The views from this high ground were wonderful and he relished the strata layers of the deep gorges and shattered cliffs, the green cloak of trees and the calls of animals. He had heard elephants below on one occasion as they bathed under a waterfall and had even seen a single, very dark leopard cross a clearing. With the sun dipping Olaf had found himself the perfect camp above high cliffs – a shallow, overhung, south-facing cave above a forested valley. He set up camp and prepared a simple evening meal of rice with a spicy sauce, finishing it off with a chocolate bar and tea. He drank a lot of tea. The sun set in the west and a huge moon rose above the misty hollows. It was so long since he had felt such peace and he wished for once he could stop the passage of time. Olaf knew visiting the mountains and hills of the world reduced a man's trouble to nothing, every step higher made the gap greater as if altitude kept the worldly woes at bay. Down in the towns and cities all of the problems and fears remained. He stood to face the moon, yawned and lost himself in thought.

By mutual agreement the group of mendicants remained at their camp next to the Indira Sagar. In India such groups were accepted as part of everyday life so Nawal Ji's Kuru was seen as nothing unusual. They followed an irregular, annual circuit across the continent, but were often sidetracked to new places. After the monsoon they tended to move south, though Nawal Ji's latest experiment with probability made this uncertain. For now, they waited. Their ailing vehicle had finally been coaxed back to Bhopal for some necessary welding in a large, old-fashioned workshop where the driver could use the equipment in return for his skills with other jobs.

Whilst at Indira Sagar the local villagers often visited for help of various kinds, both spiritual and physical, and the group were glad to give it, bartering help for basic supplies and invites to feasts when festivals were happening. Festivals ensured they often had contact with other ideological people with varying levels of faith, from the absolute to the pragmatic. The reasons for each group's itinerant existence were as different as chalk is from cheese. Some were sadhus in name only, with only a basic knowledge of the religious dogma found in Indian pantheistic society, using it to make a living. Others carried their devotions to the other extreme and suffered terrible hardship to attain purity. Nawal Ji's Kuru was different as each member had never embraced faith on face value. Doubts borne of unanswered questions had acted as an isolating medium until, one by one, they had found Nawal Ji, become part of his Kuru and found peace in the acceptance of logic, based on empirical evidence. This slow agglomeration of like-minded people made Nawal Ji happy.

In a previous existence Professor Nawal Pratap Singh had been head of astrophysics at Oxford, specialised in particle physics, eventually moving to Switzerland, where, upon the death of his wife of forty years, he suffered a partial breakdown. He retired and travelled, eventually finding his roots back in India, evolving into the unorthodox sadhu he now was – restored of mind, but changed in his attitude to the world. He had always found peace in the logic of science, applying rationality to all things, not needing to invoke a god to fill the gaps in his knowledge. Nawal had teamed up with a banished Tibetan monk in Ladakh before his present wanderings had truly begun. Over time his band had become known as the *Kuru ki Kvark* and Nawal had the *Ji* added by his constant companions. They were welcomed in all the places they stopped on their annual circuits of the country.

Nawal Ji was sitting by the shore as the small figure of Vamana approached from the camp fire with a steaming drink of chai.

"Nawal Ji," he said. "I know you are not a prophet, nor a seer of the future, nor do you have truck with such things. But how long must we wait?"

Nawal Ji smiled in his beard, eyes twinkling, and stared at the moon.

"It is a reasonable question, Vam," he said. "I am thinking something will happen. It may be a dog bite, or an asteroid strike, or a storm – who knows? I am also tired and need a rest, so *waiting*, as a word, can be the same as a resting. Let's continue to wait and allow what the moon sees to arrive. After all, it is nice here."

"Hmm," said Vam.

The sadhu and the dwarf both looked at the moon and accepted that logic required them to rest, and that rest would bring something, and what the moon could see, they could not.

Mr Gupta marched past the corner café, across the main street and into a bustling market, redolent with spices and ringing with noise. Several of the stall holders shouted out greetings, to which he waved and tried to hide his agitation. He knew the watcher was following. True to his word, William MacKeeg was with him, taking the lead.

"We need him to follow, laddie," he had said in reassuring tones.

Mr Gupta strolled to a shop on a street corner to buy a newspaper.

"We need to see him," whispered MacKeeg.

Mr Gupta had fully embraced the MacKeeg presence. Without this safety device, the cascade of memories would have made him struggle to maintain a grip on sanity. He was now confident enough to give MacKeeg physical and mental primacy, when the need arose, after all, MacKeeg alone had the skills to give him the chance of survival. Rupa and Jhatish had taken some convincing of the story Mr Gupta told. Accepting Ravi Uppal as being duplicitous to the point of murder had been hard, but being confronted with the threat of death from a lurking assassin stepped into the realms of incredulity. It was the memory stick data that finally showed the truth of it. Tamina and Kiran had been killed and the clear link was Fallen Angels and big money; this in turn implicated Ravi Uppal, Cobra and, by default, Vasupati Chopra. Father and daughter were the only people left with a grip on the fortune that had been Shastri money. With them gone, Ravi Uppal would be richer and any connection with criminal deeds expunged forever. Their execution would be the perfect crime, but for the data Tamina and Kiran had kept. The MacKeeg mind had extrapolated the truth and Mr Gupta had passed it on to those he loved. MacKeeg's plan was now under way and, as he crossed the market place to the shop, Mr Gupta knew there was no longer any room for doubt.

"What if we are wrong?" asked Mr Gupta, with little conviction.

"Then, laddie, no harm done," said MacKeeg, "but if we be right? Then it will be all ye can do to survive the night."

"What then? Call the police?"

"They'd lock y'up as a loonie and feed you on soup wi' a spoon," chuckled MacKeeg. "See in yon window ye can see him following. The game is on."

"I am scared, can't we just run? He may delay a while," said Mr Gupta as he caught a glimpse of the shadowy figure.

"Nay, it's tonight," snapped MacKeeg.

"Why?" The questions and answers raced through Mr Gupta's mind in a flash as all evidence meshed together to make probables into definites.

MacKeeg stated the obvious.

"Uppal has decided as would I have. Recce: done. Enemy in one place: yes. Only for one night: probably. Assault group in place: yes. Bang! Gone! All problems solved. Simple."

"Maybe tomorrow?" The question was weak.

"Nay – now stop this."

"How will he kill us?"

"Ye have me there," sighed MacKeeg. "I do not know…"

Mr Gupta stepped into the shop and talked to the proprietor, Mr Khan, as he purchased a paper and a bag of boiled sweets of which Rupa was particularly fond. He left and took a different street in order to make the journey home protracted. The watcher was very careful, keeping a good distance, using shadows and people to remain neutral in the background – a shopper gazing in widows, a strolling man reading a folded paper, the shadow of a shadow – but MacKeeg saw him.

"He is the assassin, come to kill."

Mr Gupta knew he was right and was terrified.

"I cannot do this," he said.

"It is not for ye, laddie," said MacKeeg. "Ye're already dead. Y'll do this for Rupa."

Mr Gupta quaked uncontrollably. His legs wobbled and he leaned against a wall to stop himself sinking onto the filthy pavement. Then, as he took deep breaths, calmness embraced him. He was seeing the world through a soldier's eyes. He really had nothing to lose and knew MacKeeg would never leave him defenceless. With a new resolve he saw how keen MacKeeg's senses were and where the advantage lay. The assassin saw an old man, not a seasoned soldier.

"Fuck him, laddie," laughed the Scot.

Mr Gupta straightened and strolled home.

Kush Karnik was startled. He was sure he had not been noticed, so the sight of Mr Gupta striding in his direction upset his cool demeanour. He relaxed as his target strode past without pause. Karnik would need to follow. Should both targets be in separate places he would have to rethink his tactics and that could make things difficult. At a safe distance, he watched Mr Gupta stroll through the market sharing words of greeting with those he knew, then entering a small shop beyond the last stall. Karnik busied himself looking at a variety of goods, anonymous in the crowd, whilst keeping an eye on the shop entrance. Mr Gupta looked frail and harmless. Karnik mused at why Vaz would want him killed, especially as the tumour in his head would surely do the trick in time. He concluded it was simply an issue of convenience. His pondering ended as Mr Gupta left the shop and wandered into a side street, paper tucked under his arm, a colourful bag of sweets in his hand. Karnik followed and watched, along streets and through a small park, his target seeming to be enjoying a walk in the moonlight before returning home. He watched the man stagger and lean against a wall, sure he was going to collapse, but he had rallied and set off once more. Perhaps the tumour was further advanced than Vaz realised? Eventually he returned to the house leaving Karnik in the shadows. Jhatish Das left, hugging his old friend before making his way to the decrepit car he had arrived in. The two men chatted casually for a while before Jhatish opened the car door, shouting a farewell to the girl inside.

"I will stop by tomorrow, Rupa!"

Karnik knew things were back on course. The Duck clanked into life, bounced through some complex turning manoeuvres and clattered off into the bustling Delhi night, one of its rear lights flickering in rhythm with the engine. Mr Gupta took a last glance at the moon and went into the house, closing the door and turning off the garden lights. After another half an hour Kush Karnik slipped quietly away. Before long The Mechanic would return.

Mr Gupta sat in total darkness. He was pensive. Dragging himself from the comfortable world of inertia had changed him, even if he was haunted by old fears. Yet Kiran had been right and her words were echoed by Wamil – he was a strong man. Had it taken the tumour to force this part of himself to the surface in the form of William MacKeeg, or was it his need to protect his only child? It was a question he did not care to ponder, he was just glad that MacKeeg was now part of him. No lights shone, all curtains were drawn and only the moonlight penetrated the chinks and cracks remaining. Upstairs in his room he had left a lamp on. Rupa's door was shut and her wheelchair was parked in a corner nearby. He closed his eyes. When he opened them, a luminous William MacKeeg was sitting opposite. Mr Gupta smiled.

"I am glad you are here William."

"*William* is it, laddie?" said MacKeeg returning the smile. "Do I detect affection in yer tone?"

"I am scared," replied Mr Gupta, "but I know you will not let me down. You have shown me the truth of things. You have taken all that I have seen and put the pieces together to make a picture I could never have contemplated. I did not even realise the pieces were there! Now you have given me the ability to do something about it all, so, yes MacKeeg, I see you as a friend."

"Back to 'MacKeeg', that's better!" laughed the Scot. "WE have done this, not me. We are ye and me, and make no mistake. But the time to wonder is past. Well past. I think y'are ready to confront everything and I shall help force the answers."

"I am scared," repeated Mr Gupta. "All my questions are simple enough, though what possible answers there are I have no clue. Will the tumour kill me? Why has this man been sent to kill us? Will he kill Rupa, regardless? Did Kiran and Tamina die for the same reasons? And ..., oh MacKeeg..., and what am I to do? What can I do? We have no time to think with that killer coming. I am so, so scared."

MacKeeg packed his pipe, lit it and stared at the blue glow of the tobacco.

"Don't ye worry about time," he said. "Time here is relative. This is taking mere seconds – brains are like that. Now I want ye to listen, laddie. Y'are me and that makes ye a soldier brave and true. And I know ye can get angry. Not wild, mad anger like.... what did the old Vikings call them...?

"Berserkers," said Mr Gupta.

"Aye, berserkers, them's the ones. Well, not like that. I mean a controlled, focussed anger, enough to drive ye on. Rupa's safety has started this. Keeping her safe is a war ye must win. Tonight is nothing to what will come."

"But I am scared," said Mr Gupta a third time. "This man who is coming is a professional killer and ..."

"Hush," soothed MacKeeg. "Let me set the world afore ye. I hear everything ye say, yet ye avoid the obvious that ye already know and ignore. So, I shall state it. Close yer eyes."

He did.

"Open them."

Mr Gupta was back on the beach, the full moon huge and bright, the planets too close, but beautiful. MacKeeg was sitting on his rock smoking. There was a change. His uniform looked worn and his kilt dusty; an Enfield rifle leaned at a steep angle against the rock. He looked as if he had been in a battle. Mr Gupta was sitting on his own rock and looked at the scene. Small waves gently kissed the sand and he felt peace descend upon him. The tightness in his guts loosened and, though he knew the answers MacKeeg would give, allowed him to speak anyway.

"This thing in yer head is incurable, ye know that, laddie?"

Mr Gupta nodded once.

"Any hope of medical intervention has disappeared from today. But, and it is a big *but*, the change it has made gives ye the chance to strike at the demons that have dogged yer life unseen. This tumour has given ye both sight and deep insight too. Y'are going to die, laddie – ye and me both, though I'm one death ahead, but we can put things right, tough as it may seem. It is strange, but without the tumour ye may have died sooner. Now we can destroy that bastard Uppal!"

"Why?" said Mr Gupta. "There is nothing for a court of law to…"

"Shut up!" MacKeeg's roar silenced him.

Mr Gupta felt absurd being chastised by himself.

"The one thing we do not have is endless time. The police could take months, years even, to sort through what evidence there is. Justice might take longer. Ye must forget *proof* as the law would want it. Proof will come tonight, right enough. What we can do is strike first.

"Ye have ignored the main motive in all this – money! Y'are so docile ye have been milked like a cow. Ravi Uppal had his wife killed. Kiran was murdered. Ye were left as window dressing to give Uppal legitimacy. Now ye are a problem. Rupa thus becomes a problem. This foul man is driven by political ambitions and he needs money to slake his thirst for power. He needs to sanitise the past. Ye and Rupa are both excess to requirements. That man out there is a hired assassin of the worst kind. He will erase ye, no matter what, and leave nothing to link this deed with Uppal. Even if he fails, nothing will touch Uppal."

"How can you be so sure?" asked Mr Gupta.

"Because it is the only possible explanation!" said MacKeeg emphatically. "And ye know it! Ye have to trust an old soldier. By the time the morning comes y'll be as sure as I."

"And Jhatish?"

"He has just done the hardest thing he will have to do. Like Lucknow we have to keep the enemy guessing. We are dead already, yet we can still do the unthinkable and beat the bastards."

Mr Gupta wavered again. Was this story proof enough? He opened his mouth to plead for more time, when the world shimmered and Kiran stepped onto the beach before them. She spoke without hesitation.

"Ravi Uppal had me killed. You must protect our darling Rupa. You are a strong man so do not be afraid. You will bring balance to all things and the universe will be right again. Listen to MacKeeg."

Tears blinded Mr Gupta. When he wiped them away Kiran had gone. The imagined safety of his mundane existence had been an illusion. Death had always stalked him. It had stalked him closer than he could ever have imagined and it took a tumour to reveal the plain truth of it. He smiled: his vision was cured; his mind was razor sharp; and he felt ridiculously well, self-pity aside. Dying was giving him a new start. It was ironic. He had known the truth all along and allowed fear of change to become a faux armour. MacKeeg had disabused him of this. He felt new hope and greater strength.

"Will he have a gun?"

"Nay," said MacKeeg.

"How do you know?"

"It has to look unplanned," said MacKeeg.

"Will I live long enough to do what I must?" he asked.

"Aye, laddie," said MacKeeg, "plenty long enough. So, are ye ready?"

"Yes," said Mr Gupta.

The night seemed eternal and fatigue crept upon them. Neither were prepared for the explosion in Rupa's room. A barely audible tinkle of glass was followed by a loud *Whoomph!* The door burst open to reveal a raging inferno. Mr Gupta leapt towards the wall of flames, but the heat gave him the truth — everything inside was lost. He had been too slow. He dropped to his hands and knees and the world began to spin away. A silhouette darkened the window and panic took hold. The Mechanic had arrived.

Mr Gupta crawled across to the chair and reached beneath, just as the door crashed open. The Mechanic was dressed in black and had no gun! MacKeeg had been right. His weapon was a length of metal wielded in a gloved hand. He came in fast, easily spotting the crouching figure of Mr Gupta silhouetted against the fire, blackened face frozen in fear. The Mechanic swung his weapon in a wide arc. Too wide. Too wide to hit an old soldier.

"*Buaidh no Bàs!*" screamed an unearthly voice.

MacKeeg leapt upwards thrusting the point of a long screwdriver through Kush Karnik's throat. It smashed through his palate and out through his temple. Karnik screamed and fell, dropping the tyre iron in a clatter to the floor. The room was filling with smoke and small fires were igniting beyond Rupa's room. MacKeeg pressed home his advantage with brutal ruthlessness, kicking the screwdriver with the heel of his shoe. Karnik howled and tried to crawl away, but there was to be no respite and no mercy. Karnik's mind could not, would not, comprehend what was happening. A kick caught him in the stomach. Winded, he rolled over. With horrified disbelief, he stared into the enraged face of Mr Gupta.

"Ye are a fucking useless assassin, laddie. One question or I'll leave ye to burn – who sent ye?"

Kush Karnik gazed through unspeakable pain at the figure above him. Survival was all now.

"Vassshh!" he gasped, through pinioned jaw and broken teeth.

Mr Gupta finally understood that all MacKeeg had told him was true. As the flames roared, incinerating his final link to the past, an uncontrollable fury filled him. He picked up the tyre iron and beat Karnik to death, continuing even when the face was gone and the flames began to scorch his clothes.

"Let's get out of here man!" shouted MacKeeg. "The fire will do for us!"

Mr Gupta regained his senses. The horror of what he had done almost broke his mind.

"Help me!" he cried as the world blazed around him.

MacKeeg took his charge into the night, grabbing a single bag from the corner, dropping the bloody tyre iron as he went. He left all that stood of his old life to burn. The moon was lower, dropping towards the west and the sky looked pink in the east.

"What does 'bwee no bas' mean?" he asked

"Victory or death," said MacKeeg.

"We have both," said Mr Gupta. "Where are we going?"

"To the station," replied MacKeeg. "The 06:00 train will be leaving soon enough."

Chapter 19

The Journey Begins

In Yamuna Naga the house had burned fiercely, the fire spreading to nearby properties which were only saved by the swift response of the fire brigade. Mr Gupta's home, however, was beyond salvation. It was razed. His shrine to Kiran and all he had loved was gone.

The Shatabdi left Delhi on time. How he had reached the station he could not recall, but his lungs still burned with the unaccustomed effort. It had been MacKeeg who had driven him beyond what he would have considered the point of exhaustion. And what a sight he must have been: a middle-aged man in crumpled cream trousers and grubby white shirt, dishevelled and dirty, hanging on to a bulging bag; bug-eyed and dribbling, shuffling along in his stout, but worn, Indian Railways issued shoes. He smelled of smoke and his thinning hair was wild and matted. The only thing he clearly remembered was the roar of the flames tearing through everything he treasured, every memory, everything he and Kiran had owned. MacKeeg had left him at the station to find his way to where he knew the train would be waiting. He mused how difficult it would be for a Victorian soldier to negotiate the complexities of the modern railway system. The picture of a computer sheet flashed through his mind.

"Bloody hell," he mumbled.

The cacophony in the early morning station had brought him back to reality. Getting to the train had been easy enough. He was known and respected by the staff and his scruffy appearance raised no eyebrows – it was early and busy. Everyone was a little jaded. His pass had gained him quick access to the Superintendents' Wash Room for which he was grateful, as he was well aware of the horrors in the public facilities. Once clean, he had finally boarded the 06:00 Bhopal Shatabdi – the very one upon which he had made his previous, fateful trip. He made his way to his favourite spot, his pass being a free ticket for any train he might choose. The kitchen boys chattered nearby as they put together breakfast packs for the passengers in First Class. He was all in. Familiar surroundings helped relax him and the moving train soon rocked him into a dreamless sleep. Miles slipped by.

The gentle shaking of his shoulder and a soft voice dragged him from the well of sleep. He knew the voice before he was fully conscious.

"Sir? Mr Gupta?" said Raj. "Wake up and enjoy the pleasures of my tea!"

Mr Gupta opened his eyes and blinked at the smiling face of the tea-boy he liked so much. He smiled back, voice straining as he stretched his arms above his head.

"How is your pencil, Raj?" asked Mr Gupta, accepting the mug of tea.

"Still unused – but ready!" chuckled Raj, pushing back his red baseball cap. "But it is agreed we will marry as soon as I get promoted to manager status. So, all my hard work must pay off, or I may burst!"

"You will make a good manager, Raj," said Mr Gupta. "Never lose your sense of humour, but be aware of old farts who may consider you an upstart."

"Yes sir!" said Raj settling opposite. "We have heard that you have been unwell, Mr Gupta. Is it true?"

Raj's constant smile ebbed away as he looked intently at the man he admired and liked. This simple question was a shock – Mr Gupta was unsure how to answer. As the fug of sleep evaporated he tried to rationalise his last few hours.

"Yes, Raj," he finally replied, sipping his tea. "I have been ill and will not be back at work for a while, but it is nothing too serious. I have had some treatment and am convalescing, so I thought I would take the opportunity to visit friends in Bhopal."

"Ah, I see," said Raj, his smile reappearing as he stood. "Well, I shall make sure you have food and tea all the way! No one will bother you here. Old Shesh is the conductor and he came through just after Agra…"

"Goodness me! We have passed Agra already?"

"Oh yes sir! And Morena," pronounced Raj. "You were very much in the Land of Nodding! Can I fetch you some food?"

"Toast would be nice," said Mr Gupta, absently.

"Toast it shall be!" said Raj and disappeared into the clatter of the kitchen.

The tea was perfect and Mr Gupta savoured every drop. His mouth and throat had been parched and tasted of eggs for some reason. He also ached in places he forgot he owned. As he settled, clutching his warm mug, he could finally gather his thoughts. He had killed a man! The memory of the thrusting screwdriver shook him as he saw the awful aftermath of the murderous attack on his life. Ravi Uppal had wanted him dead! Rupa too! Panic rose in his chest as the enormity of what he was part of threw up a mixture of feelings. Despair, sorrow, anger and confusion fought for prominence.

"Hush now, laddie."

MacKeeg was sitting opposite.

"All is well for now," he said. "But, ye have a few things to do. Don't ye talk aloud though or they may have a paddy wagon waiting for you at Bhopal."

"I am scared," said Mr Gupta. "I have lost everything and can see no advantage."

"Enough of that!" shouted MacKeeg, face twisted in anger, spittle flying with the force of the outburst. "Y'know we have to do this, soldier! Trust MacKeeg. Trust me! Y're through this opening skirmish, now we have to prepare for a war of attrition. Cobra is a two-headed dragon that needs killing!"

"An interesting analogy, but I am dying, MacKeeg," said Mr Gupta simply. "And I have become a murderer. What the hell am I supposed to do?"

He was just as forceful, a spark of anger flaring to life. For an instant he and MacKeeg were a single mind, reviewing everything. The coming together of all the intelligence of the recent past calmed him, and his nerves left. The sleep had revived him. MacKeeg sat quietly smoking and smiling.

"Tell me, laddie," he said. "What *are* we going to do?"

"Draw the dragon away from his world and into ours. Bring him after us. Make him follow."

"Aye," said MacKeeg, nodding and gesturing with his pipe. "We choose the ground and, if we do, we can cut off the heads. Uppal's is not so difficult."

"Vasupati Chopra?" said Mr Gupta.

"He will take some killing."

"He will. Yes, he will."

Mr Gupta looked at his reflection in the window behind William MacKeeg. For a moment he could see a mixture of himself and the Scot, but forced his eyes to look at himself alone. He had changed so much in such a short time. He had lost the excess weight a man in his fifties was liable to carry. His hair was longer and more ragged, his thinning pate disappearing under the uncut wisps. His moustache mingled with long stubble, now almost white to match his hair – how could the colour go so quickly? Yet his eyes looked bright without the weak, relaxed look spectacles tended to engender. He was gazing at Mr Gupta the killer. But what did a killer look like? The man he had beaten to death and left to the flames of his house had looked like an ordinary fellow. In spite of everything, his reflection still looked like that of a harmless man.

"That is our strength," said MacKeeg. "Chopra is coming to kill a feeble sheep of a man. He'll never expect to get killed for his troubles. I think we should send him a message."

The house had burned for hours. The dry, post-monsoon weather had allowed the flames to rage unchecked, scorching nearby homes and causing mayhem in a nearby alley, which had become a shanty for many poor families. Their shelters were made of timber, plastic and palm leaves; sparks had settled and caused a second conflagration that raged unchecked. The owners wailed and cried as everything they possessed burned before their eyes. The fire brigade concentrated on saving the adjoining houses, but sent a smaller unit to the alley, where they had to pull the ragged structures apart with long, hooked poles to reduce the concentrated heat and allow hoses to damp the area down. They also had to try and hold back desperate owners who defied all logic and safety in trying to rescue something of their lives. Some succeeded in grabbing the odd cook-pot or smouldering keepsake, several received burns for their effort, one elderly woman died, her heart giving out at the shock of her loss.

By mid-morning all that was left of the Gupta house was a pile of ashes and blackened bricks. Smoke still rose and firemen damped down remaining hot-spots as policemen kept people back, though even skilled scavengers would have struggled to find anything of value. The remains of the shanties had more to offer and the salvaging of useable remnants had already started. A young policeman had found a bloody tyre iron by the Gupta property's boundary wall and, in a flash of conscientious vigour, placed it in an evidence bag. He went straight to Police Chief Kamdar who was leaning against his jeep smoking, already penning a report in his mind – domestic accident, end of paperwork, then it would be the insurer's problem.

"Sir," said Sandeep, his nephew. "I have found this by the wall over there. It has blood and hair all over it."

"Looks fresh," said Kamdar absently, but his interest was aroused.

"Keep it safe and see if the forensic chaps can do something later. There is nothing here to bring them down, so I trust you to follow it up, Sandeep. Get some of the lads to ask around for witnesses and the like. All we know so far is an Anil Gupta lives here alone and he seems to be missing. Away perhaps. We will need some information." He then turned and shouted at his men. "Keep that bloody crowd back! Push the cordon further out will you Shah! Bloody hell, this is not a free-for-all! Tell them you'll shoot anyone who breaks through!" He turned back to his nephew. "Off you go then. Do some detecting!"

"Yes uncle," said Sandeep, saluting.

"Sir! Call me Sir you clod!"

"Sorry uncle, I mean Sir," shouted Sandeep over his shoulder.

This would spark an investigation which would grow rapidly, falter, then cool gently – a solution was found raising further questions, which were ignored until they went away.

Kamdar sighed, his simple report gathering complexity in his head. He lit another cigarette and went to lean against the jeep again.

"Chief Kamdar!" It was the Fire Chief. "We've found a body."

Jhatish Das manoeuvred The Duck as close to his friend's house as he could. He wept as he drove – horrified and worried in equal measure. The previous evening, he had been reluctant to leave Mr Gupta alone, but carried out his task with the tight knot of anxiety in his stomach.

"You have to go," Mr Gupta had said. "I will make my stand here. I am dying anyway and you have work to do, my dear chap. You must carry it through."

He had watched the supposed assassin follow his friend into the back streets and was there when Mr Gupta returned. From being simply a loyal friend, Jhatish had become key to a series of events he could not possibly have foreseen, nor fully understand. He was to take the memory stick to Sudhesh Shastri and give him as much information as possible, so he could start to unravel Cobra's real persona and avenge Tamina and Kiran's deaths.

"Whatever y'do, do not return here," Mr Gupta had said in that strange voice. "Ye have already done enough. I shall be in touch, dinnae ye worry about that."

But Jhatish had seen the morning news and had been unable to stay away. He was sure things had gone wrong. Absolutely sure. He left The Duck in the market and jogged towards the crowd surrounding the smoking gap where the house once stood. He pushed his way to the front ignoring protests, to gaze at the smoking heap of rubble. The destruction was astonishing – the house was gone!

"There is a body – could be more," said a man next to him.

"How did it happen?" asked Jhatish unable not to sound distressed.

Several people began to answer, eager to add what they knew or supposed to be true.

"No one knows…"

"An electrical fault, perhaps…"

"Cigarettes? Did Gupta smoke…?"

"My house was nearly set alight…"

"No one has seen Gupta…"

"His must be the body…"

All the voices coalesced into babble as Jhatish stared across the smoking ruins – then he froze. Vasupati Chopra was on the far side talking into his phone. Jhatish faded into the crowd and made his way back to The Duck, anxious, but sure he had not been seen. He should have stayed away. His horror was intensified by the mention of a body. He had set out on his errand, sure of but one thing – whether it be the assassin or Gupta, they would find only one body.

Vaz had spent a wakeful night awaiting Kush Karnik's call. Instead he received one from Ravi Uppal.

"Look at the local news!"

The fire had been raging for some time and many news cameras had arrived to record the drama, the burning shanties adding to the spectacle. It was Mr Gupta's house. Ravi was happy enough. In spite of the silence from Kush Karnik, Vaz had made sure all aspects of the plan were in place.

He had called Rat. Rat was a creature he could rely on. He confirmed the body was rapidly thawing in a back alley. The police would find a dead heroin addict with a rolled-up wad of notes in his pocket, a receipt for a tyre iron and a card with Anil Gupta's address scribbled upon it. Vaz knew they may also find a medal depicting Shiva, but nothing more. It was a simple set of events which he knew the police would quickly decipher: robbery and murder, the money spent on drugs which led to an overdose. Karnik was missing, yet everything seemed to be as was intended. What exactly had happened?

On impulse he drove to the smouldering remains of the house. After mingling with the onlookers and finding out all he could, he called Ravi.

"There is no sign of Gupta," he said. "He may have died. They have found a body."

"One?" said Ravi, uneasily.

"Maybe more," said Vaz. "It is a mess down here. I'll wait and see what turns up."

He waited well into the morning and eventually fell into conversation with a young policeman. He discovered that a bloodied weapon had been found, foul play was suspected and that there was only one body, and that so badly burnt it was hard to tell anything about the victim, though it was assumed to be a man. But where was the girl? He ventured to ask the young officer if they could use dental records to identify the body.

"That's the odd thing," Sandeep had said. "It looks as if the poor fellow died horribly three times over."

"Three?"

"Well, there is a metal rod stuck in his head, nasty that. Also, his face had been smashed in – no teeth left. Or he could have been burned to death too. However he died, it was not nice."

Vaz relaxed. This whole scenario had The Mechanic's signature written all over it – all that was missing was Karnik, and a second body. Annoyed with loose ends, Vaz was walking back to the car when his phone rang. It was Karnik at last! He accepted the call.

"About time Kush," he hissed.

"Now I know the name of the man I killed," said Mr Gupta.

The shock was absolute. Vaz struggled to comprehend what he was hearing. Gupta had killed Kush Karnik? A man even Vaz considered intimidating. He found his voice.

"I don't know what you are talking about," said Vaz, regaining control. "Is this you Anil?"

"'*All life's weaving is undone,*'" quoted Mr Gupta.

"Are you alright?" asked Vaz. The adrenaline released his Kāla mind. The uncertainty went. He had to gain some information.

"I know everything," said Mr Gupta. "Tamina. Kiran. Cobra. I know all."

"Where are you?" asked Vaz, voice now full of authority.

"I am going to bring ye to an end," came the answer.

Vaz was rattled again. The voice had changed.

"You are dying," he said. "How can *you* kill me?"

"Kush was easy," said the voice. "Ye come to me and find out."

"Let me know where you are and I will!" snapped Vaz.

"I will be in touch."

The call ended. Vaz thumped the car roof. He was furious.

Param and Taraa Singh were mortified.

"Trust me," Mr Gupta had said. "Just do this one thing and I can be at peace."

They were both tired and now stood in the crowd gazing at a stretcher being carried from the smoking rubble. They held hands like young lovers. Jhatish had left them earlier and they could think of nothing else but to witness first-hand what had happened. Old Mr Singh wept quietly and his wife held him close.

"What the hell is going on?" he sniffed. "What has Anil gone and done?"

"Ssh now," said his wife. "Ssssh. If Jhatish said all will be well, we must trust him."

"Mr Gupta said the same thing, but look at this…this mess!"

"Hush, Param, my darling man," she said. "We were told not to worry about what we may see. What we may hear. We are to wait and say nothing."

"Taraa, Taraa," said Old Mr Singh, sniffing again, "have you not thought he may be unhinged? He…he has that thing in his head. He is…he is dying…and his brain is damaged. He is on a crusade to put things right – things that sound crazy if you think about it. Is this it? Suicide in his house now all these *loose ends* are tied up? Is this why he had us do what we have?"

"No!" said his wife, squeezing him tighter. "Come, let us go home and wait. Have faith Param. Have faith."

Old Mr Singh stared a while longer at the curling wisps of smoke drifting up to the blue sky, then at the stretcher bearers struggling over the rubble. The body beneath was covered in a green sheet, the shape obvious. It was charred stiff, arms curled up and in towards the torso – it looked as if the sheet concealed a statue. The front bearer stumbled and the sheet shifted. A black arm was exposed, the hand a hideous claw. The crowd gasped. Taraa Singh pulled her husband away, holding his hand all the way back to their home, needing comfort as much as he. The sight of that roasted, clawed arm had shaken her faith, but she knew one thing above all – whoever was under that sheet, Rupa Gupta was now safe.

The Shatabdi sped south. It had passed Gwalior as Mr Gupta put his phone away. His heart had felt like a caged butterfly as he had conversed with his would-be executioner, but MacKeeg had helped him choose the words he needed for the greatest effect. It had worked. The plan was in place and Vaz had been stung. If he could stay calm and retain a semblance of sanity they really had quite an edge. Kiran was right in that he was strong and now he had the chance to avenge her murder and save his daughter. He *had* to believe he was sane for her sake. He no longer doubted the culpability of Ravi Uppal and Vasupati Chopra in the deaths of Tamina and Kiran. The assassin he killed was proof enough, as was Vaz's reaction to his call. MacKeeg had predicted it, prepared for it and saved his life. He would never doubt his MacKeeg mind again. By killing the assassin, he had struck an unlikely pre-emptive blow at Cobra and for that he was pleased.

His phone pinged as a message arrived:
Jhatish: *?*
Mr Gupta: *I am OK. Rupa?*
Jhatish: *All safe. Anything Else?*
Mr Gupta: *Tell Singhs I am fine.*
Jhatish: *Please take care.*

Mr Gupta closed his eyes and reflected on the success of their plan so far. Jhatish and the Singhs had held up their side perfectly, with no thought for their own safety. Rupa had been spirited away in Old Mr Singh's tuktuk whilst the assassin followed Mr Gupta through the market. It was a risk, but MacKeeg pointed out that Ravi Uppal would not be expecting anything but passive ignorance from their soft target. Earlier in the day, Jhatish had visited Sudhesh Shastri in his Delhi offices and appraised him of events. Sudhesh had initially been ready to intervene to stop any possible harm, but reluctantly accepted that nothing was proven as yet. He loved his family and had been shattered at the death of both his sisters. Rupa was equally adored, though the Guptas had become estranged of late. Sudhesh would now put that right. It was the data on the memory stick that gave him a jolt. He had no time for Ravi Uppal and considered him to be mean spirited and crafty. The Shastri financial services had never been used by Cobra Investments, and Sudhesh was sure he knew why – irregularities. Fallen Angels had the whiff of fakery about it. The story Jhatish told and the information he supplied sent Sudhesh into action. If there was anything illegal contained in those data, his people would find it. He agreed to look after Rupa without hesitation – his homes were big enough to keep her happy, and his security strong enough to give her safe sanctuary.

The element of surprise had been used to perfection and Mr Gupta's moves would remain unclear. Ravi Uppal would take time to understand the seriousness of his situation, but when he did, time would be short. Meanwhile, Sudhesh Shastri would use the opportunity to unravel the truth of Cobra's hidden financial irregularities. As long as Rupa was safe Mr Gupta would no longer need to involve his loved ones. He had made himself the biggest thorn in Cobra's side.

It was the second part of the plan that was the most volatile. Vasupati Chopra had to be drawn away: the dragon had to be confronted at a place of MacKeeg's choosing. He had to be slain before the tumour did its work. There was the chance hired assassins would be used, so MacKeeg had made things personal – the challenge in the call had hit home. However, success relied upon Mr Gupta running in full sight. This really was madness, he thought.

Raj had brought Mr Gupta a tray of toast, biscuits and more tea. He ate hungrily as he pondered his future. Then it struck him – he had no idea where he was ultimately going! His heart sank.

"I know where we should go, laddie," said MacKeeg from the seat opposite.

"Bhopal?" asked Mr Gupta.

"Nay, not there," said MacKeeg. "There is a story deep in your memory and it ties in with something ye have wanted to do since y'came back from England."

"I am not sure what you mean," said Mr Gupta.

"Think sandcastles!" chuckled MacKeeg.

In an instant Mr Gupta knew. His memory opened younger eyes and he was looking at a book full of painted illustrations. It was A History of the British Raj published in 1924, an old book his Uncle Nik had given him. Originally aimed at the children of expatriate British families, it explained how the East India Company developed to the point where India's affairs were governed from London. But it was a chapter about Robert Clive's adventures that he loved the most. On page 33 was a picture showing the sunset over a calm ocean, the moon shining, huge and silver, with a ship sitting at anchor, silhouetted against the sky. There was also the figure of a man sitting on a rock staring at the sinking sun – Robert Clive. He had sheltered here after a storm. Clive's Beach. It was the very place to which he fled to talk to MacKeeg, north of Goa, hidden in a cliff-bound bay. He would find it somehow.

"Clive's Beach," he muttered.

"Aye, laddie," said MacKeeg. "Our beach. If we are choosing the ground it should be somewhere we would like to end. Somewhere nice."

"The sea!" exclaimed Mr Gupta. "I've never seen the Indian Ocean!"

Mr Gupta was a boy once more. Clive, a man of ambition, stopping to stare at the beauty of an unplanned refuge in a country whose name he would become synonymous with. That picture was locked in his mind, and strong enough to have a bearing on his future.

"I want to go to the sea," he said.

Chapter 20

Olaf and Seva

In the clearing of a high wooded valley a pack of dholes had stalked a spotted deer. The attack had come in early morning, mountain mists hiding their approach, giving the old animal little chance of flight. It had put up a spirited fight, but blood loss and exhaustion saw it topple under the combined weight of the dogs. Once down it was doomed and died under the onslaught of the hungry pack. They did not settle for long. An ear-splitting roar cleaved the air as a huge tiger charged from the cover of nearby bushes scattering the dholes in disarray.

Angaar had yet to successfully hunt wild prey. On this morning he was hungry, so coming across the dholes gave him the opportunity to feed on fresh meat. He took the carcass easily. He tore at the flesh swallowing great lumps whilst keeping a wary eye on the dholes that were pacing nearby. A hyena loped into view, whilst above vultures, kites and crows circled waiting their turn. Occasionally a dhole would rush in to nip at Angaar's rump whereupon he would spin to claw at the fast retreating attacker. The wild dogs instinctively knew that as the tiger grew fuller, his resolve would weaken. Eventually, stomach bulging, Angaar stood and left the clearing ignoring the sudden rush of dholes behind him. He settled in the cool of some scrub and long grass nearby, laying his head on his front paws, shaking his ears frantically as flies settled on his bloodied fur. He dozed, ignoring the howls and yaps from the clearing where the carcass was being reduced to skin and bone.

Olaf stretched in the cold morning air. He had remained at his lofty camp longer than intended, enjoying the solitude and the magnificent views. For the first time in years he felt physically and mentally strong, enjoying life above ancient India. He had no absolute plans and was wandering south taking things as they came. Over the weeks he had travelled through Rajasthan, visited Delhi, hitched a ride to Agra and spent two days mixing with the colourful throngs of people at the Taj Mahal. Eventually he had made his way to the Western Ghats, determined to walk as far as he could high above the civilised world.

Olaf had been drawn to India. His maternal grandfather had served with the army here between the wars and Olaf possessed many old pictures of him in various places, some complete with pith helmet. He enjoyed the feeling of following the tracks of a man he had known only briefly, but had learned to love. Michael Savage had enjoyed life and made a great impression on his little grandson. He always laughed, enjoyed whiskey and beer and sang bawdy songs, much to the horror of Olaf's mother. He had died when Olaf was seven, but the fascination for Michael Savage remained and Olaf had pieced together a lot of his history from army pay books, diaries, photographs, postcards and letters. He knew where his grandfather had travelled in India and now used these places as a rough guide for his present journey. Olaf was drifting south, but there was somewhere he was determined to find. There was a picture of his grandfather sat on a rock next to the sea, naked but for that pith helmet. He was heading there.

His mother, Mary, had married a Dane, Eric Roff. Olaf's early life had been split between Copenhagen and his mother's family home in Dublin. After a surprisingly amicable divorce, mother and son settled in Ireland permanently. Eric visited regularly and laughed at his bilingual son's Irish accent, especially when speaking Danish, but had remained a caring father, often taking young Olaf away for weeks at a time, giving him a love of travel. With two such strong, unconventional influences on his life, Olaf developed an adventurous spirit.

"Olaf, you are like your grandfather", his mother had often said.

He had been like his grandfather in many other ways too, and his presence in India was more than a pilgrimage to Michael Savage. Olaf's own military past still held him in its thrall. This journey was his attempt at cleansing his mind of never-ending nightmares. He had reasoned that travel would help cure him, and India was proving to be the right place. Meeting the tiger had certainly given him a lot to think about. He wondered if his grandfather could match that particular event. In his high camp he had started to feel better. This made him smile as the sound of wild dogs and the roar of a tiger echoed up from below. It was quite a place to find one's sanity. He would move out today, he decided, keeping to the high ground as far as possible and, perhaps have a break in Goa but, before all this, he would find that beach. The coordinates were written on the back of his grandfather's picture. He occasionally descended to a village for supplies – some rice and whatever protein could be had for a few rupees. He could always trap an animal should he need to, but was loath to take a life just out of convenience. Survival was hard enough for wild creatures. He thought he could be a Buddhist should he chose to reduce himself with religion. The very thought made him laugh.

Right now, he wanted to fill his water bladder from a nearby stream. The sounds of the dhole pack down in the valley receded as he made his way along a game trail into dense undergrowth and trees. The sun had risen higher, but it was still chilly here on the hills, with patches of mist in shadowy hollows. Olaf paused briefly to let a muntjac cross his path, the small deer picking its way cautiously through the vegetation, sniffing the air. Olaf was down-wind so to the deer he was just an undefinable shape against the trees. He watched the little creature disappear noiselessly, then set off again. He could hear the stream before he saw it, but there was another accompanying sound.

"Eeesh!" The cry was followed by sobbing and mumbled words. After a few seconds a wail of anguish, then the "Eeesh!" once more. Olaf was perplexed. He felt for his knife, grasped the handle and drew it. For a big man he could move with surprising silence. He crept out into the clearing and saw a very small, thin man curled up on the stream bank. He was in obvious distress and jabbered as he tried to stand, falling each time onto his face and sobbing some more. Olaf thought he had seen more flesh on a butcher's pencil. The man was dressed in filthy green overalls and close by lay a baseball cap with what looked like the picture of a tiger emblazoned on the front. He was shod in the most threadbare sandals he had ever seen, indeed one hung loose fastened only by a single strand to a bony ankle.

"Eeesh" – softer now and muffled by the man's arm across his face. He spoke intelligible words that made little sense, "Angaar, where are you? I cannot…must not…death is lonely…"

This man had nothing with him, nothing at all, and had the trail-worn look of a refugee. Olaf put his knife away and went to the stricken figure, crouching so as not to seem intimidating.

"Hey," he said, reaching out and touching the man's shoulder. "Hey. Are you ok feller?"

The little man turned and stared at Olaf. His big eyes were full of pain – not fear or madness.

"Do you understand me?" asked Olaf, smiling.

The man struggled to a sitting position still looking at Olaf, obviously surprised at a huge, blond white man in a world of shorter, dark-skinned locals.

"Angaar," said the man.

"I'm not at all angry," chuckled Olaf. "I am friendly. Do you understand me?"

"Slowly," said the man. "Slowly and, yes, understand."

"I am Olaf. I will help you."

"Food," said the man, adding, "please."

Olaf sifted through his pockets and found a small packet of Marie biscuits he had kept from a recent train journey and two squares of chocolate still in a crumpled wrapper. He handed them to the man and noted that, though desperate, it was taken politely, with thanks. As the man nibbled at the sparse meal Olaf filled his water bladder by pumping it through a filter. He always filtered fresh water as one dose of giardiasis in a previous life had been more than enough to teach him a lesson. Once finished he held out a hand to the man.

"Come on feller," he said being careful to smile reassuringly. "Come with Olaf and I shall make you a decent breakfast."

The little man took the proffered hand, stood shakily and followed.

Olaf decided to remain at the camp for a while longer. The little man had managed to drink some tea, but continued to shiver at the back of the rock shelter until Olaf had wrapped him in his spare fleece. He rarely felt the cold in these relatively low mountains, so the loan was no hardship. He even managed to find enough dry wood to make a fire with a rock surround – the hot stones would hold the heat. Hardly a word was spoken and Olaf thought he had probably said more to the tiger, but this small man was in a daze of exhaustion, cold and hunger so it was not surprising. After more tea, food became the important thing and from somewhere in his Bergen Olaf found a half-remembered dehydrated meal labelled *Nasi Goreng*, which he cooked in his battered army canteen.

"Eat," he said handing it to his new companion. "Rice and vegetables."

The man took the canteen and with a spoon delicately ate the yellow, spicy mixture, which again impressed Olaf. Manners were rare at such times. Once the tin was half-empty the man finally looked warm and had stopped shaking. He spoke.

"I am Seva."

"And I am Olaf, as I said."

"Are you a god?" asked Seva, wide eyed.

"Jaysus, no," said Olaf laughing. "Just a feller out for a walk and enjoying these fine hills of yours."

"Oh. Thank you for the food," said Seva.

"Now don't you go worrying about that," said Olaf. "It tastes like shite, but it'll keep you going and warm your cockles."

Seva found the man's use of English hard to follow, some words utterly baffling. Seva's own native dialect was of no use in greater India so, like most people, he had learnt English just to survive, but Indian English was very different to the utterances he was now struggling to comprehend.

"What are you doing up here dressed like that, anyhow?" asked Olaf. "And what is this Project Tiger badge you've got on? You don't look much like a game warden to me."

"I am looking for Angaar," said Seva.

"Anger?" repeated Olaf.

"Ang-aar," enunciated Seva. "It is what I call my tiger."

Olaf goggled. Tigers had become a bit of a theme in his recent life. The gears in his mind finally meshed.

"Is this tiger a friendly sort?" he asked.

"To me, yes," said Seva.

"Is he dangerous?"

"He killed two very bad men," said Seva simply.

"You don't say," said Olaf with a whistle.

"I did say," said Seva, "but these men tried to kill him!"

"Oh, I see," said Olaf smiling, "that makes all the difference, so it does. And how did he do that?"

"He bit their heads."

"Fuck me," mumbled Olaf, remembering the huge tiger that had sniffed his face. "And you are his master?"

"No sahib," said Seva. "He is my friend and is ill and scared. He needs help. But I am finished now. I have no strength. Angaar is lost."

"I think you are still pretty much alive," said Olaf. "A bit on the small side and wiry, but you'll be ok. Oddly enough I have a hunch this Angaar tiger is not so far away."

Seva sat up.

"What is your meaning?" he asked.

"Well, a while back I spent the night with a tiger, so to speak. I was camped up pretty high and half asleep, when this big beast strolled by and curled up opposite me."

"Were you not scared?"

Olaf's smile was replaced with a pensive look. He had not considered such an obvious question too deeply. He knew he ought to have been worried at the time, but there was something about that tiger that failed to hit any alarm bell. The smile returned as he remembered the firm grasp he had had on his knife. If this animal had the capacity to dispatch two men by simply biting their heads, he doubted whether he could have discouraged it from such a course of action, had it so wished. Olaf had just ignored the probable risk and relied on instinct. And he had been right. The tiger had practically kissed him goodbye. It had to be this Angaar. His sojourn to India had become slightly mystical.

"I was not scared," he said chuckling. "Whether that is because I am daft, or the tiger is not keen on Viking meat, I am not sure, but he seemed to be, well, placid – you know, friendly."

"You have been touched by the gods," said Seva with wonder. "You are to play a part in his future, I am sure." Seva had continued eating during the conversation and held up the empty mess tin. "Thank you, sahib," he said.

"It's Olaf," said Olaf. "O-l-af! Easy."

"Owalf," said Seva.

"O-laff," said Olaf again.

"Olab," said Seva, triumphantly.

"Close enough," said Olaf resignedly. "Now I shall make another brew, then you can sleep."

"But I have to find Angaar," said Seva.

"All in good time," said Olaf. "You'll have more of a chance if you rest and get your strength back. You look fecked. Get some sleep and I'll have a wander and see if I can find some tiger signs."

"You can track?" asked Seva.

"Men usually," said Olaf, "but this tiger of yours is not too sneaky. I've already followed his trail on and off. My guess he is down yonder in that valley. He seems to be heading south."

"Are you helping me?" asked Seva.

"We all seem to be heading in the same direction," said Olaf. "So why not, eh? Get some zeds in. There's hot water over the fire and plenty of tea bags in the top of that stuff sack. I'll be away a couple of hours…" He stopped talking.

Seva had nestled into the huge fleece and had fallen asleep.

Olaf covered him with his tarp to make sure he stayed warm.

"Poor little fecker," he said.

The dholes moved away from the remains of their kill, making way for the waiting hyena and carrion birds. The afternoon grew warm, the chill of the high mountain valley finally being driven off by the sun's lofty glare. Insects buzzed and the hyena, vultures and crows squabbled over the carcass. A white-browed wagtail paced the sward behind the larger birds, occasionally flying up in a tumbling aerial dance to grab an insect disturbed by the throng. Hidden in the undergrowth Angaar watched the scene unfolding – sated, restful and, for once, without a dull ache inside his gut. A tiger's memory is stored in the cerebral cortex; it is not reflective, but instinctive, stimulated by senses to physical action when required. He missed Seva, the creature his mind framed as *clever monkey*, yet his plaintive search call had waned as more pressing matters crowded his world. His wilding had been rapid and the need to survive as the top predator had taken precedence; the memory of Seva would surface when related stimuli were encountered. His early life in the wild, though short, had played a part in his survival. Eating *live* food had reinvigorated him, stimulating the need to hunt with the reward of a good meal. So far, he had not gone hungry and remained in good condition, notwithstanding the chronic ache that plagued him more and more.

Angaar had no obvious range with which he could become familiar. Male tigers usually had large territories overlapping those of several females and, though the boundaries were fluid, they tended to remain on the familiar ground of their own. Where a female was involved males might trespass, but generally preferred a peaceful life. As a wanderer, Angaar was vulnerable, yet, in spite of his long walk south, he had encountered no others of his kind. Tigers were rare in the Western Ghats. His long journey was thus both empty and full of game. He was a loner by dint of circumstance. He had no reason to move on today: he had a full stomach, fresh water nearby in a log-blocked stream and his lair was cool and comfortable. He dozed.

It was the scent of the hyena that roused him. The remains of the deer were now bone, hide and sinew, but this was a fine meal for the strong-jawed scavenger. The capricious breeze finally took the hyena's acrid scent to Angaar's nostrils. The stimulus triggered latent memories of his time in the zoological gardens and that elusive creature he hated. He leapt from his lair, roaring as he charged. The hyena, a lone male, had become used to a tiger-free world and failed to react quickly enough. He made the fatal error of freezing at the terrible sound, a strip of bloody hide still hanging from tooth-filled jaws, tail curling down between his legs. In a heartbeat he turned and fled. He moved quickly, glancing over a shoulder in fear, stumbled, rolled and barely regained its feet as the weight of the tiger fell upon him. Long canines sank into the hyena's neck and powerful jaws clamped shut. The hyena yelped and howled horribly whilst trying to bite his assailant. Angaar tore, ripped and slashed, finally dropping the lifeless body to the ground. He sneezed out blood and hair from blocked nostrils then threw back his great head and roared into the sky. Freedom had given him a greater voice.

Another scent came to him. Something vague on the air. Something that made him stretch up and sniff the cool breeze. He turned and started to walk towards the plateau from where it issued.

Olaf Roff felt at peace in high hills. He fixed his position by taking several compass bearings, then walked south towards the edge of the high escarpment. The game trails were oriented in a north-south direction and he saw there was a general convergence. Each time he came to a junction he blazed a tree or bent a branch to make the return trip easier. He walked through verdant clumps of forest interspersed with green scrub and open grassland, all relatively undisturbed. He felt sure the tiger would have used one of these trails and knew there was such a beast below from the roars he had heard. He came to a puddle across the trail and there, in the soft mud, were large pug marks. Olaf crouched and looked closely. Water had not leached into the depressions and the edges were sharply defined, probably no more than a day old. On what was the right forepaw there was a clearly formed diagonal line repeated in other corresponding prints – this was from the tiger he had met. If this beast was Angaar he would be easy enough to identify. Whistling thrushes and bulbuls sang as he walked on and at one point a king cobra slithered away from its basking spot into the undergrowth. He revelled in being unfettered and free to roam without orders or reason, walking quickly and quietly, senses full of life's fecundity. He smiled as a scarlet minivet scolded from a branch above his head, small and feisty in its black and red plumage: size meant nothing in the wild world, it all depended on how the mind was wired. The little bird-man, Seva, showed this. He had courage and conviction that belied his stature, which is why Olaf would help him as best he could. Tracking a tiger was as good a reason as any to continue south, though what they would do when they found it was up for debate. Olaf needed to see what lay ahead as he knew he would need supplies and Seva would need better rest. The spoor of the tiger was obvious and led to a draw where the trail turned down into the lower valley. He saw a pile of faeces at the side of the track. Flies buzzed over the moist pile clustering round darker areas in the mass. Olaf looked and noted crimson streaks of bloody slime – this tiger certainly had something wrong with it.

"Not even dry," said Olaf, quietly to himself. "You shat here late yesterday I should say."

Just then a fearful roar and series of yelps echoed up from somewhere below. A brief pause was broken by a second tremendous roar. The whole valley was quiet for a few seconds before first insects, then birds and chattering monkeys resumed vociferous normality.

"There you are," said Olaf looking over the tree tops.

He started down the steep, winding trail that led towards the valley floor several hundred feet below. He had to slide down some stretches on his backside using overhanging branches for support, eventually stopping to rest where the terrain levelled. Here the trees thinned from forest to the scrubby ground of a long clearing. A gaur snorted and crashed away to his right and a group of hairy pigs ran ahead of him for a short way, before darting down a side trail and out of sight. The sound of running water announced the presence of a stream that ran along the far right-hand side of the clearing, fringed by a thick curtain of forest which stretched up to the southern heights beyond. To his left was another blanket of trees edging the northern side of the valley, converging in the distance with those on the other side. Olaf paused and listened, aware that somewhere close by there could be a tiger. He fingered the handle of his knife. The hairs on his neck stood on end as he breasted a rise in the ground. An explosion of sound made him jump as a cloud of birds flew up from a scattering of bloody bones. He tripped and sat down heavily. A jackal scampered past whining.

"Shite!" said Olaf.

Beyond the bones was the ravaged body of a hyena, wounds still bright red and fresh. Olaf picked himself up and approached carefully, looking around constantly for any signs of danger. He bent and put a hand a clean patch of hide – it still held the warmth of recent life. It was easy for him to follow the set of pug marks which led south-west towards the forested slopes beyond the stream. The same diagonal mark was clear on the front right pug mark. Angaar, if that was who it was, could be no more than an hour away from where Olaf stood. Or resting close by. As he was down wind Olaf knew his scent would be hard to detect, so carefully followed the trail as far as the stream – the tiger had crossed here. He felt he had gone far enough for the moment.

For the next hour he made his way down the stream to see what lay below the far line of trees. He finally came to a waterfall that plunged into a lower valley; the rocks and trail were very slippery here, so he chose to make his way up to higher ground and climbed a tree. He could just make out the hazy lowlands, miles distant, and a few buildings through the trees closer to, along with the lighter green of cultivation. Rising smoke showed it was a village. Olaf had seen enough and began his return journey.

Angaar's senses were at their sharpest. He had managed to survive thus far without too much effort, reflecting the quality of his inherited genes. He had learned fast and the lack of competition had allowed him safe passage as the top predator. His killing of the hyena was born of instinctive loathing for a lesser competitor and confidence in his own size. Now he followed an enticing aroma that continued to waft down from the heights. He left the valley behind, climbing steadily through the trees. Instinct drove him. As he went he spray-scented the trail, an innate show of territorial behaviour. Angaar plodded on ever upwards ignoring the scolding calls of monkeys and birds that heralded his passing. Behind him the sudden burst of wing beats and squawks echoed from the valley floor. He listened. There was no repeat, so he continued following his nose.

Seva woke from a dreamless sleep. His body ached, and he felt weak, but he was warm. He opened his eyes and squinted in the afternoon light which was blocked by a large silhouette. Blinking he squinted harder.

"Angaar?" he whispered.

"Not quite feller," came the reply, "but Olaf has found his trail…at least I think I have."

"Olab," said Seva.

"I'll get used to it," said Olaf. "Give me a few minutes and I'll make some tea. I could do with a cup."

He put together his cooker – a burner, hose and red fuel bottle – pumping up the pressure and struggling to light the poor-quality fuel. Eventually it roared into life and he boiled a pan of water. The tea was strong and sweet, he handed a mug to Seva.

"That'll wet your whistle," said Olaf.

Seva took the drink and sipped it.

"Thank you," he said. "You are a kind giant, Olab."

"You still look peaky," he replied. "I think we will stay here another night and get moving in the morning."

"You have seen Angaar's trail, Olab?" asked Seva.

"I tracked a tiger down to the valley. It made a meal out of a deer of some sort, then killed a hyena, by the looks of it. I heard that happen when I was down yonder. He is now climbing, but further to the south."

"It is him!" pronounced Seva. "We must go now!"

"Steady there, feller," said Olaf firmly. "This beast is moving slowly and we have time. I need to get supplies and get you rested somewhere safer. I only have enough food for a couple of meals, you have sod all and you look shagged out. We wouldn't get very far if we started charging after him right now."

Seva sagged back into his cocoon. "You are right, Olab. I am very tired. Will you still help me?"

"Can't see why not," said Olaf grinning. "We're going the same way and you seem like a nice enough chap. You can help me too. There's a village way down there and we need rice and such. I have the money, you have the lingo – so we can be a team. We may be back on the trail in two days, with some luck and ten strong policemen."

"Why do we need police?"

"Don't worry about it," chuckled Olaf. "Tell me, has this tiger of yours got any marks on his feet?"

"A scar. He was cut when he was taken from the wild. It makes a line on his foot here," said Seva holding up his right hand indicating the palm.

"That's the clincher," said Olaf. "My tiger is the same as yours. You kept pace with him somehow."

He refilled Seva's mug, then drank his tea from the battered canteen.

"I'll fix us some food. Rice, some dried meat and tomato sauce of some kind. A feast in a pot, Seva."

They sat together, both looking over the darkening world to the east, lights twinkling in the hazy distance. They sipped their tea.

"Tell me, Seva. What will you do if we find yon Angaar?" asked Olaf.

"I do not know," replied Seva absently. "But that is not a problem. Whatever will be, will be."

"That's not much of a plan," laughed Olaf. "I just hope he's happy to see you!"

Chapter 21

The Drawing of the Dragon

It was mid-morning when the Shatabdi left Gwalior Junction. Mr Gupta had finally come to grips with what had occurred. His MacKeeg mind had awoken on his other fateful journey to Bhopal, prompting him to accept things were not as they seemed. He had *always* known things were wrong and he had ignored those instinctive warnings. He had been a sheep. How could he have carried on so passively whilst Ravi Uppal had been destroying his life, killing his wife, and now almost finishing the job?

"But we have hit back, laddie," said MacKeeg. "That is what y'have to remember. Ye need not worry about me not being around. I'm here all the while. Feed on that anger. We're dying, and no mistake, but we'll take Chopra with us, and Ravi fucking Uppal will fall. They *think* ye are a sheep, so Chopra will never understand the danger. He is incapable of such thoughts."

"I know he will come," said Mr Gupta, "but when he catches up, what then? He is a natural killer. Heartless. I cannot match that... "

"But I can," asserted MacKeeg. "Look at that bastard ye saw off in Delhi. He would have killed Rupa. Tell me y'are not pleased ye inserted that screwdriver into his face. That will keep you going. If we do not see Chopra off, he'll find Rupa. Now fix that in yer mind."

Mr Gupta did. The anger was still inside, yet there was still doubt. A lifetime of passivity was hard to shake off and, no matter what atavistic depths he had, to step beyond his fixed moral compass was proving counterintuitive. He knew MacKeeg's existence transcended all possible doubts, but he remained fundamentally Gupta and, as such, found violence an uncomfortable bedfellow, though he had felt righteous in killing a man. The assassin's suffering seemed a balanced price to pay for the callous intent with which he would have burned Rupa. His course was irrevocably set. Somehow, he would have to bring Vasupati Chopra to an end, or die in the attempt. Failure was not an option - that would condemn his darling daughter to death.

"I am not scared," Mr Gupta said in his duo of voices. "He cannot kill me, I died in 1857, he is chasing a wraith, and he will end. *Buaidh no Bàs!*"

Mr Gupta could no longer resist the insanity of his dual identity. MacKeeg was his stronger half, his hidden warrior and his saviour. In an instant he was on the beach with a sword in his hand. He knew Kiran and Rupa were behind him, watching their guardian's stand against the coming Death. And Death stood before him, black with blue eyes, absorbing light from the world, relentless and unstoppable. Tall as a tree. The wind grew in strength and the chimera that was Mr Gupta and MacKeeg stood his ground. His long white hair flowed out as he raised the sword to the storm ravaged sky above, lightning making his every movement a flickering dance. The demon shape loomed higher, eyes burning with cold neon, a horror born of darkest nightmares, striding to devour all before it, drawn to the Gupta seed, bent on destruction. Above the screaming wind MacKeeg roared "Hold fast!" and the warrior, the both, bellowed at the black creature, "Fuck you!" then smiled, then laughed at the madness of giving battle to something so huge, so terrible, so unstoppable. Long, black arms lifted, claw-hands poised ready to strike the pathetic creature before it. It was the Destroyer, Kāla, and it believed all would fall and nothing could resist. All plans were to come to fruition here. But the warrior gave it pause. Mr Gupta raced at the monster screaming...*Buaidh no Bàs!...Buaidh no Bàs!...*

High above the world Mr Gupta smiled across at Kiran.

"I am not scared," he said.

"You are strong my darling man," said Kiran. "Doubt not yourself. Put everything right and end our journey."

"Will you be there?" he asked.

"I am as much part of you as your Scottish soldier," she said. "I am here. I shall be there."

MacKeeg sat on the stone opposite, the waves washed gently.

"It is done my friend," he said. "We are all the hells Chopra could dream. Let him come. Draw him on."

"And have I seen the future?" asked Mr Gupta. "For we did not strike him to the floor."

"No one can see the future," answered MacKeeg. "The world is full of journeys, but not one at a time. We will cross many trails and must accept what help comes. What ye have seen is just a mind adjusting to being a soldier. We'll not fail, laddie."

"I'm not scared," said Mr Gupta. "I'll bring him to the killing ground. To the sea, MacKeeg, to the sea."

William MacKeeg laughed and smoked. Mr Gupta smiled and watched the moon. The world shook...

"Mr Gupta," said the voice accompanying the gentle shaking of his shoulder. "Mr Gupta."

The voice grew louder as Mr Gupta's consciousness returned. He felt stiff and uncomfortable, and noticed he had been dribbling. Then, struggling into a more comfortable position farted, coughed and his nose ran.

"Bloody hell," he groaned, fruitlessly scrabbling for a tissue in his jacket pocket. Then he was fully back. A smart, smiling Sanjay Uddhav was standing before him.

"Sanjay?" said Mr Gupta, immediately feeling unkempt and aware of his misfiring social skills. "It is you! You scared me half to death."

Noticing a napkin being proffered he took it and wiped his face, carefully blew his nose and pulled himself together.

"I'm sorry to give you a shock, Mr Gupta," said Sanjay, "but you were making some odd noises so I thought I'd better get to the nub and check you out for wellness!"

"I'm still in the realms of the living," he said. "Goodness me, I must have been in quite a sleep. Where are we?"

"Halfway to Jhansi Junction, sir, but it has been slow going," said Sanjay. "There is work going on along this section of the line. Raj popped along to tell me you were aboard. I look after this train from Agra now, you see. I have secured my temporary position to a permanent one and all because of your hard mentoring! May I sit with you a while, sir?"

Mr Gupta felt rested. Indeed, he must have slept for at least three hours, yet his dreams had felt brief in spite of their intensity. He mused on the complex piece of hardware that was his brain and wondered if he could live a whole life in an hour; or, perhaps, wake to find his life had run its course. What if this was a dream? What if the beach was his reality? He abandoned this train of thought as it made his head creak.

"May I?" repeated Sanjay.

"Yes," said Mr Gupta, "of course you may. It is time I heard all your news since we last met."

Sanjay settled in MacKeeg's seat and briefed his mentor on the new job and his fortunate rise up the ranks. There was not too much to say. As he talked he gestured with a flat, black, rectangular object the size of a thin book.

"What is that thing?" asked Mr Gupta.

"This," announced Sanjay, waving what was now obviously something Mr Gupta would regard as a *computing contrivance*, "is the future!"

"For what?" asked Mr Gupta.

"It is a tablet upon which every passenger is recorded!" said Sanjay, triumphantly. "It reads the ticket barcode and stores the information. No more paper and it sends the updated data via the inboard Wi-Fi. The future for Indian Railways!"

"Does it make sure everyone has the correct seat?" asked Mr Gupta.

"No!" said Sanjay in his irrepressible way, "but I can update it on screen and send emails!"

"I think I left at the right moment," said Mr Gupta.

There was a brief silence.

"I have heard you have been ill," said Sanjay, serious now. "Very ill. And I was astounded to know you were here. Especially after the news..."

"What news?" asked Mr Gupta sharply.

Sanjay's demeanour had become solemn. His eyes were sad and he could not hide his consternation.

"The fire has been on the regional news," stated Sanjay. "Your picture was shown as a man who died. Just a short story, but I saw it. The rumour was that you were terminally ill which made me sad - then that TV item. Then Raj tells me you are on my train! And here you are smelling slightly smoky and looking worn out, talking in your sleep about the sea. What is going on, Mr Gupta?"

The strangest thing for Mr Gupta to deal with was how uplifted he felt. Listening to the story of his own demise was bad enough. Killing a man, planning a murder against ludicrous odds and carrying a malignant tumour in his head seemed to be the perfect formula for permanent, crushing depression, but he felt well. Indeed, he felt like a new man. Was it because he was two men? The latest step into his other world had caused an irreversible alteration in all realities. How could he explain to Sanjay what was going on? Yet, he had to say something.

"It is quite simple, Sanjay," he said. "I am going to the sea to die."

Sanjay's eyes widened.

"Oh my goodness," he said quietly. "But...but the fire?"

"The news has it wrong," said Mr Gupta, gambling on the paucity of facts. "My spare room caught fire and I got out. By the time the fire people arrived, it was too late. I just watched. Then I thought I had had enough. I rescued a few things and I just walked away."

"But you have to tell the authorities!" said Sanjay. "Are you really that ill? It is madness to just wander off. Madness."

"I am not mad, Sanjay," said Mr Gupta. "As soon as the fire took hold I lost everything. I have weeks to live and I want to spend them at the coast. It is that simple. At Bhopal I am staying at a friend's from where I shall call the police, my solicitor, my remaining family and those closest to me. Then - poof - I will go."

"Oh dear," said Sanjay. "I will never see you again. I have never known anything like this. What a brave decision. What do I say, sir? Can I do anything? Do you want to sit in First Class - there is a spare seat."

"No, no, no," said Mr Gupta softly. "There is no need to do anything..."

As he was speaking his MacKeeg mind forged an idea.

"...but, you can do me a favour later."

"Of course," said Sanjay without hesitation.

"If you can find me a piece of paper and a pen I'll scribble out a little task - nothing much - but it would be a great help," said Mr Gupta.

The Shatabdi eventually regained its normal high-speed. Mr Gupta had eaten a free lunch, care of Raj, and had written down his request of Sanjay. He had sorted through his bag and felt happy with the choice of items MacKeeg had insisted he needed to pack. Even though he was becoming comfortable with travelling alone, carrying just enough to see him by, he took a little extra consolation in having a roll of rupees and a phone charger. These latter items would at least allow him a level of contact with Rupa and Jhatish. Even so, deep down he knew the link would never be more than a few calls or texts, and that he would never see them again. This thought choked him into uttering a quiet cry of regret and sorrow, but this new Gupta was a changed man who refused to wallow in self-pity.

He looked at himself in the window and saw the changeling: its hair had grown and seemed whiter; the face had lost its roundness, he looked thinner; and his moustache was less defined as his unshaven face was being claimed by a beard. And no glasses, that was the hardest thing to understand. Was it possible to change physically into a new person?

"Aye, laddie," said MacKeeg who became his reflection. "By the time that devil comes to us your look will be a revelation!"

"But death," said Mr Gupta, "is a worry for me. Will I make it? Will I have the time? Will I have the strength?"

"Aye again," said MacKeeg settling back, his webbing creaking. "We've got our whole life ahead of us."

Mr Gupta chuckled and MacKeeg lit his pipe.

"By the way," said the Scot. "Using Sanjay for our little job was a good idea. We're a good team."

"A good team of one," said Mr Gupta. "I am mad, aren't I?"

"Let me tell ye something," said MacKeeg, "there is not one person in the world as is not mad. Most people need to belong to something that gives them comfort and makes them special. Once they are safe, dogma and routine take over. Anything that threatens this comfort is anathema to them. They are blind to anything in the real world – it's a threat y'see. In the end they ignore what is real. If stepping beyond that safe existence is called *madness*, then it is so. But, stepping beyond is what drives us forwards, and we hold all the advantages. Chopra belongs to his limited world. He kills anything that gets in the way; and he has never failed. In his version of normality, that is so - he can never fail. That, by any measure, is everyman's insanity.

"Look at India. Not an atheist to be seen. A person has to belong to the gods to be sane - an atheist is deemed as mad. It is the same the world over."

"...and your point is?" asked Mr Gupta.

"We are outside the glass bowl of limitation," continued MacKeeg. "We are the sanest it is possible to be. Yet, to Chopra, we are mad. The British ruled this great country by using the limitations of schism, creed, caste and tribe. All India preferred rule to unity - until Gandhi, that is. My point is, madness is impossible to define absolutely. Are we mad to draw on this killing monster? Yes. To defend all as is ours? No. Take yer fucking pick!"

MacKeeg laughed to a coughing fit which, once it had subsided, left him tearful with glee. He resumed smoking.

"I like to think I am sane," said Mr Gupta, smiling at his other self. "Gentle Mr Gupta, executioner of demons. I could never go back now, could I?"

"Nay, laddie," said MacKeeg. "Our course is set. The more we run the more he'll chase. He'll get so used to it, by the time we turn and make our stand, he'll not be able to stop. Then we'll have him..."

"...and he'll have us?" ventured Mr Gupta.

MacKeeg puffed and pondered.

"We are a small force," he said. "The logistics of moving us is easy, but we have limited resources. Thus we have to adjust tactics to suit the situation. We'll have him just where he wants us."

Mr Gupta laughed along with MacKeeg and both were reduced to tears. Outside the plains and hills drifted by, towns and villages flashed past, colourful in all their Indian gaiety. Colours defined India. Even the poorest dressed in optimistic rainbows which were worn throughout the travails of life.

Mr Gupta dozed. Even with his new resolve the pain of loss pulsed deep. Kiran was gone, that ache was familiar, and Rupa was safe, but far away and Jhatish with her. His family home, his world in Yamuna Naga which had instilled false comfort, was gone forever, and what of Amit, his brother? They had become involuntarily estranged through distance and lack of common ground, with only an occasional phone call, or even rarer lunch when their paths crossed. The Singhs would be distraught, but they had each other. He hoped they would learn to understand. All his friends had been affected, but if he was honest it could just be the start. If he failed in killing Vaz the aftermath for those who helped did not bear thinking about. It was all too horrible to dwell on. Sleep fled.

He glanced at his watch – 14:33. He picked his phone and fired another barb at Vaz.

Will call you from Bhopal. Save time - come here and die.

"We'll have him just where he wants us," MacKeeg had said. Mr Gupta smiled again.

Vasupati Chopra had retreated to the solitude of his study. He had driven slowly from the remains of Mr Gupta's house, from the unraveling of his venture, and from the taunts of a voice both familiar and alien. The rage he felt was tempered by his first ever failure. Mr Gupta had not only escaped, but knew, it seemed, everything. This harmless, helpless old man, riddled with cancer, had made him look foolish. He needed to calmly rationalise the options open to him. This was not all – Kāla was getting harder to control and Vaz knew he would eventually lose the struggle. For now, in the dimly lit sanctuary, he had regained command of his dark driver – just.

Hemlata had tried to welcome him home, but her husband brushed her aside, pausing only to bark an order.

"I want no disturbance," he said.

With that he entered his study and closed the heavy door behind him. Hemlata had seen her husband like this many times and, although not cruel, his coldness brokered no compromise. Lately though, he had changed. The glasses he wore gave him a harder, more contrived look. When they were removed his eyes looked haunted, distant and alien. Her handsome man was still there, but something undefined and disturbing lurked. She was losing him, not to another woman, but to a different reality. All she could do now was comply and, with luck, Vasupati would

305

remain her protector, loyal husband and provider. For that she would do most anything.

Later, whilst she strolled in the garden, Hemlata pondered a recent event. Her blue eye-shadow had gone missing. She had given it little thought until she found smudges of the same shade on one of her husband's shirt collars. She watched him after that. On this particular day he had been in his study for hours. *That* music was just audible and she heard the voice of the Parsi intermixed with it. She had casually walked from the lounge humming softly as Vasupati had emerged to shower, wrapped in a white bathrobe.

"What time do you want dinner my love?" she had asked.

He had turned and smiled. His long hair was down, the robe open in a long V to his naval, and he looked so handsome, so sexy, so much the man of her dreams. His smile remained as he spoke.

"I want you now," was all he said.

She was momentarily shocked, but submitted to his request without question or thought. He had pulled her into his study, locked the door and before she could adjust to the darker room was thrown with unwarranted aggression across the large wooden desk. A blue light given off by an ornate lamp made everything surreal. Vaz remained silent and she had not resisted as her sari had been torn away from behind and her underwear pulled to her ankles.

"Vaz..." she had gasped.

He tore into her. To Hemlata it was a violation. He grabbed her long hair, pulling her head back. She could not see him, but heard the grunts of effort as he maintained a hard rhythm. Surprise bloomed into fear as he released her hair and grasped her neck and started to squeeze. She had struggled, wriggling her hips and squirming, frightened for her safety, but he held on seemingly more excited with her desperate effort for release. Just as her vision filled with coloured flashes, he had roared, thrust deeper, making her groan with pain, then let her go. She had slid from the desk onto the floor gasping with relief, but shaking with fright. She noticed the music was still playing very quietly.

Pain is the right for all as impurity leaves...

The idols and carvings made the room a shadowy temple. The music filled the space.

Embrace your pain. Flow on to Chinvat...

Vaz had remained silent. He stood over her, naked, features etched with the blue glow. His gaze was fixed on the idol nearest his desk, a grotesque thing - it carried a head in one hand and a bloodied sword in the other. He spoke.

"Sometimes it is best to submit, then forget," he said. "You have helped me, now I have control..."

She rose unsteadily to her feet then stepped to the door. His hand had gripped her shoulder and he must have felt her quaking. She opened the door a crack, then turned to him, his strong grip holding her back,

"I... I understand, darling," she managed.

"You are quite safe," he had said, then smiled. He was her Vaz again.

She smiled back.

"I need to clean myself up dear," she said. "No one should see me so...so untidy."

He let her loose and she had kissed him on the cheek before bustling off to their bedroom. This had been a strange encounter; her husband tended to be a more traditional lover. As she stripped her ruined sari from her aching body a latent memory made her pause. When she had kissed him there was a smell, a taste and a colour. She looked in the mirror. There was a faint smudge of blue on her cheek. Now she was sure. His neck and lower jaw had been tinted blue - she had not seen it until she had let the white light in as she left. Vaz had used eye shadow to colour his neck. His idol had a blue neck. She would watch him ever the more, but would adjust, and serve, and submit. Most of all she would survive. The house was quiet except for the faint sound of music.

Vaz settled into his chair. The sound of Zahan soothed him. Today, for the first time, a plan had failed. *He* had failed. Now he had to gather his thoughts and plan afresh. There was no need to panic, but Ravi would soon be calling. Much as Vaz was loyal to Ravi, a man who had never let him down and gave him the freedom to grow, the power of Kāla was gradually taking precedent. Could he serve two masters? As yet there had been no conflict and nothing to require a choice, but the time was coming.

The sacrifice is made...

Vaz was beginning to realise total submission to Kāla may be inevitable.

Mankind's sacrificial man...

The music meshed with his thoughts, then choreographed their course.

Gophapa will be slain by Him...

Full, uncontrolled submission. He had an epiphany: Kāla *could not* make mistakes so it was no submission to become a god. What remained of his human resistance began to erode.

Gophapa takes ruin with him...

Panic and doubt left him and he could function once more. The music drifted on. Vaz picked up the phone and called Ravi, who answered on the second ring.

"What the fucking hell is going on Vaz?" snapped Ravi. "The news is still cycling Gupta's house fire every hour. Every bloody hour, Vaz! They say a single body has been removed. Is it Gupta? Is it? And where's the child? Talk to me, Vaz."

Vaz felt a pang of resentment. The foul up belonged to Kush Karnik and that contract had been permanently withdrawn. Vaz smiled as he thought of how well The Mechanic had literally been fired. He chuckled.

"Are you...are you...laughing?" gasped Ravi. "I'm struggling here, Vaz. Come on, give me some good news, please."

"Relax, Ravi," soothed Vaz. "There has been a delay, nothing more. I have taken personal charge of this now."

"What happened to our contractor?" asked Ravi slightly calmer, but still with an edge to his voice.

"A casualty," said Vaz, now happy to be accurate. "He failed to live up to expectations, but I'm sketchy on details. Let's meet at the club."

Vaz knew Ravi's short-lived panic had waned. They were similar that way.

"I can be there in a couple of hours," said Ravi.

It was at this moment his mobile phone beeped. He looked at the screen.

Will call you from Bhopal. Save time - come here and die.

"Gophapa has just sent a message, I'll forward it." said Vaz. "See you at the club."

"Who?" asked Ravi.

The call was ended. Balance was immediately lost again. So much energy had been expended keeping control, but this was an impossible attack on his will. Gupta was goading him! Gupta and Gophapa were one and the same! Vaz clicked on *Contact sender*, but was immediately informed the device was unavailable. Helpless, unfulfilled anger coursed through him and the door to Kāla began to thump in his mind.

Thud! Thud! Thud! Thud!

It beat in his head and was driving him mad. Oh, to let him out, to stop the effort of fighting, to give in and start an age of chaos. Vaz gripped the arms of his chair, losing his mind, consumed by rage. With a supreme effort the voice of Zahan drew his senses.

Flow on to Chinvat...

Vaz focused with all his will...

Obeisance at Chinvat, pour into the ocean of fire...

Rigid in his seat, Vaz resisted and kept the door shut, and imagined himself pressing on the heavy wooden boards, felt the heads of forged nails, felt the strength of Kāla from his dark world beyond.

Thud!...Thud!...Thud!...

Sweat poured from him as the beat faded, then stopped. Still he pushed against the huge, heavy door...

New life on a moonlit shore...

He slowly relaxed.

Stars and worlds align…

Exhausted he stopped the struggle – at peace now.

New life crawls from the Birthing Black Sea…

BOOM!

Fossa's rhythmic melody erupted with the beat of a drum. His mind exploded as a mighty force hit the door. Vaz screamed in despair. *It was not time!* He screamed again and felt the floor of his study under him. He scrabbled about, weeping and sobbing in anguish. *It was not time!* Another sound. Someone was banging on his study door. Kāla was silent inside. The door was knocked again, gentler this time. *From beneath He comes,* thought Vaz, *From the abyss He climbs.* He chuckled through his snotty mouth.

"Darling?" It was Hemlata.

The screams had been heard throughout the large house. Hemlata expected a sharp rebuff, but instead her husband called out to her.

"I need you!"

This was no demand, but a plea for comfort. Hemlata pushed open the door. Vaz was sitting on the floor with his back against a desk leg. He was dishevelled, sweaty and looked exhausted. His nose was running and his eyes were wet and bloodshot. He looked up at his wife. Then he started to cry. Great, wracking sobs. She rushed to him, knelt and cradled his head to her breast, stroking his hair and kissing the top of his head. There was no resistance as, like a child he sank into her embrace, taking comfort and feeling overwhelming love for his wife. After several minutes he quietened and raised his head, then kissed her softly on the mouth.

"You must listen carefully, Hemlata," he said. "There are many things you cannot understand, but know this, you are safe. You have security and my love. But something is happening for which I have no cure. It will take me, and I cannot resist. There is a dangerous man who can destroy us. He is called Gophapa by the low people who protect him, but I know who he is and what I must do. If I end him, all will be well. There is no alternative.

You must be prepared. Everything will revert to you and you will be safe. For me, even if I end him, I do not believe I can return. Trust no one – no one at all. Do you understand?"

"Darling man," she answered, "I do not know what you mean, but I never doubt you. I will not question or delve, but are you sure in what you say? You are just overwrought with work. Who can harm my brave, strong husband?"

"This man is already dead," said Vaz. Then gently extracting himself, stood, drawing his wife up by the hand. "I have to go now. First, I must shower. I will be home later, but may have to leave again. Thank you."

Hemlata stroked his face, kissed him on the cheek then, seeing him segue back to his usual self - strong, and fearless - she left to reassure the children.

Ravi received the Gupta message from Vaz.

Will call you from Bhopal. Save time - come here and die.

He was agitated. Using his position as Anil Gupta's chief executor, and acting the distraught relative, Ravi discovered the police were of the growing opinion he had perished in the fire. None of his neighbours gave conflicting stories: Mr Gupta had been at home all afternoon; a local shopkeeper had sold him a newspaper in the evening; no visitors were seen after dark; the lights were out before midnight. The body was burned beyond formal recognition and the facial bones were crushed and incinerated. There was little doubt it was Anil Gupta. A tyre lever had been found by the garden wall covered in fresh blood. It may, or may not be connected, but, for now, the probability was Mr Gupta was dead. Ravi Uppal had willingly accepted this, but the new message changed everything. Ravi Uppal's heart leapt in his chest. Gupta had survived, Rupa was safe and the body was that of Vaz's hired man. Ravi knew if Gupta contacted the right people his business, freedom and dreams of a political future would be gone. A film of perspiration shone on his forehead as such possibilities gripped his mind. Then he saw something else. Anil Gupta could have started his ruination already, but had not. He had fled because he wanted something. This meant there was time. There was no doubt that Vaz would track Anil Gupta down and kill him, and Ravi had the resources to guarantee that. He calmed down and thought it through: with urgency driving him on, how would Anil Gupta get to Bhopal in a day? By train! Shatabdi, no less; the familiar always made life easier for the desperate. He checked the daily Shatabdi schedule and printed a copy. Then he booked an online reservation with CityKennect Airlines for Vaz on a flight to Bhopal and finally made a call to a political ally in the city, Ranjit Kumar Roy.

"Ranjit Roy," said the voice, "how are you Ravi?"

"I need a favour," said Ravi. "How quickly can you arrange for one of your investigators to do some work in Bhopal?"

"That's easy," said Roy. "Suliman has people there. It will cost. Is there a problem?"

"Possibly," said Ravi. "I think a client is trying an insurance fraud. He has stolen some information and may have committed arson. I have no solid proof to give the police, so I need him found. Money is not a problem, but I need this started like yesterday."

"Suliman will need more than that," said Roy.

"Yot-Yot can email some pictures," said Ravi. "This man is one Anil Gupta. He will be arriving at Bhopal, probably by rail. I'm guessing he'll be on a Shatabdi from Delhi - an early one - so it will only stop at the main stations. I've looked at the schedules and the earliest he'll arrive is a little after two, but there are delays, as usual. I need someone there now! I'll give him a bonus of a thousand American dollars if he finds Gupta."

"I'll call you back within the hour," said Roy. "Get the girl to email me direct and I shall ensure they get to the right place. Anything else?"

"I just want him found, followed and watched," said Ravi. "Vaz will be down soon, he'll, contact Suliman's chap and take over security from there. The fee will be met, in full, regardless of the time taken."

"Ok, Ravi," said Roy.

In less than an hour Roy called Ravi back.

"Suliman has a man at Bhopal Junction already," said Roy. "If this Gupta is on an express from Delhi, he'll be seen. All the contact details have been passed on, but Suliman wants the thousand up front."

"Excellent!" said Ravi. "I'll wire the money immediately."

Ravi waited for Vaz at the Rothschild Club bar. Things had moved quickly and there was little more to do until Vaz and he had talked. His phone rang.

"Ravi Uppal," he said.

"Hello Mr Uppal," said the voice. "Mr Anil Gupta has paid me to send a message from this public phone in Bhopal."

"Is he alright?" sputtered Ravi.

"I am not to answer questions," said the voice. "I am to read this once then replace the receiver. He writes, *I am safe as is my daughter. I will leave a message at the reception of the Trans Continental Hotel here in Bhopal. I have backup. Send Vasupati Chopra. I know all.* That is it."

The phone went dead. Finally, Ravi felt more like himself and was sure things would work out. If Anil Gupta thought he could outwit Ravi Uppal he was about to get a shock. He immediately relayed the information to the investigator's number. He then ordered a glass of 10-year-old Talisker single malt from a hovering waiter and settled to wait for Vaz.

Chapter 22

The Pursuit Begins

Mr Gupta was exhausted. He stood outside Bhopal Junction gazing at a familiar scene - a chaos of traffic, barrows, animals and people, dominated by the ubiquitous tuktuk. Sanjay had shaken his hand as he left the station, but only after he had used the pay-phone on the main platform to deliver Mr Gupta's message. The favour complete, Sanjay quickly bustled off to continue his duties with his usual energy. Mr Gupta had told Sanjay he would go far and life had to go on, the young replacing the old, and they parted with smiles and genuine affection. He stared at the melee before him, momentarily paralysed with the stress of the last few days and the fundamental need for rest. He shuffled forward adjusting his heavy bag on his shoulder and was immediately approached by a rowdy posse of drivers. His mind closed down as the resulting cacophony assaulted his ears. He staggered, but caught himself just before blacking out.

"Get ye the fuck away ya bastards!" he shouted in desperation, the Scottish accented profanity causing a lull in proceedings. Stepping back, he selected a driver who stood away from the crowd and asked, "Would you take me to the Pan Continental, please?"

The elderly, turbaned man jumped forwards, pushed the other disgruntled drivers aside and grasped Mr Gupta by the arm.

"I will take you, sir," he said.

Then, shrugging off the vituperation pouring upon him, he expertly steered his prize to a dusty yellow and maroon tuktuk which looked well used, but sturdy.

"Don't you be minding those bastards, sir," said the driver. "They are all rude and excitable. Patience is the world of older men. Like us, sir."

"Thank you," said Mr Gupta.

"Hari," replied the driver, "my name is Hari Singh."

"Well, Hari, could you take me to..."

"The Pan Continental!" pronounced the driver.

The tuktuk roared into life and shot into the traffic with traditional reckless haste. Hari reminded Mr Gupta of Old Mr Singh, and he took a moment of comfort in the memory of their many drives together. Hari Singh was not a talkative man, so the short, but exciting journey was one of reflection rather than conversation. The vehicle came to a halt by the main gate of the hotel and Mr Singh bounced out to help Mr Gupta onto the pavement.

"The security bastards do not like tuktuks on the hotel drive, sir," explained Hari.

Mr Gupta assured him that was fine, paid the requested fare, adding a tip. He walked up the short drive to the large red-columned entrance, stepping quickly into the air-conditioned interior. Indian Railways had an ongoing account with this hotel chain, so even though Mr Gupta looked dishevelled and travel worn, his identification card and rank ensured a polite welcome. A senior colleague would be arriving in the near future, he explained to the young woman at the reception desk, and he needed to leave a message in letter form for him to pick up upon arrival. She happily gave him an envelope and paper whereupon he sat at a quiet table to write Vasupati Chopra a note, as promised.

As you have come this far I can only assume my life is forfeit. This being so I intend to meet you when I am ready. I will be travelling west from here and shall send regular messages to your phone to let you know where to follow. Eventually a message will arrive explaining where and how you will meet your end - I will not run forever.

A. G.

It was simple and, he thought, almost childishly belligerent, but if things were kept straightforward Vaz would not be able to infer anything but the truth. Mr Gupta knew well enough that his flight bore no hallmark of a preconceived plan. How could it? Vaz would only see what he wanted to see. He folded the letter and sealed it in the envelope writing, *For the attention of Vasupati Chopra of Cobra,* on the front. The receptionist took the letter and placed it in a tray specifically for patrons' messages, just below the counter. With that he left and walked out into the bustle of the city. He was achingly tired, his head felt sore and his mind foggy. He knew the tumour must be having some effect on him, was killing him, but it was too soon to collapse and give up.

"Come on, laddie," said MacKeeg falling into step beside him, resplendent in his faded uniform and smoking as usual, "we need to find somewhere to rest up. Ye've done plenty the now."

Mr Gupta gave in to the choreographed synchronicity and his companion saw him into a taxi. Upon request he was delivered to an inexpensive, four storey hotel of the driver's recommendation. The Palace Hotel was small, clean and nondescript, just what was required to remain incognito. He paid for a top floor room that overlooked the street, took the lift up and finally sat heavily in a comfortable chair by the large window. It was ajar, so the incessant street noises echoed in. He felt secure at last.

"Let's not get complacent, laddie," said MacKeeg, from where he was sitting on the bed. "Take yon chair and shove it under the door handle. Then shower and rest a while."

"I am done in," muttered Mr Gupta miserably. "Let me rest awhile, will you?"

"Life and death are separated by seconds," said MacKeeg. "That moment of rest can kill ye! We're soldiers now. We have to be. So secure yer perimeter and get clean. It is a psychological thing. Trust me, now. Trust me."

With great effort Mr Gupta secured his perimeter, stripped and showered his rapidly thinning body, then curled up under his bedcovers to drift into slumber. MacKeeg kept watch at the foot of the bed, at least somewhere in Mr Gupta's subconscious he did, allowing him to rest on every level. With the Scot safely stationed, Mr Gupta had no one to disturb him.

Ranjit Kumar Roy was a close ally of Ravi Uppal. He already held a seat for the Indian Patriotic Union, the IPU, in Madhya Pradesh. He was also CEO of a large American mineral extraction company, Barrett de Vaal, which had many interests across the sub-continent. The IPU was growing. All the key members were wealthy and their aim was gaining overall power for the right-of-centre party they represented. Roy already subscribed to the idea that knowledge begets power, so had made strong ties with a firm of private investigators with offices in several major Indian cities, Bhopal being one. Roy's initial use of the Suliman Investigation Agency, run by an IPU sympathiser, Mehmet Suliman, had been to check on industrial rivals, investors and contractors. Suliman was efficient and professional, with a fine reputation, so his company was now the preferred choice of Barrett de Vaal and, subsequently, the IPU. His investigators were some of the best in their field to be found in India. With a call from Suliman a local operative, had been dispatched to Bhopal Junction before Mr Gupta's Shatabdi had arrived. The investigator, Jag, had been sent a picture of Anil Gupta, with instructions to follow him and to relay information to one Vasupati Chopra.

Jag had waited at the station, sitting quietly on a bench reading the local paper. He very nearly failed to recognise his quarry. It was only when Mr Gupta paused by the bench to have an extended conversation with a young conductor, that Jag realised who it was. No glasses, whiter hair and unshaven, but, yes, this was Anil Gupta. Jag followed at a distance then jumped in a waiting car driven by Tarik, another of Suliman's men. They followed Mr Gupta to the Pan Continental Hotel, Suliman having already informed them this was the man's first likely stop. When Mr Gupta re-emerged, they followed the taxi to the Palace Hotel. Easy. A few rupees to the receptionist established an Anil Gupta had checked in, paying for a single night. He was oblivious of being found. As darkness descended Jag sent a message to the number he had been given, outlining developments thus far. A quick reply simply stated, *Stick with him until I get there*. Jag was happy to comply. Between them, he and Tarik could watch all night.

It was the early hours of the morning in Bhopal. MacKeeg drifted from sentry duty into Mr Gupta's dreams. In deep sleep there were no colourful visions, just flashes of thought, brief pictures of Rupa, Kiran and Jhatish. As deep sleep passed, the other world appeared. They were sitting at the beach, the sea calm and the night's sky its usual kaleidoscope of planets and stars. MacKeeg was agitated, not smoking for once. Mr Gupta knew he was troubled.

"What is the matter?" he asked.

"Something is not right," said MacKeeg. "It's been hard on us to get here, but the plan seems to be working well enough."

"So, what's not right?" asked Mr Gupta. "We managed to escape this far and we're ahead of the game. I do not know what the next step is, I'll wait for you to help with that, but we have time now."

"Why did ye put the chair under the door handle, laddie?" asked MacKeeg.

"Because you told me too," said Mr Gupta.

"Aye, that I did, but we are one," said MacKeeg, standing and starting to pace. "The only error we are making is assuming. We assume Uppal and Chopra are just sitting and waiting. How fast can this Vaz fellow get here?"

"By this evening," answered Mr Gupta, "if he takes the train. Even if he drives all night he would not reach Bhopal until mid-morning. He does not know where we are, so by the time he gets to the Pan Continental he will still have to wait for our next message."

"Aye," said MacKeeg. "There was a gap they could fill though. It was sending that first message telling the bastard to come to Bhopal that's started to bother me. Was it time enough to have someone waiting?"

"Waiting where?" asked Mr Gupta. "How could they know? Sanjay only let Ravi know where my note was less than half-an-hour before it was left. They cannot find us."

"I could have found us," said MacKeeg sitting. "It would be easy enough to work out how we were travelling. The time tables are clear enough. The Shatabdi terminates at Bhopal Junction. That gap. Someone could have been at the station and we would have missed it. We were not thinking. Fuck it!"

Mr Gupta could see the slight possibility. Then the greater probability. It was not beyond Ravi Uppal to have moved quickly. Then he had another thought.

"Vaz could fly down!" he said, alarmed now. "If we were spotted…"

"Then we need to move," said MacKeeg.

The beach segued back to the hotel room. Mr Gupta dressed quickly in the light of the street lamps, repacked his bag, threw it over his shoulder and looked out the window to the street below. A few people huddled around lamp posts, many others cycled or walked along the pavements, and some traffic was passing. Two cars were parked. One was a taxi, the driver clearly sleeping across the front seat, the other was a dark Japanese saloon under the shadow of a bushy tree protruding from an adjacent park. A cigarette glowed briefly within. A wave of panic swept over Mr Gupta. He looked at his watch - 05:03. Nothing was certain, but his inner reasoning could not be ignored. He removed the chair and opened the door slightly. The corridor was empty. He stepped out and made his way to the back of the building. There was a fire escape and the door opened easily; the building was colonial and made to a reasonable standard - Mr Gupta quietly thanked the British architect. The air was cool and it was still very dark. In the distance he could make out the glint of water from a large lake and to the east a pale sky showed dawn was not too far away. He hurried down the iron steps as quietly as possible eventually finding himself in a rear yard that opened on to a back alley. The alley was empty. He made his way to the end where it joined the main street, then he carefully looked around the corner. The dark saloon was turning in the road, rear lights facing him, then drove off into the distance. It looked as if there was nothing amiss. Mr Gupta relaxed and decided to walk towards the lake he had seen, guessing it was west as dawn was breaking behind him. At least he would see if anyone was following. He casually wandered away from the Palace Hotel, just another early riser making his way to work.

After a while he felt very hungry. He had covered a fair distance and nobody seemed to be following. He knew he would have to rest properly for a while, but circumstances were conspiring to drive him on. He had not eaten since his final snack on the train and felt weak and drained, the adrenalin of his fast departure from the hotel now being spent. For the first time he felt hunted. The sun had risen and the roads were getting busier, but more importantly shops and cafes were opening ready to catch the breakfast trade. Mr Gupta stopped in a small square centred on a single large tree, where there were plenty of cafés. He looked back up the road he had travelled, but it was now so crowded he was unsure whether he would see anyone following him anyway. He had to stop. Choosing a cafe on the corner of an adjoining street he ordered tea and a parotta, then sat in a window seat glad to be resting. Outside, the colourful and constant traffic, mechanical and human, surged about the tree in chaotic order, never ceasing, ever moving. The food arrived and Mr Gupta ate slowly enjoying every mouthful, savouring his tea and finally regaining a little confidence. By the time he started his second cup of tea he was able to rationalise his journey so far. Since the awful events in his house, he had kept control very well. The last few hours had seen the first sign of panic which, with hindsight, was an overreaction. MacKeeg would always ensure that he put caution first and keep Vaz guessing. Yet, there was no doubt, coaxing Vaz to them was going to be a dangerous feat.

Mr Gupta paid the bill and walked out into the day. He turned south, following a road away from the general direction of Bhopal's Upper Lake, which he had glimpsed earlier. Mr Gupta felt untapped stores of energy and he marvelled at the thought of becoming fit whilst, at the same time, dying. After an hour, everything had changed. He realised he had forgotten to buy water. He was becoming tired and there was a throbbing pain in his temple. His legs were heavy and he longed to rest, no matter what the risk. As the sun climbed he developed a raging thirst, clarity faded and his now robotic trudge slowed minute by minute until he ground to a halt. There were spots before his eyes, he could no longer think straight and MacKeeg had gone missing. Getting fitter whilst dying and being abandoned by an imaginary friend – he smiled at the absurdity of it all. He had reached his limit. His head ached and his nose dribbled.

"What should I do?" he asked aloud as dust from passing vehicles enveloped him.

He looked back and saw the high buildings of Bhopal well behind, as were the leafy suburbs, surprised at the distance he had covered. Next to him, beyond a fence, there was what looked like a chemical plant – all pipes, metal cylinders and pumps leading from a large silver factory. Bhopal's legacy was bound to such places. Ahead was a truck stop, a large dirt area cleared from surrounding scrub and weeds. A crudely built wood and thatch snack bar had been set up. It had stacks of bottled water, soft drinks and snacks piled up on the counter, above which a board sported one word: *Ali's*. Smoke from a cooking fire drifted up behind the structure giving hope of hot food and drink. Two rough tables with rickety chairs were set to one side, one of which was occupied. A young man in black trousers and a white shirt was serving his single customer with chapattis and dhal, chattering as he worked. A vehicle was parked nearby, the like of which was unusual, even for India. The dusty truck looked ancient, had a flat fronted cab and a badge proclaiming it to be a Bedford. Originally a flatbed lorry, this had a large wood and metal hut strapped and bolted to it, complete with an assortment of tarpaulins, pots, pans and tools attached, some precariously. It was the colours which caught Mr Gupta's eye. The original army green was the base colour, with an air force roundel on the front, but everything had been overprinted with flowers and rainbows, multi-coloured clouds and stars. Over this were more traditional Hindu pictures of gods, heroes and stylised animals, finished off with crenelated borders and edging. It looked for all the world like a shrine on wheels which had accreted several decades of cultural progress, both Western and Oriental. It was India condensed into an ancient British truck.

The short distance to this haven seemed miles to Mr Gupta. The sun was unbearably hot and he felt nauseous. With a great effort of will he began to shuffle forward, small clouds of dust forming around his feet. The scene before him wavered as his eyes lost focus. The world began to spin as he moved and he was unable to feel his legs; vertical and horizontal were now meaningless as he swayed into the road. A huge truck blared its horns as it rushed by, missing him by inches. He staggered back onto the side of the road and his eyes focused briefly on the truck stop. Time had slowed. The young waiter had stopped talking and was watching Mr Gupta's progress, alarmed and unsure what to do. It was the customer who made the first move. Mr Gupta saw a Mongol warrior racing towards him.

"Hold fast!" he screamed.

Then darkness came.

Tarik jumped. As he opened his eyes he caught sight of Anil Gupta walking quickly down the road away from the hotel. The taxi was a perfect surveillance car and seldom caused much of a stir – sleeping drivers were often to be found in their vehicles. Tarik should not have been sleeping; Jag had left him to watch the main door whilst he reconnoitred the rear of the building. As Tarik lifted his phone it rang in his hand: it was Jag.

"Did you see him?" he asked. "The bastard came out the back, I only just got a glimpse!"

Thinking quickly, adrenalin flowing, Tarik answered.

"Yes, I was just about to call", he said. "He's walking fast, but staying on the main street. Do I wait for you or what?"

"I'm here!" shouted Jag into the phone as he came scurrying around the corner. He dove into the passenger seat as Tarik started the engine.

"I see him," he said, "drive past and let me out well in front. I'll pretend to pay you and cross the road. You just drive away and park somewhere, I can follow him alone. Less obvious."

Tarik had worked with Jag before and fell in with the trusted routine – no one noticed a taxi. Mr Gupta certainly did not. Once Suliman's men had a target in their sights, seldom did they lose him. Well ahead of Mr Gupta, Jag left the taxi, made an act of payment, then crossed the road to an open shop. He went in and the taxi shot off, soon lost in the morning's increasing traffic. Mr Gupta had no reason to notice them. He had so nearly kept his advantage, yet hunters were on his trail and the killer was not too far behind.

The meeting at the Rothschild Club bar was strained. Ravi was still unsettled. He knew where Anil Gupta was heading and knew he had sewn up any loopholes in Cobra's links to him, yet he needed to know where Rupa was. How had such a disabled girl just disappeared? In business and politics Ravi had learnt to deal with the knowns first, eventually the unknown would appear. Perversely, he could make enquiries in the guise of a caring guardian, especially as it was assumed Mr Gupta had died. Yes, with his political friends, his contacts in the police and his altruistic persona he was sure he could weather any storm. Vaz had arrived, hair down and still wearing his blue glasses. They had become a fixture. And he was smiling. Ravi was beginning to think his partner had major mental health problems, he just hoped it was not some kind of breakdown.

"Vaz, have you heard anything else from our friend?" asked Ravi.

"Nothing more," Vaz replied. "What is the plan?"

"I have Suliman's fellows watching Bhopal Junction," replied Ravi. "My guess is Gupta will use the express, it's familiar, and you are flying down on a CityKennect flight at 06:50 tomorrow. At the very least you'll pick up Gupta's message and be ready to play his game, but if we're lucky Suliman could well have got him under surveillance. Take plenty of cash, the company credit cards and use whatever you need to get the job done."

"What if he goes to the authorities?" asked Vaz.

"I don't think he will," said Ravi. "The best time to have done that was immediately. He's presumed dead, for now, and he's made it clear he wants you. I am sure he is mad – that tumour. Who would believe a man who committed murder in his own house then burned it down? Who would not see how a sick brain could drive my much-loved brother-in-law to lash out at phantoms and imaginary enemies? Track him down, Vaz, and I'll weave a web so complex that if he is found by anyone else, he'll be locked up in a mental hospital until he dies."

Vaz smiled again. The coming journey would free him for a while. He was losing his fight to restrain Kāla and his irresistible need to kill. If the Kāla mind became dominant, could it be recaptured as before? Vaz had started not to care.

"It may take some time," said Vaz. "What about tools for the job? I can't take things on the plane."

"Whatever you want, make a list and I'll get Suliman to get things to you. His men are at your disposal. Here are their numbers, they already have yours. One rule, you must never contact Suliman directly," said Ravi handing over a slip of paper.

"Shall I travel incognito?" asked Vaz.

"Do what you think is right," said Ravi. "This is the last time we need to do anything like this. We have enough now. Once I'm in government money will be easier to come by and you can rest a bit. See the world. Stay hidden, get it done and that's it."

"What about the girl?" asked Vaz.

"She'll turn up," said Ravi with renewed energy. "Then, I am her guardian. She'll rot in that home and dribble until she dies. In the meantime, Uncle Ravi will use his generosity to fund more fallen angels. Just get this done, Vaz. I'll do everything else."

Vaz's logical mind knew Ravi was right, they did have enough to keep them rich forever. It was always understood that in time the whole business would become legitimate. Mahto's money had been a huge windfall and the Gupta money was the icing on the cake. Even so, the words Ravi had uttered were sickening. Logic meant nothing to a narcissistic, schizophrenic psychopath, even one who was well controlled.

This is the last time we need to do anything like this.

Vaz thought not. Kāla-Vaz thought not. The great imaginary door holding Kāla back had fractured and Vaz saw a different future for himself. The worms in his head moved; never before had this happened unless a kill was close and he had gone through a careful ritual of preparation. He kept cool and bade Ravi farewell, but the smile had gone.

Ravi was very perceptive and had studied the profound changes in his partner for some time. In spite of explicit instructions, Vaz had been unnecessarily cruel. He had seen the reports on Mahto and Sethi's murders, and shuddered at the memory. Mr Gupta was on borrowed time. Whether the tumour killed him, or Vaz did, mattered little to Ravi. Even Vaz was expendable, if necessary. He had already begun sanitising Vasupati Chopra's links to the legitimate side of Cobra. It had been easy enough, as Vaz never seemed overly interested in financial matters. Ravi was in control of everything and felt better for it. He could oversee Anil Gupta's removal from a distance and continue with his plans to create a clean business, step into government and control the space between the buildings of power. Lutyens knew what monuments could do. Ravi Uppal desired everything between: the very space in which people existed.

Hemlata watched her husband's dark car come to a halt by the lamplit front door. His words had haunted her and cold fear gripped her heart. She was scared of losing the man she loved, her provider and protector, unable to imagine a life without him. She watched to see what mood he was in. The driver's door opened and there he was – tall, upright and moving in his usual confident way. Yet, something was not right.

Vaz walked past her and spoke without breaking stride.

"Keep the house quiet," he said. "I will leave early in the morning. If I need you I shall call. Is everybody home?"

This gave Hemlata pause. Her husband's voice had changed. What could he mean?

"Only the children and the maid," she said.

"All has ended, all has gone. All life's weaving is undone..." he said, continuing his march to the study.

Those blue glasses. How she hated those blue glasses. She could not see his lovely eyes to judge his mood. Sometimes she saw fear; sometimes emptiness; rarely love, or normality as she imagined it. Hemlata had always used her intuition to make things perfect for him and stress-free for the household, but those constant blue lenses had isolated him from her. She set about making sure the children were in bed and ready to sleep, that would make her job easier. Then she told Lajita (everyone called her *La*) the maid, to stay in her small flat - a pair of rooms above the large garage, well-furnished and comfortable, but away from the main house. Sometimes La slept in the spare room near the children, but not when Vaz was as he was tonight. Hemlata watched the girl ascend the external wooden flight of steps to her quarters, then settled herself in the lounge between her

327

husband's study and the children's rooms. She began reading a book by lamplight only looking up when she heard Vaz walk to the bathroom; forty minutes later she listened as he returned and *that* music started.

Kāla was out. Ravi's words, *This is the last time we need to do anything like this,* had changed the world. In trying to keep a semblance of control Vaz turned in on himself. He had tried not speak to Hemlata when he left the car, focusing on gaining the refuge of his study, but he had spoken, using words his human side had not intended.

All life's weaving is undone...

Kāla needed to kill. The Vaz mind still struggled for dominance, but Ravi's words had broken his final strand of willpower. The mighty door of Kāla's prison had exploded into shards of jet.

How could black shards glow? thought Vaz.

Kāla was revealed in the darkness beyond, blue lit eyes staring out at freedom.

From beneath He comes...

The mind of Vasupati Chopra screamed as it was absorbed into a greater whole. The music played on in the blue-tinted world of the surviving chimera, Kāla-Vaz. Doubt was replaced by a pleasant warmth, a healing acceptance of melded desires. The worms no longer squirmed. This new mind hummed like a transformer full of power. He would pursue Gophapa and cleanse the world of him. Then all attached to him would be found and wiped from the land of the living. The music played on...

From the purity of blackness, he rises, and gains far sight from blue sky. Kāla collects lives, he will sow them......In the new World.

The shower was hot and washed him clean. Kāla-Vaz shaved his face and body, leaving only his long hair and eyebrows. He felt immensely strong, full of energy and confident of his irresistible will. He walked naked to his study and turned on a white light above an ornate mirror, edged in carved dragons and tigers, then lifted a small bottle from the desk. The liquid inside glowed blue, the clear glass splitting the white light into rainbows against the wall. It contained a blue dye he had bought from a temple in Agra. He removed the stopper and poured a little out onto a pad of cotton wool, then slowly dabbed it over the skin of his upper chest and throat. It dried with the heat of his body. He repeated the process several times then spread a layer of palm oil over his work, finally soaking the excess up with paper towels. Zahan and Fossa played on. The result gave a semi-permanent sheen of blue, not too obvious on his dark skin, leaving him sure that Shiva had been honoured and his joining with Kāla was complete. If Shiva could take a variety of forms then why not Vasupati Chopra's mortal body? Becoming Kāla-Vaz was a natural, irreversible metamorphosis. Vaz's mind was trapped in a cycle of its own logic and dogma, thus anything was justifiable: he had become his own master.

At midnight the house was silent and softly lamplit. Hemlata had fallen asleep curled up on a couch, her book left on the floor. She dreamed of the comforts of her life and hardly woke as her body received a mighty blow. A brief flicker of her eyelids, a gathering of soft light, then death took her. Kāla-Vaz stood naked over the body holding an ornate brass sword in his hand. The weapon had two edges, one keen and sharp, the other blunt, perfect to crush bone and sinew.

"I give you security and immortality my love," he said.

He had remembered his promise. She was safe with the gods and he need not protect her from whatever was coming. Just as she could never have been allowed to leave him, he could never have allowed her to carry on in this world without the man who owned her. He walked on to the children's room.

La lay quietly on her bed. The sound of a single cry had awoken her. Had it been one of the children? Hemlata would comfort them this evening if required, La knew this and would never go to the house if ordered to stay away. She respected her beloved employer's private family time so she snuggled down under the covers. Even so, that cry had unsettled her, so she remained alert, ears straining in the darkness of her room. She heard the creak of a step outside. Was Hemlata coming to knock her door? She must need help with the young ones. Perhaps one was ill? Then La would have to sit with the other. Pre-empting the knock, La switched on her bedside lamp and got up, slipping on a nightgown. She walked into the main room where the far door led onto the steps.

"Madam?" she called.

She paused and listened. Another slight creak.

"Madam?" she called again. Hope of a reassuring answer had vanished and her skin prickled with apprehension.

"Please, Madam?" she called, plaintively now.

The door burst open so suddenly, so loudly, that La's knees almost gave way. When she saw the monster beyond, she screamed. The master stood holding the severed head of his wife in his left hand and a sword in his right. He was naked, blood spattered, and expressionless, his eyes glowing blue as light reflected in his glasses. His throat was blue. Before La had chance to recover the master stepped into the room to complete his evening's work.

Chapter 23

Sahyadri

As Angaar reached the heights of the plateau the scent he had been following faded. The sun was low in the west and the long climb had made him tired. He raised his great head and tested the air, but failed to identify anything of note. The wind had dropped with the sun. He continued across the high ground, eventually finding a stream from which he took a long drink. His stomach was still full and he had no desire to hunt, so he sought a place to sleep. He ranged a little to the north eventually crossing his old trail, finding his faint scent mark and dried scat. He sprayed the tree. There were other smells here: the large man and just a hint of something familiar mixed with the residue left in a footprint. Recognition rose slowly from the recesses of his mind, but the masked odour was too slight, even for a tiger. He quartered the ground for some time, scratching tree boles and spraying bushes. Such displacement activity was prevalent in any unsettled animal. The half-familiar scents, loneliness and the debility of his chronic, worsening illness was causing stress. For a moment he walked along the trail towards Olaf's camp where Seva lay sleeping, but the distraction of a group of wild pigs breaking through the undergrowth, made him turn and trot half-heartedly after them. They raced off squealing and Angaar's pursuit petered out. He was moving south once more.

Vikram Chakrabarti and his team had mounted a search for their escaped patient, knowing without treatment the tiger would surely die. Several days passed before the crime and its bloody aftermath started to make sense. The tiger was tracked a short way into the hills before the trail gave out. Local police were half-hearted in their efforts to inform the residents of the scattered hill villages and, after a week with no sightings, things reverted to normal. Reluctantly Vikram called off the rescue attempt acknowledging that it was a pointless task – either Angaar would die quickly of inexperience and weakness, or be shot by locals out of fear. Even if found he knew he would have to put the poor creature out of its misery.

Seva was wracked with grief. After a few days he quietly left with his few belongings and was never seen at the zoo again. For the price of a month's rent in lieu of notice the blacksmith drove him up into the hills and left him on a high road a long way south from the scene of Angaar's escape. All Seva knew was his only friend needed him and was thought to be moving in that direction. He left with nothing but hope. He and Angaar were adrift in the wilderness of the Western Ghats. Seva had been unprepared for the journey, but as with any journey the unforeseen can be positive as well as negative. Olaf had found Seva. Seva needed rest and food, but would need help to find Angaar. In this he had been incredibly lucky, as Olaf was skilled in bushcraft. As night drew on the seekers and the sought slept barely three miles apart.

After weeks of rain the hills were bathed in a spell of fine weather. Inversions kept thick morning mists in the valleys, the cold capping air making the high tops and plateau refreshingly cool before the sun warmed everything, releasing the lowland of its white shroud. Plantations of tea and coffee thrived on the slopes. Here local villagers could earn a good living, hard as it was, and had a little more disposable income than many in rural India. Traditions were embraced and festivals colourful. There was a marked increase in visiting tourists, many travelling up from the resorts of Goa bringing their dollars, yens and pounds. The higher, more isolated villages, remained traditionally self-sufficient through necessity. Although many were attracted by more lucrative employment below, the familiar, quiet refuge of home still drew them back. This was so for Karukula which sat in the shadow of Mount Karoo. Karoo was not so much a mountain as a lofty, resilient spur of the eroded Deccan Traps which formed the bluffs above their valley. From here to the south the range became more mountain-like with verdant, tree covered summits and deep lush valleys leading all the way to Goa and Kerala beyond. Mount Karoo was cloaked in green. Only its stratified cliffs were bare rock, except in fissures where soil had accumulated so occasional stunted trees and shrubs could grow, serving as secure nesting sites for black eagles and buzzards. Many of these circled on the rising thermals, joining the ever-present vultures and kites in their search for prey or carrion. All the lands beneath Mount Karoo were blessed with rich soil in which crops would thrive.

Karukula was a quiet, prosperous village set in the wide Karoo Valley overlooking the distant plantations of the foothills. Land around the neat hamlet of huts and stone buildings had been cleared of encroaching forests and laid out in an irregular patchwork of fields. Some thickets of trees were left as shade for resting workers, tethering posts for animals and screens for young lovers. From the village a track wound down towards the markets and towns of the lowlands – a single umbilicus to the outside world. Above the village was a web of lesser tracks, only one of which continued up the steep climb to the wilder forests of the upper valley. From here a river careered over a series of waterfalls to join a wider torrent below which irrigated Karukula's crops. Above these falls the land became part of a protected area, ostensibly to preserve the dwindling flora and fauna of the Sahyadri, as the Western Ghats were known locally, yet still used by villagers for wood, food plants and sometimes, hunting. The upper forests held leopards which occasionally stole down to snatch a goat or village dog. Tigers were seldom thought of anymore.

Misty morning had given way to a fine day. It was still early and the local troop of grey langurs had settled in the trees clinging to the base of Karoo's cliffs feeding on a fruiting fig. A great hornbill had joined them, gently plucking each round fruit with its long beak and tossing it deftly up in the air to catch and swallow. Fruit bats were flying in from further down the valley and a group of wild pigs could be heard snaffling anything dropped to the ground. Kuldev watched and listened to the creatures from a little plot of tobacco near the upper limit of the cultivated ground. He was a small, rugged forty-four-year-old, grey hair showing at the temples and in his thick moustache. A grubby white, wide brimmed hat sat on his head and he smoked a cigarette whist leaning on a rude fence. Nearby an old mongrel dog of complex lineage panted beneath a stunted palm and further along three teenage girls, colourfully dressed, wandered up the steep path towards the tree-cloaked waterfalls. Anupa and Keya were his daughters and the third, Resham, his niece, the offspring of Vyan, his brother. Kuldev glanced in the direction of the chattering girls, smiled to himself and then frowned.

"Don't go too far, girls!" he called after them. "And be careful climbing up there, it is slippery!"

Anupa turned, laughing. As the oldest she was the leader.

"Alright father!" she called back waving. "We are visiting the Great Banyan to sing to the monkeys!"

The girls laughed, a sound Kuldev loved as it reminded him of youth and light and hope. He still had hope for many things, but was comfortable enough. He had been blessed with two lovely daughters and a son, also Kuldev, who at the age of ten was bright as a button and was attending the school down in the Maskrey Plantation. The Great Banyan was not too far off and the girls often went there to sing to the monkeys, ask for favours and leave small offerings. Their many chores were complete so he did not begrudge them this simple joy. The dog raised its ears at the shouting, uttered a hoarse *"wuff"*, then settled back to rest.

"Those young things," said Kuldev to the dog. "Makes you feel tired just watching them, eh Dog?"

The dog had always been known as Dog. He *wuffed* once more and wagged his tail. Kuldev finished smoking, took one more glance at the colourful trio and grabbed his hoe from where it leaned against the fence.

Anupa reached the top of the climb and looked back across the open space in the trees towards the village. She could just make out a cluster of roofs and smoke rising from the cooking fires. Keya and Resham were not far behind, their noisy progress momentarily masked by the cascading water plunging down towards their valley. Anupa led on through thicker forest, the path weaving around great trees full of calling birds and scolding monkeys, towards the special grove of the Great Banyan. She turned off the main trail and pushed through a clump of bushes which opened out into a spacious cathedral of living wood. The walls were an intricate weave of aerial roots leading to trunks and foliage high overhead. It was a natural amphitheatre of strong religious importance for Karukula, a place to pray and ask for favours. Nilgiri langurs inhabited this grove. They were rare in this region, but were revered, so prospered in the forested upper Karoo Valley, for they were considered to be the reincarnated ancestors of all the village families. The individual trees fruited at different times, so the dark, handsome Nilgiris' favoured whatever tree was full of ripe figs, but they always returned to the Great Banyan. It dominated the grove and covered a huge area, soaring higher than any of its progeny. This was where the girls were heading, the vast wooden cavern silencing their endless chatter. They stopped just before the Great Banyan's foremost roots, bowed, hands together and then settled on the leafy floor. Resham unwrapped a bundle she had been carrying and unravelled a colourful square of cloth. Upon this she placed several palm-wrapped parcels, strips of patterned rags and a bottle of water. As they gazed up the black faces of several Nilgiris looked back with excited interest. The three girls began to sing their song, all in tune, all in time, filling the void with a beautiful melody of love, hopes and dreams, asking the wise Nilgiris to hear them and talk to the sacred tree upon which they lived. They sang for a handsome husband, a powerful man who shone like the sun, a prince and a hero bedecked all in gold. They sang and they smiled, finally giving way to giggles, a sound as lovely as the old song.

"We are so silly," chuckled Keya. "I think we may end up with a monkey if we can't sing without laughing."

"Rubbish," chuckled Resham, "we'll all get a shining prince!"

"A doctor would suit me," managed Anupa between titters. "As long as he was handsome!"

Resham stood and tied a gaily-patterned rag to one of the Great Banyan's roots.

"There," she said. "That's my wish, now do yours."

The others followed suit, then stood back to admire their work.

"Will it work do you think?" asked Keya.

"It depends on the mood of the Nilgiris," said Anupa looking up at the inquisitive black faces high above. "Maybe Arjuna will come down from heaven all golden and handsome!"

"Who would he pick? giggled Resham.

"Anupa!" said Keya. "She is the oldest."

"We would get a vanara," said Resham in mock horror, then dissolving into fits of laughter again.

"Arjuna may select a vanara for Keya!" said Anupa.

"Oh no!" said Keya. "What a terrible thing to say in front of the Nilgiris." She looked up into the branches of the Great Banyan and shouted up to the langurs. "Do not listen, Nilgiris! Send me a prince! Monkey-men are nice, but not as a husband!"

Resham took the parcels and placed them at the foot of the Great Banyan's vast tangle of roots, then the girls retreated to watch. The Nilgiris knew the parcels contained a mixture of rice, vegetables and fruit and were cautiously edging down towards the ground via branch and root. The three girls began to hum the melody once more which made the Nilgiris pause, but only briefly. They had been through this process many times and knew the girls and their song. With practised ease the beautiful creatures dropped to the floor and began gathering the parcels, carefully unwrapping them and devouring the contents, keeping a watchful eye on the singers.

As the girls hummed and watched there was a sudden change in the langurs' demeanour - they froze, uttered sharp cries of astonishment and then fled into the trees as quickly as they could. The creatures had looked beyond Anupa, Keya and Resham causing them to turn quickly. They all screamed as one. Just at the head of the track Arjuna stood, glowing and golden, with a vanara over his shoulder.

Olaf woke early, stoked up the fire, stretched out his stiff limbs and yawned loudly. It was only after he started to boil some water that he noticed the little man had not moved, but was shivering in his bundle of clothes. He stepped across to Seva and crouched down gently shaking his shoulder.

"Hey, feller," he said. "You ok? You look like shite."

Seva's eyes flickered and he struggled to a sitting position. He coughed, chest rattling, then looked about him.

"Olab," he said weakly. "I think I am very ill. I am sorry sahib."

"Jaysus," replied Olaf, smiling, "don't go apologising. Let's have a look at you."

Olaf put a hand on Seva's forehead then felt around his neck and jaw.

"I think you have some form of flu," he said. "You are pretty damned hot and your glands are up. That comes through wearing yourself out. Can you walk?"

"I think so, Olab," said Seva. "But I do feel very ill."

"Well, we have to get down to yonder village," said Olaf. "We need supplies and you need rest. We'll have a brew and see how you shape up."

Olaf prepared some tea and placed a full tin mug into Seva's unsteady hands. The small man sipped it thankfully, yawning after every swallow. Olaf then riffled through his pack until he withdrew a strip of tablets, popping two out into the palm of his hand and offering them to Seva.

"These'll help a bit," he said. "Can you eat?"

Seva swallowed the tablets and replied, "I am not hungry."

"I didn't ask you if you are hungry," said Olaf. "I said *can you eat*?"

"A little, Olab sahib," said Seva.

The big man made up a pan of soup, fortifying it with rice and dried vegetables, pouring a good helping into Seva's now empty mug.

"Drink it all," said Olaf. "You will need it afore the day is out."

He consumed the rest from the pan, belched and packed up the camp. Seva managed to climb out of his cocoon and leaned against the rock wall. Olaf quickly got everything into his pack and kicked out the fire making sure nothing was left to burn. Then he turned his attention to Seva who looked tiny and out of place in this wild highland of jungle and rocks. He walked across the open area to a stand of small trees and, using his knife, cut a stout staff and cleaned it of any sharp protrusions. He returned to the camp and handed it to Seva.

"We have to get down so you can rest," he said. "It will take while so you'll need this. I'll carry everything else, you just plod along as best you can."

"What about Angaar?" asked Seva.

"The only way you'll ever find him is by recovering from your present state," said Olaf. "Once you are back on your feet I promise I'll help you find him, if we can. Killing yourself in the process will do no good at all. I'm fecked if I know what you'll do if you find him anyhow. Dance a tango?"

"What is a *tincow*?" asked Seva.

Olaf chuckled. "You are a funny feller, Seva. Not to worry about all that, let's get moving. The quicker we get down, the faster we can come back up. Then we can hunt a tiger."

"You will still help me?" asked Seva.

Olaf took a deep breath.

"Look, feller," he said. "I have a few months to kill and a place to find not too far from here. I've only a rough plan, but I will eventually get to Goa where there's some pretty girls and nice hotels. In the meantime, I am heading for a beach my granddad visited years back, and as yon tiger and you seem to be heading the same way, well, there's no harm in teaming up. You look like you need a friend, and I don't mind a nice chap like yourself coming along. Come on my lad, let's get down this mountain and see if we can't regroup."

The two men started their long walk, Olaf hefting the Bergen, and Seva, still swaddled in his borrowed fleece, limping beside him leaning on the staff. It was obvious from the start that Seva was going to find the walk tough, but Olaf was impressed that the small man soldiered on without complaint. Even so, it was noon before they approached the edge of the plateau, Olaf pausing briefly to wait for his companion and point at the ground.

"See this dung?" he said. "That's your tiger's."

He took off his Bergen and had a good look at the ground and surrounding trees. Then he crouched at a spot on the edge of the track and beckoned Seva over.

"I never noticed this on the way back up yesterday, so I think old tiger has been back," he said, smiling. "He's scratched yon tree and has left new pug marks. See the scar in this one?"

Seva leaned heavily on his staff, but gamely took in all that Olaf explained and pointed out.

"Yes, Olab," he said. "It is him! So, he was here yesterday when we were at the camp?"

"I reckon so," said Olaf, standing and walking back the way they came. He paused again some way off. "Yes, he walked this far then turned back, there's nothing after this point."

"Why does he use this track and not the forest?" asked Seva.

"Same reason we do," said Olaf. "It's easier."

Seva found the energy to laugh then coughed for a long time. Olaf gave him some water and another two tablets.

"They're only paracetamol, but they'll help a bit," he said. "Are you ok to go on?"

"Yes, Olab," he answered weakly. "Angaar is very close. I have to keep going. There is nothing else for me."

Olaf led Seva onto the steep, barely discernible path which led to the wide valley below. The forest was buzzing with insects, ringing with the cries of birds and monkeys, and rustling with the occasional larger beast. A troop of lion-tailed macaques crossed their path at one point, so they stopped to rest and watch.

"They are rare beasties," said Olaf. "I read a lot about the Ghats before I came out, and there ain't many of these fellers left in the world."

"They are beautiful," said Seva. "Why are there so few?"

"Because humans think the world should be beaten into shape," said Olaf. "People have a terrible tendency to fuck things up for no logical reason. Kill, chop, burn, break, feck up. All we are, Seva, are shaved chimps with a gun."

"They wanted to kill Angaar," said Seva. "But I gave him a chance. He killed them, now he is dying. But he's free."

There was a long silence. The macaques disappeared into the forest and the sea of treetops below waved in the breeze.

"So, you are going to find this tiger and comfort him," stated Olaf. "That's not a bad plan."

"I think that is so," said Seva. "But he has a purpose and we will see that too."

"Tell me about old Angaar," said Olaf. "The miles go by quicker that way."

And so, Seva told Olaf Angaar's story.

There were still tigers in the Sahyadri. The few reserves set aside to conserve this great cat were well run and protected, but in the thicker forests beyond, a small, very wary population lived almost undetected. Any missing livestock was usually blamed on the more common leopards, and tigers were seldom thought of, thus not considered. Natural selection had given this remnant sharpened senses when it came to human beings, so they were all but invisible and kept to the steeper slopes. The land to the south of Mount Karoo would be difficult to cultivate and until the lush plains and foothills failed to feed a growing population, the forests were relatively safe. People did pass through on well-marked tracks and unsurfaced, single lane roads, but only local villagers used the natural environment to supplement their traditional way of life. In recent years there had been an international drive to conserve large parts of the Western Ghats, so there was hope for these large remnants of primary habitat. It was into this wilderness that Angaar approached from the higher plateau and it was on the forested slopes of a wide, steep sided valley, his senses were spiked with something irresistible. He had followed a game trail frequented by wild pigs, gaur, deer and lesser creatures when he paused at a fallen tree in a small clearing. The smell of tiger was strong, the super-concentrated origin of the vague scent he had followed from the high ground. The irresistible perfume released hormones into his system and his primary imperative took control. He had found the territory of a female and there was enough information in the copious scent marking to identify that she was close to oestrous. Angaar paced up and down the fallen trunk sniffing. He clawed and sprayed a nearby tree and rubbed his neck in the fascinating odour of the female who had so recently been here. A short way back up the trail he squatted down and left a scat as a clear and pungent signal of his existence. Eventually he was satisfied his intentions were well displayed then started his pursuit in earnest. The female's territory was defined by the valleys and forested slopes between hills stretching west towards the coast. It covered a large area, but was narrow and long, enclosing the wildest, least trodden parts. Hunting was good here if a tiger knew the ground and there were plenty of hiding places on the higher slopes in which to lay up undisturbed. At times Angaar caught the scent of people, but only faint traces of urine by the trail or old camp sites used in traversing the Ghats.

It was hunger that eventually halted his steady progress, and the instinct to hunt which took him towards the river below. He had found a well-trodden trail leading down to where animal calls echoed and the scent of game led. Turning off the trail over steep, densely forested ground, he quietly made his way to a point where a thick stand of bamboo hid him from the water's edge. Keeping low he crawled closer to the water margin and settled to take in the scene. The river was slower and wider here, as two valleys converged with a lesser stream joining the larger, pooling and forming a marsh at the confluence, before it became a single, faster watercourse where the valley narrowed a mile or so further on. The game trail ended at a long marshy waterhole where animals of all kinds visited through the day to drink. As he watched a group of spotted deer, a lone gaur and a herd of wild pigs occupied the muddy margins. Three elephants watered on the far bank. Angaar focused on the closer creatures. So far he had been lucky in his travels and had survived well on fresh carrion, domestic animals and stolen kills, but he had inevitably reached the point where he had to hunt. He settled, hidden within the bamboo thicket. As time passed the elephants disappeared into the forest, hardly making a sound; the gaur and deer moved further down the river. It was the noisy group of pigs that Angaar watched. They finished drinking, but unlike the other animals, moved closer to his hiding place to take advantage of a wallow. Of the fifteen pigs, six were younger and less wary than the large adults, and gambolled to the pool of liquid mud nipping at each other, squealing and dashing about in uncontrolled fits of exuberance. The adults hung back watching and sniffing the air, taking their time to cover the same ground, occasionally rooting around for tubers in the riverine clay. The youngsters reached the wallow and ploughed in, rolling and grunting in pleasure. Angaar watched and waited; it was a long way to make a charge. After several minutes three large sows and a boar usurped the wallow, the youngsters protesting noisily, but gave way to those further up the hierarchy – the old boar was not to be messed with. The herd remained wary, those awaiting the pleasures of the mud sniffing the air and listening. Gradually, calm settled over the group, curled tails dropped and nosing through the earth took precedence. Those in the wallow relaxed further, relying on the balance of the herd to sound a warning of danger.

The day drew on and the valley became warm. The pigs started to drowse in the heat, and the wallow filled to overflowing. A small group wandered back into the forest and the sub-group of youngsters drifted to the river's margins. A lone, subservient boar had started to root in the earth closer to Angaar's hiding place. He fixed his amber eyes upon it, staying low and gathering his rear legs beneath him. The rooting boar gradually moved closer until it was just ten yards from him. Downriver a deer barked out an alarm and all the pigs froze and gazed in the direction of the noise, sniffing the air and listening. Although Angaar was down wind of the herd, the breeze was capricious and the element of surprise would soon be lost. Time stood still as the herd gazed away from the tiger all attention focused towards that alarm call. The pigs were poised and could move very quickly from a standing start. Gradually they settled and at this point, just as the adrenalin rush had eased, Angaar charged and roared. The pigs scattered in all directions, but perversely Angaar's target ran towards him in confusion, swerving at the last moment, realising its fatal mistake. A single huge paw reached out and swiped the boar's legs from beneath it, whereupon Angaar turned, and in single fluid movement, clamped his jaws upon its throat. The stricken boar kicked and struggled, but it used precious oxygen and quickly succumbed to hypoxia before expiring. Angaar began to feed from his kill where it died, ignoring the distant shapes of jackals and already circling vultures and kites.

He only looked up when another tiger emerged from the forest beyond the smaller stream. Angaar stood and sniffed the air, quickly establishing she was a female and started to approach which elicited a low growl from her in response. He paused and she waded through the water, but circled Angaar indirectly making for the body of the boar. He growled deeply and turned his head to track her course. Her odour was intoxicating, so much so that he looked passively on as she reached the carcass and, ever watchful, started to eat. Instinctively Angaar paced carefully towards the tigress, but stopped short of a complete approach, lay down and began to lick the back of his great paws – a display of non-aggression. She growled again, yet there was no ferocity in her demeanour and she continued to feed. The first stages of tiger courtship had commenced. Sometime later the tigress stood and dragged the boar's remains into the bamboo thicket, then walked back, passed Angaar, and made across the stream into the forest. He stood and followed at a safe distance.

The hours dragged for Olaf. Seva was still struggling, even though they had reached easier ground. The descent from the high plateau had been agonisingly slow and the small man was obviously suffering, yet never complained nor asked for a rest. What had taken Olaf a couple of hours the previous day had taken them three times as long and it was obvious they would need to find shelter without reaching the distant village. Seva's cough rattled in his chest. Olaf called a halt at a stream and helped Seva sit down on a flat rock.

"You look pretty done in, feller," he said. "I think we will be camping out again. The village is still a good few hours away. As soon as I find a good spot we can rest up and drink some tea."

"Sorry, Olab sahib," said Seva. "I can try. We can get there."

Olaf laughed and crouched down so he could talk to Seva without being overbearing. The story Seva had told him of his life with Angaar, his deep love of the beast and its brutal treatment at the hands of the men who tried to abduct it, had made a deep impression. This man, a nonentity in his homeland, had courage, integrity and a deep-seated loyalty to his feline friend. Olaf had had comrades he trusted with his life, had relied upon the judgement of men in battle, and had a deep confidence in his own ability, but he doubted he had ever had a friend who would give up everything to make sure his passing was not alone. Seva's adventure was reckless and ill conceived, but it was equally honest, with no gain but the knowledge that his friend, Angaar, could have comfort. The little bird-man might be slightly mad, but then, so was Olaf. After all, tracking down a very big Bengal tiger might well prove to be the maddest venture of his lifetime. And Olaf had a debt to pay. He carried a burden that tortured him every day. Though not religious, he was seeking redemption.

"You look here, Seva," he said, placing a hand on Seva's shoulder. "Sorry is a word oft used, but seldom meant. It is also a sign of subservience in some, but we're better than that. There is nothing to be sorry about. We are a team right now and so it shall remain until our parting. I'll filter some water, you chew on one of these hardtack biscuits. It tastes like a hamster's bedding and will break yer jaw, but it's supposed to be full of energy."

Seva took the square biscuit and nibbled the edge experimentally.

"It is hard," he said.

"If you can get through that, yer a better man than I am Gunga Din," said Olaf, chuckling as he filtered stream water into his bottles.

"Who is this Gunga Deen?" asked Seva.

"Jaysus, feller, you know, I'm not that sure. I think he was an Indian soldier who was braver than his British officers. Kipling wrote a poem about him."

"Ah," said Seva. "You are a soldier, I can see it."

That surprised Olaf. With his long hair and rapidly growing beard he thought he looked more like a hippy.

"What gave me away?" he asked.

"Everything you do is confident and second nature," said Seva. "You cope in any circumstance, but these are learned skills that have meshed with your natural abilities. You must be more than an ordinary soldier, I think. You have more stories to tell than me."

"You read men well," said Olaf. "Is that learned?"

"I think it is," said Seva, coughing again. "I am small and was always bottom of the pile. It helped me avoid trouble. I learned this very quickly."

Silence followed as Seva crunched on the biscuit and Olaf filled his various containers. Then they resumed their trek, Olaf walking ahead munching a biscuit of his own, Seva limping behind relying heavily on his staff. The shadow of the plateau began to creep up behind them as the sun sank towards the west, just as they reached the clearing where dholes had made their kill, only to be robbed by Angaar.

"See those bones over there?" said Olaf. "Our tiger fed on that. The other scraps yonder shows he took exception to a hyena and pretty near bit his head off. Old Angaar is well clued up for a zoo creature."

"He is more than that, Olab," said Seva. "He was born in the wild and weaned before he came to any zoo. Just like a soldier he was taught things, by his mother, and he remembers how to be wild. Even more than that, he has a fire inside that never went out. He has a destiny with death, but a path in life."

"Then we are all similar creatures," laughed Olaf. "There is me, and there's he, and there's thee, Gunga Din."

"You may be right, Olab," said Seva, "but I am no Gunga Deen."

"You are to me, Seva. You are to me."

As they crossed the clearing Seva lagged behind. Olaf waited and scanned the forest edges. He could see a thin margin of trees tightly packed against a low rocky outcrop, a hardy strata layer that had resisted erosion. It looked as if it would give a reasonable amount of shelter. As Seva reached him he relaxed and rubbed his blond beard.

"I think we have to stop here, Seva," he said studying the sky. "We can't make the village and we need to be safe and cosy come night."

"I am a burden, Olab," said Seva miserably. "But you are right, I need to stop now."

"What's another night under the stars to us, Gunga Din?" said Olaf happily. "We be warriors. We be comrades. And we stay together to weave tales for the camp fire. We'll be right. I reckon we can set up home over by the rocks yonder."

He led a grateful Seva the short distance to the trees and slipped off the Bergen. Using his knife, he cut away some vegetation where the rock met the ground and stamped out a flat area between two large trees. Seva sat watching, enthralled as the giant, blond man built a fire, lighting it with nothing more than a piece of metal, ignited his strange cooker and boiled enough water for the both of them. He made tea and sweetened it with sugar, then crumbled a tiny cube and several of the hard biscuits into the remaining water, adding some powder from a small plastic, screw-top container. As this simmered he handed two more of the white tablets to Seva.

"There you go, Seva," he said. "The sugar in the brew will give you a lift and these will keep your temperature down a bit."

"You are good at this," said Seva. "How are you making a meal with nothing?"

Olaf laughed.

"Well now," he said stirring the gloop in the pan, "the biscuits will set in the old guts, but will keep you going. There's nothing in the rules that say you can't use a stock cube and curry powder. It's all we have, but it's better than cat or rat, and I've eaten both in my time."

"You ate a cat?" asked Seva.

"Well, it was him or me!" said Olaf. "I was starving and he trotted past. He would have gnawed on me had I been freshly dead."

"What did it taste like?" asked Seva.

"Curry, mainly," chuckled Olaf, "a bit like this jollop."

Seva laughed and dissolved into a coughing fit, recovering only after sipping at his tea. The two men ate. Afterwards Olaf directed Seva to the place by the rock.

"You sleep here," he said. "Have my sleeping bag and I'll kip next to the fire."

Seva was too tired to argue and was asleep before full dark. Olaf walked to the clearing and watched the sky grow navy blue, then black; he loved watching the stars appear and the odd meteor flashing across the atmosphere. After a long while he returned to the camp and settled down using the Bergen as a pillow and his tarp for a ground sheet.

Chapter 24

Hunted

"Is he dead?" asked Ali.

"No, just fainted I think," said Tsering. "Help me get him into the truck."

Mr Gupta had collapsed in the dust close to Ali's truck stop and now lay with his head on the lap of the man he had seen as a Mongol warrior. Tsering was not, but it was an easy mistake to make as his sun-browned, Oriental features set him apart in this region of India. He hefted Mr Gupta into a sitting position and grabbed him beneath the arms; Ali grasped the ankles and together they managed to reach the back of the colourful Bedford.

"Doors!" shouted Tsering.

A taxi had pulled up and two men jumped out and approached the struggling men. One deftly opened the large rear doors of the truck and assisted Tsering and Ali get Mr Gupta's lifeless body up and onto a single mattress set in a wooden frame.

"Is he dead?" asked Jag.

"No, no," said Tsering. "He needs hydrating, get me a bottle of water."

Ali trotted over to his shop and grabbed a bottle from the counter, and gave it to Tsering.

"No charge!" said Ali.

"Hmmph," said Tsering as he unscrewed it, "probably well water anyway."

Ali looked hurt. Tarik re-joined Jag outside and stood back as Tsering lifted Mr Gupta's head and started to drip water into his mouth. He automatically swallowed, though remained oblivious to his surroundings.

"What now?" whispered Tarik.

"We stick to our plan," replied Jag. "One of us needs to meet our client, one of us needs to keep tabs on the fellow."

"Did you manage to get a transmitter into the wagon?" asked Tarik.

"Better," said Jag. "It's in Gupta's bag."

"You are good," said Tarik relaxing. "So who does what?"

"Let's see what happens here and plan when we know where things stand. He might die," said Jag.

"Do we still get the bonus?" asked Tarik.

"Four questions are too many," said Jag. "We will be paid. Now let's see what's happening."

The flatbed upon which the cabin had been bolted was high off the ground, but with both doors wide open the scene inside was easy enough to see. Tsering was still dripping water into Mr Gupta's mouth and the patient seemed to have regained some colour. After a while Tsering stood and fished around in several of the rough, fitted cupboards and alcoves and pulled out a small electric fan which he plugged into a hidden socket. He positioned it to blow air over his patient's body, from which he had stripped the jacket and shoes. Finally, he propped up Mr Gupta's head and shoulders with a cushion, before jumping back onto the ground.

"Is he ok?" asked Ali.

"I don't know," said Tsering. "He looks worn out and is sleeping. He's not comatose; at least I think not. Do you chaps know anything about him?"

Jag was first to answer.

"We were just stopping for some food," he said. "Doesn't he have anything on him? What's in his bag?"

"Watch me do this," said Tsering. "I want witnesses to see I steal nothing."

He went through the jacket pockets and found credit cards and a wallet.

"His name is Anil Gupta," announced Tsering.

Then he looked through the bag which Jag had retrieved.

"Nothing more than a few clothes and stuff," said Tsering. "Ali, I think I should take him to Nawal Ji. Vam knows more than me about medical things."

"Why not take him to the hospital?" asked Tarik.

Tsering thought for a while and glanced at Mr Gupta's motionless body.

"Just a feeling," he said. "This man looks like he will be alright. I think Nawal Ji is expecting him."

"Where have you all camped this time?" asked Ali.

"Indira Sagar," said Tsering. "We've a spot by the water. I only came back to get a spring welded. This old Queen Lizzie is not easy to get fixed. I'll let this fellow rest for a bit."

"Shall I fix you all some food?" asked Ali.

"Why not?" said Jag. "That's why we stopped anyway."

They settled under the thatched awning and idled away the time, Tsering occasionally checking to make sure Mr Gupta was not any worse and to administer more water. Jag steered the conversation as best he could, getting as much information as possible. The driver said little, but watched a great deal. Jag established that Tsering was of Tibetan origin and was part of an itinerant group who travelled in the truck. This was not unusual in India. Eventually Jag remembered a comment Tsering had made.

"You said he was expected. How can that be if you do not know him?" he asked.

"Who knows how a sadhu's mind works," answered Tsering. "Nawal Ji is different and works using something he calls Kvark. He will know if this is the man."

Any further conversation was halted by a cry of anguish from the back of the truck, followed by two shouted words.

"Hold fast!"

As Mr Gupta collapsed in the dust, the Mongol warrior raced into his other world. He tore along the beach towards Mr Gupta and William MacKeeg, where they were standing by the calm sea beneath a huge moon. Mr Gupta was terrified.

"Hold fast," said MacKeeg quietly. "Trust me now, laddie."

The charging man ran through them and faded to nothingness beyond. Mr Gupta was exhausted, even in this other world which had become his haven. There was heaviness in his heart and, although MacKeeg was an equal part of him in all worlds, he was still full of doubt and knew his strength was failing. This whole unlikely quest looked set to fizzle out in vainglorious defeat, leaving his family and friends exposed to horrors beyond their understanding. This possibility rallied his spirit a little.

"The illness is not such to break ye yet, laddie," soothed MacKeeg. "Don't mistake the weariness of labour for the kiss of doom. It is time to rest up a little, after all 'tis what ye needed and wanted, so dinnae ye start mithering now it's arrived."

"Then what the bloody hell is that?" said Mr Gupta pointing at the silvery water.

Both men stared at the black shape in the distance. It was the misshapen head and wide shoulders of the black demon that plagued an earlier dream. This time it hunkered in the sea, blue glowing eyes reflected in distorting wavelets that rippled from the all-consuming blankness of its body. It seemed to be moving imperceptibly towards them, cautiously and inexorably. It had poisoned their sanctuary. Mr Gupta knew there was to be a reckoning in both worlds.

"That," said MacKeeg, "is the echo of our plan. He comes and there is no stopping him, but we must draw him on. We have more to do and there is still time. What you see is the same as that Mongol fellow. A wraith; a shadow. Nothing more. Do not fear it, laddie."

The demon heaved itself upright. On bent, muscular legs it started wading through the water, screaming with the voices of a million tormented souls, eyes flashing and clawed hands grasping. It loomed huge over the two men and reached for Mr Gupta. He cried out in fear and anguish as blackness enveloped him. From somewhere far distant MacKeeg yelled, "Hold fast!" and the monster evaporated into nightmares unborn.

He awoke fevered, but alert, and felt the softness of a mattress beneath him. His eyes were open though his vision took some moments to return. And there was the Mongol looking down, wide faced, with a smudge of moustache above the corners of his mouth. This was not a warrior, just a man dressed in a t-shirt and jeans, his almond eyes full of concern.

"How do you feel, Anil?" he asked.

Mr Gupta had but sketchy memories of his recent march along the hot, dusty road, but realised his collapse had been caused by simple exhaustion, notwithstanding the relentless drama of the other world. The tumour's progress was yet to become something he could perceive beyond a basic awareness. He took in his surroundings: a cabin decked in ornate hangings, tassels, swags and tails; carved wood shelves and compact furniture; lamps, idols and cushions; all immersed in a pleasant aroma of spices, joss sticks and engine oil. He remembered the fantastically decorated truck.

"Who are you?" he asked.

"Tsering. I have some medical knowledge, but I think you are just a bit travel worn. How do you feel?"

Mr Gupta struggled to a sitting position.

"Fine, but thirsty," he said. "Where are we?"

"The same place as you fell," said Tsering. "Ali's place. We have not moved."

"My bag...?" said Mr Gupta.

"...is safe and next to you," said Tsering. "I found your name in your wallet and looked through your bag. Nothing has been taken."

"Thank you," said Mr Gupta. He took the bottle of water Tsering held out and drank it dry, belching quietly at the end.

"Where do you want to go?" asked Tsering. "Are you lost or something?"

"No, not at all," said Mr Gupta. "I am journeying to the Western Ghats – a sort of vacation. Call me a pilgrim, I suppose, if you want."

"Nawal Ji is expecting you," said Tsering in a matter-of-fact way. "Would you like to meet him?"

Mr Gupta baulked at this. He was drawing trouble towards him and knew it would be grotesque to involve innocents. He stared through the open doors at the traffic and reflected on this for a moment.

"He cannot be expecting me," said Mr Gupta. "My world is one of trouble and it is still running its course. I think I should do this alone."

Tsering laughed at this, the change in his inscrutable features was quite startling.

"In Tibet my life was trouble, and it still pursues me," he said, "and it is the same for all in the Kvark. So I think a night with us can do no harm, and you would be well on the way to the Ghats too – we are camped at Indira Sagar and you will be welcome. I could do with the company of someone with a story. The drive is long and slow in this Queen Lizzie."

"Just to Indira Sagar," said Mr Gupta, having no energy for an argument. "You are very kind. What is this Kvark and how can this Nawal Ji expect me? It makes no sense."

"He has told us a change is coming," said Tsering, "perhaps not you by name, but by implication. We are waiting for an indication where to travel and you have a direction in your head, so you are what Nawal Ji is expecting. He will explain the Kvark, for it is beyond me."

Tsering helped Mr Gupta to his feet and then down onto the dusty ground. Ali, Jag and Tarik watched from nearby.

"Is he alright?" asked Ali.

"Yes, make some chai," ordered Tsering.

Mr Gupta was helped to a chair and his bag and jacket were placed on a table in front of him. Chai appeared and the other men drew up chairs.

"Do you want a lift to the city?" asked Jag, hoping for an easy completion to his task.

"No," replied Mr Gupta. "It is a kind offer, but I have no need to return there. For now, I shall go with Mr Tsering, here, as we appear to be travelling the same way."

"Where are you heading?" asked Ali.

"To the sea," said Mr Gupta. "To the sea where a man called Robert Clive once went. Just to see. Nothing more."

Jag and Tarik finished their chai, then walked back to their car.

"What now?" asked Tarik.

"I'll follow in the taxi using the tracker," said Jag. "You phone the boss and let him know what's happening. If he tells you to wait for our client, then so be it. I'll let our client know all is in hand and between them they can decide what to do. This is more than simply following a man. Indira Sagar is a long way and if this Gupta chap is heading for the coast, it will complicate matters. I'll be glad when we can hand this over. Something's not right. Gupta is no criminal. He looks more like a victim. That voice was odd."

"Yes," said Tarik, "it was very strange. And you are right, he looks all in. I wonder what he has done?"

"Takes all kinds," said Jag, "and if he's pissed off one of Suliman's clients then there are big amounts of money involved. Or information. In the end it revolves around money and power and money."

"I just want the money," said Tarik.

A while later Mr Gupta felt much better. He had relieved himself copiously in the undergrowth, his urine pale enough to show the effects of dehydration had passed. He climbed up into the passenger seat of the ancient Bedford settling into the creaking seat next to Tsering. Ali handed his bag up. The truck roared into life, belching a plume of black smoke through the side-venting exhaust pipe, before lurching slowly onto the road. Inside the bag a tiny transmitter, wrapped like a boiled sweet, pulsed once every twenty seconds, sending a signal to the receiver in the faux taxi.

Jag sent a message to the client's number.

Target under observation moving south on the NH69. Transmitter located on target, signal clear.

A reply took some time in coming, but when it did it was unambiguous.

Do not lose him. I will be there. Transmit locations as necessary.

Jag drove off, following at a safe distance, leaving Tarik to await instructions.

The truck rumbled south towards Indira Sagar. Inside, Mr Gupta remained unaware that he had lost most of his advantage.

***

The plane touched down at Raj Bhoj Airport just after nine o'clock. In seat 5A Vasupati Chopra of Cobra Investments had been listening to music on his smart phone. His mind relaxed as he focused on the comforting sounds of Zahan's *Chaos Birthing*. He had ignored the cabin crew and only drank water for the short flight. His hair was down, he wore his blue glasses and all black clothes; the blue sheen around his neck was not obvious and had drawn little attention, not that he cared. He had left his human life and those who were nearest him. He carried no thoughts of them. It was a swift trip through the arrivals hall and baggage reclaim area, and he stepped into a waiting car well before ten o'clock. The driver was one of Suliman's and took Vaz straight to the Pan Continental Hotel. Here he was given Mr Gupta's written message:

As you have come this far I can only assume my life is forfeit. This being so I intend to meet you when I am ready. I will be travelling west from here and shall send a daily message to your phone as to where I've been. Eventually a message will arrive explaining where you will meet your end - I will not run forever.

Vaz smiled. He had been in touch with Suliman's men and knew Anil Gupta was being followed. The message seemed naive in light of this. He decided a little more help would not go amiss, so sat in the foyer and called an old acquaintance.

"Engineer," came the answering voice.

"Sachet, it's Vaz" he said. "I need the Engineer's help, full costs, no questions."

"Go on," said Engineer.

"A vehicle fit for a long journey and some hardware," said Vaz. "There could be some issues in the way, but ultimately just one. I will deal with that, you just do your usual job."

"I need a few hours," said Engineer. "Where shall I meet you?"

"I will be at the Pan Continental," said Vaz. "I'll fill you in when you get here."

The call ended. Vaz dismissed his driver and booked into a room. He was supremely confident about finding and killing Mr Gupta and was excited that he was relatively close. But something troubled him. This insignificant old man had killed Kush Karnik. Karnik was a true professional and reliable too, yet he was gone. Had it been a lucky break? Probably, but here he was dancing to Mr Gupta's tune. Even with the power of Cobra and Suliman, this ragged old fool was still out there. Mr Gupta had yet to send a message. Could he be aware of being followed? By the time Vaz was called by the girl at reception, he knew Jag was tracking an old lorry south to Indira Sagar. Confident though he was, there remained a hint of unease.

When Sachet Engineer arrived, they shook hands.

"Well, Vaz," said Engineer, "you look different. Are you leaping into the world of politics with Ravi Uppal, or just hamming it up for a Bollywood role?"

"The look suits the latest job," said Vaz simply. "Sit down and I'll talk you through it."

Engineer was taller than average, but not a big man. He was trim and looked fit with bright, intelligent eyes and a neatly cut shock of black hair. He wore dark combat trousers and military style shirt and boots. Sachet Engineer was a private mercenary. He did not serve any army, but sold his skills to those who needed help in simplifying their business, especially if it entailed the removal of rivals, debtors, informers or anyone of similar ilk. Engineer had a moral compass and there were rules to his services. Children were exempt, as were those he deemed innocents or unconnected, though it was his dynamic assessments on the ground as to how that may unfold. Ultimately money ruled and India was a rich hunting ground. Vaz and Engineer's business had converged several times over the years, and their rise from poverty had been similar. But where Engineer was more practical and considered himself as a technician, he saw Vaz as a pure assassin. Engineer knew Vaz could be unpredictable under pressure and had avoided working with him too closely. However, when Vaz wanted help the job had to be complex and this meant no quibbles over the fee. Easy money.

"Ravi has got Suliman's men tracking a man," said Vaz. "This man is dangerous to us, has too much information and may be part of a multi-million-rupee fraud. He killed Karnik..."

"You're joking!" interrupted Engineer. "This man must be bloody dangerous."

"No, not really," said Vaz. "He is frail and has a brain tumour. He's dying. But not fast enough. He has information that could harm Cobra and stop Ravi's love affair with politics. And he has threatened to kill me. That is an affront."

"So he is to be removed," said Engineer. "Do you foresee any collateral damage, as our American friends would say?"

"With this man anything is possible," said Vaz. "The job will fall into your loose ethical parameters, but you will be paid an extra five thousand dollars for any unforeseen removal that may need to happen. The only rule is I will remove the target."

"Shall I call Aktar and Kepi?" asked Engineer.

"It would be wise to have a little insurance," said Vaz. "Bring them."

"I want the main fee up front, then I will be all yours," said Engineer.

"I can arrange that now," said Vaz lifting his phone. "The standard twenty thousand dollars now, all expenses paid and the collateral money as and when."

"I'll watch you do it," said Engineer smiling.

In ten minutes, the money was wired into his private account.

"I'm all yours," he said. "Now who is this nasty man?"

"Gupta," replied Vaz. "A Mr Anil Gupta."

By mid-afternoon Tsering had driven his old Bedford QL through Hoshangabad and was approaching Harda. Mr Gupta had nodded off after a few minutes and the cab had been silent, Tsering not being one for radio. The truck's rumbling engine was not the original, the QL was of 1930s vintage, so it had died years before. Tsering had recovered a newer engine from another wreck, and had fitted it one long summer up in Leh. With this the *Queen Lizzie*, as the British Army had affectionately called the QL, could rumble along at close to forty miles an hour if the road was slightly downhill, but was not designed for rapid travel. Mechanically it caused few major problems, the recent spring replacement being a rarity, and Tsering was a good engineer.

Harda was busy. There was a large market blocking several side streets and the main through road took the brunt of diverted traffic, all jammed around a central clock tower and monument. As the lorry eased forward a man on a bicycle, loaded with an impossibly massive bag of onions, shot across the road causing Tsering to brake suddenly, evincing a cacophony of horns, yells and screeching tyres. The jolt woke Mr Gupta who rubbed his eyes whilst he gathered his thoughts.

"Sorry, Mr Gupta," said Tsering, "these people have a death wish."

"Where are we?" asked Mr Gupta.

"Crawling through Harda," replied Tsering easing the lorry past the monument.

Mr Gupta yawned. He had not dreamed at all and felt rested and comfortable. The cab smelled of old leather, spices and oil, the clanking engine giving the impression of this being a machine of long lineage and tough use. The high cab gave Mr Gupta a vantage point allowing unhindered views across the market and crowded streets. Eventually they emerged unscathed onto the relatively open road with only the odd cow or breakdown to slow them up. Mr Gupta realised it was time to send some messages, so dug through his bag to retrieve his phone. It still held a good charge. The old Nokia was a device he understood – basic and uncomplicated. Looking at it he felt how tenuous his link with all he knew was. The small, blue phone gave him a little comfort.

First, he sent Rupa a message:

I am fine. You must help Uncle Sudhesh as much as you can. He will keep you safe. I love you my Rupa.

Next, he had to reassure Jhatish:

I am in a safe place. Plans are going well. Sudhesh will take care of that end.

He could not put more. The strain upon his emotions was too great and he would try to explain too much. Several incoming messages flashed, most from Jhatish, but two were from Ravi:

We are all worried. Where are you?

Followed by:

Please get in touch, the police think you are dead. I can help you. Rupa has disappeared.

The knowledge that Ravi was directly involved in this nightmare made the messages hard to read. There was nothing from Vaz. That did not surprise him, but he knew he was somewhere behind and getting closer. Should he send him a message? He dropped his hands into his lap and closed his eyes to think.

"He'll be in Bhopal the now," said MacKeeg.

"Should I send it?" asked Mr Gupta. "Where shall I tell him I'm going?"

"Ye're safe for the time being," said MacKeeg. "Taunt him and see if he responds."

Mr Gupta typed out the words:

Bhopal was nice but the sea is better. Come and see the sea with me.

Nothing more seemed necessary. He sent it and put the phone away.

"Who is hunting you?" asked Tsering.

The question startled Mr Gupta. He knew immediately he had been speaking aloud.

"Who on Earth would hunt me?" asked Mr Gupta. "I am nobody of importance."

The words were thin and lacked honesty. This drew a smile from Tsering.

"You are safe," he said. "You will see that soon. But I know that look. You are being hunted. You used two voices, each clearly different. That I do not understand, but I think you could be a sadhu. I think you fit with Nawal Ji. The other you is dangerous, he with the strange voice, and perhaps you are right. Whoever hunts you may be grasping the tiger's tail."

"I am no sadhu," said Mr Gupta. "Nor am I a tiger."

"Sadhus just are," said Tsering. "I think you are. There is nothing you can do to change this. As for being a tiger, well maybe you are, maybe not, but you may be a shape-changer. I have heard of such things. You are more than you seem and that is certain."

Mr Gupta gave a tired chuckle.

"You could be right. That makes as much sense as anything. But every step I take lessens me, Tsering. And every step brings my awful task closer."

361

"You are a sadhu," stated Tsering. "You speak like Puneet, but you are more like Nawal Ji. You are the one he talked of. You have a destination and are trusting in fate to deliver you. That is how it seems to me. Of course, Nawal Ji will call that nonsense and say things about probability, yet I can see you are linked to us."

"I just want to go to the sea," said Mr Gupta. "Everything will end there for me."

"And for the monster you draw?" asked Tsering.

Mr Gupta was again taken by surprise. Vaz was a monster. In his other world that was how he appeared. This Tibetan could deduce he was being followed, of that Mr Gupta was sure, but to use the verb *draw* was unsettling. For that was exactly how MacKeeg described their plan. Tsering had also been correct about the journey he had undertaken – Bhopal was the only real staging post he had ever had in his head; Clive's Beach was hundreds of miles away and he had never thought about the logistics of getting there. He wondered if his two realities were bleeding into each other.

"What if you are right?" said Mr Gupta. "My presence would put you in danger. I cannot do that to anyone."

"You will understand," was all Tsering would say.

It was evening when Tsering steered the Queen Lizzie off the highway onto a rough track, the suspension creaking and occasionally bouncing the two men clear of their seats. The sky was still bright, but the low sun no longer lit up the woods through which they drove, so progress was slow. The headlamps were not very strong and Mr Gupta surmised that Tsering must know the way reasonably well as he drove with confidence. In places the track had stretches of broken Tarmac which suggesting this may have once been far more suitable for traffic.

"This was a road to a small farming community," said Tsering, glancing sideways. "When the great dam was built lots of people were moved out, roads ended at the water's edge. The extent of the new lake could never be precisely worked out, so many never got compensated. But India has more electricity."

Mr Gupta nodded. He had heard the stories, but knew the lights had to stay on and that India would soon forget minor injustices to those with no political voice. He also knew the huge reservoir of Indira Sagar must lie up ahead, as must Tsering's people.

"How many of you are there?" asked Mr Gupta.

"Just five, including me," said Tsering. "You will make it six."

Mr Gupta allowed that presumption to go unchallenged as the whole situation, both inside and outside his head, seemed far more complex than he could realistically grasp.

"And who are the individuals?" he asked.

"You will know soon enough," said Tsering pointing ahead. "We are there."

Out on the main highway Jag pulled his taxi onto a patch of rough ground opposite the turning from where the signal showed the transmitter was located. He had driven past a few minutes earlier before realising his mistake and turning back, now he checked both his satnav and road atlas and smiled. This old road was a dead end stopping at the lake. A lone child carrying a bundle was just visible through the trees indicating the presence of at least one family living nearby. Perhaps there was a village? The signal had stopped and dark was falling, so Jag guessed this was where Mr Gupta would be spending the night. He decided to send a message to his client.

Target settled at Indira Sagar. Easy to locate.

Several minutes later came the reply.

Will follow in the morning. Send location updates.

Jag was tired but knew there would not be much more of this job left to do. Tarik had made his way back to the city as Suliman had informed him his role was over, and a brief call by Jag revealed a happy man with his promised bonus.

"You will get more," Tarik had told him.

Jag set the tracker to alert him if it moved more than 400 metres from its present location, then settled back to doze.

Vaz rested on the large hotel bed. He was in a semi-sleep contemplating life beyond his recent metamorphosis from human to god and the battles to be fought. He was still tied by necessity to his previous life and still felt loyal to Ravi, but now he had the freedom born of an unalterable decision. The god inside seethed with a hunger which was hard to resist. Shiva needed a human vessel and Vaz was the chosen one. But was human frailty also inherited? Kāla would not err, but this human form could. Eventually the shell that was Vasupati Chopra would be left behind. At some level Vaz knew he was insane, but becoming a god surely made insanity and genius one and the same? The phone beeped.

Bhopal was nice but the sea is better. Come and see the sea with me.

Rage bloomed and the small, guttering flame of human uncertainty retreated. He resisted answering the message. Silence would drive Gupta mad, leading to fatal hesitation. Apart from that, he knew where Anil Gupta was. That was the funniest thing of all. It was like betting on a game of cricket from the past – the score was already known. This was no test, but there was a way of making the task significant. He could meet this man on his own ground. He could race to overhaul Mr Gupta, or draw it out and remove the only thing this man had left – destiny. He would kill Gophapa by that sea, wherever it proved to be. His phone buzzed with an incoming call. It was Ravi.

"Vaz?" he said. "I need some news."

"Everything is well, Ravi," said Vaz. "I know exactly where he is. He has just sent me a message urging me to join him by the sea."

"Vaz, are you being amusing again?" asked Ravi, irritated.

"Not at all, Ravi," he replied. "I am convinced he has lost his mind, so that will be a great help in making him disappear."

"Ok, you are probably right," said Ravi. "So, is he close?"

"He has left the city," said Vaz, "but he is being watched. Suliman has good people, they have placed a tracking device on him somehow, and a man is watching."

"So where is he compared to you?" said Ravi.

"I'm in Bhopal. He is with some do-gooders by the Indira Sagar lake," said Vaz. "He will be tracked until I catch up. At that point I will remove him as quietly as possible."

"Don't take too long," said Ravi. "I am still trying to find the girl, but that may have to wait. The police are sure Gupta died in the house, which makes us holders of unique information. He has certainly not contacted them, after all he would have a body to explain away and his mind is riddled with disease. The data here has been sanitised and any dealings we have had with the family are sound. Cobra is unaffected. The Fallen Angel information is the tough one. If he has a copy of the data my bitch first wife lifted, it could cause us problems. Vaz, this is not a game."

"I know," said Vaz calmly. "But you are wrong. It is a game for him. All he wants is me. That is what he will receive. Do not worry. By the way, I have employed the Engineer."

"What?" said Ravi. "This is not a fucking war! We are talking about a single, sick old man, not an army."

"Relax, Ravi," said Vaz. "If you have taken care of your end, trust me to do my job."

"OK," said Ravi, calm again. "By the way, Suneeti has been trying to call Hemlata. Is there a phone problem?"

Vaz became silent for a moment. How could he tell Ravi his family had moved on and that his own life ended at the same time? Should he tell Ravi he was now a changeling?

"As all life ends, the seeds remain," sang Vaz quietly.

"What was...? Are you singing man?" asked Ravi incredulously.

Vaz chuckled at where his thread of thought had taken him.

"Hemlata and the kids are away in Hyderabad," said Vaz, upbeat now. "She gave me sore ears about me going away again, so she has taken an expensive trip to her aunt's villa."

"Hmmm, right," said Ravi. "Keep me informed. And Vaz."

"Yes, Ravi."

"Quiet obliteration," said Ravi slowly. "Not a public, noisy execution. Minimal attention. Is that clear?"

"Yes," said Vaz.

Vaz ended the call; Kāla-Vaz lay down. He had already decided to follow Mr Gupta to the sea. He had time and he had resources. And he also had Engineer.

Chapter 25

Arnesh Ji and the Kuru Ki Kvark

The Queen Lizzie entered a clearing next to the great lake, the evening sky reflecting on its calm surface. Scattered about were the remains of old farm buildings that had escaped immersion when the lake reached full capacity. Encroaching shrubs and trees fought to reclaim what was left. This was where the Kuru ki Kvark had set up home. Mr Gupta had not expected anything more than a rough camp, but this was something more. A large, thatched barn had survived intact with one of its long sides open to the centre of the clearing, facing the lake. The inside was lit by several electric bulbs hanging irregularly from the roof beams illuminating two people sitting at a table. To one side was a thatched hut garlanded with flowers in which shone a single oil lamp on an ancient dark-wood table, its lambent light causing shadows to dance around the interior. Mr Gupta thought he glimpsed a figure within. Tsering turned the lorry, parking it next to the third substantial structure in the clearing. It was nothing more than a tumbledown garage with a rusty corrugated roof, filled with drums and parts of machinery in varying stages of decay.

"Come and meet the misfits," said Tsering, dropping lightly to the floor.

Mr Gupta clambered down carefully, his bag over his shoulder and followed his rescuer to the open barn. An elderly man stepped out to greet them followed by the prettiest woman he had ever seen. The man was of average height and skinny, with the long grey hair and beard of a sadhu. He had a stylised sun painted upon his forehead, loose fitting homespun robes and worn sandals on his big feet. He put out a hand which Mr Gupta shook gently.

"And who has Tsering brought to us tonight?" he asked, smiling.

"This is Mr Gupta," came the answer.

"Then welcome Mr Gupta, I am Nawal," said Nawal. "What is ours is yours. I have been expecting you."

"Thank you for your kindness," said Mr Gupta. "But I find it odd you were expecting me. Even I did not know I would be here."

"Come in and have some food," said Nawal steering Mr Gupta into the building. "All will be explained. I will keep it simple, but not too simple, as Einstein would say."

The woman was not introduced, but smiled and set about filling a bowl with some of the contents of a pot suspended over a cooking fire. She placed it on the table with a piece of flat bread and Mr Gupta was guided to a chair before it.

"Goodness me," he said. "You are very kind."

"There is water in the jug," said the woman quietly.

She fetched a second bowl and placed it in front of Tsering who began eating immediately. Mr Gupta followed suit finding the spicy vegetable stew to be delicious, so much so that he delighted in every mouthful. Nawal sat and watched.

"Talika is a master with simple ingredients," said Tsering. "She has a great gift."

"This is the best meal I have eaten for years," said Mr Gupta to Talika. "Thank you."

She smiled and nodded her own thanks.

After the food, as Talika brewed some tea, Nawal spoke.

"You make the Kuru ki Kvark six. The other two will be with us before full dark. You will like them I am sure as they have similar minds to us. You, Mr Gupta, are to be our signpost, so I know they will like you."

"I think they may be loonies, laddie," whispered MacKeeg.

Mr Gupta looked out expecting MacKeeg to be standing on the shore, laughing at his own joke, but the figure walking from the lake's shore was not him. He was very tall and looked similar to Nawal, with longer, more ragged hair and beard, tied with coloured cords forming tufts and pony tails, the ends of which had been died green. His forehead was painted yellow with three horizontal stripes of red and he sported a dab of blue on the bridge of his nose; he walked with a long staff, but was upright and had bright eyes. He strode silently into the barn.

"Puneet," said Nawal. "This is our signpost, Mr Gupta."

Puneet looked down, nodded, then walked to the far corner and sat cross-legged on a piece of patterned carpet, staring out into the night.

"Puneet is a yogi of sorts," said Nawal. "He is also a sadhu and does not talk until the night is established. This, I think, is more of an eccentricity than a spiritual thing, but he is a good man. Shall we join him? Talika, would you be so kind as to serve our tea over there? Can you sit on the ground, or would you like to use a stool?"

"I think a stool may be necessary," said Mr Gupta who had not sat willingly on the floor since childhood.

Tsering, Nawal and Talika sat in a semi-circle with Puneet and waited for Mr Gupta to settle on a low stool padded with a piece of foam rubber. In the centre was a section of tree-trunk which made a useful table.

"Nawal Ji will speak," said a deep, bass voice which made Mr Gupta jump. Puneet had spoken. It was full dark.

"Mr Gupta," said Nawal. "This must be confusing for you, but the one thing you should remember is we are your friends. You can trust us as we are happy to help. Ask the other you what he thinks, then the next few days could go easier."

Although Mr Gupta was bone weary, he was constantly receiving little jolts from the insight of his new acquaintances. He blinked. MacKeeg was there sitting on the carpet closing the circle.

"Well, MacKeeg," said Mr Gupta, "what do we think? I am tired. So tired."

MacKeeg puffed on his pipe blowing smoke into the circle. Mr Gupta supposed they might all be in his mind, but the journey in the Queen Lizzie had been real enough.

"Och, laddie,' said MacKeeg, looking over the four others, "they are what they say, right enough. Time will establish the truth of this. I see no device in these people, and the lassie is a beauty. Anyhow, they are intriguing, but they have not said anything supernatural."

"But they knew you were there..."

"The Tibetan told them you were a divided person," chuckled MacKeeg. "He heard you jawing to me in yon contraption."

Mr Gupta suddenly saw the truth of this. Tsering said they were expecting change and saw him as the catalyst for that. The rest was educated reasoning. MacKeeg disappeared.

"This other is correct," said Nawal. "That is exactly what the Kuru ki Kvark is all about. We are not mystics, nor prophets, nor seers of any kind."

"But you said you were expecting me," said Mr Gupta. "And as we agree with the logic of MacKeeg, that could paint you as charlatans. I thank you for helping me thus far, but you have no concept of what danger I will bring with me. Do not think this is a game to play? Death follows me, so I must move on tomorrow."

"Does Death drive a taxi?" asked a squeaky, creaky voice from the open side of the barn, just beyond the light.

Mr Gupta jumped anew. They all turned. A tiny man stepped into the light carrying a bundle which he dropped to one side. He was dressed in dusty jeans, white vest and sandals; he had a loosely wrapped turban on his head.

"Corn cobs, tobacco and flour," said the dwarf. "The farmer thanks you for fixing the pump, Tsering, and you for the blessing Nawal Ji. All I got was a groan when I treated his arse grapes."

"Welcome home Vam," said Nawal. "Vamana is my very own avadhuta and has been collecting gifts from the village further along the road. He is also a good healer. Now, Vam, how can Death drive a taxi?"

"There is one tucked away at the end of the track," said Vam. "The man sitting at the wheel is watching, and as there is nothing here but us, and as the lorry is the only thing to have driven this way, I assumed he was watching for us. I see we have the guest you promised, master, and he talks of being followed, so it is just logic."

"Well, does Death drive a taxi?" asked Puneet.

Mr Gupta could not corral his thoughts for a moment. MacKeeg had left the field to him again, but the Scot was still in his mind and his new perception had not wavered. Taxis were so common that they were all but invisible in India. Who noticed them? He briefly thought of Kiran's death and saw the truth of it. Relaxing he let his mind open and his thoughts settle and saw another truth. There had been a taxi outside the Palace Hotel when he fled on the wave of paranoia MacKeeg had painted as caution. And when he had recovered at Ali's there was a taxi in the dusty parking area. The two men, friendly as they were, had driven up in it as he had collapsed, Tsering had told him as much, and had helped get him into the Queen Lizzie. MacKeeg had been right – Ravi Uppal had eyes everywhere and could well have known his every move since the station. Furthermore, Vaz was probably less than a day away at the most, and Death did come in a taxi – at least its herald did. He stood up.

"They have found me quickly," he said. "I cannot stay here. There is a killer coming and he does not care for anyone. You are all in danger, trust me on this."

"Sit down!" said Nawal, sharply.

Mr Gupta complied.

"It is time for you to understand us," continued Nawal, gently now. "Quite simply, we will help you. You need rest, that much must be clear to you, and there is nowhere to go on foot. Tsering, were you followed?"

"No," said Tsering confidently. "I watched and checked many times. No one could have stayed far back and tailed us, they would have to stay close, especially in the towns. The road was clear behind when I turned onto our track."

"Tell me about the events where you came across Mr Gupta," said Nawal. "Leave nothing out."

Tsering related the story of first seeing the distressed Mr Gupta, his recovery and their subsequent trip to Indira Sagar. He included the help from the two men from the taxi, but insisted he had not been followed. Nawal stayed silent and thoughtful for a while before speaking.

"What do we think?" he asked, addressing the group.

"If Mr Gupta is being followed and taxis are involved, the one waiting is confirmation," said Vam.

"The question is, *how* did they find you?" said Puneet. "If the driver is waiting, he must know you are here. How?"

"And why?" asked the gentle voice of Talika.

"And who are they?" asked Vam.

They all looked at Mr Gupta. Was it only this morning he had scurried from his hotel in Bhopal? Time seemed compressed and energy reserves were depleting faster to keep up. Two days ago, he had fled Delhi. Even with MacKeeg's help he was still running, but not fast enough. How could he hope to kill Vaz when he could barely stay on his feet for more than a few hours? He had reached the end of the road with no hope of choosing his ground, nor standing by the sea, or ensuring his loved ones' safety. Under the gaze of this odd group of people he felt exposed, his body worn and sick. For a moment he could feel the tumour eating his mind, reducing him to nothing. He was at a loss as to what he should do. He felt despair filling him, the prick of nascent tears in his eyes and the emptiness of total defeat. Just as his spirit teetered at the edge of oblivion, MacKeeg poured through him and strength returned. A flash of recall reminded him of the anger he had clung to, and it was back, warming him and restoring his confidence so much so that the Kuru ki Kvark saw him smile.

"Laddie," said MacKeeg, "I think ye can trust these strange folk. If Chopra and Uppal have tracked us, and that taxi holds their scout, ye have no choice. So answer their questions, especially if they mean to help. It's the least I would do, and that's a quantity I specialise in."

MacKeeg laughed at his jest, this coinciding with Mr Gupta's smile.

"MacKeeg says I can trust you," said Mr Gupta, "and he has never let me down. I am not the warrior he is, so my daughter's life depends on him. I trust MacKeeg to do this. I trust his judgement of you. I have told you Death is coming, but the whole story will take a while to relate. All those close to me will die if I fail to kill a man. This man is capable of terrible things and I have drawn him to me in order to kill him first. So, before you offer more help, be very aware of the possible repercussions."

"Then we must tell you about us," said Nawal. "And we shall, but first let's give ourselves time. You have been tracked, Mr Gupta."

"How?" he replied.

"A professional would not leave things to chance, especially on these roads," said Nawal. "If the man in the taxi knows you are here, then it is not intuition he is using. Could they have put an electronic device on the truck?"

"Maybe," said Tsering. "If they did they only had a moment. I'll take a look. Should I deal with the taxi too?"

"Not yet," said Nawal, "but check the lorry."

Tsering stood and walked out into the darkness; a few moments later his movements around the Queen Lizzie could be traced by the beam of a small torch.

"How do we gain time?" asked Mr Gupta.

"We have to leave," said Nawal. "I think we have to do so tonight."

Tsering walked back into the barn.

"Nothing," he said.

"Where else could a device be?" asked Puneet.

"Maybe there is none," said Vam. "What does your Kvarks make of this, master?"

"One day you will understand," said Nawal, chuckling. "Mr Gupta. Vam here means logic. Shall we see how it works? Vam prefers the thought of magic, but logic is the great mover. Let us suppose there is a transmitter. These men only had seconds to plant it. If it was on the lorry it would be easy enough to find, and it is not there. What is left?"

"Me," said Mr Gupta.

"You," said Nawal.

"His bag," said Tsering with growing realisation. "It was sat in the dust long enough. Nawal Ji, if you are right I think you have more than the Kvark!"

Mr Gupta picked up his bag and emptied it on the carpet. He slowly replaced his few belongings, but there was nothing to see. Or was there? A wrapped sweet, flat and round marked *Butterscotch*.

"I don't know what this is," he said picking the object up. It was heavier than it should be. He passed it to Tsering, who carefully unwrapped it. There in the palm of his hand was a black, silver rimmed disc of metal and plastic.

"Nawal Ji," said Tsering, "you are the king of sadhus."

"Logic," said Nawal. "Nothing more. Now we can leave."

"How?" asked Mr Gupta. "There is only one road in."

"Villagers always find easier ways," said Nawal. "There is a rough old track, running from the lake, overgrown but passable, which starts a little distance away. It comes out on the highway a few miles further west. Our Queen Lizzie can do it, can't she Tsering?"

"Slowly, but easily," he replied.

"Mr Gupta," said Nawal. "You are exhausted. Try to sleep awhile and we will pack up. Vam, I have a job for you."

All the members of the Kuru ki Kvark slipped into a well-practised routine, and the lorry was loaded in under than two hours. Vam, who had disappeared for most of that time, trotted into the clearing as the engine started. Talika woke Mr Gupta and their retreat into the darkness began.

Jag dozed through most of the night. He had confidence in his tracking system having used it many times in the past, but he still checked the transmitter's location regularly. It had remained static next to the lake half-a-mile or so down the overgrown road, so he was sure that this was a semi-permanent camp. As the sun rose a flock of parakeets flew over the taxi, leaving their roost to search for fruit in the remnants of orchards around the drowned valley. Jag started and woke from a long snooze, but relaxed when he saw the static signal flash on his hand-held screen. He decided to send a message to his client.

Subject still static at Indira Sagar. Will send directions on request.

The reply was quick, but lacked urgency, which surprised Jag.

Keep him under surveillance. Will catch up this evening.

If his client was in Bhopal he could have been there by the early afternoon. Jag groaned quietly, steeling himself for a longer wait than he had expected. He decided to phone Tarik.

"Who the hell is this?" grumbled Tarik, his voice thick with sleep.

"Jag. I have to wait here until later. I still have the old chap on tracker," said Jag. "Has Suliman said when he's paying me?"

"Got mine pretty quickly," said Tarik. "The boss sent a car and the driver gave me an envelope. The old man called and told me to take the rest of the week off. As I said, I reckon you'll get more, you lucky bastard. I heard a rumour The Engineer has been contracted."

"For one old man?" said Jag in wonder. "This Gupta chap must be a dangerous man. I can't see it myself."

"When you coming back?" asked Tarik.

"Tonight, if the target stays where he is," answered Jag, "Tomorrow if the target moves. I'm guessing there must be a camp by the lake. Anyway, one road in, one road out and the tracker is working nicely. Once the client's here I'm gone. Any idea who he is?"

"Something to do with Ravi Uppal," said Tarik. "One thing though, if The Engineer is involved this Gupta is going to have a bad day. Give me a call when you're back in Bhopal."

Tarik hung up. Jag got out of the taxi and relieved himself under the trees. As he wandered back he realised a taxi may not be not so usual in the countryside, so spent a few minutes unclipping the sign from the roof and threw it in the boot. He was confident the car was hardly noticeable and looked innocent enough, so he slipped back into the driver's seat. He reasoned that if the lorry re-emerged, he could wait and follow the tracker from a good distance. The signal was still steady, strong and static so he settled down to wait.

Mr Gupta was so tired he had to be helped into the cab of the Queen Lizzie. The others remained outside: Vam was sent along the track to keep watch; Puneet, Talika and Nawal wandered off behind the barn carrying small torches. Tsering started the engine. Plastic bags taped over the headlamps gave him just enough light to drive by. He kept the engine just above idling speed and slipped the clutch. The Queen Lizzie edged forward with a rhythmic *gerrrom-gerrrom-gerrrom…* towards the lake, then into the shallows paralleling the shore.

"Don't worry, Arnesh Ji," said Tsering. "The old track runs from the lake and we'll pick it up in a few minutes. I've done this before."

"What did you call me?" asked Mr Gupta.

"Arnesh Ji," said Tsering. "It is your name now you are with us. It gives anonymity and respect, and it fits."

"How?" asked Mr Gupta.

"It means *Lord of the Sea*," said Tsering. "That is where you said you want to go. The sea"

"I still do not understand why you are getting involved," said Mr Gupta. "I am dying anyway. It makes no sense to make this some kind of spiritual crusade. There is no value to it."

"All I can say is you fit our need to pursue order through chaos," said Tsering. "As for spirits, well none of us have any notion of them. Now, let me concentrate Arnesh Ji. I have done this before, as I said, but only when the water was lower."

With that the truck bumped into a submerged hole, lurched, righted itself and was steered out of the water onto the promised track which was almost hidden by encroaching shrubs and trees. The compacted gravel and stone surface had sprouted a crop of weeds so was barely visible in the dim lights. The others walked slowly ahead with their torches. The Queen Lizzie forced its way through undergrowth which scraped against its metal sides, the noise muted by surrounding trees.

The Queen Lizzie emerged onto a metalled side road leading to the main highway just as Vam caught them up. It was still dark. Nawal climbed into the cab next to Mr Gupta, the others made themselves comfortable in the back. Tsering then took a convoluted route using lesser roads, passing occasional groups of farm labourers walking in the darkness to their fields. They all waved and smiled, Vam waved frantically back shouting light-hearted greetings which brought laughter and more waves. For the first time in days Mr Gupta felt able to relax. Tsering was ever alert and drove as quickly as the Queen Lizzie was capable. As dawn broke they were more than eighty miles from Indira Sagar, the taxi and the transmitter. Eventually they joined a main highway and continued south towards what Nawal had told Mr Gupta was *our little place in the hills – Hingoli way*. Mr Gupta finally succumbed to sleep.

He was awoken by Nawal in mid-afternoon. He came to, his neck stiff and his head aching, but felt rested and very hungry. Tsering was pulling the truck into an ancient petrol station stopping next to the pumps.

"Queen Lizzie is thirsty," said Nawal smiling. "This is not very far from our destination and we can eat here. It is cheap and the food is good."

They all clambered out onto the dusty ground and Puneet led the way to a group of tumbledown huts where were people cooking. As it was now daylight he did not speak, just bowed at the sweating man at the stove of one of the central buildings and sat at a plastic table to wait. Talika ordered a simple but plentiful meal for all of them and joined the others where they had settled next to the silent sadhu.

"How do we pay?" asked Mr Gupta. "I have some money."

"We have adequate funds," said Nawal. "For now, accept you are our guest. Believe me it is no hardship for us."

"You are now free to direct us, Arnesh Ji," said Vam. "That is your only task."

"I still do not understand," said Mr Gupta.

"You must not worry," said Talika. "As soon as we settle, Nawal Ji will explain."

She placed a soft hand reassuringly upon his and a jolt shot through him. She gently pulled her hand away, but the touch remained etched in his skin. He looked at her and, for an instant, saw Kiran. The spell was broken by the clattering Queen Lizzie which Tsering parked a short distance away. He climbed out and joined them just as a young boy arrived with the first part of their lunch – a pile of rice and a pile of banana leaves. Banana leaves saved on the expense of plates and could be fed to the cows once used. Steaming dishes of food arrived soon after and they all began to eat.

"Where is this place you told Tsering of?" asked Nawal through a mouthful of rice. "He said you considered yourself a pilgrim."

"I only know it as Clive's Beach," said Mr Gupta. "I know it is north of Goa, and south of Mumbai, close to where the mountains are nearest the shore. I read that Robert Clive once spent some time there. I have never seen the Indian Ocean, so it seems as good a place as any to confront my destiny. It is no more complex than that."

"I know where it is," said Nawal.

Mr Gupta could not be more surprised. He had had some notion of reaching a town on the way and finding directions for this beach in a library somewhere, but things had happened so fast he thought any beach may have to do. To speak openly of his random selection of a venue to die seemed fanciful, especially as he had no clue if it existed beyond books. The coincidences were mounting in his world.

"Where?" he asked.

"It is on the coast west of Mount Karoo," said Nawal. "This is another example of the laws of probability, which may help explain our philosophy. Coincidence, Arnesh Ji, can seem preordained and you have, as I told the others, become our signpost. We shall make for Karukula where they know us. From there you can reach the coast."

"This does seem oddly fatalistic," said Mr Gupta. "I'm finding everything very difficult to take in."

"Do not worry, Arnesh Ji," said Vam. "This kind of thing happens to us all the time. Remember I saw the taxi before I knew you? That's just having your eyes and mind open at the same time. Puneet would explain, but I think you will have to wait until the owls are hooting."

"Enough," said Nawal. "Let's get to Seraraya."

Seraraya sat atop a hill giving views across Hingoli and beyond. The rough road to this haven twisted and turned through woods and wild grassland. The ancient Bedford QL wheezed and grumbled its way to a collection of huge boulders, which lay close to the summit, surrounded by stunted trees. In the distant past, flat slabs of rock had been hoisted up to form an irregular roof using the boulders as walls. Over the years, gaps had been filled using stones and earth making dry, weather-resistant habitable cells of good size. They formed a rough *C* with the north facing gap giving a spectacular view of the surrounding country. From below, the stones were visible for some distance and, as it stood out as a pale circle surrounded by green, the locals referred to it as *Aankh*, the *Eye*. It was occasionally used by Sufis, sadhus, other holy men and various mendicants, but for now was deserted.

"This is Seraraya," said Nawal. "We will stay here for a while and rest."

"It is an odd place," said Mr Gupta.

"Yes," said Nawal. "It has been used for centuries and was once a permanent shrine to some local god. Now it is only visited for festivals and special days, so we often come here to rest. It is always quiet after the monsoon."

The truck was offloaded. A large awning was affixed to the rear cabin and stretched across to one of the flat roofs where it was held in place by some heavy stones. A rudimentary kitchen was set up and three of the cells cleaned and furnished ready for use as sleeping quarters. Water was brought from a small stream in the woods and very soon Tsering had made a fire bounded by stones in the obvious fire pit at the centre of the clearing. Around this, long ago, flat rocks had been arranged as seats, the surfaces of which had been worn smooth by generations of bottoms. Mr Gupta helped as best he could, but floundered and stumbled in his weariness. He felt useless and tired and, above all, old. Then his shoe split.

"Bloody hell!" he said.

"Have you no new clothes?" asked a gentle voice. It was Talika.

"I did not plan too well," said Mr Gupta. "I never thought I would have to walk as much. I have a change of clothes, well, a fresh shirt, but needed time to buy things, and, of course, I have not. I am so tired, Talika, so very tired."

"We can find you some clothes," she replied, smiling so radiantly Mr Gupta blushed. "And I make sandals of very high quality, all the men wear them, so I shall make sure you have a pair. Sometimes, Arnesh Ji, you are not alone. You can rest here before we make the long journey to the Sahyadri."

She placed her hand reassuringly upon his shoulder and this time he did not flinch, enjoyed the moment and felt much better for it.

They sat around the fire watching the sky change from light blue to star-spangled black. Below, the darkening land followed suit with lights winking on in distant towns and villages. Lines of headlights sketched out roads and highways. It was chilly at this higher altitude, so Mr Gupta was given a thick blanket to wrap around his shoulders. Talika chose to sit next to him. The fire was warm, the tea sweet and the night still.

"It is time to tell Arnesh Ji about us," said Tsering. "Before he falls asleep."

"It is time," said Puneet, his voice restored with the darkness.

"Are you happy to listen now?" asked Nawal.

"Yes," said Mr Gupta.

Nawal smiled and stared at the fire, his face lit by its flickering light. He told the story.

"The Kuru ki Kvark is a name we gave ourselves. It is a little bit of a joke, but sounds fantastical enough to give us the air of mystery, and in India that helps a great deal. First, though, I will begin in Switzerland. I was a particle physicist and worked on the Large Hadron Collider in the early days. Do not look so amazed, Arnesh Ji, for you know more than most that people are full of surprises. I am a professor…or rather, *was*. We were studying space-time's theoretical effects on particles, then, ironically, real time caught up with me. One day I stepped back and for the first time saw the mountains. I had sought the data to support the Standard Model of the universe, and did my part in no small way, but had never looked closer to home. All about me were younger men, bright and eager and full of endeavour, and there was I in my mid-sixties having an epiphany. I wanted to relax and see the world, so I sold up, banked the money and travelled for a while, learning about everything I could, from geology, to philosophy, to social anthropology. I saw a kakapo in New Zealand, the Ring of Brodgar in Orkney, tasted the best seafood in the world in Puerto Montt and set foot on Elephant Island. I stopped cutting my hair or shaving and felt free. Eventually I wandered the Himalaya near Leh for a year or so, celebrating my seventieth birthday in a shepherd's hut in the high passes near Stok. I lived with these hardy men for a whole summer and just thought about life, the universe and humanity. I had been married once, but it did not endure my work, so I was alone in the world, yet never felt sad. I thought of science, philosophers, theories, hypotheses and of religion. It was in that high pass, Gangpoche, sitting on a rock in the sun overlooking the Tokpo River, that I decided to remain in my homeland. I always had good health and the travelling had made me leaner and fitter, as you see me now, so I decided to ignore getting old. That would take care of itself. The shepherds thought me a sadhu as I could answer so many basic questions about existence, but grew anxious as I tried to explain my atheism. They could not see a world without the gods. I made the mistake of trying to explain quarks one stormy evening, after which they assumed a quark was a god of some kind. Only they could not pronounce it properly. I became the Sadhu of *Kvark*!

"So, upon that rock I thought about our place in the world, who we are and where we are going. It took me a while. Eventually I saw something new. My thoughts polarised. When I left my summer companions, and whilst I wandered down the steep gorge to Stok, I decided on what the remaining years of my life would be spent doing. I would see how the laws of probability would work as a guide to the rest of my life. In effect, I had become an astrophysical sadhu and found how it was probability that inspired religion, not spirits."

"Then he met me," said Tsering.

"I am getting there," said Nawal firmly. "I had a lift from Stok with some soldiers who dropped me in Leh. They treated me with great respect. You see, looking like a holy man made life easier. In a backstreet I found a small hotel to stay in. Whilst trying to rest I became irritated by the sound of metallic hammering from outside. That is where I met Tsering. He was fitting a monstrous engine into the Queen Lizzie and I was taken with its look. I did not mention the noise, but rather fell into conversation and passed him various oily tools. The vehicle had been used by travellers from Europe on an overland journey, but it had died in Leh and was abandoned. Our friendship was sealed when I helped him wire up the old lorry and he realised I was no useless codger. We ate together and talked of many things. He proved to be good company and I convinced him not to sell the lorry, but to drive south with me to see where it would take us. I had money, he had no family, no plans and no direction, so the Kuru ki Kvark was created and was mobile. The two of us invaded a land of a billion people. Tsering had escaped Tibet before the Chinese could shoot him..."

"All because I was a monk," spat Tsering.

"All because you became a freedom fighter," added Nawal, "but that is quite a story in itself. In Shimla we found a grumpy and unpopular yogi, quite a rare combination, and Puneet joined us."

"It was that or starve to death," mumbled Puneet.

"Well you are hardly going to have gifts of food if you cannot teach," said Vam. "A yogi who refuses to talk in civilised hours may well starve,"

Puneet gave a grunt, but said no more.

"Then Vam and Talika tagged along after a stay in Bangalore," said Nawal. "Vam is a qualified doctor, but was worn out with his tendency to work for nothing and give away everything he had."

"And Talika?" asked Mr Gupta.

There was an uncomfortable silence. Before it grew to embarrassment Talika smiled and spoke.

"I am a widow with no prospects," she said. "My husband's family took everything and left me on the street to beg, or starve. I was a teacher of English, but it meant nothing once a widow. I nearly succumbed to becoming a street woman, but Vam helped me and I assisted him in his work. He was an avadhuta, a special sadhu who could heal, and he became well known. I am now a sadhvi and we joined the Kvark as we are of the same mind."

"To all intents and purposes, we have nothing," said Nawal. "We do have a rather fluid, annual routine which takes us to places where we offer our services in return for companionship, food and the necessities of life. For each of my companions the reasons for being here are different, and they are free to go if they wish, but we have become used to each other. I am the selfish one. All I do is find empirical proof to support my theory of the effects of chance on human cultures. It would take time to explain it all, but an example is what we are doing now. In Bhopal we had no firm plans after the festivals. I said we would wait as probability would guide us. As we are all godless and free, these good people were sceptical, so I suggested we follow the directions of a stranger. And thus, you were expected, but perhaps not prophesied in the metaphysical sense. The first nomads had to follow something, why shouldn't we follow you?"

A cough from beyond the glow of the campfire stopped the conversation.

"Come," said Nawal.

An old man shuffled into the light holding the hand of a little girl.

"Nawal Ji," he croaked, raising his free arm in a stiff wave. "I saw the light and knew the Kvark was back."

"Welcome, Pallab," said Nawal. "Come and sit with us."

"My granddaughter has a sore eye," said Pallab. "It will not heal. Can the Kvark help her?"

Mr Gupta watched his new companions with interest. Talika sat the girl on her lap as Vam looked at the child's eye. He then searched in the lorry and returned with a small tube of antibiotic cream. He anointed the girl's eye very gently – an odd sight as she was nearly as tall as he – and gave the tube to the old man explaining how to use it. Pallab and his granddaughter were fed, then they set off into the night.

"It is ironic, Arnesh Ji," said Nawal, "that we may become a godless religion and save the world."

"Then why risk it all for me?" asked Mr Gupta.

"Because you need more help than most," said Puneet.

Chapter 26

Convergence

The matt-black Shogun wove an intricate course through the Bhopal rush-hour, barely missing pedestrians with its lethal crash bars. Sachet Engineer knew the city well and wanted to avoid the inevitable traffic jams on the main thoroughfares. Beside him Vaz sat in silence, lost in thought. Ravi had tried to contact him early in the morning, he always needed information, this is what had kept him ahead of the game, but for once he would have to wait. Vaz was agitated. Could it be this easy? A dying man had somehow killed Kush Karnik, had outmanoeuvred him, taunted him with a level of confidence that beggared belief and was now just waiting to be caught? Something was wrong. Anil Gupta wanted to get to the sea, not a lake, so why was he still there waiting? He could have become debilitated by the tumour, but Vaz did not think so. This truly was a game where advantage would ebb and flow between players and right now Vaz should be holding a significant advantage. Could he be mistaken? Whatever the case his position in the game would soon be revealed.

Engineer had arrived at the hotel in time for breakfast. He was surprised at the odd look Vaz had acquired, dressed in black, blue glasses and the slight blue sheen on his skin around the collar of his shirt. He also knew the man was unpredictable, and very dangerous, but a significant amount of money bought a complete service, so he mentioned nothing. After eating, Engineer took Vaz to look in the back of the Shogun. He lifted the false floor just enough for Vaz to see several weapons set snugly in dense foam rubber. There were also a lot of varied supplies just in case, Engineer had explained, the journey took longer than planned. He summarised the arsenal to Vaz.

"I knew you couldn't bring anything on the plane, so took the trouble to put enough items in for us both," he said. "Combat knives, medikits, plenty of compo rations and packs to carry things in. An SA80, a couple Glock 17s, a GPS and plenty of rounds for us both. The Glock is beautiful, really lovely. It feels warm. We've enough hardware to win a small war. It should just about do the job."

"I've never used an SA80," said Vaz. "Isn't it complex and fragile?"

"No," said Engineer. "All the faults have been ironed out and this is a new model. Pretty well anyone with a bit of brains can make a good shot at four hundred metres."

"I want to be closer than that," said Vaz.

"As you know where this Gupta is I assume it will be sorted in a couple of days," ventured Engineer.

"I'm not so sure," said Vaz. "This man is more than he seems. Where are the others, by the way?"

"They will meet us on the road as soon as I give them a call," said Engineer.

Once they set off, Vaz inserted the ear buds from his phone and drifted into a reverie of familiar music and incantations.

Praise Kāla who cannot die, The Destroyer has built the new world...

Is that not what had happened? The world was different now. He strode amongst mortals with absolute power over their lives. Kāla had given him this and now his existence had clear meaning. He knew he had been preordained to start the World's journey through the Age of Destruction; to make things begin again. A narrative spontaneously rang through his mind, given voice by Zahan Bulsara...

...And Shiva stepped onto the blighted earth which had grown stale in his nostrils. All creation crouched before him in abeyance, except mankind who had grown arrogant and forgetful. A man was sent from the demon world as a

challenge to destiny. He sowed scandal and lies and planned the death of Shiva. Shiva became the soul of a man and declared him the physical incarnation of Kāla. Humanity was diseased and Kāla was hungry for souls, but the demon's disciple had to die first. Then the world of men could die and be reborn in a new age. Shiva declared the pursuit of Gophapa would bring them to a blighted shore. Upon that place would be a great shadow and both Gophapa and Kāla would see the sun eaten and a storm of fire roar down upon them. One would be consumed on the shores of the Birthing Black Sea...'

Vaz opened his eyes. He felt the weight of uncertainty on his back. Was there anything to fear? No, never fear.

"We'll reach the lake well before dark," said Engineer.

"Good," said Vaz. "Perhaps Indira Sagar is *the Birthing Black Sea.*"

"Are you alright?" asked Engineer.

"Yes," said Vaz. "I miss my children."

"You'll be back with them soon," said Engineer.

"Yes." said Vaz. "Yes, I will."

Olaf sank to his knees lowering the limp body of Seva to the ground as the three girls fled screaming through the undergrowth towards the village. He was exhausted. Seva weighed very little, but after several hours of staggering down rough tracks in the warmth of the day, the small man felt as heavy as an elephant. He crouched panting for a long while then stood and stretched, dropping his Bergen onto the ground with a heavy thud.

"I tell you what feller," he said to the unconscious Seva. "After all this effort I hope you repay me by not dying."

He wiped his face with a dirty hand and took in his surroundings. It was like a great cathedral echoing with the distant sound of water and gentle susurration of the wind in the high canopy. He looked up into the faces of the Nilgiris and smiled.

"How ya doing fellers?" he called.

The monkeys blinked and stared. He walked to where the girls had left the offerings and picked up one of the remaining parcels, sniffed it, and pushed the contents into his mouth. It was surprisingly good. Olaf washed it down with a swig from the opened bottle of water taking the rest to his companion. He carefully raised Seva's head and dripped water into his mouth. Seva swallowed without opening his eyes. He was feverish and delirious so Olaf had no choice but to carry him; it was that or leave him to a lingering death, or be killed by a predator. He had been on his last legs as he approached the steep path to the village, but the sound of singing had brought him to the clearing. He smiled as he thought of the shock he had given those poor girls. Then one of the girls returned.

Anupa had stopped Keya and Resham by the falls.

"I think this man is in trouble," she said. "We should help him."

"Oh no, Anupa," cried Resham, "we must run home and get our fathers."

"Yes," said Keya, "I am so frightened. I never thought Arjuna would really come for me. We should never, ever have wished upon the Nilgiris. The vanara was so small."

"Please, can't we go?' pleaded Resham. "This monster may be here any second!"

Anupa had been driven more by her companions' reaction rather than her own fear. As she rationalised what she had actually seen, she could see the truth of it. The giant man had been exhausted, not fearsome at all, and the figure he carried was just a small person, not a vanara. She had never seen a golden-haired man before and guessed him to be European, a handsome one at that, but he had looked so tired. She determined to find the truth.

"You two go and get father and Uncle Vyan," she said. "I will creep back and see if the golden man is alright."

Squealing protest brought a firm rebuke from Anupa and the two girls eventually scurried down towards the village. She tiptoed back to the Great Banyan.

Olaf looked up and smiled, but the girl just stared with wide eyes, uncertain and ready to flee.

"I'm too tired to carry my friend any further," said Olaf sitting down heavily next to Seva. "Do you speak English?"

Anupa was transfixed. The man was different from any European she had seen before, but it was his clear blue eyes that held her. He looked handsome and young, but also time-worn and wise, with mischief in his smile, but sadness in those eyes. She stepped fully into the amphitheatre of the Great Banyan and stood tall.

"I speak English," she said.

"I am sorry to have frightened you," said Olaf, remaining seated in the dust. "I have eaten some of the monkey food."

"It is alright," said Anupa. "The others have gone to bring men. I thought you needed help. You did scare them."

Olaf rose to his feet, slowly so as not to seem too intimidating. The girl was little more than an inch or two above Seva's height. He towered over her and was impressed how she stood her ground. He stepped forward and offered his grimy hand to this brave young woman.

"I am Olaf," he said.

Anupa hesitated. This giant had left a good distance between them so she felt sure she could run safely away. To step closer would remove any such advantage. She stared at the proffered hand, glanced over her shoulder, then back, unsure what to do.

"Is your friend hurt?" she asked.

"He is ill," replied Olaf. "Seva needs some rest and medicine. There's not much about up in the mountains."

The girl made up her mind, strode forward and offered her hand.

"I am Anupa from Karukula," she said.

Olaf took her hand and shook it gently.

"I'm pleased to meet you, Anupa," he said. "I am Olaf. Olaf Roff from Ireland and Denmark, but Ireland mainly."

"Olab," said Anupa.

"Close enough," said Olaf.

Anupa crouched next to Seva and felt his head. It was hot. The man was very ill.

"He must have water," said Anupa.

"If you stay here I'll fetch some," said Olaf digging his filter and a bottle from the Bergen.

"Yes," she said.

By the time he returned Anupa had made Seva a pillow using rolled up clothing from the pack. She took the water and helped Seva drink a little. His eyes were open and he looked haggard, but not so deathly pale.

"You must be magic, Anupa," said Olaf. "I was sure he was fecked."

"*Fecked*?" said Anupa. "I do not know this one."

"Er, it means nearly dead," said Olaf smiling. "Or tired. Or broken. It is a word I use to describe such things."

"Well he is fecked," said Anupa, delighted with the new word. "But not fecked dead. Is that the right way?"

"It'll do," said Olaf.

He eased himself onto the ground again and sighed. His head hung forward and his long hair formed a curtain over his face. Anupa though him to be the most beautiful man she had ever seen. She had a million questions, but knew they would have to wait, especially as a quiet snoring showed Olaf to have drifted into sleep. She looked up at the Nilgiris who still gazed down with their concerned little faces and wondered if wishes could come true, then dismissed the idea as fancy. A short while later several men crept into the clearing followed by Resham and Keya, a donkey and an old dog.

Mr Gupta's body finally gave in to the sleep it craved. He was wrapped in a cocoon of blankets, warm and snug in one of the rock shelters high on Seraraya. He had been helped there by Tsering and was being watched by Talika. She passed the time by working on a pair of new sandals. The Kuru had discussed Mr Gupta late into the night. He told them he was dying, but they were unsure if he meant he was condemned by the killer or by something else. Whatever the case, he needed their help and care. That night Talika slept at Mr Gupta's feet.

Mr Gupta was with MacKeeg in the permanent night on the peaceful shore. This haven from all the bother that came with people, made him consider the possibility of turning existence on its head, making India the dream from which to wake. The Scot sat on his rock and smoked as he gazed up at the alien sky. Mr Gupta sat down in his usual place and sighed, glad that time here had little meaning. Above him the moon was still full and planets dotted the sky. Whatever the truth of it, this was a beautiful place.

"We have been given back a wee bit of time, laddie," said MacKeeg. "I think we should use it wisely." Then mischievously added, "She's a braw lassie, don't ye think?"

"What? Who?" said Mr Gupta.

MacKeeg grinned. Mr Gupta blushed.

"Oh," he muttered.

"Aye, the pretty lassie ye're sleeping with, the now," said MacKeeg chuckling. "Och, don't take on so, I'm only jesting with ye."

"She fell asleep next to me back there, is that what you mean?"

"Aye, and ye know it right enough," said MacKeeg. "And ye know what that means, laddie?"

"What?" asked Mr Gupta.

"Ye are still very much alive!" said MacKeeg.

Mr Gupta allowed himself a smile, then thought of Kiran. His mind filled with the cares he had briefly forgotten. With the tide of woe came doubt and the edge of despair. He remembered this rest was in readiness for doing battle with the only man he had ever wished harm upon. He wondered how much time he had left before the tumour finally did more than cure his sight and expand his mind. Any hope of a surgical remedy, that straw of hope he once eagerly grasped at, was no longer an option. He had effectively condemned himself to death.

"But the prize, laddie," said MacKeeg. "The prize for this one-way journey is freedom and justice. These are not commodities to devalue by the drain of self-pity."

"I know, MacKeeg," said Mr Gupta. "It is just I have had no time to tell Rupa all is well. Nor Jhatish or the Singhs. I sent Rupa to Sudhesh as a form of *fait accompli* and took it for granted Jhatish would appraise him of the detail. Sudhesh made positive sounds, but I cannot forget how estranged I became after Kiran was murdered."

He used the term *murdered* freely now.

"I have always had so much time, but never found enough to finish things properly. Rupa knew what I was doing and had the strength to let me send her to safety. I love her for that, but miss her so very much. And Kiran. My darling, my love, my life. I never had time in the end even to kiss her goodbye. Did she know, MacKeeg? Did she know I loved her?"

"Aye, laddie," replied MacKeeg. "She knew y'down to the core. She loved ye because she always knew y'ta be as ye are now. It was thee, laddie, who did not believe that, not she. Rupa has her mother's sharp mind and knows the same. What we are doing is ridding the world of a blight. Nothing more. How do ye think the epic tales of legend begin? They all start with quests such as this. We need to rest here and, in the morn, get the phone working. Talk to Nawal Ji, tell him everything and explain ye need to draw this devil Chopra on to his destruction. It seems we need to get to this Karukula as soon as we can and then I can work out a battle plan. Further to yer question about Kiran, ye forget the power of your new insight, your memory and its effect on this lovely world ye find yourself in the now."

And it was so. He stood under the planets on the silver beach where a figure walked towards him. Kiran looked lovely and smiled at her husband raising her hands to beckon an embrace. He gave himself to her comfort, breathed in the smell of her fragrance and began to cry, burying his face in her neck. Kiran hugged him tightly as he wept the tears of undistilled grief as all life's sadness poured from him. Loneliness was the worst pain he had endured and here, on this silver shore, he knew there was no going back, no trail left to the life that had been his final comfort. Kiran stroked his hair and hushed him as sobs wracked his body. Time stopped and nothing more mattered. He gave in to all pain and accepted the greatest comfort. She kissed him gently and he lifted his head. Now there was strength growing once more as the grief ebbed away and he gazed into those beautiful eyes.

"Darling Anil," said Kiran, wiping the tears from his cheeks with a soft hand. "You are strong enough to see this through. Do not leave us as fading memories. You can save our little girl and bring Cobra to an end because you have the courage, and because we have to end the deaths. We cannot have been the only ones and will not be the last, unless you end Vaz and bring down Ravi. Now rest and build your strength."

He stared into her eyes and loved her more. She lifted her face to his and kissed him softly, lingering as desire filled him, bringing with it energy and a new-found confidence. They sank onto the soft sand and were young again and the world whirled and colours merged as the warmth of their bodies took them to another place. Mr Gupta had never felt stronger and knew he could carry on.

Jag had decided to drive to a nearby village to buy food and drink, but in the night, someone had scattered roofing tacks under the car. As soon as it moved the rear tyres punctured. It had been a deliberate act, but why? The tracker showed a steady, static signal, but he felt the first pangs of doubt. He hurried over to the rough track which led to the edge of the lake and looked for some signs of a vehicle's passing, not that it could have passed him without being obvious. A new layer of dust had drifted into the tracks from yesterday. There had been no vehicle using this road and the lorry had to be where the transmitter showed it to be. If it were to move now, however, he would be stuck so his anxiety increased. He decided to send a message.

Where are you?

The message was answered quickly.

Less than an hour. Is target still in place?

He answered.

Yes.

There was no more.

Jag decided to contact Suliman, something he rarely did. The phone was answered after a few moments.

"What do you want, Jag?" came the gruff voice.

"The client will be here soon, but I have two flat tyres, can you send Tarik down to help?" he asked.

There was a short silence, and when Suliman spoke he sounded gentler.

"The client has the Engineer with him, Jag," he said. "We have our fee, so I want you out of it as soon as you can. Call Tarik and get him to pick you up. Find a hotel if it's too late and charge it to the company, get the car fixed and then get back here. If the Engineer is involved our work is over. Tell Vasupati Chopra that our job ends once they locate the target. I have other work you can get stuck into. Time is money. And Jag?"

"Yes boss."

"Don't get involved with these two anymore than necessary," urged Suliman. "They are bloody dangerous."

Tarik reluctantly agreed to drive down to the lake that evening after the promise of a good hotel on company expenses. Jag felt a little better. He knew of the Engineer and that his involvement would mean violence in its severest form. That was something Suliman distanced himself from. He felt sorry for Anil Gupta as he had seemed a gentle soul.

It was mid-afternoon when Engineer brought the Shogun to a halt next to Jag, closely followed by a dusty, grey Mahindra Classic jeep. Engineer and Vaz got out, the former shaking Jag's hand, the latter standing aloof.

"Where is he?" asked Vaz.

"You can just see the start of the old road," said Jag gesturing to a gap in the trees. "The signal's remained constant since they got there, so I'm guessing there is a camp of some kind. The lorry is a big one and this is the only way out."

"How long is the road?" asked Engineer.

"About half-a-mile before it disappears into the reservoir," said Jag. "Google Earth shows it well enough. A cluster of old buildings at the end and nothing more."

"Have you been seen?" asked Vaz.

"No," said Jag.

Two men climbed out of the jeep to join the group. The driver, Aktar, was short, stocky, with a pock-marked face and nose. His companion and cousin, Kepi, was younger, taller, with the bloodshot eyes and detached look of a pot smoker. Kepi walked with a languid swagger as opposed to Aktar's rolling gait. Each had a pistol tucked in their belts. They listened attentively.

"How do you want to do this?" asked Engineer. "Straight in, or a recce from cover?"

"I think a careful look," said Vaz. "We can figure it out from there."

"Ok," said Engineer, "we'll just take the Glocks. You can come too," he said to Jag.

"Not if there's guns," said Jag firmly.

Vaz had stepped towards the car. He had noticed it was low at the back, so crouched to get a better look.

"Someone didn't want you to go too far," chuckled Kepi.

"Must've been invisible for you not to notice," added Aktar.

"Who did this?" asked Vaz.

Jag's heart sank.

"I don't know," he said, abashed.

"I think we may have a problem," said Vaz.

Engineer joined him. The tacks had been simple but effective. He looked across at the gap in the trees, then at Jag.

"Show me the layout," he said.

Jag grabbed his tracker and selected a satellite view of the old road and lake. There was the cluster of buildings, the winding road and nothing to show another exit. Changing screens Jag pointed out the pulsing signal.

"That is in Gupta's bag," said Jag. "I have not moved since they went down there, and nor have they."

Vaz knew things were not as they seemed. The punctured tyres were indicative of something he was growing more aware of – Anil Gupta seemed to be protected by something supernatural. Kāla was restless, his rage near the surface. The need to kill was harder and harder to suppress with less and less logical reasoning required to excuse the desire, and more hunger to drive it.

"You are coming with us," said Vaz.

Jag could see no way out. He prayed he would not have to witness anything brutal. Engineer pulled out two lethal looking guns from the rear of the Shogun, handing one to Vaz with a spare magazine. They both tucked a knife into their belts.

"Let's go," said Engineer.

He led the way along the track with Jag following miserably behind. After ten minutes they reached the final bend and could hear waves lapping the shore. Engineer crept forward, sighed, then stood and led them into the clearing. It was devoid of life with no sign of a large, ornate lorry. Engineer and Vaz checked the barn, whilst Aktar and Kepi searched the outbuildings and perimeter. Vaz stopped by a wooden post where an orange carrier bag had been hung. He lifted it down and looked inside. He pulled out the transmitter and a scrap of paper.

"What does it say?" asked Engineer.

"Have a look," said Vaz.

On the paper was a neatly written sentence: *The mind is superior to technology - or was it magic?*

"So, how long have they been gone?" asked Vaz.

Engineer checked the ground, skirted the shore and disappeared beyond the buildings. Jag stayed by the road next to the trees trying to figure out what had happened. Vaz stood silently, the sky reflecting in blue lenses, his breeze-blown hair the only movement. A few moments later, Engineer reappeared from the landward side of the barn, closely followed by the other two.

"There is an overgrown track back there," he said. "They took the lorry along the shallows and joined it where it enters the water. Not easy, but doable, obviously. Some of the broken leaves have dried out a bit and the flattened grass is bouncing back, there're also new cobwebs across the track. It means they left early last night. If they haven't stopped, that's ten hours at thirty miles an hour. They could be anywhere in a two or three-hundred-mile radius. If they dropped Gupta off somewhere, he could have taken a train and be another three hundred miles away by morning. It's your call Vaz."

"He will be in touch," said Vaz calmly. "Any advantage we had has gone. I think we find a hotel and wait. Your fee is safe."

"That's alright with me," said Engineer tucking the gun into his belt.

"I will wait for Tarik," said Jag.

He felt safer now Engineer was back and Vaz sounded pragmatic.

Engineer led the way back along the track and Jag stepped aside, thinking it may be best to let them go on without him. Vaz stopped.

"Sorry about that," said Jag.

Vaz shot him in the face.

Kuldev liked the golden giant. When Keya and Resham had come rushing into the village he had been convinced his lovely Anupa had been fatally injured, or abducted. Once he managed to calm the girls and extract the full story, he felt a lot easier. He, Vyan and a neighbour, Umang, set out with a donkey to help what purported to be an injured man in the care of a golden giant. The men remained sceptical until they reached the vaulted clearing of the Great Banyan. Anupa was indeed standing and talking confidently, in English Kuldev noted with pride, with a very big golden haired European. Dog wandered over, sniffed the giant's leg, wagged a raddled tail and settled at his feet. If Dog approved, Kuldev was sure there was no harm in him, large as he was. Umang had some knowledge of healing as he had served in the army for several years in his youth, so squatted by Seva to do a cursory examination. Before long Seva had been loaded onto the donkey and carefully led down the precarious path to Karukula. Kuldev followed with the giant, three excited girls and Dog, for whom nothing seemed to phase nor excite. Conversation was a little stilted as the descent was demanding and English was very much a second language for the villagers. This, coupled with the need to get Seva to a safe place, meant pleasantries would wait. Upon reaching the village he was helped to an empty hut, normally reserved for visiting doctors, dignitaries and invited guests. It was basic but clean.

Sameeksha, Kuldev's wife, and the three girls, under Umang's direction made Seva comfortable on an old, cream, metal-framed bed, making sure he had clean water to drink. Vyan left to fetch the doctor from the Maskrey Plantation with orders to invoke the regular free supply of tobacco as payment from Kuldev. In the meantime, an old Beechams Powders was administered, it being the only drug in Umang's aged medical tin. Seva was conscious, but weak and remained quiet apart from keeping up a regular *thank you* mantra for each administration of care. The men retired to Kuldev's mud-brick and thatch house where Olaf slumped into a chair on the veranda.

"You must not worry," said Kuldev, carefully forming the unpractised words. "You stay as a guest until Sevak is well. We have no riches, but enough for comfort. Karukula is a good place."

"Thank you, I don't need much," said Olaf. "I'm not sure where I go from here. I need some rest, but I'm not Seva's travel companion. I found him collapsed up on the plateau and was making sure he was safe. He is a nice feller."

"*Feller?*" said Kuldev.

"Man," said Olaf. "Anyhow, I am Olaf," he said shaking each of their hands.

"Olab," said Kuldev.

"Olab," said Umang.

"Close enough," said Olaf.

"I am Kuldev, and this is Umang."

Anupa and Keya arrived with a selection of foods which they placed on the table before the men. Olaf noticed Anupa smiling at him and returned it with a big grin, which made her blush and Keya giggle as they retreated.

"Forgive my daughters," said Kuldev. "They are young and find you not normal. I think that is not the right words."

"Unusual?" offered Olaf.

"Yes," said Kuldev. "You can sleep in Seva's hut, but no bed."

"I can get comfortable," said Olaf. "For now, I just need a clean-up and this food."

399

"Clean at river is good, Olab," said Umang. "Doctor here in hour maybe quickly."

Once the food had gone Olaf thanked the men again and went to check on Seva. Sameeksha had made him comfortable and he looked a little better.

"I am weak, Olab," he said. "I have aches in my ribs."

"That sounds quite nasty," said Olaf.

"The lady says you bruised me when you carried me," said Seva with a wry smile.

"Jaysus," laughed Olaf.

Later he made his way to the tumbling river. He stripped and washed the grime from his body in a deep pool. It was clear and icy cold. He plunged beneath the surface enjoying the sounds, the weightlessness, the cleansing and the momentary isolation of the water world. Afterwards he dried himself on a small, absorbent towel, then dressed in the last of his fresh clothes – shorts and a t-shirt. He spent the next hour scrubbing his pile of trail-soiled laundry, spreading it out in the afternoon sunshine to dry.

"Olab?"

The soft voice startled him. It was Anupa.

"Hello lass," he said. "Just getting things clean."

"This is women's work, Olab," she said smiling. "You have golden hair on your legs!"

"I guess so," he said. "It's a Viking curse."

"It is nice," she said. "But there is news. The doctor is here and he has told us the Kuru ki Kvark is coming tomorrow. They are in the Maskrey Village."

"He was quick," said Olaf.

"He has a motorbike," said Anupa.

"Oh," said Olaf. "Then what's this other stuff?"

"The Kuru ki Kvark visit us after the monsoons some years," said Anupa. "They stay and help and teach us things. Nawal Ji likes to talk about logic and kvarks and Vam is like a doctor too. Doctor Mistry loves it when they come. He says it raises the tone. And they have a pilgrim with them who is on a quest. Come and meet the Doctor, and call me Anupa. I am an adult, not a girl."

She turned and marched off. Olaf followed enjoying the swing of her hips and the tickle of unborn laughter in the pit of his stomach. The cold water had revived him and the spring was back in his step.

⁂

The sleep that came after meeting Kiran in his other world was total, dreamless and reviving. Mr Gupta opened his eyes and relished the all-encompassing comfort and warmth. His body ached from the enforced exercise of the last week, but he stretched and savoured the easing of tight muscles. Then he froze. Talika lay next to him. Without a sound she rose on an elbow, kissed him lightly on the cheek, slipped from the covers and stood up. She wore a single figure-hugging wrap.

"You were crying out in your sleep, Anil," she whispered. "I held you until you quietened. You will be well now."

She hurried away towards the kitchen. Dawn had not yet broken, but the sky was light in the east and the breeze was soft and cool. A clean pile of clothes had been left next to him with a beautifully finished pair of soft leather sandals, each with an intricate stylised sun pattern etched into the leather. It was then he realised he was completely naked. Had his dream of Kiran been real, transcending both worlds?

"Aye, laddie," came MacKeeg's voice on the wind. "Don't sully it..."

In spite of a collision of emotions, Mr Gupta realised he felt rather happy. Kiran and Talika could be interchangeable in this duel existence, but felt he should not think about it too much. He pulled on his freshly laundered underwear, a dhoti, white shirt and sandals. He walked out into the open and took a moment to look at his reflected self in a puddle of water. The transformation from pudgy railway supervisor to faux sadhu looked complete. He did not recognise himself, yet in spite of a severe weight loss and woolly, white beard, he looked well. Nawal was sitting silhouetted, facing the dawn at the open edge of the clearing, so he joined him sat down unbidden. They looked at the red horizon, the occasional light flashing through the morning mist and the final stars fading overhead. They remained this way until a satellite, bright in the hidden sun's rays, passed over from the dawn to the retreating night, glowing brighter against the dark, and then winking out as it passed into shadow.

"That was the International Space Station," said Nawal. "I was waiting for that."

"I though you may be meditating," said Mr Gupta.

"An overused word," said Nawal. "People really mean *thinking* when they say it. Think in a shop, think on a rock – what is the difference?"

"I thought there was a difference in depth and focus," said Mr Gupta.

"Phaw!" laughed Nawal. "That is the diktat from authority. Put on strange clothes, tell people they are special, invoke visions and inspired writings and the frightened herd will follow. Always, always look at the evidence. *Cogitate, think, ponder, meditate, consider.* All valid words that pretty much mean the same thing. That is mankind's greatest problem. We complicate where we should simplify and usually with one aim."

"That being?" asked Mr Gupta.

"To invent authority from which to confound, instil fear and control," said Nawal.

"And this from a professor of physics?" said Mr Gupta.

Nawal laughed.

"So, what is your story Arnesh Ji?" he asked.

"It is long and chaotic," said Mr Gupta. "MacKeeg says I should trust you, but it still feels as if I may burden you with my own doom. It could be contagious and lead to further deaths."

"All you are doing is speaking," said Nawal. "All I can do is listen. I have no power, but I am inquisitive."

Mr Gupta looked out across the world and found it easy to finally narrate his tale and with its telling the burden lessened. He left nothing out, even including his convictions about the dealings of Ravi Uppal and the murderous actions of Vasupati Chopra. At the end he realised it was the first time he saw everything in chronological order. The theory he and MacKeeg had constructed was in no place wanting, the part left was the ending which only had scope for one possible outcome and two deaths. The sun was a huge orange ball lifting clear of the mist as he finished.

"And what of that which you have left behind?" asked Nawal.

"Of that I have no control," said Mr Gupta. "I have to rely on friends and family to bring Ravi Uppal down. My payment to them is their lives by ending Vaz. It has been forced upon me, but I have MacKeeg."

"Today things change, Arnesh Ji," said Nawal placing a hand on his arm. "The Queen Lizzie has several electronic surprises we installed over the years. Phone signal amplifiers, charging facilities, satellite links and access to the World Wide Web. You can contact all those you need including this monster Vaz. Keep him moving. We will bring him close to Karukula, but from there things will depend on events and probabilities I cannot yet see. He must follow if he is as you said."

"When do we leave for this place?" asked Mr Gupta.

"Now!" said Nawal rising to his feet. "We can get there in three days or so, but in the meantime, I smell breakfast! And Talika is singing! That is something I have not heard for a long time."

Mr Gupta blushed as he followed Nawal who glanced over his shoulder once and winked.

"Not very sadhu-like," muttered MacKeeg.

Chapter 27

All Life's Weaving is Undone

The extensive grounds of the great house enclosed green, wooded hills and rolling parkland. The boundary was marked by a red-brick wall some ten feet in height, capped by yellow stone. At regular intervals piers reinforced the structure, each of these topped by a selection of figures – elephants, stylised eggs, grotesque faces – anything the builder had felt was suited. Alakapuri was accessed via a huge masonry archway, with heavy wrought iron gates flanked by half-sized stone elephants decked out in finest ceremonial regalia. Beyond the wall the hills of Dehradun stretched away to join the Rajaji National Park to the north, home to real elephants, giving fine panoramic views to the owner of the former palace. It had been purchased from a minor rajah, who had fallen upon hard times, by Kishor Nalin Shastri in 1938. It had remained the family home since then, though much improved and modernised to reflect the banking family's opulence. Kishor had died here in 1986, two days after his hundredth birthday, and was mourned by his two sons, Sudhesh and, his namesake, Nalin.

Both sons inherited the property and, although each owned a large house in Delhi from which the family business was run, they regularly came home to Alakapuri, it being more than big enough for their families. The brothers were gentle but driven and pushed the business to new heights, yet remained very much family men. Sudhesh had one son, also Sudhesh, and Nalin two daughters, Tamina and Kiran. Upon Sudhesh senior's death aged 83, his son took over his side of the business, and when Nalin died in his 88th year, it became his in its entirety. Nalin's daughters chose not to become involved in banking, Tamina marrying an up-and-coming financial and legal professional, Ravi Uppal, and Kiran marrying one Anil Gupta, son of a rich merchant. Sudhesh junior had left the thought of marriage late, but recently became engaged to a much younger woman, the daughter of a South African shipping magnate, and the wedding was rumoured to be planned for the following summer.

All three cousins remained close and the women visited Alakapuri when they could, but preferred to meet Sudhesh in Delhi when he was there. He was as good natured as his father and understood the need for his cousins to make their own lives, always remembered birthdays and anniversaries, and often reminded them they had an open invitation to the family home. He mourned the loss of Kiran's stillborn son and was inconsolable when Tamina was killed. He grew cold towards Ravi Uppal when he remarried so quickly and Sudhesh's curiosity was piqued enough to find out Ravi's new wife had been pregnant whilst Tamina was still alive. There was no evidence of foul play and eventually he marked Ravi Uppal down as a man with low morals and no natural dignity. Yet he still felt uncomfortable reading the news that Ravi was stepping into politics and found Fallen Angels to be anathema to the founder's normal modus operandi.

Rupa's birth was at first a trial for him, allowing unconscious bias to judge her disability as being definitive of a lifetime's burden. But he had been wrong. Frequent visits with Kiran allowed Sudhesh to realise Rupa had a unique personality and exceptionally high intellect. It was her ability to laugh at herself that finally made Sudhesh comfortable with Rupa and he had learned to love her, enjoying the brightness her visits always brought. Alakapuri had an extensive ground floor and a suite of rooms had been modified for Rupa's needs. Sudhesh had been one of Rupa's sponsors for her education in the Beaufort Homes system along with Ravi Uppal, but kept a lower profile than the latter due to natural modesty.

It was Kiran's death that had caused the most pain. Her loss left him as the last of his generation in their family and he missed her so. Then there was another loss as his friend, Anil Gupta withdrew from the wider world to mourn, dealing with it by immersing himself in the comfort of familiar routine. Sudhesh did not interfere, realising that grief was personal and a trial to endure through indefinite time. Thus it had been a surprise to get a call from Mr Gupta asking for Rupa to be looked after and for Sudhesh to cast his eye over some data appertaining to Fallen Angels and possible illegal dealings with the charity by Cobra Investments. He had agreed without hesitation giving Jhatish Das a place to stay for a while, the latter having been charged with telling Sudhesh the whole story, including their suspicions about Ravi Uppal's involvement in murder.

"And Sudhesh," Mr Gupta had concluded. "You will hear some odd things about me in the near future. The truth is with Jhatish. However, I am terminally ill, so I need to charge you with the safety of my daughter and friends. Death also follows me in the shape of Vasupati Chopra, Ravi's partner, and he will stop at nothing to destroy me. Leave him to me. Sudhesh, your job is to bring Cobra down if you can…if you want to."

Sudhesh agreed to wait for Jhatish's imminent arrival for answers, barring one.

"Tell me, Anil," he had said, troubled by the threads of truth linked to his own suspicions. "Are Uppal and Chopra in any way involved in the deaths of Tamina and Kiran?"

"Yes," he had said. "Of this I have no doubt."

"I have long had my suspicions, Anil," said Sudhesh, anger giving his voice an edge, "so you must not worry. I will use everything I have to protect my family. Jhatish and Rupa will remain here at Alakapuri for as long as it takes. If Ravi Uppal is involved in this, I promise I will destroy him."

With that, Anil Gupta had ended the call.

The Duck had waddled into the grounds of Alakapuri at mid-morning the following day and Rupa and Jhatish were welcomed. Sarasa had been allowed to accompany Rupa as Sudhesh had arranging to cover her salary with the Beaufort Homes Trust for the duration. Jhatish was whisked away to a private office where he told Sudhesh everything Mr Gupta had relayed to him. The tale seemed fantastical until the television pictures of the Gupta home had made a brief slot on the news, then Sudhesh realised the truth of it all. His accountants were given the data from Kiran's memory stick to pour over, and a friend in the Indian Intelligence Service contacted. By the end of the day a spotlight had fallen upon Ravi Uppal and investigations had started.

Sachet Engineer was not easily rattled, but the gunshot which ended Jag's life made his legs buckle. He had spun round raising his Glock, bringing the weapon to bear before realising what Vaz had done. He could not comprehend the rashness of this execution. Engineer hurried back down the track to where Vaz crouched next to the dead man. Vaz removed his hand from the bloodied face, wiped it in the dirt and stood. Aktar and Kepi trotted up, each startled, but not overly concerned.

Kepi scratched his nose and smiled, "Suliman will be pissed off," he said.

"Why did you kill him?" gasped Engineer.

There was no immediate reply from Vaz. His face remained blank, blue glasses reflecting the surrounding trees. Engineer believed for a moment his companion was having a catatonic fit of some sort. *Vaz is mad*, he thought. He was unable to take his eyes from the ruined head of Jag. The single round from the Glock had entered Jag's face under his left eye and taken a large part of his brain and skull with it. The dust of the track was now soaking up a huge pool of blood.

"Vaz!" snapped Engineer. Still nothing.

His mind was elsewhere. Kāla's hunger had left. In the distance Vaz could hear Engineer, and some part of him registered the gravity of this murder, but he had no control this time. The chattering idiot had failed and Kāla had acted. It had felt so good to take that life. He had wanted to make him suffer, tie him to a tree and flay him, but time was short. The internal spotlight of analysis found no feeling, no remorse, no blame, only righteousness. Kāla-Vaz he was and a god has nothing to worry about and no one to answer to. Anil Gupta had to die, then he would rule the new world.

"Fucking hell!" Engineer shook Vaz's arm. "Why did you kill the poor bastard?"

"He let us down," said Vaz smiling, his golden tooth flashing. "We just leave everything as it is and let the police try and figure it out. We are safe enough. I will have to wait for Gupta to contact me."

"Your boss knows! Suliman knows! Who knows what information this chap sent out?" said Engineer. "What a bloody mess! Still, this is an isolated place. Let's get a hotel further south and keep away from Bhopal."

Vaz was already walking up the track towards the main road. Engineer bent and searched Jag's body for a phone and removed it. Something caught his eye — a dull glint in Jag's mouth. Had he been wearing a brace on his teeth? He shrugged and hurried on. Back at the road, Engineer and his men tidied up as best they could. From the back of the Shogun came a roll of blue and white tape with *Police - do not cross* repeatedly printed along its length. They tied a strip across the entrance of the old road and wrapped some around Jag's car too – it would cause more confusion. Engineer joined Vaz back in the Shogun.

"I'm heading for Jalna. If we're being coaxed south we may as well pre-empt the issue, unless you have any suggestions," he said. "And by the way, that dead man is an unexpected removal, so you owe me another five thousand."

Engineer drove quickly, followed by Aktar and Kepi in the jeep. Vaz remained quiet until his phone started buzzing. Vaz answered.

"Hello Ravi."

"Vaz!" barked Ravi. "Where are you? Is all going well?"

"Yes. We will catch Gophapa soon."

"Gophapa? ... Look, I need you to get this done quickly," said Ravi. "I am starting to feel uneasy about the whole thing."

"There is nothing to worry about, Ravi," said Vaz. "Even if trouble comes I will wipe it away. Ignore them all."

"What are you talking about, Vaz?" asked Ravi.

"I will come back once Gupta is destroyed," said Vaz. "We have all the power. *The sacrifice is made, mankind's sacrificial man, Gophapa will be slain by Him, Gophapa takes ruin with him. Tarnished silver. patinated gold, my Lord watches, my Lord sees...* The next time we talk we will be in the realms of the mighty ones."

Vaz ended the call. Engineer raised an eyebrow making a mental note to keep his Glock close to hand.

Locals had noticed the Chopra home had been silent for several days. It was not unusual for the family to be away, but there was generally a mower to be heard, or a trade van going through the gates. The local gardener had been unable to enter the grounds and had complained at length to his wife about loss of earnings and the highhandedness of the Chopras. Curiosity turned to alarm when a large flock of kites and vultures began to circle the property. It was Lajita's mother who eventually contacted the police, when frequent calls to her daughter went unanswered. At first, they had ignored the woman, but she eventually turned up at their headquarters and caused such a scene that it was agreed to send a car out to make sure all was well.

The two investigating officers could not open the main gate, so had entered the grounds through a hole in the fence, crawling through shrubbery before emerging hot and dirty on the other side. The flock of birds above was oppressively huge and the policemen realised something was very wrong. There was no answer when the doorbell was rung, but being unlocked, the men entered calling out as they searched the deserted house. Outside, one searched the garage and outbuildings, the other the grounds. There was little to see in the huge, tidy garage, but as the policeman reached the top of the external stairs to the small flat above, he froze and drew his pistol. The door was open and the scene inside was chaotic, with toppled chairs and furniture, and dried pools and splashes of what was most likely blood. The rooms were deserted. A shout from the far end of the manicured lawn drew the policeman away from the grimly painted room and down into the garden. He saw his partner vomiting into a flower bed. He hurried across the lawn and noticed smoke billowing from the top of an old well. The smoke buzzed. He realised it was a cloud of flies just as the smell sent him reeling into the flower border to join his companion. Within an hour a further six police vehicles had arrived at the Chopra home, the gate was forced open and the property sealed off from the public.

Inspector Ram Naresh Singh stepped from his car onto the drive, scratched his nose and rasped his beard. It had been a busy week and he had not slept well. In the space of two days he had rubber stamped a covert investigation into parliamentary candidate Ravi Uppal's business dealings and now was visiting the scene of what seemed to be a mass murder at the home of his business partner, Vasupati Chopra. There were also links to the strange case of one Anil Gupta, his possible assassination and probable escape. And that was definitely connected to a dead body which lay burned to charcoal in the city morgue. Usually cases such as this were slow in coming together, but in this instance, he had had a mountain of information materialise in no time at all. He ran a podgy finger around the inside of his neat, white turban, dabbed a handkerchief to his brow, hitched up his trousers under an ample stomach and walked past the uniformed officer stationed at the main door who fired off a quick salute. The Inspector was nicknamed *Toad* by his colleagues and subordinates, though never within earshot. He may be short and squat, but had an astute mind and ferocious tongue if his ire was piqued. The large entrance hall was cordoned off with yellow tape and a middle-aged woman with hair swept back into a ponytail, wearing a white disposable suit and blue plastic overshoes stepped forward to greet him.

"Good morning Ram," she said. "You look harassed."

"Surinda, I blinking am," he said, squeezing her hand. "What do we have here?"

Surinda Kaur was in her early forties, a career policewoman, now detective, and in Ram's opinion the best in Delhi.

"Four bodies," she said lifting the tape and leading Ram into the garden. "The four body bags over there contain Chopra's wife – decapitated, two children and the maid. Preliminary examination by the forensic chaps show the wife and children had been beaten with a narrow, blunt instrument aimed at the head. Quick deaths I would guess. The wife's decapitation happened post mortem on the lawn by the look of it. The maid has wounds indicative of a struggle, but I need to wait for a full autopsy report to be sure. They are pretty smelly, but the well they were dumped in had been capped a short way down, so they were easy, but unpleasant, to retrieve. Vasupati Chopra is missing so I guess he is number one suspect. Unless he turns up dead too."

Ram stopped at a safe distance, the smell already stomach turning.

"I will have to see his business partner later to ask some questions," he said. "In the meantime, I want you to look at the Gupta case in tandem to this."

"Is there a connection?" asked Surinda.

"Let's get away from this stink and I'll tell you about a call I had earlier this week," said Ram. "It may help us to solve several riddles at once."

"Including the finger prints on that tyre iron matching the body in the alley?" she asked.

"Bloody hell, I'd forgotten that," said Ram. "There is a chance it is all related and that is why we need a good chat."

They returned to the front of the house and stood in the cooling shade of some nearby trees.

"Do you know the name Shastri?" he asked.

"Aren't they part of the investments sector?" replied Surinda. "Bankers. One of the big financial houses?"

"Correct," said Ram. "Well, Sudhesh Shastri, the remaining eponymous owner, contacted me a few days ago and we met up. It concerned Anil Gupta, his late cousin's widower, and Ravi Uppal who runs Cobra Investments with Chopra, which in turn supports the famous Fallen Angels charity."

"I have heard of Ravi Uppal recently," said Surinda. "He's to be an IPU candidate in Delhi at the next election. Already rich, now grabbing for power. His altruism is becoming well known."

"Spot on," said Ram. "Ravi Uppal was married to the second Shastri cousin, sister of Gupta's wife. She was murdered in Mumbai years back. The owner of this charnel house is Ravi Uppal's business partner..."

"...who is Vasupati Chopra!" exclaimed Surinda.

"Exactly! One big circle. Sudhesh Shastri has found some huge anomalies in the Fallen Angels finances. These records were passed on to him via Anil Gupta, from his wife who acted as Fallen Angels accountant for a while, as did her sister."

"Goodness," said Surinda. "That is a lot of coincidences. So Gupta is dead too, and you think it is all linked?"

"I know it is," said Ram. "You have only heard the half of it. According to Shastri, and he has proof, Gupta is alive and fleeing in fear of his life from Chopra. The body found at Gupta's house was, allegedly, a hit man sent by Uppal to silence him. All this landed on my desk over the last week, but these murders make no sense. If, and I emphasise the *if*, all this really is connected, we have the biggest case we've ever tackled on our hands."

They were still deep in conversation when a young police officer rushed over to them.

"Sir, Chopra flew out of Delhi to Bhopal nearly a week ago, according to Mr Uppal," he said. "Mr Uppal is demanding to know what is happening. He is very agitated."

"I bet he is," said Ram. "Surinda, do you fancy coming with me to see this future Member of Parliament?"

"Yes," she said, "Detective Prabhu can carry on here. I want to see what this Ravi Uppal looks like."

Umesh Prabhu had been enthralled at the site of the murder. He was bright, with a quick mind and had impressed Surinda Kaur over the last couple of years. Tall, trim and fresh faced, he had recently grown a moustache to *engender respect*, so he said, which had made her laugh. Umesh was good. When he entered Vasupati Chopra's bizarre study, he was immediately sure this man was more than just eccentric. After some careful searching he discovered that the large brass figure of Shiva was an ornate lid to a hidden chamber. The first item he removed was a passport in the name of Lalit Mahto. Umesh remembered a recent double murder in Agra. He delved deeper.

The Rajpath looked no different. Traffic was heavy and the hawkers were selling their usual array of rubbish and refreshments. Halfway along the route from the India Gate to the far seat of government, Ravi Uppal was sitting under a tree with a knot of anxiety in his stomach. He gazed at Edwin Lutyens's grand works and considered failure of his plans for the first time. He had been so careful for so long, yet his partner seemed intent on destroying everything they had built. Vaz had long stopped answering his phone and had effectively disappeared after his final nonsensically cryptic message. Ravi had completed sanitising Cobra's records of links to

Vaz's misdeeds, but he was no longer confident of its effectiveness in face of his partner's recklessly open actions. Ravi sauntered towards the far buildings. It had been the call from Ranjit Kumar Roy which had given Ravi palpitations. Ranjit had informed him that Mehmet Suliman had refused any more help in finding Anil Gupta.

"Why?" Ravi had asked, heart sinking.

"It has become too dangerous," said Ranjit. Then there was a long pause. "Is your partner mixed up with gangsters?"

This was an unexpected question which Ravi found difficult to answer.

"No," he said without conviction. "What is going on?"

"I'll tell you what is going on," Ranjit had barked. "Suliman does not like it when one of his top investigators gets executed!"

"What?" said Ravi, shocked.

"Chopra has been working with a mercenary Suliman would not touch with a barge pole," raged Ranjit. "His man had found this fraudster of yours, waited for your man, and then silence! Suliman tells me his operative was found by his partner with his face shot off! There is no sign of Chopra or the mercenary. Suliman has threatened to give all the information he has to the authorities, implicating the IPU in illegal activities. Believe me, Ravi, he can do the party terrible damage."

"How much money would it take to calm him, Ranjit?" said Ravi, coldly.

"It is not about fucking money!" raged Ranjit. "This is about survival! Fucking hell, Ravi, this fellow Jag was the son of Suliman's sister! His bloody nephew! Get this through your head. Under my direction the Indian Patriotic Union will put out a statement today saying you are no longer being considered as their Delhi candidate. You are to be expelled from membership and, with luck that will placate Suliman. Unless you rein in Chopra I will make sure I cooperate with the police and cleanse the party of this unnecessary stain."

Ravi Uppal was shaken and unsure what to say. His dream was at the very least on hold, at worst destroyed. He could hardly think. He could not accept the sudden and irreversible change in his fortunes.

"Everyone has a price, Ranjit," he said. "I can find a lot of dollars. Please hold fire on any statements, after all I have pumped a lot of those dollars into the party and you have never questioned their origins." Now confident in what he knew about the IPU's less than overt finances, Ravi grew angry too. "Take this on board Ranjit, if I fucking go, you will all fucking go! Remember, I have enough information here to make life very uncomfortable. Tell Suliman it is down to Gupta that his nephew was killed, and he has become desperate. Make up something, you are good at that. Offer him a good compensation package and remind him that I too know what it is like to lose a loved one through violence. As for Vaz, well I will keep trying to rein him in."

There was the sound of deep breathing over the phone as Ranjit saw the awful truth in Ravi's statement. He set emotion aside.

"I tell you what, Ravi," he said in a low voice. "I will give you two days to sort this mess out. The IPU Chair, Manish Patel, is arriving from Hyderabad in the morning. We will fly up to Delhi for a meeting with all the big players, including your main backer, Dr Pallab Bhanot, and you will be top of the agenda. It will be in camera, but, get this Ravi, the outcome will make or break you, and you will know soon enough what the decision is. Suliman only deals directly with me, but he knows Patel and Bhanot very well. If, and I mean *if*, Suliman can be placated, you can be one of the most powerful figures in the IPU within a year – a safe Delhi seat and government salary as well as continuing your own business. *But* it means *you* have to be squeaky-clean and Chopra brought back to Delhi. Forget Gupta. You may be able to bring me down – and don't think it will be easy, Ravi – but the IPU has great power and hefty backers. Call me with good news tomorrow. That is all!"

For the first time in more than a decade Ravi Uppal had felt powerless.

As he strolled past the armed guards stationed outside the Secretariat Building he had still not resolved his problem.

"Are you alright, sir?"

It was a young soldier he had not noticed.

"Er, yes, thank you," said Ravi.

"You look a bit confused," said the soldier. "If you need directions I can't help, but you will need to go back towards the main road in a few minutes as the Police Commissioner's convoy is due. The policemen down there may help you with directions."

"I shall do that," said Ravi, an idea forming as he strode off. If he reported Vaz to the authorities, doing his patriotic duty by implicating him in unsanctioned criminal activity, he may come out looking like the innocent victim of a madman. It could work. There was absolutely nothing linking him with the Gupta event. As he strode past the group of policemen he nodded in greeting, then hailed a cab. He would return to the office and try to reach Vaz – then simply call a policeman.

No matter how carefully Ravi Uppal worked, his one error had already borne prodigious fruit. The murder of his wife to fund the nascent Cobra Investments had been well planned and, literally, executed, but he had missed the disc. Tamina had replaced it with that damned Zahan album, and her sister had been too clever. Removing Kiran Gupta had been a gamble, but her husband had placed that disc in his hand, seeming almost too good to be true, and so it was proving to be. He should never have brought Kiran into Fallen Angels and now he was plugging gaps he should not have needed to. All of these troubles would be manageable if Vaz had been his usual efficient self. Then, Anil Gupta had outsmarted them all! A man who had achieved nothing, had no ambition, no strength and nothing to drive him; a man who had a terminal brain tumour and a crippled child; this man had somehow dispatched a professional assassin, made his daughter disappear and then had the gall to taunt them. He had actually challenged them. There was no doubt Vaz would catch and kill him, but what was to gain? Anil Gupta was either deranged and lucky, or very clever and clinically dangerous. Ravi could not believe the latter. He was sure his luck would eventually run out or his cancer would gain the upper hand.

Ravi worked late at his office, long after Jyoti had left, every hour sending Vaz a message or phoning him. He left the building after midnight and arrived home very tired, but sure he had isolated himself from Vaz's actions, which give him some breathing space. There were no records left to implicate Cobra in anything more than legitimate business. There was absolutely no trail for the authorities to follow. He was even gaining in confidence that the information Anil Gupta had on Fallen Angels would be worthless on its own. Where was the evidence of any fraud? At most it was circumstantial and disparate. Yet, he went to sleep still angry at his one error.

The Kuru ki Kvark was leaving Seraraya. Whilst the Queen Lizzie was being loaded, Tsering led Mr Gupta to the back of the lorry and helped him climb inside. He went to a bench which backed on to the cab and lifted the upholstered seat. It was filled with an array of wires, sockets, plastic boxes with USB ports and flashing LEDs, and a portable aerial and dish. Clipped to the side was a vintage British Army Webley Mk VI revolver.

"This is our communications system," said Tsering with some pride. "Nawal Ji and I built it over the years. We have a laptop, internet access, charging points, satellite connections and can pick up most microwave transmitters. It keeps us up-to-date with things. Puneet sometimes gets me to plug in our television so he can watch the soaps!"

"Puneet watches soap operas?" asked Mr Gupta, bemused.

"Only the dreadful ones," chuckled Tsering. "Nawal Ji says you have a phone that may need charging."

"Yes," replied Mr Gupta. "I had forgotten. I will have to make some calls when we are a bit further south, so it will be handy."

"I know this is important," said Tsering. "You will be able to contact anyone you need. I also have this." Tsering lifted a hefty device of yellow and black. "It is a GPS!" he stated. "With this you can work out directions for the man who is following you."

Mr Gupta longed to hear Rupa's voice and to talk to Jhatish. His existence had been simple since Kiran was murdered and he had felt safe in its very blandness. He missed Old Mr Singh and his wife's motherly cosseting. He missed the simple act of leaving Delhi station and finding Old Mr Singh always ready to take him home. He hoped they were well. He hoped for so many things. But here he was.

"Why the gun?" he asked.

"One never knows," said Tsering. "Nawal Ji is very wise, and as yet his way has kept us safe, but this pistol is well cared for and may well improve the laws of probability one fine day."

The day was hot, the road dusty and the main highways busy. Tsering drove steadily all morning, eventually finding quieter roads to use south of Udgir. The roads were less undulating here, leading across the Bhima River and the Karnataka Plateau. On Nawal's instruction Tsering took a side road just before Ganagapur, where they set up camp in a small farming village. The locals welcomed them as old friends. Whilst Tsering, Vam and Talika fussed over their hosts, administering ointments and fixing recalcitrant machinery, Nawal and Mr Gupta sat in the shade and talked.

"Now the time has come, I realise I will be sending my last messages," said Mr Gupta with a sigh. "The rest at Seraraya was good for my body, but I cannot rid my mind of the insanity of my situation. I think I'm going mad. All I want is to spend my last days with Rupa and my dear friends."

"You have to accept the brain's reaction to constant pressure," said Nawal.

"I do not understand," said Mr Gupta.

"Alright Arnesh Ji, I shall explain. The heart is an organ that pumps blood, the eyes organs for sight and the brain is an organ for thinking. That is its function, end of story. At a more primal level it also interprets what we see, and being primates, we tend to see patterns that suggest what may be. The rustle in the grass could be a lion. The log in the water a crocodile. Initial information for safety, followed quickly by logical, thoughtful interpretation of what really is there. Apophenia or pareidolia is what scientists call that primitive function. At times of great stress, the mind needs to make sense of what has happened and can make us lazy thinkers. The primal brain may be dominant. Logic is hard work. Religion relies on that process, replacing logical thought with blind faith of authority. All it has to do is convince people they are special, adding an unmerited importance to mankind, and from that point lazy thinking becomes standard.

"You, Arnesh Ji, are different, as is your daughter from what you have told me. Right now, you are at the midpoint in thought where your mind is dominated by emotion and it craves an easy option. It is not controlled by logic. Take a moment. Answer me this: why are you here and what is your goal?"

Mr Gupta knew that he longed for the *perceived* security of the life he led after Kiran died, ignoring the incipient peril creeping up on him. The pull to give up was strong, and his mind felt ready to find an excuse to do so. Without the tumour, without the enforced use of his MacKeeg mind, he and Rupa could have been killed and not one shred of evidence would show a link to Ravi Uppal. He had been stricken at the perfect time to exact retribution. The improbable had happened without the interference of the fates. He smiled as he realised his thought process had moved on just as Nawal had suggested. Allowing lazy thinking to break his spirit could never be an option.

"Does this mean I am being enlightened?" he said, smiling.

"It certainly does," said Nawal. "Do not give natural emotions a supernatural origin, nor believe that you have been the puppet of some unseen weaver of your future path. So, why *are* you doing what you are?"

"I am exacting revenge the only way I can," said Mr Gupta. "I am dying, but need to know I leave Rupa and my friends safe from harm. But…" he paused to gather his thoughts, "…but there *is* something more. Chopra murdered my wife, of that I am sure. He has killed others too, ordered by Ravi, but I am not a court of law, so have no need to prove it beyond reasonable doubt. That he is coming to kill me is proof enough. MacKeeg has drawn Chopra into the open using me as bait. Nawal, I *want* to kill this man. Is that such a terrible thing to crave?"

"No," said Nawal emphatically. "Believe it or not it is perfectly natural. You are protecting your DNA. This killer has taken your resistance personally and sounds unhinged."

"That is to my advantage," said Mr Gupta. "I have used it to draw him on. Then again, there has been no direct contact since Delhi."

"Then it is time there was," said Nawal. "Let's get the phone working!"

Chapter 28

Endings

Alakapuri was a haven for Rupa and her Uncle Jhatish. Sudhesh Shastri had become ever more animated in his resolve to bring Ravi Uppal to justice. The great house was visited by a succession of detectives, who had been drafted in to investigate what was becoming a large and complex case. Sudhesh eventually left for his Delhi house to assist in unscrambling the bogus Fallen Angel data. He was also to visit Chaitanya Ghosh, Delhi's Commissioner of Police. The right-wing policies of the IPU had caused consternation in Parliament, especially as further success gave them the opportunity to dictate a balance of power. If Ravi Uppal, their new high-profile candidate, could be brought down, the media would link his misdemeanours with the IPU, and Commissioner Ghosh would look favourably upon this. Disparity in government could harm India and he was sworn to prevent irregularities such as this. The hard evidence supplied by Mr Gupta had delivered Ravi Uppal into the Commissioner's hands, but care would need to be taken unravelling the suspected money laundering system. The data indicated classic piggyback scams were in action, channelling money to foreign accounts, to return as clean American dollars. The Commissioner had already arranged for Cobra's IT system to be seized and Ravi Uppal's security systems had been partially decoded. Sudhesh Shastri knew information could never be completely erased and his team, along with the Commissioner's police experts, would eventually put every piece together. Even so, they were more than aware it could take years to develop a case.

A white Bentley delivered Sudhesh to Commissioner Ghosh's offices. He was excited with the news on Cobra, but carried the burden of Anil Gupta's sorrows with him. The link between Ravi Uppal and the deaths of Tamina and Kiran, as well as the pending assassination of Mr Gupta, could not be proven. The circumstantial evidence was great, but a good barrister could make it inadmissible with ease. Sudhesh was shown into the Commissioner's mahogany-panelled office which was redolent in coffee, beeswax and spice. Commissioner Ghosh was tall, trim and wore his ceremonial uniform with pride. His greying hair was swept back and tidy, and his luxurious moustache turned up as he smiled.

"Sudhesh!" he said, shaking his hand with genuine affection. "Come in and sit down! The coffee is fresh and the biscuits delightful."

"Chaitanya, you look very well," said Sudhesh, settling in a padded chair and pouring himself a black coffee.

"Survival is the key!" laughed Chaitanya. "And I seem to have the knack. It must be all the rich bankers I know!" He laughed again.

"So, are we in for a long, drawn out affair with Uppal?" asked Sudhesh. "Do we yet have enough to bring the bastard to book? He has been clever. It looks like millions are unaccounted for. And dollars, not rupees."

Chaitanya continued to smile, then leaned upon his desk and steepled his fingers.

"We have enough to stop Ravi Uppal's step into politics, but the circumstantial evidence and plausible connections to murder could never stand up in court." Chaitanya's smile broadened and he leaned further forward, conspiratorially. "But..."

"You have something," said Sudhesh with some excitement.

"Yes!" said Chaitanya. "I will tell you a story. A few days ago, a whole family were brutally murdered. The remains of the mother, maid and two sons were found dumped in a well in the garden. The house belongs to Vasupati Chopra..."

"Uppal's partner?" asked Sudhesh.

"Yes," continued Chaitanya. "And Chopra is missing. According to you he is pursuing Anil Gupta in order to kill him and stop any link being made between Cobra Investments and criminal activity. But, of course, that is a tough tale to believe. Until, that is, a young detective discovered a cache of items at the Chopra home. Tell me, have you heard of a serial killer the media refer to as Kāla?"

"No," said Sudhesh. "What of him?"

"Well, he is irregular in his killings, but distinct in his calling card. Each of his victims are found with a metal medallion of Shiva on their person. Up until the Chopra killings we had nothing to focus on, then Detective Prabhu found a pile of them in a bronze urn mixed with some interesting effects from a selection of murder victims, this at the Chopra house. Four medallions were flung down the well with the bodies."

"So, they may have been the victim of this serial killer?" said Sudhesh.

"Yes," said Chaitanya sitting back. "Vasupati Chopra's study is full of Shiva images and collected personal effects of at least seven victims, but only one of these give witness to its owner. The passport of one Lalit Mahto – a retired pilot who was killed in his home in Agra. *And* he was a Cobra client."

"Are you saying Uppal is linked to this?" asked Sudhesh.

"Inspector Ram Singh and his team have stumbled across more. The finger prints on a tyre leaver at Anil Gupta's house matched those of a man found dead of a drug overdose a few days later. We initially thought this was a closed case and the murderer had died by accident, until a Shiva medal turned up in his pocket wrapped in two one thousand-rupee notes. Right now, Detectives Prabhu and Kaur are sifting the evidence gathered at crime scenes linked to your family, Cobra, or both. We have Chopra's prints which may well match those found at the Mahto house, but there is a lot to go through. I can say Ravi Uppal may stall us on the fraud case, but that would be a secondary felony compared to complicity in murder!"

"And my cousins?" asked Sudhesh.

"Prabhu, Kaur and Singh will leave no stone unturned, old friend," said Chaitanya. "But I have not finished. A murdered private detective has turned up with a Shiva medallion in his mouth. His partner had driven out to find him on instruction of his boss, one Mehmet Suliman of the Suliman Intelligence Agency, also the victim's uncle. Suliman is raging and says his nephew had been helping a Mr Vaida of Cobra Investments. The victim had been shot in the face. We think Chopra and Vaida are one and the same. This murdered detective's body was found by Indira Sagar south of Bhopal!"

"Where Anil fled to after the fire," said Sudhesh breathlessly.

"Quite," said Chaitanya. "So, your version of the fire and escape by Anil Gupta, and his insistence of being pursued by Cobra's assassin, Vasupati Chopra, looks pretty real right now. Ravi Uppal is to be arrested in the morning."

"And what of Chopra?" asked Sudhesh.

"He is prime suspect in at least four murders," stated Chaitanya matter-of-factly. "He will be arrested on sight!"

"But Anil has no chance against this man," said Sudhesh in despair. "We must help him."

"Where is he?" asked Chaitanya.

"I do not know," said Sudhesh.

"No," said the Commissioner standing. "After Bhopal he disappears, and that seems to be his plan, from what you have said. Unless we find some trace of Vasupati Chopra, Anil Gupta is on his own."

In the back of the Queen Lizzie, an enthralled Nawal listened to a surreal conversation.

"Och, come on now laddie," said MacKeeg. "This is the part in which we discover if we be soldiers on a mission, or useless excuses for a man."

"I know, MacKeeg," said Mr Gupta, "but up until now we have just been running. Now I will discover if the plan, such as it ever was, is working. What if Vaz is in Delhi? What if Sudhesh has failed to find a hearing ear? Have my friends already become victims of my failure?"

"Just keep in mind what y'know," said MacKeeg. "Uppal and Chopra killed Kiran and wanted ye dead. And Rupa, by-the-way. Y'should call Jhatish first. It was his task to take Rupa to safety, so he will know what is happening. I will guide ye when it is Uppal and Chopra's turn."

"It is time," Nawal said.

Jhatish sat in a large, airy lounge on the ground floor of the main house of Alakapuri. Sudhesh had called him frequently from Delhi updating him as to the progress of the destruction of Ravi Uppal. Close by, Rupa was sitting in her chair staring out at the distant forested hills. She had become quiet and Sarasa fussed about her, but Rupa's usually constant high spirits had been dulled. She was anxious about her father. She knew he was far beyond any help and thus sacrificing himself for her safety. It was a fight he could not possibly win. Rupa had refused to be defined by her condition – it was what it was and no bar to her intellect – but now her inability to function in an able-bodied world made her feel helpless.

"Uncle Jhatish?" she said. "I have tried to screw up my eyes and bring William MacKeeg to me, but there is nothing there. I concentrated so hard. I feel if I can summon him he may tell me all is well. Will I ever see Daddy again?"

Jhatish snapped out of a reverie. He had seen the sadness building.

"I cannot answer that, Rupa," he said. "As for this Scottish fellow, well, he belongs to your father. You know that. The odd thing is it makes me feel Anil is safe. He is...hmm, it is hard to say..."

"Different," stated Rupa. "He killed the bad man, didn't he?"

"Yes," said Jhatish. "Your father has been three men. With Kiran he was quietly happy, one of a pair. After... After he was alone he kept his gentleness but seemed lost, though no less devoted to you. But now, since his illness, he has become something new. This thing in his head has produced a man who knows his future is short, and that would destroy most, yet with Anil it has made him stronger. Rupa, I do not think we will see your father again, but he is righting some terrible wrongs. He could have left it to the police, but then you both would have died. How he figured that out I do not know, and how he bettered a hired assassin? It is beyond me. He..." Jhatish choked on his words for a moment. "He has started to destroy Ravi Uppal. That foulest of men. It is Chopra who scares me. Your father is his target and what will happen is in the hands of the gods. No, I think we will not see him again, but he will call us, of that I am in no doubt."

Rupa wept. Jhatish wiped her face, kissed her head and saw such grief in her eyes his heart melted. At this moment he knew how Mr Gupta had found the strength to make his startling transformation ready to avenge great wrongs. To commit murder was heinous beyond words, but to rob a child of hope, love and innocence, to dull that spark of joyfulness, just for money, was unforgivable. Jhatish was not given to anger, yet hoped his friend would succeed in the physical destruction of Vasupati Chopra. Before he could form words of comfort, the phone rang.

Whilst Tsering busied himself with the communication equipment, Mr Gupta paced up and down in the dust with Nawal looking on.

"Are you a sadhu?" asked a soft voice.

Mr Gupta had been accosted by a group of five small children – two tiny, naked tots; two larger girls who looked like twins; and an older boy of perhaps six. It was the boy who had spoken.

"I suppose I am," said Mr Gupta.

"To be with Nawal Ji, you must be very wise," continued the boy. "Can you do blessings?"

"This is Arnesh Ji," said Nawal. "He is a very important sadhu, for he rids the world of sadness. His blessings are rarely given as he needs his energy to fight bad things. Arnesh Ji can deliver the sweetest of blessings."

The children goggled.

"Do you want your *special bag*?"

The question was addressed to Mr Gupta, who caught the other's wink.

"Have you all been good children?" asked Mr Gupta, warming to the task.

"Yes!" came three voices, the tots being too small to utter more than moist squeaks.

"Then I think the special bag is in order."

Nawal fished in his robes and produced a white paper bag, handing it to Mr Gupta. Inside was a mass of sticky boiled sweets of various colours. He looked down at the shiny faces and his heart swelled with emotion. Such little things with the whole of life ahead, standing in the dust waiting for a sweet.

"As you are all good children I give you the blessing of sweet things," intoned Mr Gupta. He handed the bag to the older boy. "You must share these equally with the others as you are the oldest and have that duty. Do you understand?"

"Oh yes sir," said the boy carefully taking the bag. "Thank you. Will you be here tomorrow?"

"It is already tomorrow," said Mr Gupta absently.

"Then you will be," said the boy running off, followed by his little tribe.

Mr Gupta watched as the children sat under a nearby tree and was pleased to see the older boy sharing the sweets out.

"Such is life," said Nawal. "A few sweets and the world is right. Then along comes dogma, superstition and the gods, children become adults and, I fear, rather hopeless."

"So, I am a sadhu?" said Mr Gupta.

"More than that, Arnesh Ji," said Nawal. "You have taken on a task which, when completed, will remove a nasty blot from humanity's none too savoury record. And you are dying. And you are accompanied by an invisible advisor and remain very sane, which, to me, is fascinating. All of this will become legend."

"Now comes the hardest thing of all," said Mr Gupta. "I must talk to Rupa."

They walked to the truck and collected Mr Gupta's phone. He made the call.

"Hello?" said Jhatish.

"It is me," said Mr Gupta.

"Anil?" said Jhatish. "My goodness, it is you! How are you? Where are you? What is happening? Rupa is here. We have been so worried! I ..."

"My dearest friend," said Mr Gupta, "please stay calm. I will answer all your questions, but first can Rupa hear me?"

"Yes, I will put the speaker on," said Jhatish. "There, now Rupa can hear."

"Rupa?" said Mr Gupta. "My darling girl, are you alright?"

"Yes Daddy," she replied. "I have missed you. This whole thing seems unreal."

"I know. I know," said Mr Gupta. "You need to know I am well and being looked after by some nice people. They are pilgrims, of a sort, and they have given me a new name – Arnesh Ji."

"Why?" asked Jhatish.

"Because it helps keep me anonymous, to a point, but it is of no matter," said Mr Gupta. "This is so difficult for me. I do not know what time I have left, but need to know how things are there."

"Sudhesh has been marvellous," said Jhatish. "He hates Ravi Uppal and there is more than enough evidence to ruin him. He is to be arrested!"

Could it have been so easy? Mr Gupta dismissed that thought. It had taken a foiled murder plot and the miracle of MacKeeg to bring things to this point. His own life was forfeit whatever eventually happened.

"Will the charges stick, do you think?" he asked.

"I am sure they will," said Jhatish. "The memory stick gave the key to unlocking his fraudulent actions, but it is the link to murder that will do for him."

"Murder?" said Mr Gupta, incredulous. "How?"

Jhatish talked him through the events unravelling at the now notorious Chopra home. Sudhesh had initially phoned updates through to Alakapuri, but now the local media were creating headlines about the charnel house, with graphic descriptions, both factual and fictitious. The local Chief Inspector, Ram Naresh Singh, had appeared on the television with the Police Commissioner, linking the killings with a long sought serial killer and their search for the main suspect, Vasupati Chopra.

"And this has touched Ravi?" asked Mr Gupta.

"Yes, that is what I meant," said Jhatish. "Ravi Uppal's new political profile with the IPU and his ownership of Cobra Investments has given reporters plenty to speculate about now that Chopra is being sought. One paper even predicts the arrest!"

"So, Vaz has helped to bring Ravi down," said Mr Gupta. "I never thought he was capable of killing his own family. Why would he do that?"

"No one seems to know," said Jhatish, aware that an even greater weight had descended upon his friend's shoulders. "Whatever comes of this I think it is time you came home. Chopra must be in hiding by now. If he was innocent, he would have given himself up. You have won Anil, you have won!"

The words were left in the air unanswered and Jhatish knew his friend would not return. Anil Gupta was far removed from the man he had been.

Jhatish could not bear the silence. "Is it revenge?" he asked.

More silence.

"Daddy?" said Rupa. "I love you and want you here before the end. But I know what you have to do and do not know how you can defeat such a man. If he killed so many, including his own family, and has no fear, nor conscience, how can you match him?"

Mr Gupta sighed and his other voice answered.

"Calm yourself lassie," said MacKeeg. "Ye know the one advantage we have is Chopra's underestimation of me. And, Jhatish, it is not about revenge alone. This Chopra is affronted and will not stop until he catches up. Then he will kill me, if he can. If he does then everyone else will become a target, Rupa first. Weigh it all up. Do we gamble that the authorities will find him? Or do we destroy him on our terms? Killing me will be a provable murder, so my death may still hold the key. And I am an old soldier, ye remember that."

"You are not real!" cried Rupa. "I want my Daddy!"

Her father spoke.

"My darling, dearest girl," he said softly. "I love you more than life, of that have no doubt. I loved your mother so too. I do not understand what has happened to me, but it is the tumour that seems to have set my course. It is too late to stop its progress. Mr Radhika was optimistic at first, but knew surgery would have at best diminished me and that would not have stopped Ravi. Without this other me, this deep insight, this extended, doubled mind I see as MacKeeg, we would have been in the gravest peril. At least I have managed to start the destruction of Cobra in its entirety. Uncle Sudhesh is by default your new guardian, and is happy to be so, and dear Jhatish joint executor of my estate. I should have trusted my family to him from the start, but hindsight is always brightest at a distance. To hear you in such distress is enough to make me come home, but I would then bring death back with me. You know that. With MacKeeg I have the chance to avenge your mother's *murder* – that word is so hard to say – but it was Uppal and Chopra who carried this out, without question. What I did not realise was that Chopra is a twisted creature. He seems to love killing. I cannot believe he has killed his own little ones.

"I cannot come home, my darling girl. I can make a promise, however. I will make sure that my friends bring word to you of my passing. I am not frightened any more. Darling Rupa, I have found courage and a rage I could never have before imagined. I will use it to bring Vasupati Chopra to book. Your role in this is to be strong for me, darling girl. I do not know if I can go on without your understanding… I really do not. I need that strength."

Jhatish remained quiet, wiping Rupa's face. She sat slumped in her chair listening, the burden of her condition bearing her down. Jhatish expected more histrionics once the gravity of what his friend had said to his daughter found its mark. In this there was a glimmer of hope, as he felt the outpouring of emotion would be too great to ignore and Mr Gupta would return. Then Rupa sat up and all had changed. She smiled at him.

"Always bubbles!" she laughed. "Wipe!"

He did and sorrow disappeared.

"Daddy," she said, "are your new friends nice?"

"Why, yes," said Mr Gupta. "And I trust them."

"Then you must make sure the whole story is told to us here. I am not little anymore and think I can cope, but only if I know your story. So your friends must promise."

"They do," said Mr Gupta. "Nawal Ji of the Kuru ki Kvark is beside me and will keep this promise."

"Then you must do this thing for all of us," said Rupa with renewed resolve. "Keep me and Mummy inside your head with MacKeeg and we will be indestructible."

"Thank you, Rupa," he said. "Jhatish, keep Sudhesh in the picture. Vaz is some miles behind, but I will entice him on. I will try to call again from the Sahyadri. Goodbye for now."

"I will keep the promise," said Nawal. "The next two calls will be easier."

"I have MacKeeg and Rupa's blessing," said Mr Gupta. "Let us see what an old chap can achieve."

IPU Party Chair, Manish Patel had flown in to Delhi gripping a copy of the Times of India. In the Political Supplement the IPU, Cobra Investments, Ravi Uppal and a serial killer, probably one Vasupati Chopra, had been woven together under the disturbing headline, *IPU Linked to*

Delhi's Underworld. Dr Pallab Bhanot, the party's biggest sponsor, met him in Arrivals and they went together to the waiting car. In the short journey to party headquarters they had reached the same conclusion about Ravi Uppal – deselection and damage limitation. The once golden boy was too hot to handle. A press release was authorised immediately. Ranjit Kumar Roy had phoned Ravi with the news that morning and, in a terse exchange, it was made clear that any political friendships had now been severed. His dreams of power had disappeared, literally overnight.

Ravi Uppal sat in his spacious garden. He watched the striped squirrels on his lawn and the house crows quartering the ground amongst them. Yet his mind was elsewhere. This, for the moment, was his whole world. A dragonfly, large and clattering, landed on a chair and swivelled its head around looking for prey. Ravi was sipping a large glass of Talisker Single Malt with ice, something he seldom did in the working day. His eyes were puffy through lack of sleep and he felt traumatised. He could not grasp unfolding events. He stared at the dragonfly trying to focus his thoughts. After the cryptic, unhinged comments of his last call Vaz had simply disappeared. Ranjit Kumar Roy had publicly denounced him and the news from the Chopras' home was devastating. Ravi could control many things, yet the media were unstoppable. This had been what had done for him. He was sure the police had leaked information to the news corporations, resulting in the sudden rash of stories linking serial killers and every unrelated, unprovable crime to Cobra. The newspaper headlines were only limited by the reporters' wild imaginations.

Earlier, Jyoti had called to tell him the office had been sealed off by the police. An armed guard had been posted and several men were inside – an IT specialist unit, so she was informed. Vaz's madness had made everything he had erased irrelevant. No one could second guess insanity. He told her to go home and take a few days leave. Before he had time to do anything else, three vehicles came up his long drive, two police jeeps and a large, unmarked saloon. Inspector Ram Singh and his partner Detective Kaur introduced themselves. Suneeti had been chivvied to a lounge with their son and a nervously smiling Ravi had received them in his large, airy office overlooking his extensive grounds.

"What can I help you with, Inspector?" had been Ravi's first question.

The next hour was an impossible nightmare. This dumpy man knew more about Vasupati Chopra than Ravi did. Much, much more. He talked about links to a serial killer and, worst of all, Lalit Mahto, all the time circling the space left by Vaz. Vaz was a killer and these two interrogators had proof enough to have him arrested on sight, or shot dead in the process. And each revelation was ended with a direct question as to what Ravi knew. Denial was king, qualified in answers carefully spoken, gently easing the guilt onto his partner. Where Inspector Singh paused, his stony-faced companion asked for confirmatory information, especially when Ravi prevaricated. They had kept him on edge all through the interview, but he felt he had handled things quite well. Then Inspector Singh had dropped a bombshell.

"We have in our possession new information, originally from Anil Gupta. It is data on the finances of Fallen Angels. This has already been studied by the Shastri banking accountants, upon our behest, and the results passed on to Commissioner Ghosh. Tell me, do you know where Mr Gupta is?"

"And," added Detective Kaur, "is Mehmet Suliman's accusations of you and Vasupati Chopra being involved in the murder of his nephew based on any sort of fact?"

Ravi Uppal's resolve had crumbled.

"I want to talk to my lawyer," was all he could think of saying.

As Ravi mulled over events, a pied bird swooped down from a tree and snatched the drowsing dragonfly from its perch. He could hear the click of its snapping beak. Then it flew to a nearby shrub and impaled the doomed insect onto a thorn, legs still kicking whilst life expired. It was a long-tailed shrike which Ravi knew in his childhood as a butcher bird. He remembered telling Vaz how being a hunter was the only way to succeed, how dragonflies dominated the space, but this bird had confounded his metaphor. That policeman, Inspector Singh, had been just like this butcher bird and, somehow, Tamina and Kiran Shastri had provided the thorn. Above all, Anil Gupta had proved deadlier than his psychopathic partner, which was still an unpalatable truth. He hoped Vaz killed him. He poured another drink. For now, under house arrest, all he could do was plan an escape – somehow. His phone played Wagner's Ride of the Valkyries, a tune that now seemed overly pretentious in his present situation. He did not recognise the number, hesitated, sipped his drink, and then answered.

"Ravi Uppal."

"You should never have been so greedy," said Mr Gupta.

"You!" was all Ravi Uppal could manage.

"You took Kiran from me, for what?"

"What have you done, Anil?" gasped Ravi. "After all I have done for you!"

Mr Gupta laughed. "You killed my wife and nearly killed my daughter. You want me to be grateful for that? The ruination coming to you is earned, Ravi, but it is secondary."

"You bastard!" shouted Ravi, temper surfacing swiftly from a river of alcohol. "I will get out of this! You'll see! Data can be falsified. There is no evidence against me that will stick – it can be construed as a set-up."

"Sudhesh Shastri may not see you dead, but, mark my words, your dreams will be erased, stupid, greedy man," said Mr Gupta. MacKeeg added, "Ye are a piece o'shite and not worth a tinker's fart!"

"I hope Vaz guts you!" raged Ravi. "Kiran was nothing but a fool and you are worse, because you lived on to waste your miserable life. Nothing will stick, you'll see! When Vaz gets there remember as you die, I am still here!"

"Och, ye are a coward," said MacKeeg. "Ye could never do the job yourself, not even women!"

Ravi felt the sting of truth, but ranted on, "Power means delegation, Gupta. I delegated, Vaz acted. You will die, whether it is the tumour or Vasupati Chopra. He has no conscience and is no longer mine to control, but he is after you. Relentless and unstoppable. But think of this, I will remove Rupa when you are gone, as I did my bitch wife and her ridiculous sister. Live with that!"

It was Mr Gupta's unaltered voice that answered.

"You are nothing," he said. "You will hear nothing more from me."

The line went dead. Ravi Uppal finished his whisky and rubbed his eyes. Looking up he saw a short, squat figure walking towards him. The butcher bird flew off.

"Ravi Uppal," said Inspector Singh. "Modern technology is wonderful and these mobile devices makes listening in so easy. A court sanctioned surveillance warrant allows me to say, you are under arrest for involvement in the murders of Tamina Uppal, née Shastri, and Kiran Gupta, née Shastri. Anything you say..."

Two large policemen waited to take Ravi away.

In Jalna, Sachet Engineer was sitting quietly in his hotel room looking out at India bustling by. He had just checked his bank account and nodded with approval at his new balance. Vasupati Chopra had been quick to pay his dues, yet Engineer was not happy. A few enquiries gave him the bad news that the man killed was related to Mehmet Suliman. Engineer would have to stay ahead of the game. He had no faith that Vaz could make a rational decision, but also knew he could gain a lot more in financial bonuses if he stuck with it. Engineer decided to take out insurance. He called Mehmet Suliman.

"Suliman," growled the voice on the other end of the phone.

"It is Engineer."

Silence. Then an exhalation of breath.

"I am in no mood for talking to you," said Suliman's. "You of all people! The Engineer has always been trusted so how can you be involved in my nephew's execution?"

Engineer stayed calm.

"You know this is not my style. I had nothing to do with the killing. I just accepted a job from Chopra, as I've done before, but this time with him, not for him. Something is wrong here, Mehmet, very wrong."

"You are telling me," growled Suliman. "Ravi Uppal is in great trouble, but that is not the point. Did you know Chopra's family have all been murdered?"

"Bloody hell!" he managed, genuinely shocked. "Who..."

"Chopra killed them, so I have discovered," said Suliman. "He is to be arrested and charged. He is insane, Engineer, totally rat-shit mad."

"I am so sorry," said Engineer. "In this business there are risks, but right now I am a little, shall we say, *compromised*."

There was a pause.

"Kill him for me," said Suliman. "Prove your worth. No one else knows you are part of this. I will let it be known you have been sent to apprehend my nephew's killer. I will pay you twenty thousand dollars American. If not, I will bring you down with Chopra."

Engineer let the threat hang in the air and ignored it. He was not scared of Suliman, but knew his own reputation was at stake. Also, being paid twice was very attractive.

"I would want half the money now," Engineer said. "Killing a man like Vasupati Chopra is not so easy."

"I will wire the money in the next hour if you agree," growled Suliman. "Half now, half when you prove to me he's dead. And do not cross me, Engineer, you hear?"

"Deal," said Engineer. "I will send the account details and check the deposit this evening."

"When will you do it?" asked Suliman.

"Once we are away from prying eyes," said Engineer. "I think the fellow we are chasing will lead us to the right place."

Whilst Engineer negotiated his new contract, Vaz lay naked in the half-light of his curtained room. The dominance of the Kāla mind was total and worms no longer writhed out the rhythm of conflicting halves. He lay mumbling the words of the prophet, Zahan.

"He will stop the World turning. He can make himself Demon or Angel. In gigantic form He reaches the all of mankind's realm. He is all pasts and all futures. He can kill and resurrect. He hears the thoughts from other worlds. He is Kāla and He is all of us, our Hive Mind.

Zahan had channelled the rhythms of the Zoroastrian past into the consciousness of a deranged psychopath. Somewhere in Vasupati Chopra's dysfunctional brain, Zahan's words meshed with partially remembered pieces of the Bhagavad-Gita, giving the foundation for the irreversible emergence of Kāla-Vaz. He had needed a reason to give in to his homicidal desires without moral conflict, and he had found it. He was God! God is the creator, owner and dictator of morals with no one to answer to, which meant he could choose to give in to capricious desire as he wished. Using such one-dimensional logic, as Kāla-Vaz he was convinced he held the power over death and life, with the ability to recreate his family when his war with humanity was won. Vaz's insatiable desire to kill was now an unquestionable, self-ordained right. Engineer was on his guard, but even he could hardly appreciate just how volatile Vaz was.

The phone buzzed. Vaz stirred, soft light from the street picked out the blue staining around his throat and neck. He stretched out an arm, grabbed the phone, saw *Gupta* in the caller I.D. and answered.

"Speak," he said.

"Ravi Uppal is starting to pay his dues," said Mr Gupta. "It is nearly time you met your end Vasupati Chopra."

Vaz sat upright and swung around to sit on the edge of the bed.

"I await your instructions," he said, calmly.

"I know you are mad," Mr Gupta continued. "I know you are a mindless murderer, but to slay your own family puts you in a class of depravity uniquely your own. You have a chance to survive – run whilst you can."

"Your death is required, little man. I will come to you – *Only Angels defeat Death...*"

"To the sea, Vasupati Chopra, to the sea."

"Where are you, Gophapa?"

"Head towards Miraj and ye will be in the right place to reach me," came the other voice. "Fear only for thyself, Vasupati Chopra."

This last pierced the calm.

"I will destroy you!" raged Vaz, voice hissing, spittle flying. "All will end with you and the world can start again!"

Laughter was the only answer. For a moment Vasupati Chopra thought his prey may be possessed.

Evening in Jalna gave way to night. The moon was waning and soft clouds scudded across its bright gibbous face which reflected in the Kundalika River. Lights from high rise blocks added faux stars to the aqueous scene as families prepared to retire to soft beds. All-encompassing India tucked the poor and homeless around the affluents' town houses, moths to a flame of riches – close enough to touch, proximity giving wealth the role of a hoped-for beneficent infection. Nestled amongst the trees, night sleepers curled under ragged covers, discomfort numbed by cheap alcohol. After midnight few people wandered in wakefulness. By the river, a half-naked holy man was sitting cross-legged, meditating beside his worldly goods — a clay dish, wooden staff and sandals. The moonlight was strong at the river's edge, away from the blackness beneath the trees. Vishnu was pouring brightness upon him, lifting his mind away from his frail body. A shadow fell across his bearded face, not fleeting, but persistent, breaking the man's inward focus. Flickering eyelids opened, revealing the dark silhouette of a shadow-man. Hints of blue sparkled where its eyes would be.

"Peace," whispered the holy man.

An iron hand clasped his throat killing more words aborning. Lifted with gravity-defying strength, a hunting knife pierced his abdomen. The pain overrode his fall to the silver washed ground, where a slimy, puddling blackness grew. With failing vision, he saw the figure loom over him, moonlight flashing on blue-lit eyes. *A demon has killed me*, was his last viable thought. Something metallic and sour grated between his teeth as pain left and life fled into darkness.

Chapter 29

All Roads Lead

The tigress walked alone along the river and entered a side valley at the centre of her territory. The big male had remained with her for days and would be the sire of her cubs. She was no longer in oestrus. She felt the change in her body and the male had become excess to requirements. She had driven him off with fierce growls and swipes with her claws. Angaar's interest had waned with her enchanting scent.

Angaar was tired. A young male, smaller, but charged with the desire to mate, had also been drawn to the female's territory and had challenged him on many occasions. Angaar's size alone had kept the young pretender at bay, but wounds around his neck and face showed he had not been unscathed. Now, primal instincts sated, he walked slowly upwards panting in the humid air, his mind a confusion of foggy scent-memories. His stomach hurt. There were no stimuli to give him direction and as he left the forest for higher, scrubby, rock-strewn ground, he sniffed the air. No smell of clever monkey – sour enemy or sweet, spicy friend – nor enticing female, nothing but mountain air laced with the odour of dry grass and a faint waft of ozone.

"*Geerumph!*" he sighed quietly.

His breathing eased and his thin flanks stilled as he turned west between some stunted trees on the edge of the deep valley. A deer barked and he turned his head towards the far sound. This was when the young male charged from higher ground, down wind and undetected. Angaar turned quickly, not freezing at the ferocious roar, taking the impact in the left shoulder, the momentum knocking both tigers down the slope. The roaring stopped suddenly as they hit a rocky outcrop the impact throwing them apart. This saved Angaar's life. The young male had broken a rib which punctured a lung and left him panting in the dust; his broken body had cushioned his old rival from serious harm. Angaar was spent, gasping in air and sneezing as he stood on sagging legs. Blood dripped from new wounds, the red drops displacing little plumes of dust as they hit the ground. He knew his foe had suffered a mortal injury, could smell the faecal stench of a released sphincter, so, without a glance walked into the cover of trees. Monkeys scolded as he lay in a cool thicket protected from the sun by the green canopy. He slept.

It was full dark when he awoke. His stomach pulsed with a dull ache which had become a constant companion. Thirst raked his throat driving the pain of his wounds into a far corner of acceptance. He rose and stretched, muscles popping along his back. His hind legs sagged a little. Nearby he found a muddy pool and lapped gritty water. Then he defecated leaving a scat, shiny with slime and wet with dark blood. His legs sagging anew. He bent around and licked as his haunches, unsure of where the discomfort lay. Angaar was dying. With an effort he stood and walked out into the open, stomach growling as hunger pangs added to his distress. The night was still and silver-washed by the bright gibbous moon. It was quiet on the ridge as Angaar stopped to taste the air. Nothing but faint residues of long passed prey, moist vegetation and that salty hint from somewhere beyond the hills. He panted again and sank into the grass to cool his belly. His rest was disturbed by a frantic buzzing. A cloud of flies, shiny in the moon's glow, had begun to work on his dead rival's carcass. As soon as Angaar approached, flies settled upon his fresh wounds, causing him to sneeze and shake his great head. He hesitated, instinctively knowing the meat would not taste sweet, but finally gave in to cavernous hunger.

The calls Mr Gupta made from the small village near Ganagapur had exhausted him. The tumour felt like a loose weight behind his left eye – large, malignant and inescapable. His new friends made sure he wanted for nothing, but they could see he was ailing and they were worried. He slept a dreamless sleep for a full afternoon and night under a colourful awning on a comfortable bed of cushions and blankets. Talika never left Mr Gupta's side, holding his hand through the night. He had become special to her; his story of incredible courage in the face of unimaginable grief, had mirrored her own past. Her flight had no obvious end; his had the greater burden of imminent, inescapable death, even if he was successful in his unlikely quest. Death followed him and death waited – running from one drew him closer to the other – and he carried death in that tumour in his head. As she had held him through that long night at Seraraya, his febrile narrative from that other world had given her insight to what a struggle he was bound to each and every day. The echo of the long dead Kiran telling him he was strong enough to carry this onerous task through, proved to her the strength she had seen had not been an illusion. That Talika's journey had brought her to the same point in time as Mr Gupta, Arnesh Ji as she now thought of him, made her smile at the impossibility of trying to understand life. She squeezed his hand as thoughts of her life grew bright in her mind.

Talika had been an English teacher before her marriage to a local rich man, her senior by many years, who fell for her looks, but was dismissive of her intellect. Her job was to produce children. Had she done this it would have sufficed as a future, but her husband had been both impotent and cruel, the one directly linked to the other. He had loved her beauty, then hated her for it. He became jealous of other men's glances and graduated from cold, cutting remarks, to direct assaults. His family turned against her, considering barrenness a curse. Her life became bleak and desperate, until the night she watched him die. He had taken to twisting her arm and pinching her cheeks during his frequent, frustration-borne outbursts. On this fateful evening he had returned home drunk and angry. Talika was alone in their great house, the servants having a rare night off, so she bore the full force of his poor humour. He ranted into her face about her worthless housekeeping, useless family and fictitious whoring. Spittle flew as he raged and pursued her tearful retreat into the kitchen where, cornered by a violent man, she pushed him but once in the chest. He stepped back and toppled, eyes rolling and face a rictus of shock, rage, and then fear. His heart had reached a crescendo and the pressure had burst his aorta. He sank clutching his chest mouthing the word *please* before slowly, very slowly, giving up his life. Talika just watched, making no effort to save or comfort him. He left her nothing from his vast estate, so she had fled with only curses and vitriol in her ears.

Though not old, in most people's eyes she was an outcast. A penniless widow was of no use in a patriarchal society. Being a part of the *Kuru ki Kvark* had given her a new life in which she was treated as an equal. Her body had not yet succumbed to the winding down of her biological clock, so submitting to this gentle, brave man had felt perfectly natural. She was comforting mother and, amazingly to her, willing lover, even if she had been taken as the vision of another. Talika had little truck with fate, but helping Arnesh Ji had given her a spike of personal redemption in the unfulfilled life she had led.

The journey south began at dawn. Mr Gupta was helped onto the Queen Lizzie in a fugue state. They were heading for the Sahyadri where the village of Karukula lay high in the valley below Mount Karoo, which marked the trail to the hidden beach. Through the long journey, Mr Gupta remained oblivious to what was happening. As the mountain hove into view his friends took stock.

"I am worried," growled Puneet.

"You must be to talk in daylight," said Nawal. "What do you think Vam?"

"Rest is good," said the little man. "He will eventually succumb to this tumour, but his eyes react to light and all his vital signs are good."

"He is thin now," said Nawal, "and looks every part the sadhu with that ragged beard. But you are right Vam, he does not look like a dying man. It is almost like a hibernation."

"I think he is regaining his strength," said Talika. "I have sat with him and watched. Look, he is dreaming now. You can see his eyes move beneath the lids. Before he seemed to be comatose."

"I wonder what world he is in?" said Puneet.

Mr Gupta saw blackness segue to grey as his surroundings registered. He was standing on the white beach beneath that surreal night sky with its huge moon and planets. Bright stars shone and all were reflected in the calm sea washing the shore. The awful ache in his head had gone and he felt rested. William MacKeeg sat nearby on the usual rock smoking his blue-burning pipe. A breeze whispered in Mr Gupta's hair and it felt cool across his skin. He realised he held a staff on his left hand, a straight branch stripped of bark, smooth and comforting to lean on. He felt changed again.

"Ye are killing dragons, laddie," said MacKeeg blowing out a plume of smoke. "We are near the beginning of our last journey and I think y'will be ready."

"We have come this far together," said Mr Gupta. "You have kept me alive and turned me into a murderer. It is hard to believe poor old Mr Gupta can be such a thing."

MacKeeg laughed, "Nay, nay laddie. Not a murderer. I have made ye a soldier!"

Mr Gupta settled beside his friend. Looking out at the silver-etched horizon he realised it did not matter one way or the other, so long as the dragon he killed was Vasupati Chopra. Somewhere in his mind he knew that they approached Mount Karoo and from there he would find a killing ground. And, of course, his dying ground. The spangled sea darkened and clouds swirled and grew, pushing a storm before it. Mr Gupta's hair flowed back as the breeze increased and the air chilled. He knew what was coming.

"Is it him again?" he asked absently.

"Aye."

"Hold fast?"

"Aye again."

Mr Gupta stood and walked a few paces and turned to the wind.

"I have nothing to say to you!" His new energy projected his voice over the whole world. "Killer of women! Killer of children! Craven, black-hearted coward! I – will – kill – thee!"

The clouds grew black and swirled faster, driving the sky back into the universe, stars dimming, planets retreating. The moon grew red. As the clouds touched the water a swirling black hole grew from which the demon rose, massive and dark with cold, blue burning eyes firing shafts of light across all time. The blood-moon tinged the sea-sparkles with crimson as the grotesque figure stood. In one clawed hand it held a scimitar, in the other a cluster of severed heads which it lifted high, necks dripping into tainted water. Mr Gupta's mind reeled and his strength wavered as he looked into the faces swinging above him; the rolled-up, dead eyes and lifeless flesh retained enough features to register. He knew them! Some already dead, some still alive: Kiran; Tamina; a woman and children; Rupa and Jhatish. But the horror had not finished. As the heads slowly revolved his own face came to the fore, pale and putrid, wriggling with black, worm-like threads, tongue lolling. The eyes rolled down and stared at him as the ruined lips moved and a croaking voice spoke.

"So will you end! You are mine to harvesssst..."

The sibilant utterance echoed, a sound which filled the universe. The demon began to wade towards the beach, sword rising.

"Your mind throws up some real nightmares, laddie. Why don't ye tell it to fuck off!" suggested MacKeeg.

"Get the bloody hell away!" shouted Mr Gupta. "This is only your idea of my future, demon. In mine you will harvest nothing but your own death!"

"Nay bad," said MacKeeg. "But now ye have pissed it off."

The world exploded into a kaleidoscope of colour and the universe drew close again – moon, stars and planets filled the sky. The demon was gone.

"It has gone," said Mr Gupta.

"*Get the bloody hell away?*" mimicked MacKeeg, grinning. "Ye would never make a Glaswegian! Look yonder."

There was a dark mass further along the beach. Deep tracks led from the sea to where it lay like a huge, polished, black rock, the moonlight picking out hints of emerald. The amorphous shape moved and unwound from its matrix, a long tail and neck lifted from the sand and four clawed legs hefted the body up into a crocodilian crouch. It was a dragon, the only hint of the demon its glowing blue eyes.

"Bloody hell," moaned Mr Gupta.

"See yon beastie?" said MacKeeg pointing with his pipe. "He is your dragon. All ye have to do is kill it."

"That does not make me feel much better," said Mr Gupta.

The dragon made no move and stood, head cocked to one side as if it were listening. A noise, a shuffling, from the bushes beyond the beach caused Mr Gupta to turn and look. Something was coming and whatever it was had given the dragon pause. With a roar it fled into a wisp of turbulent air. Peace returned and all was calm once more.

"What was coming?" ventured Mr Gupta.

"Nemesis!" said MacKeeg. "How do ye feel?"

"Much, much better. Is it time to wake in the world?"

"Nearly."

"Who is Gophapa?"

"Och. A human sacrifice," said MacKeeg.

"Bloody hell," said Mr Gupta, again.

Everything swirled around him. *Crack!* He was above the Earth gazing down into the blue of the atmosphere. It was such an alien place to be. Yet he felt at peace and knew Kiran was next to him. He felt her hand grasp his and he turned to smile at her beautiful face.

"It is alright my darling," she said. "You can finish this. The monsters were just nightmares – all your fears condensed into pictures – nothing more. You are ready for the journey."

"Yes," he replied, feeling himself tumbling back to consciousness. "Never leave me, Kiran."

As the world span away, he felt her hand still holding his.

"I will always be part of you my darling," came her voice from so far away. "Always here...always here..."

"...here. We are here Arnesh Ji."

Mr Gupta jumped in his sleep, his mind falling through the stratosphere, nothing but air beneath – then firm bed. The smile he had given Kiran remained as he opened his eyes.

"We have reached the Maskrey Plantation," said Talika as she held his hand. "Mount Karoo looks beautiful."

The truck's final juddering halt had dragged Mr Gupta into wakefulness.

"I am hungry," he said sitting up.

"Then you are well," said Talika and she kissed his cheek.

Tsering helped him down. They had parked in a clearing near the main entrance of the large plantation – hundreds of hectares of tea stretched up onto the slopes of Mount Karoo. The entrance had no gates, just a huge archway of stone, brick and carved masonry. Everywhere was green with trees, shrubs and flowering plants; the grass was lush and the steady flow of workers colourful and happy. Various stalls had been set up to take advantage of such lucrative traffic making a small but vibrant market attached to the great estate. Beyond this was a neatly laid out village for the Maskrey employees. A large van was parked nearby emblazoned with the words *Indian Network News - national & international.* They were interviewing a man in an expensive looking blue suit; a white Rolls Royce with waiting chauffeur indicated his importance.

"We are on TV!" growled Puneet, his daylight vow of silence forgotten once more.

They had reached Miraj in record time, had booked into a good hotel and waited on the whims of Mr Anil Gupta. Aktar kept a close eye on Kepi as his young partner had the habit of disappearing into the seedier parts of a town. If sober and not stoned he was a perfect wing man, so a shared room was the only guarantee of keeping him sharp.

Engineer fretted. Vaz had become implacable, taciturn and, ostensibly, tireless. The blue-lensed glasses he wore removed any sign of humanity from his face. Engineer used eyes to keep his edge. Eyes never lied. Reading a target's eyes had saved him more than once. Sitting alone in a back-street restaurant, sipping a post-prandial beer, he pondered his options for killing Vaz. He was spinning Suliman a line about *choosing the ground*, knowing if he completed the Gupta job before executing Vaz, he could have his cake and eat it. Two big paydays. He could not let Aktar and Kepi in on his double deal as they would want a big cut and could resort to blackmail. He was also wise enough to know killing Vaz would be no push over, confident though Engineer was in his own abilities. But. It was that *but* that had made Engineer fret. It was as if the Vasupati Chopra he had previously worked with and for, had been replaced by a simulacrum, devoid of all but basic, muted emotions. Atavistic instincts fired constant warnings into Engineer's nervous system. It was the same feeling as walking into a dark cemetery – knowing you were safe did not stop the unease. Logic didn't always win.

Time's End, World Beginnings echoed through the ear buds of Vaz's phone. He had played the hour-long verse over and over as he lay in the dark. Engineer had been right in his pondering. There was no thread of humanity left in Vaz. Kāla had filled him completely. Even body hair felt wrong for a god, so each night he removed any new growth keeping only his long, raven-black hair – all the gods had long hair, but smooth bodies. The blue dye around his neck had faded a little and in doing so looked more natural. He now decreed Ravi Uppal had been but a key used to unlock the door to Kāla, nothing more. As Kāla-Vaz he was self-governed and free of all the shackles of duty to a master. His psychotic reasoning, driven by the need to kill, had bypassed any moral compass. It supplied him with a dogma underpinned by his own authority as a god: it was a self-perpetuating faith which could never be broken. Engineer had only scratched the surface of how unpredictably dangerous Vaz had become. Kāla-Vaz no longer deliberated about feeding his hunger to kill. He paid each one with his coin, so what more could such feeble creatures desire? One thing he had not sacrificed was caution, however, so he took great care with his choice of victims. He knew the end of time would come and was convinced Anil Gupta's death would restore the world. His was a new beginning for everyone, including his harvested souls – such was his self-justifying mantra. He wanted to kill again soon, and why wait? He dressed and stepped from the hotel into the night.

Kāla's choice was a legless beggar who propelling himself by swinging his shortened body between long, gnarled arms, leg stumps attached to a board: a human tripod of surprising manoeuvrability. As the beggar swept around a dark corner a rock hit him full in the face. He was semi-conscious as he was dragged deeper into the gloom. Then he was briefly weightless before landing on his back in shallow, stagnant water. This shocked him back to consciousness. Broken teeth rattled in his mouth as he gasped for air, blowing out blood and bile. He gasped a single breath. Oxygen sharpened his dulled mind, which struggled for reason and a plan before the weight of a foot pushed him under. A minute of consciousness pre-empted long seconds of relentless, hopeless struggle.

Vaz ate a meal in his room, glancing occasionally at his phone wondering if his god-mind should make it ring. That it would be Gupta, he had no doubt. He turned the television on just to see the World's turmoil. The rolling stories provided a background babble.

...with the exchange of fire across the border in Kashmir...

He ate, and watched, and looked at the phone once more. Could he?

...and political ambitions of Binseswar Maskrey Sah reached a climax in the Karoo regional assembly, after which he spoke to Indian Network News outside his estate.

He thought hard and became sure he could not only change the world, but bend the destiny of men to his advantage. Could he?

...Rajdeep speaking to him earlier this afternoon.

And then his mind registered what his eyes were watching. He was not interested in the interview, but in the background an old, very distinctly painted truck had been parked. A thin man in homespun robes was being helped from the back: the hair was almost white and longer; he was thinner by far. Then the man glanced across at the camera. He could bend destiny! Mr Gupta was at Karoo, at the Maskrey Estate. Today!

Early in the morning the convoy was on the move south. They had the advantage once more.

Chapter 30

Redemption

Seva cried out in his sleep, an anguished keening, followed by a rattling cough. Olaf sat up and crawled over to his slight companion. The lambent light from an oil lamp cast a yellow tinge to the inside of the hut, but it was enough for Olaf to see Seva was in great distress. Dr Mistry had left a general antibiotic for any infection, but announced that the problem was a *virus of some sort, brought on by weakness* which would take a lot of rest to recover from. Seva could not be moved, should be given plenty of clean water and kept at a steady temperature. Dr Mistry said he would return the following day. Olaf knew night-times were the hardest for a patient. He had seen it with injured soldiers: long, endless nights of fear and short tempers, then, magically, all was well as the sun rose. Seva cried again and opened his eyes wide.

"I am scared, Olab," he said. "Angaar will die alone. I cannot find him. I will die here, Olab."

Tears formed in Seva's yellowing eyes, his anguish clear to see. Olaf was amazed that this tiny man could suffer so much, yet only think of his tiger's wellbeing.

"You have to rest and get better," said Olaf. "We can look for yon Angaar when you are on your feet again."

"No!" The shout was emphatic. "I will die here. Promise you will try, Olab, please."

Seva grasped Olaf's wrist in his despair.

"I don't know where I'd look," said Olaf.

"Go to your picture. Find the signs. Promise and I will be happy."

Olaf smiled. He was going to find the beach in his father's photograph, so to look on the way would be no hardship.

"I promise," he said squeezing Seva's hand.

Seva sank back onto his bed and closed his eyes. The rattle in his chest sounded bad and Olaf feared the worst. He opened a flap in his Bergen and pulled out the old, dog-eared picture of his grandfather sitting on a rock by a beach somewhere to the west. On the back, in faded pencil, were the coordinates by which to find it. To get there was not so difficult, and the trails were clear enough, but it had to be on foot. He may be able to pick up the tiger's trail. The least he could do was try. He glanced at Seva again. He had the look of death about him. Olaf had seen this drift from life many times when exhaustion dulls the will to hang on. Sometimes, he knew, getting through that pivotal hard night could make or break a man. Olaf's promise could well have reduced the need for Seva to keep fighting. He stepped out into the grey twilight to watch the sun rise.

"Hello, Olab,"

Anupa was up early leading a goat to pasture. Its bell clonked as it walked, a kid scurried close behind. The sun rose above the horizon, turning the world golden.

"How you doing, Anupa?" he said smiling.

"You are golden again," she said squinting at his silhouetted shape. "Are you here for a hidden purpose? I think you may be."

"Just walking," he replied. "Walking away from bad things."

"You smile and look sad, Olab," she said, face stern, but, he thought, beautiful in its innocence. "Are you in trouble? What bad things?"

He stepped down onto the track and ruffled the goat's neck, chuckling as he moved.

"Booze, battles and bodies," he said stooping to stroke the kid. The mother turned and bleated.

"Do not worry, she is only making sure the baby is safe," said Anupa. "You are a soldier?"

"*Were*," he corrected. "Now I want to find my roots and figure out what difference I can make."

"In India?"

"You ask a lot of questions," he said kindly. "My grandfather served in the Royal Artillery Signallers in Rajasthan between the wars. He was an adventurer and explored the mountains in his down time. There is a secluded beach to the west of here where Robert Clive went ashore when the East Indiaman he was on took refuge in a storm. He was travelling from Bombay to Calcutta. A letter to his family describes it as *strangely peaceful* so he stayed for a few days. Clive recorded the coordinates, so Granddad scribbled them down and found it with his batman. He may have travelled up this valley for all I know. Clive's Beach is not widely known, so I'm hoping it remains *strangely peaceful*."

The goat's bell clonked as it started to browse, the kid suckled, tail a-blur with pleasure.

"When will you leave?"

"I have to wait until Seva is up and about," he said. "He wants me to look for his friend."

"In the hills?"

"Ah so," said Olaf slipping into his vernacular.

"Will he not be in danger?"

Olaf chuckled again and turned to face the dawn.

"Nope," he said. "You see, his friend is a bloody great tiger!"

A further question was stopped by a crash from the hut door. Seva had managed to rise and stagger to the small veranda where he fell heavily.

"Olab!" he gasped staring at the sunlit man. "Your promise!"

Olaf covered the distance to him in three bounds, crouching to hold Seva as blood dripped from his mouth. With surprising strength Seva grabbed Olaf's wrist and stared into his eyes.

"Promise! Do not forget...he is alone..."

"I will look for old Angaar, feller," said Olaf. "A promise to a friend is unbreakable to me. Now let's get you..."

Seva exhaled and his hand fell to the floor. He died quietly in Olaf's arms.

"Booze, battles and bodies," whispered Olaf. A tear formed as he remembered his sorrows, seeking out a reason to justify weeping with grief and regret. The single drop ran down his cheek into his beard.

"You poor feller," he said lowering Seva gently to the floor.

A soft hand touched the damp trail of that single tear. Olaf looked up into Anupa's face and smiled in his sad way.

"Find his friend and find your roots, Olab," she whispered. "Then come back with the story. Promise?"

Olaf nodded. He had now made the same promise twice. What he would do if he found the tiger he was not sure, but, as per his philosophy, he would cross that bridge if he came to it. Olaf stood and looked to the big sun on the horizon. He did glow in the dawn light. Anupa hoped the Great Banyan and the Nilgiris kept her feeling as she did now, foolish though it was. Olaf sighed and turned to the girl beside him. He smiled again.

It amused Nawal that the capricious laws of probability had given rise to belief in fate, superstition and astrology, a faith which controlled many people's lives. He realised this reflected a child-like need to ignore the finality of death. To be told, by authority, one was the beneficiary of a greater being's attention was all that was needed to stop clear thought. He also knew the same people had no real idea of time and the infinite universe, their ignorance being a comfort and bastion against a more severe reality. The analogy he used was of a man concentrating on a single one of the trillions of gut bacteria in his body, bestowing favour upon that fleeting speck whilst ignoring the greater whole. It took blind faith not to see the preposterousness of such wilful ignorance. However, if that faith was strong enough a man could believe in anything he chose, and allow himself to do anything he wanted to impose it upon others.

Vaz was such a man. The second puncture the Shogun suffered outside of Baaghwadi he considered to be the doing of a meddlesome mind. It seemed Anil Gupta had enough power to delay the inevitable, but Vaz remained calm. He felt this was proof of his conviction that he was entering a final battle before the world could be reborn. It was a skewed and terrible logic. Engineer, Aktar and Kepi had taken the wheels down into the town to get the tyres repaired, so Vaz was left watching the sun rise. Kāla was with him.

"*Do you trust them?*" asked Kāla.

"No," answered Vaz. "But men like Engineer live for money, and will do most anything to acquire it. As long as he's paid he will be a good soldier."

"*I do not trust him,*" came the reply. "*He watches you too closely.*"

"We will watch him," said Vaz.

"*I think Engineer would betray us,*" said the voice vibrating in Vaz's skull. "*We must use him, then discard him and his companions.*"

"It will be so, for we have willed it."

Vaz stood in the glow of the morning sun. Mr Gupta's death would spark the Earth's new beginning and nobody could be allowed to get in the way.

Dr Mistry had arrived at first light and was distraught at the news of Seva's death. He examined the body and tutted over the wasted frame. He felt sure pneumonia was to blame, weak as Seva was, and could only wonder at the distance he had managed to travel, sure such effort had sealed his fate. They buried Seva in a grove of mangos overlooking the distant Maskrey Estate, in a grave marked by a cairn of rocks.

"Every time you farm this patch, add another stone for luck," Olaf had said. "He was a nice feller."

All the villagers had helped build the rough memorial. Seva had been buried in his clothes, his cap on his chest. Olaf had placed Seva's old sandals on top of the cairn, weighted with a rock. Since his appearance at the Great Banyan, Olaf's story had already been exaggerated enough to become legend. His size and golden hair, coupled with his gentle nature made him a heroic figure. In the fullness of time his exploits would make Karukula a special place. Seva's cairn would become a shrine for pilgrims who had heard of the converging paths of dreams and fate, and the acting out of a battle between good and evil. The arrival of the Kuru ki Kvark was latterly considered a further portent of the events that followed – *in hindsight*, as Nawal Ji was wont to say with a smile. Whatever tales were woven, Seva's death was merely the prelude to fantastical events.

Dog shuffled up to the head of the narrow track and cocked a leg against the doctor's small motorcycle. He heard the sound of approaching mules, woofed half-heartedly, yawned and settled down to wait. Thus alerted, every other dog took up the chorus to warn the village of approaching visitors. The mules had been hired from the Maskrey Village and carried the Kuru ki Kvark with their supplies, including medication, tools and gifts to help ameliorate any pressure on the villagers' resources. Olaf smiled as he watched the train arrive and the excited clamour of the people who were respectfully glum a short while earlier.

"Olab, you must come and meet the Kvark." Kuldev stood in the doorway his hat in hand as a mark of respect for his guest's recent loss.

"That I will, Kuldev," said Olaf. "Seva is gone so there is nothing more to do."

"You must stay as long as you like," said Kuldev. "The villagers already think you are blessed and lucky, and they tell me to say this."

Olaf picked up his picture of his grandfather on the beach.

"I will hang on a wee bit longer, but will be setting off here next. It is back over the mountains." He showed the old print to Kuldev.

"We call it the Beach of Sighs," said Kuldev absently.

"You know it?" asked Olaf, surprised.

"Yes, but it is a hard walk. I went as a child with my grandfather. In his day there was money in guiding British travellers, but now there is little need to go. Vyan and I may be the only ones left here to have been."

"Why the Beach of Sighs?" asked Olaf.

"Because it is the first thing a man does when he sees it, and the sound he makes when he has to leave."

"Strangely peaceful," muttered Olaf.

"I think those words are true. Come and meet Nawal Ji."

Five people had arrived with the mules. Olaf was surprised. He had expected a group of missionaries from some American sect for some reason, or at least their representatives with white toothy smiles and matching shirts. The newcomers were obviously from the subcontinent. Two looked like sadhus, with long white hair and beards, one constantly smiling, the other taller, taciturn and stern. A dwarf, busy and vociferous, directed proceedings, the muleteers complying without question, suggesting familiarity and a level of respect. Finally, there was a man and woman. She was beautiful, naturally so, colourfully dressed and attentive of the man. Olaf detected an affection between the two. The man was dressed similarly to the other sadhus, but was restless and when he saw Olaf he raised an eyebrow and stared wide-eyed. All this was taken in at a glance as Kuldev steered Olaf to the smiling sadhu.

"Nawal Ji," said Kuldev, hat in hand. "This is Olab, our new friend."

Olaf and Nawal shook hands.

"How you doing?"

"Very well, Olaf - at least that is your name pronounced, I assume?"

"I was getting used to the Olab," smiled Olaf.

461

"You look like a Viking and sound like a chap from the Emerald Isle," said Nawal. "The South I would guess. Scandinavian and Irish – a volatile mixture."

"You are an educated man," said Olaf. "Not a born sadhu that's for sure. Mammy was a Dublin girl; Denmark produced my Daddy."

"Umang told us of the death of your friend," said Nawal. "Perhaps we came too late. It is sad."

"Pneumonia, so the doctor says," said Olaf. "Without a hospital he had little chance. I had to drag him some miles from the high plateau. It was luck alone that I found him."

A voice made Olaf turn.

"I am Arnesh Ji," said Mr Gupta still staring intently. "But I think you should know my name is Anil Gupta. Tell me, have you any Scottish ancestors?"

"Olaf," said Olaf shaking hands. "I'm a lot Hibernian, and a good deal Scandinavian, but not Caledonian to my own knowledge. Why do you ask?"

"You look like a younger version of someone I know," said Mr Gupta.

The Karukula community absorbed their visitors with ease. With little debate, Talika was given the privacy of Seva's vacant room and the men were lodged in the remaining room and on the wide veranda. They made comfortable beds on the floor. Talika helped Mr Gupta arrange his bedding nearby. As the rest of the group busied themselves with the village heads and established the parameters of their stay, Mr Gupta settled down to rest. Olaf stood to one side, uneasy in the melee, consoled with thoughts of his imminent journey to his beach, as well as the improbable search for the tiger.

"Arnesh Ji wanted to be near you," came a soft voice from behind him. It was Talika.

"I seem to be popular all of a sudden," said Olaf. He held out a hand shook hers gently. "Olaf."

"Talika," she said. "He thinks you are very much like William MacKeeg."

Olaf looked flummoxed. Ever since meeting the huge tiger, his carefree walk to Goa had attracted troubles unbidden which he did not doubt were about to be added to. Talika placed a reassuring hand on his arm.

"Do not worry," she said, "Arnesh Ji is very special and brave. He is not what he seems and will leave us soon I am afraid."

"I am sure you will explain things, but I will be leaving soon too, now Seva has died." Olaf's need for company had dwindled and painful memories had resurfaced. He did not want that to happen. "I'm going to the coast and searching for a tiger on the way."

"You say mysterious things," said Talika. Then she looked askance. "Mr Gupta goes to the sea. How strange."

Olaf would never remember the man's sadhu name, so would always know him as *Mr Gupta*. Little could either have realised they would never spend another day apart whilst they both lived.

Talika walked back to the guest hut and Olaf made his way to the high point above the trail. Dog was sitting in a patch of sunshine watching bulbuls chattering in the treetops below.

"How you doing feller?" said Olaf stooping to ruffle the coarse fur of Dog's neck.

Wuff said Dog, tail bumping the earth twice in a cursory gesture of pleasure. Dog liked Olaf.

"I get the feeling that I'm attracting the bad stuff again, Dog," he said absently, rasping his beard. Dog yawned and settled. "Maybe redemption isn't in booze and isolation, but in more bodies? I think a fellow like me could never hide where I stick out like a sore thumb."

Wuff said Dog.

"You talk more sense than I do Gunga Din."

Dog yawned again and chuffed his chops. Olaf sat next to him and waited for the day to fade. Anupa watched with bright eyes from the goat pen, fascinated by the way the setting sunlight gave Olaf a golden halo.

Impossible dreams made her smile and sing as she made her way home.

At sunset Mr Gupta sent his pursuer a penultimate message. Tsering had assured him he would have signal enough.

We begin the final journey. Go to the bridge at Baaghwadi then I shall give you directions to find me.

The bridge had been earmarked by Nawal and Tsering as a point close enough to Clive's Beach for Vaz to find it, but far enough north to be clear of Karukula.

We begin the final journey. Go to the bridge at Baaghwadi then I shall give you directions to find me.

Vaz laughed and answered.

I will be there.

He laughed again: Gupta was doomed. Whilst waiting for Engineer's men to return, Vaz had been busy finding contact numbers for the Maskrey Plantation gatehouse. He introduced himself as a TV reporter for a rival of *Indian Network News,* looking to do a report on Binseswar Maskrey Sah's benevolent employment policy, his drive into the heart of Indian politics, and the local support he was getting. Could he get an appointment with his press officer to talk things through? There was a stilted, but positive reply. A final point revolved around making sure the colours of India were on show and was the unique vehicle seen on the rival news report still there?

"Oh, Nawal Ji's chaps' lorry? Yes, they will be around for a while. I think they are making a visit to Karukula."

"Karukula?" said Vaz.

"A village up in the Karoo Valley," replied the gateman.

"Great. The lorry looked perfect as a backdrop," enthused Vaz. "Who is this Nawal fellow? Could he be worth an interview?"

"He knows Mr Sah well, but you must arrange that separately." The gatekeeper's tone had become quizzical. "Who shall I say is calling?"

"Mr Vaida of the Fuchs Corporation," said Vaz.

He provisionally booked an appointment with their HR Department, the carrot of publicity too important to reject. Vaz laughed again at Mr Gupta's feeble attempt at entrapment. Nothing could stand against destiny, especially when Kāla controlled it.

The night was still and pleasantly warm, the Milky Way bright enough to show Mount Karoo as a brooding shadow above the village. An impromptu feast had begun, with tables, chairs and food appearing, every family contributing to welcome the Kuru ki Kvark. Nawal was a celebrated friend. He brought good luck, technical expertise, an array of tales, and help by way of aid for the infirm. The villagers of Karukula were happy to share what they had in exchange for the good fortune perceived and received.

Olaf was nowhere to be seen. Anupa left to find him, Keya and Resham's knowing giggles echoing in her ears. Kuldev and Sameeksha were not unaware of this fascination, but any man who was kind and strong enough to carry a stranger across mountains, then have insight to trust Karukulans without reservation, was to have such respect returned. Their daughter could do worse, Kuldev had intimated to his wife. Olaf had an understanding which was rare in European men. He saw people, not race, creed or disability, was polite, respectful and made people smile. Above all else Olaf had a delightful air of innocence which females of all ages found irresistible – Sameeksha certainly did. Ribald whispers and stolen glances followed Olaf through the village as he strode by, naively unaware of the spell he cast on grandmothers, mothers and daughters. He had magnified the feel-good factor of Nawal's arrival.

Olaf was all these things and more, but as in all men he had flaws. One he fought on a regular basis was his dragon, his Siren calling over dark waters. He lay in the darkness next to Dog in a cold sweat, shaking as craving and willpower battled for supremacy. Sobriety had saved him, but alcohol had been his serum to oblivion. Without it the flashbacks came. The sounds, smells and visions of blood and torn bodies — women, children, a baby and an old man. No Taliban these, just innocents seeking shelter from the horrors around them. The metallic *click* that triggered Olaf's automatic reflex had been a bloody Zippo lighter. An ancient grandfather lighting their single candle, not a weapon being made ready to kill. Olaf had thrown the fragmentation grenade just as the lighter illuminated the scene in the cave. He could not take it back. The children were just scared of the dark. He saw them all, in every unguarded moment...again...and again...and again.

"Olaf?"

He leapt to his feet disorientated, crouching ready to strike out. The craving and horror retreated as he remembered where he was, and who had spoken. Anupa was frozen, wide eyed, fists clenched, but did not step back. He registered that she had pronounced his name correctly, and it was the loveliest thing he had ever heard. He sniffed back his sorrows and smiled, which made everything better. Anupa smiled back and in it was understanding, reassurance and the promise of a different antidote. His dragon had gone, the Sirens were silenced. For now.

"Olaf, you cry?" said Anupa. "For Seva?"

Olaf sniffed again, still smiling, "Maybe, but I'm fine now. Ain't that right Dog?"

Dog chuffed through his chops, stood, stretched, wagged his tail once then glanced over towards the noise of the festivities.

"You must come and eat, Olaf," said Anupa. She raised her hand and brushed the dampness from his cheeks. "Be only strong for the people to see. It makes for them happiness."

The world was right again and he fell in beside her to walk to the village square.

"You bring good feeling," said Anupa, leaving Olaf to wonder whether it was personal or general. Her basic English hid any subtle nuance that could be a clue.

Olaf's arrival prompted smiles. He sat between Nawal and Mr Gupta at a rough cane table full of home cooked food. There was beer available, but most people seemed to drink water, fruit juice or chai. His earlier cravings over, the beer was easily ignored and Olaf sat quietly listening to the babble of conversation. A gentle hubbub was interrupted by a voice which made Olaf start.

"Ye are a soldier, laddie."

It was a statement, not a question. For a moment the sound of a Scottish accent in a hill village in India seemed so incongruous that Olaf's mind could not accept the proof of his own ears. He turned to find the source of the voice, saw only dark faces. Then it registered. Mr Gupta had spoken.

"Sorry?" was all Olaf could manage.

"I referred to you being a soldier," said Mr Gupta in his own voice. "Please forgive me if I am being intrusive, but Talika has told me you travel west soon, as do I, and as time is of the essence I need to find out if you may consider having a companion for part of the trip."

"I am going to what the locals call the Beach of Sighs," said Olaf, "and on the way looking for a tiger." He left the statement without further clarification – it seemed that sort of an evening.

"I am going to Clive's Beach to kill a man," said Mr Gupta.

That trumped anything Olaf may have added, so he laughed.

"I *was* a soldier," he said. "Now I'm towards the end of a walk through my past. I'm here because I met a man who needed help, now he's gone. I am not, however, a guide for hire, especially as you plan murder."

Olaf stared hard at Mr Gupta. The night had taken on a surreal quality. Nawal looked on enjoying the unfolding drama. He knew waiting at Indira Sagar for a human signpost could prove interesting, but he never thought the resulting effects could be so uniquely fascinating. Olaf was caught in the same series of improbable events.

"Arnesh Ji is dying," said Nawal. "His wife was murdered. He rescued his daughter from an assassination attempt, killing the assailant. Now he is being pursued by the killer and that is why he has to take the initiative, but he has limited time. Any assistance from you removes the need to place his destiny in the hands of the innocent."

Olaf looked from one to the other, then sat back. Redemption, it seemed, resided in the Karoo Valley. A week ago, his first instinct would have been to avoid anything remotely flavoured with commitment, but the tiger had somehow nudged his course and Seva had moved him to embrace duty for the first time in years. Something about Karukula, its people and the arrival of this odd group, coupled with Talika's insight and Anupa's attention, had made him feel a part of something worth sticking with. Redemption may well be commitment to help where he could and right other wrongs. He fished in his pocket and placed the old photograph on the table.

"That is my grandfather. This is exactly where I am heading. Now, where are you wanting to go? I think you need to let me know what I might be signing up to."

The photograph had a profound effect on Mr Gupta. It was *his* beach captured long ago. Olaf's father was sitting on *MacKeeg's* rock. Mr Gupta could hear the sea. As he looked the picture changed, the waves started moving, the day turned to night and the man became MacKeeg, monochrome with sepia tints, hair blowing in the breeze. He felt sand beneath his sandals...

William MacKeeg looked older. He drew on his short pipe and motioned to the neighbouring rock. Mr Gupta sat down and looked at his constant companion, then glanced along the beach with its backdrop of shrubs and jungle. Something moved in the thick cover, but no demon stalked the sand or waded in the shallows.

"I fear the tumour is doing its work and time is no longer with us," said MacKeeg. "It is madness that this picture is exactly where we sit and where we go. Then again, everything is madness now. Yon soldier can get us there. What think ye lad?"

"What is in the bushes?" asked Mr Gupta.

"Nemesis, as I said before," laughed the Scot. "I think it shall kill one of us."

He gestured once more and as Mr Gupta turned his head he saw the great black demon, still and awful, watching the movement. It turned shining blue eyes to him, opened its maw and spoke.

"Death will catch us all. The faster we run the quicker we are caught!"

The sound was impure. It sapped Mr Gupta's strength. The bushes rustled a final time and with a single blink the beach was clear.

"We need the soldier," said MacKeeg. "So be honest with him. When Chopra comes people will die and we've taken enough chances with others' lives."

"Yes," said Mr Gupta. "Time is short." After a pause, "He looks like you, William."

"Aye, when I was young perhaps. When I died. Now look at us, laddie, all to fuck and nowhere to go!"

"Except the sea," said Mr Gupta.

Olaf listened perplexed. Mr Gupta conversed with himself in two voices, not just different, but continents apart. Then there was the third voice, the hissing warning. *The faster we run the quicker we are caught.* That rang true to Olaf at this moment. He had fled death across a sea of alcohol, then, sober, ran to find his roots, the distance from that charnel cave greater, but ever closer. You cannot run from that which you carry.

469

Mr Gupta spoke slowly as he came back to reality.

"I... have...to...fight..."

"...a demon." Olaf completed the sentence. "Tell me all and we'll go to the beach together."

"It is too dangerous to complete the whole journey with me," said Mr Gupta.

"I'm going to the beach, and chasing a tiger as I go," said Olaf. "Adding a demon will be little more of a burden. Now, tell me the whole thing."

Later, on the veranda of their hut, each of the Kuru ki Kvark helped Mr Gupta tell the tale, strange as it was, to Olaf. It persuaded him redemption really was here. How a gentle man, so stricken, had endured so much and travelled so far was beyond him. Olaf even accepted that the unseen William MacKeeg, whatever he represented, was a key part of it all. Nawal explained how the tumour had seemingly unlocked Mr Gupta's whole mind, and, he continued, the mind thus opened was a formidable weapon. Olaf listened and found the information about the many murders disturbing, and the attempt on Mr Gupta's life and his escape, enthralling. Finally, he heard of where Vasupati Chopra was heading and how he would then be lured to the beach. That sounded the simplest part, but he knew plans were always simple to construct.

"This Vaz feller," said Olaf. "Is there any way he could... he could find you before he is meant to?"

"Improbable," said Nawal. "Even MacKeeg cannot see how he could, and he has been right all along."

"So, you walk with me to the beach, then I leave you to kill the killer," said Olaf. "You, a fellow who has had some lucky breaks, who takes on the impossible, as well as being hampered with a fatal brain cancer, that may strike him down at any time."

"Aye," said the MacKeeg voice. "But ye can run afore it happens."

Olaf stood and looked out into the night.

"I'll do it," he said. "But there can be no rules. In war you can never be sure. You have forgotten one detail, however. How are you going to kill him?"

The silence said it all.

Chapter 31

Mr Gupta goes to the Sea

Anupa watched from the last field along the trail to the waterfall. Resham and Keya stood close by, but for once the chatter of good-humoured teasing was missing. They had seen a change in their older companion and knew it would be cruel to torment her today. Her father, Olaf and Arnesh Ji were going to the Beach of Sighs. Keya moved closer and clasped her sister's arm. Their father led Vidi, the only mule in Karukula, who was loaded with supplies for the journey.

"Why are you worried Anupa?" asked Keya. "Father will be back in three days. The others a little after that."

"There is more to it," said Anupa as the men approached. "The talk is of Arnesh Ji going to die there. Olaf will go with him, but I do not know if he will come back."

The final words faltered as emotion stifled her voice. *Stupid, stupid, stupid*, she had kept telling herself, but to no avail. Some part of her had attached itself to this beautiful man and all her being contrived ways to try to be noticed, accepted and loved. The thought of never seeing Olaf again was unbearable. Her father stopped and kissed his two girls.

"I will be back once I see them to the Baagh Valley," he said stroking Anupa's hair. "It is a job and the money is good. Tsering is fixing up a water-powered generator for us too, so helping has its advantages."

"It will be alright?" she asked.

"It is a journey, nothing more."

He started to guide Vidi up the track towards the falls. Arnesh Ji walked behind with the aid of a carved white banyan-root pole given to him by Umang. He seemed stooped under a great, invisible weight and he talked to himself a lot. Anupa was sure this man was not mad, but he could be possessed. He smiled as he walked by.

"Never fear, lassie," said his other voice. "I'll make sure the big man comes back this way."

Then he winked. His left eye was pink, something she had not noticed before.

And then the huge figure of Olaf was standing there effortlessly carrying his Bergen.

"Olaf," she said, her words drying up as she kept her emotions in check.

The big man smiled and she was lost again. She reached out and grasped his hand, kissing his palm gently, then blushed and caught her breath. She stepped back, jaw set and held her tears.

"Anupa," said Olaf. "I don't know what will happen on this jaunt, but I promised to come back and tell you the story, remember? Then I shall tell you all and you may see me differently."

He walked on covering the ground quickly. Dog wandered behind to the steeper track, then stopped and sat, yawning, wagging his drooping tail.

Wuff he managed before lying down in the morning sunshine.

The Maskrey Village woke up to a rural beat somewhat less frenetic than in the big cities. Though built as a model residential settlement, no shops, cafés or entertainment were factored in, so it was surrounded by the inevitable shanties that added a ragged swaddling to good intentions. The only official store was that run by the Maskrey Estate, there to glean profit from those it paid, reasonable though its prices were. With so many gaps in a thriving community, enterprising Indians created businesses to serve the populace. A constant market massed in the main square surrounding the central wrought iron clock, selling everything from food to crudely made idols, bolts of multi-coloured cloth to caged birds. The outer shanties were interspersed with fenced compounds housing workshops for any process or service which could make money. Yet poverty and riches lived in harmony as the Estate was benevolent and few lived in desperation. Estate Security provided a local police force which kept undesirables away with a renowned robustness, though open to pecuniary inducement to ignore breached trading rules where no harm could be foreseen. As the dawn lit the verdant hinterland, cocks crowed and ubiquitous rats scurried for cover. Occasional cows munched their cud as they lay in the road watching the village stir into life. Few gave the dusty jeep that slowly drove around the streets a second glance.

Aktar and Kepi were looking for the colourful truck. Meanwhile, Vaz and Engineer drove up to the estate's entrance to question the gatekeeper. Engineer explained that they had a delivery of supplies for a certain Nawal Ji, but were unable to find them. It was all Vaz had to go on when it came to names, but the long shot paid dividends.

"Oh yes, sir," said the gatekeeper donning her cap. "The Kuru ki Kvark are up at Karukula for a few days, maybe longer. Nawal Ji is with them. I think the lorry is in a garage somewhere having repairs done. They are good people."

Engineer pressed a little more but the gatekeeper knew nothing else, though she pointed high up at the jagged outline of Mount Karoo, explaining where the village was.

As he jumped into the Shogun, Engineer's phone buzzed.

"It is Aktar, boss," came the gruff voice. "We found the truck. It's in a compound on the west side. The rear axle is off and it looks like a lot of structural welding is being done. It won't be moving for a while."

"Is anyone about?" asked Engineer.

"Too early," came the reply. "Let's meet at the square and eat. I'm fucking hungry."

Engineer looked at Vaz. He was transfixed on the mountain.

"Gupta is up there," he said. "It is where fear would take him – closer to the gods."

"The Bedford is in a garage in pieces," said Engineer starting the Shogun. "And you are right, he's up there with his new friends. A village called Karukula at the head of the main valley. You can just see part of the trail from here. Let's join the others and we can talk over breakfast."

"Have you a good map of this part of the Ghats?" asked Vaz.

"A detailed one produced by the military," said Engineer. "I thought we may need it."

They found a place to eat in a back street and paid the owner to keep the closed sign on the door whilst they talked. Engineer spread a map out amongst the empty dishes and Vaz finally became animated. He put his finger on the village.

"Do you see?" he said triumphantly.

"What?" said Engineer.

"Looks hilly," said Kepi sniffing moistly.

"The valley is high up," growled Aktar. "Is this where our target is?"

Vaz looked disappointed. He had immediately seen everything. He returned to his stoic look inured to the ignorance before him. He gestured to a point further north.

"Here is the Baaghwadi Bridge," he said, then traced a line south, stopping at a deep river valley. "Gupta wanted me there to coax me, where? To the sea."

"I don't get it," said Engineer.

The finger moved east.

"The Baaghwadi joins this valley which leads through a steep gorge to the sea," said Vaz confidently. "But follow it from there back over the mountains, and what do you come to?"

Engineer stared, and then he saw.

"Karukula," he said smiling. "You could be right. Maybe he's going to make his way from the village to that beach to set an ambush. But how can we be sure?"

"Because it is so," said Vaz. The others looked askance at his tone. "We must go to the village."

Karukula was a small community that thrived on the familiar, so the natural rhythm of life quickly returned to simple rustic normality. Nawal Ji, Puneet, Vam and Talika were old friends, so meshed seamlessly into the daily routines. It was widely accepted that Kuldev would be back in a couple of days. Olaf and Arnesh Ji's journey was viewed as a pilgrimage, the Beach of Sighs being considered a holy place. Although the Great Banyan had served Karukula's spiritual needs for centuries, the distant beach still held a significant place in the villagers' folklore and superstitions. Even so, only Talika and Anupa were apt to glance pensively up at the cloudy plateau, each with thoughts of how destiny may unravel for two special men.

Mr Gupta had grasped Vidi's rope harness on the climb, mumbling as he went. It was MacKeeg that encouraged him onwards. Olaf was surprised at how stoically his companion walked once they had cleared the steep path by the waterfall, but found the intermittent schizophrenic conversation unnerving. Kuldev led the mule on a slack rein. Vidi had seen it all before and would walk steadily all day without displaying the mutinous nature of his kind. They stopped at the Great Banyan under the watchful gaze of the Nilgiris. Kuldev placed an offering of fruit before the phalanx of aerial roots still fluttering with his daughters' colourful tokens of hope.

"Keep the village safe!" he called up at earnest black faces. "Keep this a place of protection for my children!"

"They are quite beautiful," said Mr Gupta, watching as the monkeys descended cautiously towards the offering.

"This place is special," said Kuldev. "It belongs to Karukula and has kept the village safe for a thousand years. The Nilgiris are custodians – if they remain, Karukula remains."

"A powerful place," said Olaf. "Maybe its protection will follow us."

They moved on.

It took some hours before they reached the less densely packed trees of the upper valley where Olaf led them to the campsite he and Seva had used. With luck, from here, they could reach the beach in three days. Mr Gupta brought up the rear, a ghostly simulacrum of his former self. The tumour's relentless progress burned bright from his bloodshot eye and laid waste to his body. Yet he plodded on.

He hovered between realities. The bright moonlight shone through a broken canopy of trees, lighting the way. MacKeeg was beside him looking tired, his colour washed out, but his demeanour unchanged. He marched with a rifle over his shoulder, upright and trail worn, grimly focussed on the path ahead. Mr Gupta knew he was the burden MacKeeg carried.

"I do not know if I can finish this journey. The thing in my head feels like it's sent roots through my body to suck me dry."

"Stop mithering, laddie," said MacKeeg without breaking stride. "All ye have to do is live a few more days."

"Olaf is right," said Mr Gupta. "How do we kill Vaz? How do I end this? I am dying, MacKeeg, and dying too quickly."

"Aye, that is true," said MacKeeg, "but ye mistake lack of fitness for the final throws of death!" He laughed. "Think positive! At least y'll be fitter at the end, than afore ye started!"

At this Mr Gupta laughed too as MacKeeg worked a little jig into his marching. They walked together into a glade, with huge planets above and comets cutting the star-speckled sky, the reality of the Upper Karoo Valley influencing their place in this other world. Mr Gupta longed for the relative security his beach, but also knew he was not dead yet. Rather than failure, they were in the unlikely position of fulfilling their quest. It made the question *How do we kill Vaz?* more urgent. They had no weapons. In spite of MacKeeg being a soldier, he was only a manifestation of Mr Gupta's injured mind.

"We'll improvise…," said MacKeeg fading away as the real world finally took precedence.

"We'll improvise…," said Mr Gupta colliding with the back of the mule.

Vidi's fetlock twitched and he snorted gently. They were in a huge clearing flanked by forested slopes that led up to rounded peaks and a jagged ridge-line which marked the start of the high plateau. Mr Gupta's mind adjusted to reality. The buzz of insects and calls of birds filled his ears. In the distance a deer bounded off and he was sure he saw several dogs running over a rise as monkeys crashed about in the canopy behind him. He was enjoying being in this wild place and could not remember being so far from civilisation in his life. Olaf strode ahead to the top of the rise then beckoned them to follow. The higher ground gave a better view of the open valley and the tumbling, youthful Karoo River. It was as if the veil of civilisation had been whipped away and India's prehistoric face had been exposed. The clearing stretched into the distance, a sea of yellow-green grassland with clumps of trees and lush vegetation, hemmed in by forest. The three men stood in silence taking in the scene. Several sambar and spotted deer grazed with a herd of wild pigs, whilst egrets and storks stalked the ground behind them. Overhead hawks and bats dotted the sky whilst a huge bull elephant stood drinking from the Karoo River, tusks draped in ribbons of aquatic plants, his wet hide shining in the evening sunshine. As they looked the bull waded across the water and disappeared into the trees without a sound.

"I had forgotten about this place," said Kuldev.

"It was a little bit further up that the tiger killed a hyena," said Olaf.

"We're close to the same camp I found on the way down."

"I never knew such a world existed," said Mr Gupta. "It is good I came this way."

"As long as that big feller stays in the forest," laughed Olaf.

They reached the rocky outcrop set back in the trees just as the nightjars started to hawk for moths and call *uk-krukoo* to each other, and a lone scops owl emitted a questioning *whuk?* from higher up the valley. Whilst Kuldev and Olaf unloaded the mule, Mr Gupta wandered into the clearing. A spotted deer bounded off into the gloaming and dholes barked from somewhere in the distant shadows.

"Chital," came MacKeeg's voice from beside Mr Gupta. "Yon deer. They're called *chital* as well as *spotted deer*."

"I knew that," said Mr Gupta absently. "I feel as if we are in a dream. And something is wrong. What we think will happen, will not."

"Aye, laddie," said MacKeeg. "That is what bothers me. Chopra. We felt safe up until now, as we thought we dictated the game, but..."

"...something happened that we may have missed," said Mr Gupta.

As Olaf, Kuldev and Mr Gupta started their journey, Vaz was planning his move on Karukula. In any settlement there is an underworld where money could usurp tenuous moral values and the Maskrey Village was no exception. With little effort, Aktar found three young locals who would guide them to the high valley. Yadu grew cannabis in a secluded clearing on a south-facing slope to the north of the Karukula. For a modest sum he agreed to take Aktar and his companions to a point overlooking the village using a hidden path. Yadu did his business from a small fenced compound frequented by red eyed men, all parting with money for the dope they needed to get through the day. Business was good, but easy money was always welcome. Yadu enlisted his two partners, Har and Daksh. They barely raised an eyebrow when Engineer loaded a mule with their weapons, but Vaz gave off such an air of menace that he was left well alone.

They left the compound in the darkness of early morning. The steep, winding track eventually gave way to a small clearing surrounded by trees and shrubs, hidden and easy to protect. From here Yadu led his four clients up a steep slope to the edge of a ridge which overlooked Karukula. Dawn was breaking as they looked down at the village.

"It's smaller than I thought," said Engineer. "We need to see if the target is there first." He lifted a pair of binoculars to his eyes.

"I think a little scouting party may be in order," said Vaz.

Nawal was sitting watching the sun rise. Their stay at Karukula would be for more than just a few days. The Queen Lizzie was taking time to repair and Tsering was away getting yet another illusive part. He was also considering Anil Gupta. His tale was not in doubt, and the fact that it stretched the laws of probability a long way was both attractive, and worrying. They had transported a man to the start of his final journey, evading danger at Indira Sagar, but after that things had become surreal. Nawal was applying his principles to the possibility that Mr Gupta's story was, in part, delusion. Did Vasupati Chopra need to kill a dying man? Nawal's great joy was to explore all possibilities, so for a moment he wondered if they were all part of a communal paranoia. The sun was up and the darkness of the forested slope to the north was being pushed back by the first light. A blue flash. This sent his doubts fleeing. Who would be watching Karukula at this time of the day? Mr Gupta's demon had blue shining eyes.

"What are you looking at?" asked Puneet. He had walked out to join Nawal.

"We are being watched, Puneet. Answer this: how could Arnesh Ji's nightmare find us here?"

"Is it possible?" asked Puneet.

"Yes, of course," said Nawal. "So how?"

"Telepathy?" mumbled Puneet.

"Lines of communication..." replied Nawal trailing off in thought. "I think I need to send Vam on an errand."

A short while later Vam scuttled off down the long track to the Maskrey Village. Nawal knew they faced the possibility of direct violence and, for once, lacked the logic to subdue his growing fear.

Anupa had dressed in a blue sari, edged in gold. It was too good to wear whilst leading the goat, but she wanted to look her best every day in case Olaf returned. For once she had sought solitude so led the goat to pasture whilst Resham and Keya ground wheat for the day's bread. Just beyond a far plot the goat grazed in a tangle of vegetation, helping to clear a patch for a little more tobacco next year. Once tethered she looked up the trail to the Great Banyan and felt its pull. It would only take an hour or so to make a round trip. She set off to make a small offering and tie a piece of her blue sari to the tree. She would be back before anyone knew she had gone. Moving quickly, she scampered along enjoying the sight of colourful birds and the roar of the cascading Karoo River. As she paused to look back over the village, strong hands clamped across her face and dragged her back.

An hour later two men strolled from the trees into Karukula.

The mule stood chewing dry fodder, whipping its tail to ward off a cloud of early morning flies. A pied wagtail hawked from the beast's broad back, tumbling in the air to catch the less wary insects. Olaf and Kuldev had left Mr Gupta to sleep as they prepared a meal and boiled water for tea, but now they were looking down at his blanket wrapped form with concern. Mr Gupta was pallid and still. His eyes moved rapidly beneath the lids and his breathing was laboured. Olaf bent to wake him up just as Mr Gupta's crimson eyes opened.

"MacKeeg!" he shouted.

Kuldev gasped and stepped back.

The whole world was raging, roaring and dark. Mr Gupta staggered in the wind, the noise in his ears ringing like a thousand bells. Blue lights began to flicker in the swirling storm. Despair crushed his heart and hot tears bulged in his eyes only to be torn away by the relentless tempest. The blue lights began to take a form Mr Gupta recognised. His stomach leapt as the demon's eyes shone from the veil of black rain. Its voice screamed:

"I AM HERE! I AM HERE! I...AM...HERE!"

Searing pain tore through both worlds as the tumour pressed upon the cortex of his brain.

I cannot die now, he thought. *Not yet. Not yet.*

He closed his eyes and tumbled through time and space, hitting the sand with a thump. The storm eased and the blue eyes were swirling away as the beach took shape around him. The grey silhouette of MacKeeg stood close by, strong and unbroken.

"Come, laddie," he called holding out a hand.

Mr Gupta struggled to sit up and could not speak. *He is here!* he thought, numb and dumb with terror. He could not breathe. Eventually the need for oxygen took over and a breath was found to give both life and voice.

"MacKeeg!" he called taking the hand of his companion.

The hand was firm and his strength returned.

"Are you with us feller?" asked Olaf taking Mr Gupta's hand.

"Something is wrong," said Mr Gupta.

"That is an understatement," said Olaf, smiling. "Everything about the pair of us is bloody wrong! Try not to make too much sense of things or we'll end up running around screaming for the rest of the day."

Mr Gupta rummaged in the bedding for his phone. No signal. How could there be in these wild hills?

"Without a phone my stupid plan is useless," he said. "I have to call Chopra."

"Up on the plateau you'll get something," said Olaf. "Modern India is the same as anywhere else. People can be homeless, but phone masts grow like trees."

"I don't think the man hunting me is at the Baaghwadi Bridge," said Mr Gupta struggling to his feet. "He is here!"

Olaf raised an eyebrow. "How do you make that out?"

"I don't know," said Mr Gupta sagging against his staff. "Something has happened that I have missed."

"Well, the beach is two days' easy march away," said Olaf. "The bridge is a goodly step from our beach. If you tell this Chopra where you want to meet him, he'll still be on the way whilst we build sand castles. We..."

"There is no *We*," said Mr Gupta firmly. "You and Kuldev will leave me there. It is not your fight. Enough people have been killed because of this monstrous man and my dithering."

"OK," said Olaf. "All I meant was, we can do nothing until we get up onto the high ground. Let's eat and get on. By the way, your eyes look awful. How are you feeling?"

"I'm dying too quickly," said Mr Gupta. "But I do not want my dying to become the poison which destroys my friends and family. Chopra must die too. Somehow I will bring him to an end, but I have missed something. If I have got this wrong the poison may already have started its work."

"Could it reach Karukula?" Kuldev's question floated unanswered in the air.

The villagers were used to receiving visitors. Most were welcomed with a cheerful informality, especially if they were tourists with money to spend. There were times however, where formality was observed, should a dignitary or policeman make a call, then greetings were left to one of the senior members of the village. The latest arrivals were armed and looked dangerous, so Vyan went out to meet them. Nawal watched from his veranda with growing unease. They were dressed in black cargo pants and military style boots. The shorter man, armed with a rifle, had neatly trimmed hair and a friendly smile. The taller one had long, straight hair and round, metallic-blue glasses — there was nothing remotely comforting in his demeanour. They both carried pistols. Talika stepped from the hut and stood next to Nawal, the latter rising slowly to his feet. He knew just who this frightening figure was.

"That is him," whispered Talika quietly.

"Yes," said Nawal, finally decoding the flash of blue he had seen earlier. "This is Mr Gupta's pursuer. He's not at Baaghwadi. I should have known."

They watched as the tall man talked to Vyan who grew tense, looked in Nawal's direction and gestured him over.

"These men are looking for a man called Anil Gupta," said Vyan.

"He is a criminal wanted for fraud," said the taller man, without doubt Vasupati Chopra.

"Are you from the police?" asked Nawal.

"I represent Cobra Investments," said Vaz. "He is a murderer, fraudster and very dangerous. I know he has been with your group," he said directly to Nawal. "I need him here now!"

"I do not know the man you describe," said Nawal, honestly.

"Don't take me for an idiot!" snapped Vaz. "I want him now!"

Several villagers emerged from their homes to watch the scene, uneasy at the raised voice. Engineer levelled his rifle and it became apparent this may not end well.

"There is no need for violence," said Vyan. "This man is not here."

Vaz pulled out his Glock and shot Vyan through the thigh. He screamed, then sagged to the floor gripping the wound, blood pouring through his fingers. Resham rushed across to help her father.

"That was not necessary!" shouted Umang, joining the girl.

Villagers either melted away or stepped towards the drama, angry, scared and unsure what to do. Engineer pointed his rifle at the nearest group.

"Stay where you are!" he said coldly. "Kepi!"

A skinny man emerged from the vegetation nearby, smiling through bad teeth, casually holding an old revolver.

"Yes boss," he said moistly, wiping his nose on a sleeve.

"Hold your gun at that girl's head," said Vaz pointing at Resham. "We will look through the huts for Gupta. If I find him, shoot her. If they try anything, shoot her."

The search took a few minutes and Vaz grew angrier when nothing was found. He had seen Mr Gupta with the two old men and woman on the television. He gestured Talika and Puneet into the square and they made their way to Nawal's side.

"So, he's gone," said Engineer. "You said he would be."

"Yes," said Vaz staring up the valley. He knew and foretold everything, but needed more information. "Shoot him," said Vaz to Kepi, pointing at Puneet.

Kepi hesitated. He had hurt people before, but never killed anyone. It seemed especially absurd to do so in front of so many witnesses.

"Wait!" The shout came from Engineer. "Don't forget our hostage."

Vaz raised a hand, relieving Kepi of his dilemma.

"You know Gupta," said Vaz. "You have established that I will not listen to lies. I need to know when he left, and where he is going. First you must all listen to something?"

He turned and walked towards the wooded slope overlooking the village where Nawal had seen the flash of blue. Vaz raised an arm and waved. A piercing scream ululated down from somewhere up in the trees. It petered out to a sob.

"That was a girl we have as a guest," said Vaz. "She wears a blue and gold sari."

Sameeksha cried in anguish as she realised it was her daughter's voice. Keya held her mother and trembled as she looked up into the trees to where her sister must be.

"Now, some quick answers," said Vaz. "Gupta: where is he going, who is with him and how long ago did he leave?"

There was no gain harming the village by pointless bravado, so Nawal answered.

"He left yesterday making for a cove they call the Beach of Sighs. He is with a villager and his mule. The idea is to leave Mr Gupta there, where he plans to die. He is very ill."

Vaz smiled. "But you know more old man," he said. "He has told you about me and his twisted version of events. My companions will stay here as your guests whilst I go and find this friend of yours. The girl will be my guarantee of your good behaviour. If there are any attempts to free her she will be killed and I will personally execute every last one of you."

He raised his gun and shot Puneet through the forehead. The move was fast and final. Screams and groans came from all and Nawal cried in sorrow, kneeling at the side of his dead friend.

"You are a monster!" hissed Umang.

Vaz's head turned, the blank, blue stare settling on the man who had insulted him. Putting the gun away he strode over and kicked Umang in the ribs. He fell and vomited in the dust. Vaz bent over him and dragged Umang to his feet staring directly into his eyes.

"You feel your strength in the experience of pain. God may seem like a monster to a fool," said Vaz evenly.

"A fool who thinks he is a god, is a monster," spat Umang.

Rage bloomed and Vaz dropped Umang into the dust. He snatched Engineer's SA80 and turned it on Umang and fired a rapid burst into him.

Pok-pok-pok, pok-pok-pok!

The execution was brutal, bloody and horrifying. Umang lay in a growing pool of blood.

"It will be the girl next, so let me have all the details."

Nawal told him what he wanted to know. Whilst Anupa's fate was in the hands of such brutal men, Karukula would remain a compliant place of fear. Engineer had seen it all before, but even he was shaken by the ease with which Vaz could kill innocent men. His greatest concern was being implicated in this murder.

By noon Vaz and Engineer had started their pursuit of Mr Gupta. They commandeered Yadu's mule and, to the great distress of Nawal, dragged the bereft Talika with them. She was tethered by a length of rope to the mule's saddle with the choice of walking, or being dragged. Nawal drew some comfort in seeing her remain upright and proud, knowing she could endure in a harsh world. Anupa was left with Aktar and Kepi at the Great Banyan, and Yadu, Har and Daksh would seal off Karukula. Anyone who approached would be told the village was in quarantine due to an outbreak of tuberculosis which Nawal's team would monitor. Karukula was effectively cut off.

They were allowed to bury Puneet and Umang near Seva's cairn. Sorrow had brought the village to its knees and fear kept it there. Yet not one person mentioned the golden giant. How could anyone beyond the village have ever known such a man existed?

The mongoose tore through the undergrowth in pursuit of a fleeing rat.

The rat stood little chance having been surprised dozing in the afternoon sunshine, but it knew the trails and jinked this way and that, leaping and twisting, running for its life. The distance between hunter and prey was reducing rapidly when the rat ran out onto the steep track and under a dusty boot to the cover beyond. The boot hit the ground as the mongoose broke cover and ran into Olaf's foot, spun in the dust, chattered indignantly, then returned from whence it came. Olaf grinned and wiped his forehead with the back of his hand.

"Now there's something you don't see every day," he said.

His Bergen was heavy and he was glad to see he was close to the top of the steep trail. Turning, he looked down towards his companions. Kuldev and Mr Gupta were half an hour behind, but still climbing steadily with the help of Vidi. Olaf had ranged ahead to check their route and find somewhere to camp. He completed the ascent with long easy strides occasionally tracing arrows in the dust for the others to follow.

The plateau worked its magic again with views across the Sahyadri stretching away north and south, dipping to the west where the sea lay. He dropped the Bergen at the side of the trail and jogged a short way. Yes, he could see the misty, moist air marking the top of the valley that would lead down to the sea. Just below the ridge he could see a clear area where they could spend the night.

The sun was setting as they made camp. Mr Gupta was so weary he could only sit and watch his companions' efforts. His phone buzzed — he had a signal! The displayed message shocked him to the core.

I am not stupid... I am here... I am harvesting those behind and am coming for you.

He dropped the phone into the dust and fell into the other world.

"He is behind us!" shouted Mr Gupta. "What did we miss?"

MacKeeg stood close looking back towards Karukula, then turned to Mr Gupta.

"Remember when we arrived, laddie? What did we see?"

Mr Gupta sat down in the dust. His head thumped. His eyes hurt and his vision swirled. He vomited bile from his soured stomach. Then he knew.

"Indian Network News!" he groaned. "He saw us on the television. As simple as that."

"Och, he had to find us eventually," said MacKeeg.

"But not to bring harm to innocent people," said Mr Gupta. "He must be at the village! What can we do?"

The tumour he carried had cursed and blessed, making clarity a two-edged sword. He knew what Vaz could do.

Strong hands grabbed him and sat him up against the bole of a tree. He opened his eyes. Olaf had the phone and knew exactly what the message meant. His thoughts were of Seva and the change that meeting had wrought, and of the people torn apart in the cave. He knew where his redemption lay. He answered the text.

Clive's Beach. Beach of Sighs. Waiting for you. No more messages.

He hit the send button and turned to Mr Gupta.

"He'll follow now."

"The village?" said Mr Gupta.

"Whatever has happened cannot be changed, feller," said Olaf. "Kuldev..."

"I must go back," he said.

"It is best to face the threat here," replied Olaf. "He won't be alone. Can you call Nawal?"

Mr Gupta's face dropped.

"I...I never knew their number," he said.

Chapter 32

The Sea

Delays had kept the man invisible and safe. He had listened to the gossip at the Maskrey Village, then climbed the slopes of Mount Karoo unseen. There he had watched and waited. Finally, the watcher waded through the cold waters of the tumbling Karoo River.

A cool wind soughed through the sparse grasses of the high plateau keeping the night air clear of creeping mists. The sky was open in vaulted splendour, the light of the waning moon no longer enough to blot out the sparkling universe. Kuldev slept fitfully propped against a rock, waiting for the first light of dawn so he could return to Karukula. The story of Arnesh Ji's plight and destiny had seemed nothing but words for re-telling in the comfort of the village once he had gone. The reality of the monster hunting him had suddenly become real, and the message on the phone, *I am harvesting those behind and am coming for you*, planted the seeds of a nightmare. Kuldev's whole world was the village and the words brought his spirit low. Nawal Ji had spent much time explaining away superstitions during his many visits, but Karukula was built upon legend and deep-set tradition. Kuldev still made offerings to the Great Banyan as tithes for good harvests, or to ensure good fortune where hope was not enough. His fitful sleep was punctuated by disturbing dreams and wakeful stress.

Nearby Mr Gupta's dreams filled every gap between wakefulness and sleep; he had no peace. Reality in one world changed the other, the cool breeze here transmuted into the chill of terror there, blowing over flat sands next to an oily, silver sea. The planets and stars glowed behind the thin cloud blanketing the silver-lit night sky. Gone were the rocks and palms; gone his companion; gone all hope and the will to live; just beach and sea and horizon, a cold world empty of future. Here, Mr Gupta lay damp and cold, keeping his burning head against the grainy beach. He wished to die. But life was still strong and so he wept for all his loss and his doomed friends, and the peril he had brought to Karukula. He wept at the tenacity of life and what that still meant for him. He wept as he knew there would be no rest so raised his head. The unbroken horizon glowed as a faux dawn took hold. Terrors gripped Mr Gupta as no burning sun rose with its corona, just a black eclipse blocking out all but a halo of fire. The fire burned blue with the icy coldness of extinction. His face froze as he looked upon a world a million light-years away, gripped in the gravity well of a dead sun. The semi-circle of black was a hole in the sky. As Mr Gupta watched it turned, rolling upwards, growing bigger. Two almond eyes burning blue. No sun this, but the demon, massive and unstoppable. The black beast rose and filled the sky, rippling clouds and screaming in a thousand voices.

"*I AM HERE! I AM HERE! I AM HERE!*"

Its sword dripped oily water and the harvest of heads still dangled from a clawed hand. Mr Gupta cringed before this bleak reality. Just as despair threatened to drive him insane, the world blurred and an all too familiar *crack!* echoed through his mind.

He looked down on Island Earth, blue and shining against the backdrop of the universe. There was no pain here, just peace.

"You have come so far my darling," said Kiran softly, taking his hand.

"He has won, Kiran," said Mr Gupta. "This thing in my head has run its course, has blessed me, and now takes its toll."

"Yet you are still here," she replied, smiling. "What you see is just what may be, not what is. Don't you see this is not real? The demon will come to the sea, and the destruction left behind is down to him alone. You cannot wish your life to an end for you still have the strength to live to that final day."

Mr Gupta felt warmth return, the love of his wife replacing self-pity. With it came hope. With it came strength.

"I love you," he said.

And with that he was back on the beach. The demon remained towering in the shallows, yet it seemed diminished, uncertain, unsure, looking at something in the trees crashing through the undergrowth. The demon wailed.

"Och, what took ye?" said MacKeeg from his rock.

"What is coming?" asked Mr Gupta.

"The end," came the reply. "All we can do is soldier on, laddie. Are ye ready?"

Mr Gupta looked back along the shore. The demon had gone. His mind held on to his vision of Kiran and the strength it had given him.

"Yes," he answered.

"Then it's time ye woke up. Wake up…"

"…Time to wake up, feller."

Olaf was shaking Mr Gupta's shoulder. He opened the red pools that were his eyes and smiled weakly. Kuldev was ready to leave, looking at the man he considered a sadhu of immense importance.

"Arnesh Ji. Sometimes, before a disease is cured, it takes many lives. No single person can be blamed for that. You will stop this, I know, and you are blessed with sight beyond ours. Your eyes are proof of this. I will never see you again. My part is to try and save a few. Your burden is greater, for you must rid the world of this demon."

With that he set off towards Karukula.

"Stay high!" called Olaf after him.

Kuldev raised an arm in acknowledgement. He had no wish to stumble across the demon. He had a family to protect.

Vaz was a man possessed. He had insisted on marching as far as possible after they found the site of their prey's camp down in the valley. When darkness fell they stopped for the night halfway up the trail to the plateau. It was early when they had risen and mist hid the valley beneath. The mule stood passively as Engineer tightened straps and balanced the load. Rocks, loosened by his boots, tumbled down the steep slope into the undergrowth. Engineer had looked very carefully, but could not really distinguish too much from the tracks left. His mind had been closed by the information the villagers gave, so saw only two sets of footprints, one booted, Mr Gupta, he assumed, and the plain imprint of sandals from the captive girl's father. There was dung and hoof marks, so all looked as it should. Vaz had left Engineer to pack up and disappeared behind some low trees to check the route ahead. Talika had suffered in the night as she had been given but one thin blanket to protect her from the bare earth. She now stood handcuffed and tethered to the mule's saddle once more.

"Are you alright?" asked Engineer as he worked.

"Yes," she said quietly.

He stopped and looked at her dusty face, admiring the way she stood defiantly upright.

"He is mad," he continued in low tones. "I am not like him."

"You kill for money, so you are," she said.

Engineer had been shaken by the executions in the village which implicated him in more pointless murders. He was ready to dispatch

Vasupati Chopra, but he wanted this woman to witness the execution, that way Engineer's reputation would be enhanced as a saviour, rather than a murderer. She had to trust him.

"Listen," he said, leaning against the mule. "What happened in the village was beyond my control. I am *not* like him." Then in a whisper, "I am going to kill him today."

Talika stared in disbelief.

"He killed someone back at the big lake. The victim was related to a very powerful man, and I work for him now. I was trying to bide my time until we were away from prying eyes, but now I see I should have tried before...before the village."

Engineer looked genuinely stressed and remorseful.

"Why tell me?" asked Talika.

"Because if I do this you will live. If not, he will kill you and everyone in the village. I need your help," he said.

"What should I do?" she asked.

Vaz watched through binoculars. He looked down at his GPS and was confident he could find the beach with ease. Something in Engineer's body language and the woman's reactions intimated a meaningful conversation was taking place.

"Today he will turn," said the Kāla mind.

"I know," said the Vaz mind.

"I have willed him to fail."

"Then I will wait."

He turned and continued upwards. In his madness, Vasupati Chopra thought himself impervious to any human schemes. That he remained free was proof of this; that Shiva spoke through him proved this; that he was close to an elusive quarry was proof of this; and that his mind had controlled fate by showing him where Mr Gupta was via television, was proof of this. He reached the edge of the plateau and looked at the Sahyadri stretching away on all sides, mist filling the valleys making each peak an island, blue-tinged by his lenses. He felt his chest fill with the power of Kāla and the absolute certainty he was indestructible, irresistible and omnipotent. He knew Engineer would try to kill him because Engineer was afraid. He was squeamish in the face of death. Vaz had seen this. He also knew Engineer could not kill him. At this one point Vaz may have invited his own failure, but the laws of probability cannot be gainsaid.

Mr Gupta shuffled along on thin legs, clothed in homespun dhoti and robes, stout sandals on large, dusty feet, leaning upon a beautifully carved staff. His hair and straggly beard were white and his once dark skin had become pallid. Crimson eyes glowed with the heat of the tumour. Olaf was worried. He had been buoyed by the quest and forgot logistics. He had to face the unknown with a mule, a knife and a dying man. One thing was certain, Mr Gupta was no longer capable of killing anyone but himself. Olaf glanced down into the verdant valley which would lead to the beach they sought. He scratched his beard and looked at Mr Gupta.

"How you doing?" he asked.

"I cannot make it," said Mr Gupta.

"Ok," said Olaf. "Can you see the haze beyond the valley?"

Mr Gupta nodded.

"That is the sea. I reckon a good day marching and we'd be there. But you look fecked, so what to do?"

Mr Gupta leaned on his staff and sighed. He was so close, but realised the journey to the sea and the killing of Vasupati Chopra was an impossible dream. Even MacKeeg had abandoned him.

"Have you ever ridden a horse?" asked Olaf.

"Once, in England," came the reply. "It was not a great success, they have no brakes you see."

And Mr Gupta found himself laughing with Olaf. They laughed and laughed until they sagged to the ground. It felt good. Langurs joined in from the canopy below, and birds squawked and cheeped, lizards scurried away and Vidi snorted in mulish irritation at the fools beside him. So there they sat, a day from the sea, death stalking every plan, kicking up dust on a high plateau. Two men who had not laughed for many a year. Two men with nothing in common but a journey and a beach, with no plans for life beyond. Olaf shuffled over and put a great arm around Mr Gupta. He hugged him as the laughter subsided into little quakes of giggles.

"You know what, feller?" he said. "You will get to that fucking beach. If you can laugh, you can ride."

"And *fucking* Chopra?" asked Mr Gupta.

"He's just a man," said Olaf simply.

"Let's go to the sea," said Mr Gupta.

Olaf reduced the load on Vidi's back. He made a cache of the gear that was surplus to requirements, and fashioned a seat on the pannier frame upon which Mr Gupta could sit. They ate a small meal then set off once more. Vidi took it all in his stride with his usual, stoic sure-footedness, the man upon his back of no consequence.

Mr Gupta's thoughts warped with the invasive cancer. He could no longer see the bounds between one world and the next. Olaf marching ahead merged with the figure of William MacKeeg, becoming one and the same being. Everything around him was wonderful with blue-necked parakeets, drongos, bulbuls and kingfishers zooming amongst the green trees. Elephants trumpeted and gaurs grunted as they passed through the lower valley. Through deep gorges where macaques shouted down from rocks, yapping out warnings to the creatures who lived there. At one point he stared directly into the wide eyes of a loris, gazing from a hole in a great fig tree, which hung over the depths in which the tumbling waters of two rivers joined in a maelstrom of foam.

"That's the Baagh Valley," said Olaf, pointing towards the steaming gorge. "Your mate back there would have used that, but we could never have sent a message to bring him to us. No signal."

Mr Gupta looked back at Olaf with his crimson stare.

"Yet he is coming," he said. "Isn't life strange?"

They set off once more. Riding had allowed Mr Gupta to rest and once they stopped in the late afternoon he had to be awoken from a long sleep.

"Look up there," said Olaf pointing.

The gorge was narrower and the river roared louder, though well below and hidden in dense forest. High above Mr Gupta could see the underside of a metal bridge, beneath which bats roosted and moss and liverworts dangled.

"The Monsoon Railway," Olaf announced.

"Bloody hell," said Mr Gupta.

"Yep. And it means we're not too far from the beach."

They rounded a bend in the narrow track and found a small stone hut, windowless and doorless, but with a sound roof. A rusty *Indian Railways* sign leaned against the wall.

"I think we can stop now," said Olaf. "A good meal and a sleep will do us no harm."

They stopped out of necessity. Talika, shod only in sandals, had torn feet where stones and thorny plants had taken a toll. She had fallen several times, but the mule dragged her until she stood up. Vaz had marched ahead expressionless, relentless, showing no sign of fatigue. The tracks they followed were very clear. Now Engineer could see the boot prints were big, bigger than the average Indian. They were following three people. He kept this to himself. There was no need to share information with the man he would soon kill. After her final fall Talika could not regain her feet and let out a yelp which stopped them all. Vaz turned towards the noise.

"Cut her loose," he said. "If she falls again I'll kill her."

Engineer walked to Talika and cut the tether with his combat knife.

"Water, please," she asked remaining on the ground.

Vaz nodded then turned his back as Engineer walked to the mule. He quickly released the SA80 and stepped into the open, pointing the short barrel at Vaz from waist height. Vaz turned side on and stared.

"Suliman?"

"Sorry, Vaz," said Engineer. "It's not about the money so much as you going rogue. You are a psycho."

Vaz did not move. He stood tall. His mind filled with that same blast of endorphins he felt earlier. He felt euphoric as he knew he was immortal. A rare smile crept to his lips. He spoke.

"We were right," said the Vaz mind.

"Now the Jack is out of its box," laughed the Kāla mind.

"He will fail," said the minds together.

As Engineer lifted the rifle he noticed the magazine was loose. It fell out. Vaz raised his Glock and shot him through the knee. Engineer crumpled and screamed, grabbing his leg. As he rolled back into the bushes something struck his neck. A krait had bitten him. Engineer let out a cry of frustration and pain, but still had the sense to scrabble for the Glock in his belt, tearing the hissing snake away at the same time. A kick caught him in the arm, cracking the bone above the elbow. Engineer scrabbled in the dirt, rolled onto his back and looked up. Vaz stood over him staring impassively through blue lenses.

"Manyar venom is very strong," he said. "The bleeding from your leg will drag it through quickly."

Vaz bent and removed Engineer's knife and gun, then stepped away watching the dying man and the shaking woman. Talika prepared for death. She knew what this man was capable of. Vaz, however, made no further aggressive moves. He seemed fascinated with Engineer groaning on the floor.

"What are you waiting for?" he said. "Let's get this farce over with. Just let the woman go."

Vaz crouched and smiled, gold tooth flashing.

"I will not kill her," he said. "Nor you."

Engineer felt burning in the pit of his stomach as the krait venom took hold. He doubled over and vomited then groaned as the loose bones in his knee ground together. Vaz pulled him over and found the handcuff key in his top pocket.

"Bring those cuffs here," he ordered Talika.

She stood, lifted them from the mule's saddle and took them to Vaz. Keeping the Glock aimed straight at her stomach, he took them, then punched her. She fell and felt the weight of Vaz's boot on her arm. The bone creaked. He clipped one of the cuffs to her wrist and the other to Engineer's.

"You wanted to look after her, now you can," he said. "If she's still here when I get back, I will cut her throat."

He left, taking everything with him.

Talika sniffed back tears.

"I messed up," croaked Engineer.

"I cannot believe he let us live," said Talika.

Engineer snorted. "I will be dead before noon."

"But surely I can help." Talika replied.

"Don't you see?" said Engineer lifting his shackled wrist. "When I'm dead, you have two choices. Wait in the hot sun for that bastard to come back and kill you, if you survive that long. Or carry my body with you to safety. Maybe you could gnaw through my wrist, but do it before I stink or it could be unhealthy."

Engineer coughed and rolled onto his back. He never spoke again.

Mr Gupta had spent an uncomfortable night in the hut suspended between wakefulness and sleep. His world was a delirium of colours and unending pain. The quest was at an end and he tried to tell Olaf to leave him. Yet the big man had been gentle and gave him tea and a little rice which served to bring him back to the world. They marched on, Mr Gupta sitting hunched over a padded pommel, swaying gently to the mule's steady walk. MacKeeg was back beside him.

"How ye doin, laddie?" asked the Scot.

"Not so well, William," Mr Gupta replied.

"He'll make it," said Olaf.

"Och, he will at that," said MacKeeg laughing. "I feel right enough, so he must have a fair old spark left."

"This is my last day," said Mr Gupta. "You both know that. But you have been good companions and I thank you both."

"I haven't done anything yet," said Olaf bringing them to a stop.

"Will you look at that!" said MacKeeg.

Mr Gupta stared over Vidi's head. Just below them the track opened out onto the crescent of a sandy bay shielded by rugged cliffs, fringed by green jungle. And beyond that, the sea. Both of Mr Gupta's worlds came together and tears formed in his bloodshot eyes.

"It is beautiful," he said.

"It is that," said Olaf. "Let's get you settled, then I can do some scouting."

On the short journey to the beach Mr Gupta forgot all pain and, for a while, embraced life and all it held out. Sunbirds flashed iridescent in the morning sun and a myriad of butterflies danced before them. Treepies, parakeets, flycatchers and bulbuls squawked and sang as they passed by, with cicadas and crickets adding to the fanfare of life. The trees and bushes thinned to reveal the beach. Clive's Beach. The Beach of Sighs. All as Mr Gupta had imagined, complete with two rocks, sitting upon one of which was MacKeeg, smoking. If MacKeeg was full of life then, reasoned Mr Gupta, he was not done for yet. Olaf stopped beneath the trees at the beach's edge, where clear ground made a perfect camp. He helped Mr Gupta down and settled him on soft grass, back against a palm trunk.

"Thank you, Olaf," he said. "I can watch the sun set from here. It is time you escaped. Maybe Chopra will face justice once he has finished with this madness. Perhaps the victory is the time he has wasted and dear Sudhesh and Jhatish have closed the door on all the pain. Oh my, oh my. I am just about finished. I can stay here and be happy now."

Olaf unloaded Vidi and rubbed him down with some dried leaves. The mule wandered off to the end of his long tether and drank from a small stream. Olaf brewed some tea and sat on a log sharing the moment with Mr Gupta.

"My granddad would smile to see me here," he said.

"You can smile for him," said Mr Gupta.

"I guess that's about it," said Olaf. "A pilgrimage is always for yourself."

Olaf stood up, delved in his Bergen, pulled out his knife and pushed it through his belt.

"Goodbye, Olaf." Mr Gupta smiled and stared at the sea between the trees.

"I'll see you later," said Olaf, walking back towards the gorge. "I have to see a man about a horse."

Chapter 33

Only Angels Defeat Death

Time had stopped. Mr Gupta remained where Olaf had left him, a mind trapped inside a dying body. He looked at his thin brown legs, then at his sandals, admiring for the first time the intricate stitching Talika had used to finished them. The nails on his toes were thick and yellow, worn down by the rough trail and no longer suited to smart shoes. He could see wisps of his white hair in his peripheral vision – how long it had grown, how frail the body beneath his borrowed clothes. The pain had ebbed. All that was left was a dull ache behind his eyes and numbness in a body that felt like a heavy sack. Yet now, in these last hours, his double mind was sharper than ever. It raced with thoughts and visions of everything his life had been and he realised the joys outweighed the sorrows. This inexplicable tumour was ending his life, but it had bestowed upon him insight and memory so strong, so real that he had lost all fear. Could a dying man want for more? He thought not. He gave up control and fell into the refuge of the alternative beach, which settled about him, giving him enough strength to move his body one more time.

In one world a frail sadhu rose unsteadily leaning on his staff; in the other Mr Gupta stood, whole and strong, pausing to savour the sea breeze and look up at the universe above. He walked onto the beach staring at the sky, where stars and galaxies sparkled and comets flared. The planets were huge and the moon's cratered surface seemed close enough to touch. A silver sea rippled in the warm wind, wavelets making no sound against the sand.

Mr Gupta sat next to MacKeeg who was no longer a faded image, but full colour and complete.

"Here we are, laddie," he said, blowing out a plume of smoke. "We are at the sea in both worlds and pretty much done with everything. A convergence and an end."

"Is it really finished?" said Mr Gupta. "It seems we have failed to rid the world of that creature behind us."

"Yon Olaf may help us with that," said MacKeeg. "He has become part of this."

"It is not his fight," said Mr Gupta. "I wish he would just go. My journey has left a trail of death. I wanted it all to end here."

"Och, he's a soldier," said MacKeeg. "I've seen this before. A man like that will never solve his issues by running. He has to confront his fear and beat it before he can rest."

"Like me?" said Mr Gupta.

"Aye. Like us."

"And Rupa?" There was a catch in Mr Gupta's voice.

MacKeeg turned to his friend and patted his shoulder. There was comfort in the touch.

"Ye listen to an old Highlander," he said. "Ye cannot cover every eventuality in life no matter how ye try. How much more can ye give when it is your life that has been spent? That is a great enough fee, is it not? No man can give more. Young Rupa has greater protection now than ever before. She is alive because of ye, not despite ye. Uppal's world has crumbled and Chopra has nothing to go back to with only your death to chase. There is no joy in seeing a man die, so be satisfied he will have a long walk back to perdition with no friends along the way. So, what the now? We wait. And if we drift into death, well, we may not even notice the join."

Both men smiled and turned to watch the universe.

Olaf passed the railway hut on the narrow path. He had determined that he could get to the wider valley in time to watch for any pursuers and take it from there. A train passed over the bridge high above him raining rust down into his eyes. As he wiped the flecks away with his fingers he walked into something soft, warm and yielding – a mule! Squinting through clearing vision, with the noisy carriages clattering overhead his mind failed to grasp the unexpected. As he reached for the loose rope attached to the creature's bridle his mind exploded into a million stars as someone hit him with a rock. Falling into the gorge he held on to the rope which stopped him abruptly. His mind cleared and muscles bulged. The mule's front hooves were right at the edge just above him, its head arching down under his weight. He looked up into blue lenses as the man who he knew must be Vasupati Chopra looked down at him. Blood ran into Olaf's eyes as he tried to keep still, but the mule edged closer, the whites of its eyes showing alarm as it fought to move backwards. The noise of the train faded.

"You are unexpected," said Vaz. "Where's Gupta?"

Olaf said nothing. Vaz produced a knife.

"I would say you will fall a hundred feet," said Vaz. "Your choice."

Olaf stared back with an intensity that gave Vaz a moment of discomfort. The weakness passed and he leaned forward.

"I think you are a dangerous man. Let me tell you something." Vaz paused briefly. "*Only Angels Defeat Death*. Are you a golden angel?"

At that moment the whole ledge gave way and the mule burled over, squealing. Olaf felt himself fly into space.

Vaz lay on his back looking up at the bridge. He scrambled to his feet light-headed with shock. Then he relaxed and confidence returned. He could not be killed! Stepping carefully, he looked down into the gorge but could see nothing, the canopy of trees below hiding the roaring river. Mule and man were gone. Who was he? Another flicker of doubt. The mule was carrying all the supplies.

"You are all you need," said the Kāla mind.

Something was different. He realised his blue world had gone. His glasses lay in the dirt a short distance away, one lens cracked. He put them on. Anil Gupta was ahead somewhere, which was all that mattered. With Gophapa's death the world could start again.

All things end. Mr Gupta felt sure of this, but looking up at the universe he also knew time was so immeasurable that to mere mortals it might as well be infinite. He drew comfort from this. Death was approaching and with it the end of everything Mr Gupta could ever be, but still he smiled at the beauty of the cosmos. He loved the fact that his atoms were made from stardust, and they would return to the universe to create new things. On, and on, and on, and on. Insignificant he may be, but how complex this last act of his life had become, how primitive the desire for revenge. Above everything he wanted to see those he loved again, but only the sea remained. Loud keening, a truly terrible sound, sliced through tranquillity.

"He is here!" said MacKeeg, jumping up and turning.

He helped Mr Gupta to his feet and together they looked across the beach to the edge of the jungle where the demon stood, black against the green, blue eyes flaring in the sunshine. Mr Gupta saw Vasupati Chopra in his true form. Gone was any pretence. The monster who stood before him was the man who had killed his wife. The man who had wanted Rupa destroyed. The man whose aim, no matter how corrupt and improbable, was to kill him, and then all those he loved. Vasupati Chopra held a wicked looking knife. He stepped out onto the beach and smiled.

"*I do not know whether to gut you or just watch you die!*" he screamed.

Mr Gupta had changed so much that Vaz was taken by surprise, but the joy at being so close surpassed all else. He let out a cry of victory. To Vaz it was the roar of Kāla breaking free to consume this most troublesome man. Yet, far from being frightened, Mr Gupta stood to face him. The red eyed stare transfixed Vaz. Doubt stirred.

"*New life crawls from the Birthing Black Sea. The sacrifice is made, mankind's sacrificial man, Gophapa will be slain by Him, Gophapa takes ruin with him.*" he said.

Mr Gupta leaned on his staff and sighed.

"The journey has been too long for riddles. All that death, Vaz, what good has it done? What good will my death serve?"

"*It will start the world again,*" hissed Vaz. "*It will take weakness away and bring back the dead as an army fit for this God to rule!*"

Mr Gupta said nothing, but straightened up as reality shifted once more. Vaz looked like a small, twisted version of the huge demon. MacKeeg whispered into his ear.

"Nemesis."

The undercurrent of doubt Vaz felt remained as he watched this frail man standing firm, head held to one side listening. Mr Gupta was just not scared. Vaz's delusions were crumbling. Words drifted through his mind as he sought the key to unleash the final act.

"*Time is severed from mankind,*" he spat. Then, "*Darkness cleanses, darkness is pain, darkness is death. Pain leaves with death. Both shine with blackness… Life hurts more than death. At the point of death is purity, the pain is over. This I shall give you.*"

Mr Gupta stared and MacKeeg joined in.

"All ye are is a back-street thug," he said. "Ye killed Kiran. For what? A little bit of money. Tamina. I guess that was down to ye too. It seems ye also butchered your own family. Now, tell me, boy, what does that show ye to be? A god, or the snivelling piece of shite that ye are?"

It was not meant to be like this. Vaz felt the shift inside as the final question in that strange voice stated an undeniable fact. In increasing snaps of rationality Vaz could see his killing was just a simple pleasure, his actions nothing more than a twisted mind feeding on a simple, but awful, addiction. The crimson stare, black through his glasses, held Vaz.

"All you are is a hired killer," said Mr Gupta. "Nothing more. What makes you worse is the enjoyment you find in other people's suffering. Taking my life will not help you."

Leaning against his staff Mr Gupta summoned the last of his strength. He was not willing to die like a sheep.

"Come and try ye abomination, and see MacKeeg spit in yer eye!"

Vaz took a step, but hesitated. He did not want to move closer. Everything was different. He did not like the bay, the sea or the beach. He felt for his Glock. It was gone! It must be back on the trail. Mr Gupta took a step towards him. Why wasn't he scared? Taking a deep breath Vaz closed his eyes and found the dregs of Kāla's hunger. All doubts were quelled as anger took over. Anger at the insults. Anger at being made to feel like a fool. Rage at having to face the truth.

"Kāla cannot die!" he howled.

Vaz charged.

"*Summum nec metuam diem nec optem*...Hold fast!" yelled MacKeeg.

The final MacLeod battle cry had taken the last of Mr Gupta's strength. All he could do now was watch death coming. The demon ran howling towards him, but he did not care. Time slowed and he turned to William MacKeeg.

"Do we know Latin now?"

"Och, 'tis our motto, '*May I neither dread nor desire the last day.*' It sorta fits, dinnae ye think?"

"Thank you," said Mr Gupta. "I think you have made me a man."

"Och, ye always were," smiled MacKeeg. "All I did was bypass your empathy nerve. Deep down ye're as big a bastard as me!"

They laughed together. Then they stopped to listen.

"Nemesis?" asked Mr Gupta.

"Your senses picked it up," said MacKeeg. "Something is coming."

Then he heard it, the sound of something crashing through the jungle towards the beach. The demon heard it too. Time stopped. Onto the sand charged a huge tiger, tail up and muscles bulging. The demon screamed and changed course, running towards the water. Demon no more, Vaz looked over his shoulder as he fled and stumbled. The tiger was upon him and, as he fell, Vaz instinctively struck out with the knife. He missed his mark and the knife flew into the air as the tiger bore him down, tearing, biting and roaring. Claws tore open his chest and stomach, teeth ripped his face. His delusion of indestructible godhood fell away as pain reduced him to flesh and blood, sinew and bone. He was lifted by his neck and shaken, dragged, dropped and left. One remaining displaced eye stared at the horror of his own body. He could not be alive, surely? He could still feel everything! He had no tongue! His mind was white with terror and it screamed, and screamed and screamed.

The tiger approached the thin man. This clever monkey's smell was clean and sweet. The thing he had just left was of a different kind. Angaar had been resting by the beach for days, his illness so advanced he could no longer hunt. He had been waiting for death. Mr Gupta's sweet scent had moved him, but it was the bitter smell of Vaz that had driven him to attack.

"Geerumph."

Angaar's call was soft as he purred and sniffed the proffered hand. What could Mr Gupta do? What he had witnessed could never be explained, now this fearsome beast was rubbing its bloody head against his hip. Angaar coughed and fresh blood dribbled onto the beach and he sagged into the sand. Mr Gupta sat down against the rock and took the great head in his hands and stroked its face.

"Poor old thing," he said, "poor, poor old thing."

The tiger's body was thin and its coat matted. The eyes were glassy.

"Grumph!" chuffed Angaar.

Mr Gupta leaned back as his head thumped in pain and his body's strength drained away. He felt the tiger purring and smiled at the wonder of it all. The wonder of all this beauty just waiting to be seen, yet all men do is paint themselves into cramped lives with dogma and daftness. That is what he had done, but had broken free and put right some of the hurts, purely by opening his mind. If MacKeeg had been a well of memory, then this tiger was improbability writ large; not the answer to a prayer, but the answer to an equation.

Angaar purred and Mr Gupta smiled.

"Anil."

Kiran stood beside him.

"Is it time to go?" he asked.

"Yes, my darling man."

"Are you coming with me?"

"I have never left you."

"Then let us go, Kiran."

"I love you Mr Gupta."

"Then everything is wonderful," he replied.

Epilogue

I

Vaz wished for death. All that was left was pain. He watched insects settle on the raw flesh of his body in their thousands and his mind started screaming again. The sun was so hot, but he had no tongue with which to lick non-existent lips. The dry maw crawled with flies. After an eternity, a shadow fell across his eye. The dead golden angel. He was smiling.

"Only Angels defeat Death," it said.

Vaz stared. It was all he could do. A cooling salve washed around his neck. Water? A small wave broke over Vaz's head and filled the hollow which once was a mouth. The tide was rising. He blinked away water and the angel had gone. Another wave and his empty mouth filled. He swallowed and swallowed, the water flushing through his gaping abdomen. Desperately he tried to drink an ocean. The screaming started again as the tide flowed.

II

The smell of Engineer would drive her mad, she knew. Talika had given up dragging the body, her wrist was raw, and her muscles exhausted. The night had been a torment of mosquitoes and cold, but morning brought the hot sun. She lay with her shackled wrist outstretched to be as far from the body as she could get. A mule snorted. She opened her dust-caked eyes and saw Olaf hurrying towards her. Then slipped into darkness.

III

It was many weeks later that Talika told the remaining members of the Kuru and the villagers the full story of her rescue. Together they wove a tale for recounting over, and over again, which became a part of Karukula's folklore. When loved ones died people began to say *they left for the Beach of Sighs*. What safer place for souls to be than under the care of Arnesh Ji and his tiger protector, Angaar. It was said these two gods remained in the rocks, guarding the way to the village from demons. The logic of the tale could never stop the accreted embroidery of superstition. Nawal wrote the story down as best he could, gleaned from the accounts of Kuldev, Olaf, Talika, Anupa, and, of course, his own experiences.

◆

The Narrative of Nawal Ji.

The mule had hit the forest canopy first so the hole into which Olaf fell was cleared of major obstacles and as the rope tore from his grasp he rolled through a nest of branches and shrubs, stopping, torn but not broken, close to the river. He had followed the gorge to the jungle, limping out into the camp where Vidi still stood dozing. He could see a shapeless mass beyond the trees at the water's edge. Olaf followed huge pug marks across the sand, one with a scar. Blue glasses lay broken in one of the depressions. Vaz was torn to shreds. His abdomen was split with intestines and organs spilled onto the damp sand. A single, clear eye stared from a ruined, jawless face. Olaf had never seen so many flies. A faint wet click from the head. A breath? Olaf looked into the eye - there was still life in it. He smiled.

"Only Angels defeat Death," he said.

He left Vasupati Chopra to the sea, that single eye full of horror.

Olaf's attention was then drawn to a nearby tableau which he could never rationalise. He approached and wondered. Mr Gupta was sitting against a rock with his left hand upon a tiger's head. Both looked peaceful, and both were dead. Olaf crouched and rasped his beard.

"Well fellers, I guess redemption is all of us here and promises kept. Seva send his regards."

He stayed there for a while to pay his respects and was the only witness of this final scene.

Olaf left the camp early the next day. The sea had cleansed the beach. Mr Gupta and the tiger remained, strangely free of corruption, with but a single emerald fly perched on the white staff like a jewel. Olaf picked up the staff, then started. Mr Gupta had written two words in the sand. TELL RUPA. Had the words been there the day before? Olaf could not be sure, but nodded and tacitly agreed to the final request. Vidi was well rested and biddable, sure-footedly skirting the missing path where Olaf had fallen. Vidi knew he was heading home.

◆

They found Talika. She had dragged her burden off the trail, but Vidi's snort and raised ears had indicated something to be investigated. With no keys to release her, Olaf resorted to severing Engineer's hand by means of the knife he had recovered from the beach, and a heavy rock. Vidi bore his new burden stoically. With water and some biscuits Talika recovered well enough to walk the final mile to the clearing in the Karoo Valley. Tales were exchanged and Talika cried for Mr Gupta. That night Olaf became the soldier he had always been: it is impossible to leave something you carry with you. He left Talika safe in the clearing, explaining that he had to scout ahead to see if any of Vaz's poison was left at the village. Talika reluctantly submitted.

◆

The villagers tried to continue life as normal, for the sake of the children and as a balm for constant stress. Anupa was the key: whilst in the hands of Aktar and Kepi, the villagers could be cowed, bullied and humiliated, and as time passed their three young gaolers warmed to the task. No one would risk *looking for her in case it led to her murder. Vyan felt sick at the thought of his niece being in the hands of such men. His wound was well tended, but he was in constant pain, was worried about Kuldev and was angry at his own inability to act. Yadu, Har and Daksh had taken to smoking a lot of their own dope and developed a boldness to go with the guns Aktar had supplied. None more so than the unkempt Daksh. Vyan saw the way he watched his daughter, so kept her close. Umang, Kuldev and he had always been the headmen in Karukula. With Umang dead and his brother missing, Vyan felt helpless and emasculated. On the sixth morning everything changed.*

Kepi had called a meeting the evening before. He told them Aktar was planning to leave the next day as too much time had passed and he knew they could not keep a whole village in line forever. He knew the authorities could soon get involved. Aktar and Kepi would wait for a call from Engineer in Gokak. Yadu, Har and Daksh could do as they wished. Anupa would remain hostage until things settled and all money had been paid by Vaz or Engineer. Failing that, the villagers would pay for the girl, or she could be sold.

Resham had left the village early, knowing the three men seldom put in an appearance until late morning. She needed to wash her clothes. As she neared the river, Daksh stepped from cover holding his gun. He was stoned and leered, bloodshot eyes half shut. No words were spoken as he threw himself at the girl, pushed her to the ground and clamped his hand across her mouth. Resham was horrified. Daksh disregarded the gun and tore at her clothes as she struggled. There was a shout. Kuldev had arrived. Enraged, he pulled his niece's attacker off throwing him to the ground. Daksh grabbed the gun. He aimed at Kuldev, but it was Daksh who died. Tsering, the watcher, shot him with his old Webley Mk VI revolver.

The report stirred the village and in moments everyone was in the square, several ran towards the river. Yadu and Har shouted for order. Har fired into the air.

"Anyone moves and I will kill them," said Yadu.

"You boys have gone too far," said Vyan. "Drugs are bad, but murder?"

"Shut up!" snapped Yadu. "Once this is over you just get on with your lives, and remember, we will be watching."

Kuldev walked into the village and silence reigned. He was tattered and dusty, and had the gleam of anger in his eyes.

"Where is Anupa?" he asked.

"She will not be harmed if you do as you're told," said Har with false bravado. "What was the shot?"

"Your comrade is dead," said Kuldev. "Vyan. Your daughter is safe."

Vyan hobbled towards the river ignoring the guns.

"They killed Umang," someone shouted.

"And Puneet!" said another.

"Chopra did, not us!" shouted Yadu. "Be careful now, the others have the girl!"

Tsering stepped from cover and shot Yadu through the ribs. He died of his wounds, crying quietly. Har turned and fled. The villagers chased him, all thought of danger eclipsed by anger. It was said Har ran, fell and broke his neck. That was the story.

◆

The shots from the village could only mean trouble, so Aktar determined to escape via Yadu's plantation. Anupa was dragged to her feet by Kepi. The cathedral of the Great Banyan was a mess. Aktar would be glad to leave.

"Get the bitch moving!" were Aktar's last words.

The appearance of a huge, blond man stopped Kepi in his tracks. He watched this apparition wrench Aktar's head back and thrust a knife into his throat. Death was quick. Kepi dropped the girl and fled with his rifle over his shoulder. Anupa cried and stared at her awful warrior, but could not have loved him more. Olaf did not stop, shouting, "Stay there!" before plunging after Kepi.

The men of the village led by Kuldev and Tsering had reached the falls as Kepi hove into view. Kepi hesitated, then chose his single pursuer as the least

515

dangerous option. He fired his rifle at the crowd, missing everyone in his panic, and charged back up the track firing and screaming as he went. Olaf seemed to materialise from thin air, pulled the rifle from Kepi's hands and punched him in the throat. The villagers watched the final scene from below. Olaf appeared at a high point above the falls with Kepi held above his head, then threw the screaming man into the maelstrom below.

Nawal had no reason to believe this story was not so.

IV

Olaf left them to put things right. That is what he told Anupa. Nobody asked too much of the girl, but they knew she loved him. Kuldev and Sameeksha later discovered that Olaf said he would return. Anupa promised to wait, and she did. But that is another story.

Nobody blamed Nawal Ji for the horrors brought by Vaz and they actively encouraged the remaining Kuru members stay for several months so they could heal together. It had been Vam who had summoned Tsering, and Tsering who watched the village, waiting for a chance to act. Kuldev had arrived and forced the Tibetan's hand, but all had worked out for the best. The events spawned a new legend and turned quickly into superstitious dogma. The villagers considered Arnesh Ji and his tiger to be their protectors against outside evils. That probably had a hand in the creation of the myths that amused Nawal. Yet, though he held the laws of probability tight, he would never be critical of the need of simple people to diminish their own worth by putting it down to spiritual intervention. He almost believed it himself.

The Kuru ki Kvark left after Arnesh was born. They had to follow Olaf to Alakapuri.

V

Sudhesh, Rupa and Jhatish had waved Olaf goodbye months before the old Queen Lizzie clattered up to the gates of Alakapuri. It was here the final stories were told.

Ravi Uppal had hanged himself in his cell a few days before his trial. His dream of owning space had diminished into a small brick room in which he could not live. Sudhesh Shastri pursued everything to a legal conclusion and had financial recompense taken from Cobra Investments' assets with a ruthless ease none would challenge. Vasupati Chopra became front page news for months, but no one ever found out what his fate had been.

It was Talika who started the real process of healing. Her baby was quiet and bright-eyed. Once a celebratory meal was over, it was she who finally found the confidence to speak to Rupa.

"My son is called Arnesh," she said, carrying him across to her.

"He is beautiful," said Rupa laughing at her own dancing limbs, so much like the kicking child's. "That was Daddy's Kuru name!"

"Your father was a brave man, and loved you dearly," said Talika. "Everything he has done, was done to keep you safe, and to succeed was beyond courage. Olaf told you his last words written on the beach?"

"*Tell Rupa,*" she said, followed by, "wipe!"

Jhatish obliged, Rupa smiled and the baby blew bubbles.

"We are the same!" chuckled Rupa.

Talika laughed.

"You are, darling girl. There was one moment in my life where I became part of your world. And it is still with us. Rupa, Arnesh is your brother."

The silence was total. Talika had never told anyone of her secret, even if her friends had guessed. They knew Rupa must be the first to be told.

Rupa held out a shaking hand and touched her brother.

"Then everything is wonderful," she said.

VI

In the Baaghwadi, high on the slopes in a shallow cave, the mewling of a tiger cub, fresh born, sounded briefly. It was soon licked clean and joined its two siblings at their mother's teats. The night was clear and a bright moon shone down. The tigress looked up purring at the feel of her new youngsters suckling.

"Geerumph."

Her brief call echoed back as the Universe looked on.